BEFORE THE KISS . . .

The Beau tugged off Miss Sheringham's hat and watched as a yard of soft, silky chestnut hair slid across her shoulders.

He gave her no chance to deny him, simply captured her mouth with his and teased her supple lips. He ended the kiss, but did not step back.

A breath shuddered out of her.

"I have never been kissed by a rake," she murmured, touching her fingertips to her damp lips.

"Was it everything you expected?" he asked, his eyes glinting with humor.

"I am not in a position to judge," she admitted. "I have nothing with which to compare it."

The Beau stood stunned for a second, then threw back his head and roared with laughter. Miss Sheringham was truly delightful. Enormously entertaining.

"Come on, brat. It is time we got you to bed."

"Are you planning to join me there?" she asked with an arch look.

The Beau shook his head as he reached down for her hat. "Oh, no, my dear. Not me. You are entirely too dangerous."

After the Kiss

MAVERICK HEART

"A STUNNING LOOK AT HUMAN FOIBLES AND FERVOR. This adventurous, passionate read is first-rate from first to last page. Ms. Johnston's tale is brimming with poignant emotions and exciting action blended into a sensuous, tension-filled romance that is impossible to put down."
—*Affaire de Coeur*

"Joan Johnston gives us a double dose of romance with a mature love story and one of young love. Readers will find themselves truly captivated by both romances and the excitement of the chase and the passion."—*Romantic Times*

THE INHERITANCE

"AN ENGROSSING STORY."—*Brazosport Facts*

"WELL-WRITTEN . . . A TREMENDOUS TALE . . . THE CHARACTERS ARE ALL FIRST-RATE."—*Affaire de Coeur*

Also by Joan Johnston

A LOVING DEFIANCE
COLTER'S WIFE
*SWEETWATER SEDUCTION
*THE BAREFOOT BRIDE
*KID CALHOUN
*OUTLAW'S BRIDE
*THE INHERITANCE
*MAVERICK HEART
*CAPTIVE
I PROMISE

Sisters of the Lone Star Trilogy

Available from Dell

JOAN JOHNSTON

AFTER the KISS

A Dell Book

This book is dedicated
to my editor, Mary Ellen O'Neill
and
to Marjorie Braman and Leslie Schnur,
who introduced Dell's fabulous
Four of Hearts
and
to all the wonderful marketing folks,
sales reps, creative artists,
support staff, and publicists at Dell
who helped make it such a success.

Published by
Dell Publishing
a division of
Bantam Doubleday Dell Publishing Group, Inc.
1540 Broadway
New York, New York 10036

ISBN: 0-440-22201-X

Printed in the United States of America

Published simultaneously in Canada

March 1997

10 9 8 7 6 5 4 3 2 1

OPM

BEFORE THE KISS

The Beau

Prologue

"MATCHMAKING IS A DANGEROUS BUSINESS."

"I know that, Livy. But sometimes drastic measures are necessary." Charlotte, Countess of Denbigh, sat crosswise in a wingback chair in the drawing room of Somersville Manor, swinging her patent-leather-clad feet back and forth. Although married to an earl for nearly a year, and a venerable eighteen years of age, Charlotte refused to be bound by the traditional way of doing things, even sitting in a chair. Life was so much more interesting, she thought, when things did not turn out as one expected.

Charlotte watched fascinated as her best friend and sister-in-law, Olivia, Duchess of Braddock, held her firstborn son to her breast. William, titled Earl of Comarty at birth, suckled noisily beneath a lace-edged cloth that veiled his gusty enjoyment of breakfast.

"Does it hurt?" Charlotte asked, drawn for a moment from the subject at hand by her curiosity about nursing a child.

"It did a little at first. Not anymore," Olivia said, smiling tenderly at her two-month-old son and brushing aside a lock of his golden hair.

1

"Have you let Reeve watch?"

"Charlotte!" A pink flush began at Olivia's throat and headed for her cheeks. She kept her eyes downcast. "Whether I let my husband watch while I—"

"Have you?" Charlotte insisted, her gaze steady upon her friend, demanding an answer. She had a reason for asking. She might need to make such a decision herself sometime soon.

Olivia nodded, then looked up so Charlotte could see the inner glow of joy that lit her eyes. "Reeve loves to watch. He says . . . The silly man thinks I'm beautiful," she confessed breathlessly.

"You are," Charlotte said quietly. "Motherhood agrees with you."

Olivia gave her a questioning look. Charlotte ignored Livy's silent request for information, turning her head to stare into a crackling fire that took the edge from an unusually chilly May morning. She was not yet ready to divulge the truth.

In fact, Charlotte was in an "interesting condition," although she had so far kept the joyful secret to herself. The instant her husband discovered she was with child, Lion would insist—all in the name of protecting her and the babe—that they return home to Denbigh Castle from their visit with the Duke and Duchess of Braddock.

Charlotte had something important she wanted to accomplish first.

The house party that would shortly be forming at Somersville Manor in Sussex included a number of eligible bachelors Charlotte had asked Olivia to invite for a particular young lady's perusal. Charlotte greatly feared it was going to be as difficult to direct Miss

Elizabeth Sheringham toward one of the many marital prospects available, as it would be to convince the prospects what a precious find Eliza would be.

"You met Eliza during the Christmas holiday," Charlotte said, turning her attention back to matchmaking. "What did you think of her?"

"Miss Sheringham is a lovely girl who—"

"Stubble it," Charlotte interrupted. "I want your *honest* opinion."

Olivia sighed at being put on the spot, but conceded, "She did seem a bit . . . sharp-tongued."

"The result of an agile wit," Charlotte said.

"I can understand why Miss Sheringham is ready to trade a barb for a jest," Olivia said. "It could not have been easy growing up under such a cloud of scandal. To this day no one knows the real reason why the Earl of Sheringham disinherited Eliza's father, only that it was something so awful the earl refused ever to receive his only son—or his son's wife and daughter—at Ravenwood again. Under the circumstances, it is no wonder the girl has no regard for—"

"The rigid rules of Society?"

"Anyone," Olivia finished. "However, when a person is hounded by gossip, as she must be, one must expect some—"

"Retaliation?"

"Rancor when the tabbies talk," Oliva continued, as though Charlotte had not spoken. "With no one but a blind, elderly aunt to keep her acid tongue in check, Miss Sheringham appears to be headed neck-or-nothing toward social disaster."

"Most likely she is," Charlotte agreed cheerfully. She shook her head in mock woefulness. "Such a piti-

3

ful lack of decorum." She grinned and added, "It is what I love most about her."

"Of course," Olivia said, smiling ruefully. "She reminds you of you."

"Exactly," Charlotte said with a laugh. "You must see it will take a very special man to recognize her for the marvelous wife she will make."

Olivia's brow furrowed. "I am afraid the situation is quite hopeless, Charlie. What gentleman would dare entangle himself with such a scandal-in-the-making?"

"Captain Lord Marcus Wharton, the Duke of Blackthorne's younger brother," Charlotte announced.

Olivia jerked in disbelief, but caught herself before the baby lost hold of his source of sustenance. "*The Beau?!* You must be joking! Captain Wharton is a rakehell and a rogue. A devoted Corinthian. And worst of all, *a confirmed bachelor!* What can you be thinking?"

"That he's absolutely perfect for Eliza."

"Miss Sheringham—even with her trenchant tongue—deserves better," Olivia countered.

"Rakes make the best husbands," Charlotte argued, sliding from her chair onto her knees in the thick Aubusson carpet at Olivia's feet. The chore was made easier because she still wore the breeches she had donned to ride that morning. "Look at you and Reeve. You're happy as larks."

"Reeve is . . . was . . . My situation is totally different."

"Why? How?"

"Reeve was ready for a leg-shackle when I met him and had a need to set up his nursery. Captain

Wharton is still, shall we say, enjoying life somewhat too heartily," Olivia said.

"He is thirty," Charlotte said. "Lion was a year younger when we married."

"Lion was responsible for a sister and servants and a great deal of property for many years before that. Captain Wharton has no one's interest at heart but his own."

Olivia switched the baby to the opposite breast and carefully rearranged the lace-edged cloth before continuing. "Have you forgotten the Beau is a soldier, Charlie? And that Napoleon has recently escaped from Elba. Captain Wharton might be called back to battle at any time," Olivia said. "Surely you would not wish Miss Sheringham to marry him under such circumstances."

Charlotte paused. This was the argument against Captain Wharton she had found most difficult to overcome in her own mind. Not only was the Beau a soldier, but he was said to be dashingly brave and gallant—well, all right, foolhardy—in the face of danger. The reckless fellow was likely to get himself killed in battle, and Charlotte would be forced to go through this entire process with Eliza all over again.

"Eliza has not even met him yet," Charlotte said, reaching out a forefinger to William and watching as his tiny fingers closed strongly around it. "And here you are finding reasons why he will not make a good husband."

"Be reasonable, Charlie. Look at him. And at her."

Charlotte caressed the baby's soft knuckles with her thumb as she considered Olivia's words. Livy was right to think Miss Sheringham and the Beau were mismatched in physical favor. With her odd-featured face and towering form, it was impossible to dismiss Miss Sheringham's corporeal shortcomings as inconsequential.

On the other hand, Captain Wharton had been named "the Beau" by the *ton* with good reason. He was the epitome of male perfection—virile, muscular, with the features and body of an Adonis, and the vivid blue eyes and golden blond hair so favored by the English.

Personally, Charlotte preferred dark-haired men. However, she was not English, but American. She pursed her lips thoughtfully. So was Eliza. Or rather, half American. Raised by an American mother and a disinherited English father, Eliza had grown up disdainful enough of English customs not to care what color the Beau's eyes and hair were. Surely even Eliza could not fail to notice the Beau was handsome and be attracted to him. Charlotte was convinced that only a man as unfettered by the manners and morals of Society as Eliza was herself—like the Beau—would be willing to marry her.

Captain Wharton had other manly attributes that were certain to please someone as unconventional as Miss Elizabeth Sheringham. The Beau was a noted whipster, a member of the Four-in-Hand Club, handy with his fives in Gentleman Jackson's saloon, unbeatable with a foil, a dead shot, and charming enough to be forgiven his wild behavior and still accepted in the homes of all the most particular hostesses of the *ton*.

As an added advantage, Lord Marcus was also in line to inherit a dukedom from the current holder of the title, a widowed elder brother who had twin daughters and showed no inclination to remarry. With

Eliza's pockets to let, she could use a husband of substance to support her.

Best of all, the Beau's reputation was so iniquitous, Miss Sheringham's father was a saint by comparison.

"Will you at least help me throw Miss Sheringham and the Beau together for these two weeks?" Charlotte asked.

"To what purpose? This is a plan fraught with disaster," Olivia warned.

"What is fraught with disaster?"

The two women turned to watch their husbands enter the drawing room. Both men were impeccably dressed in the form-fitting fashions that showed off the male figure in all its glory, Reeve dressed in buff and brown, Lion in bottle green and buckskin. Reeve was a shade taller, with blond hair and blue eyes, while Lion was broader-shouldered and had black hair and gray eyes. They once had been formidable adversaries but now, related by marriage, had found a common ground to bind them as friends.

Charlotte rose, surprised at how much effort it took to free her finger from the baby's grip. She took a step backward toward the fire, knowing from the look on Lion's face, and from the tone of his voice when he had spoken, that she had better come up with some diverting explanation for Olivia's comment.

Reeve crossed directly to Olivia and bent to brush a hand across the area hidden behind the cloth, either the baby's cheek or his wife's breast, Charlotte was not sure which—until Livy's blush gave it away.

Charlotte continued watching as Livy's eyes met Reeve's and saw the smile of welcome on her sister-in-law's face as her husband's mouth lowered to hers.

7

Before their lips could meet, a beloved face appeared before Charlotte and demanded her attention.

"What disaster?" Lion asked. His palms settled on the mantel, capturing her within his embrace before the fire.

She tried looking innocent, but a year of marriage had taught him too much about her. He had rescued her from any number of scrapes and seemed resigned to a lifetime of such endeavor.

"What calamity are you planning now, my dear?"

Charlotte wriggled as his warm breath tickled her ear. "Only a little matchmaking, my lord."

Lion lifted her chin with his forefinger, forcing her gaze up to his. "Who is it this time?" he asked with the hint of a smile teasing the corners of his lips and sparkling in his eyes.

"At least we are out of the running," Reeve said to Lion from his perch on the arm of the wingback chair in which Olivia sat nursing William.

Lion slipped an arm around Charlotte's waist, turning her so they faced the other couple, and gazed down at his wife. "Well, Charlotte? What lucky devil have you chosen to be the fortunate recipient of your matchmaking?"

"The Beau."

The two men exchanged astonished looks.

"And what lady have you chosen to bless with such male perfection?" Lion asked.

"Miss Elizabeth Sheringham."

Lion exhaled in an explosion of laughter.

"It is nothing to laugh about," Charlotte said indignantly. "Miss Sheringham needs a husband, and Captain Wharton would do better with a wife."

"There you have it, Lion. As simple as shooting ducks in pond," Reeve said, slapping his knee at the jest of two such implausible figures becoming man and wife. The sharp sound disturbed the heir, who made his complaint known with a yowl. Further discourse was impossible, and within moments Olivia and Reeve had abandoned the room, leaving Charlotte and Lion to finish the discussion by themselves.

Once alone, Charlotte pressed her advantage, that is to say, pressed her lovely figure against Lion's body from chest to thighs, wrapped her arms around his neck, and said, her mouth against his, "Please, Lion. Let me try. You will be here to help if things go awry."

"*If* things go awry? It is a certainty. That termagant's tongue has the bite of an adder. If she threatens the Beau, he will show no mercy."

"I guarantee she will match him, spite for spite. The Beau will be charmed," Charlotte insisted.

"I will not be privy to such maneuvering, Charlotte. Besides, Captain Wharton's elder brother, the duke, is a friend of mine. I would not be able to look Blackthorne in the eye knowing what you have planned for his brother during the next two weeks."

Charlotte knew from the rumbly sound of Lion's voice, and the heavy-lidded look of his eyes, that victory was close at hand. It needed only a little urging to win the day.

"Eliza and the Beau are perfect for each other, my lord."

"No, Charlotte," Lion said. "And that is my final word on the subject."

Charlotte settled her mouth against her husband's

9

and rubbed gently until his lips were damp, and she could taste him. Her body curled inside with desire. He pulled her close to feel his arousal, and she momentarily lost her train of thought. She forced herself to concentrate.

"Please, Lion. Let me try."

"Please will not work here, Charlotte."

"Pretty please. I helped Reeve and Olivia get together, and that did not turn out so badly."

Lion growled low in his throat. He bound her tightly against him, his mouth ravaging hers, taking what he needed and offering her a promise of more.

"Please, Lion."

It was her own plea she whispered this time, but as he picked her up and headed toward the door, the words on his lips were the answer she had sought.

"Very well, Charlie. You may try matchmaking one more time."

Chapter 1

"*I* WILL NEVER MARRY. EVER. YOU, OF ALL PEOPLE, must know why."

"We must forget the past, Marcus, and plan for the future." Alastair, sixth Duke of Blackthorne, sat with shoulders ramrod straight, his back a precise three inches from the wooden slats of the chair behind his desk in the library. Seeing him, one would have thought Alastair was the soldier rather than Marcus.

Alastair entwined his fingers in a single, white-knuckled knot and placed them in the center of the polished walnut surface. "You must marry and breed an heir, Marcus. Otherwise, Blackthorne Abbey will pass eventually to that imbecilic fop Albert and be dissipated by his excesses."

Captain Lord Marcus Wharton, on leave of duty from the Prince of Wales's own 10th Royal Hussars, contemplated the plea of his elder brother as he took a sip of brandy. He slouched down in the cushioned chair across the room in a way he knew irritated his brother, and crossed his booted feet at the ankles. "If Cousin Bertie inherits, it means both of us are dead. Why should we care what happens to these moldy old stones when we are gone?"

"Consider, if you please, Regina and Rebecca."

"You can, and I am certain will, leave your daughters with substantial trust funds to provide for their needs," Marcus said.

An awkward silence ensued this brief discussion of Lady Regina and Lady Rebecca. From almost the day of their birth eight years before, the twin girls were rumored to be the daughters, not of the Duke of Blackthorne, but of his younger brother, Lord Marcus. The gossip was fueled by numerous drunken declarations made by Penthia, Duchess of Blackthorne, herself and had not ended even when Her Grace died in a fall down the stairs these three years past.

The two brothers had never discussed the subject. Marcus, because he knew the truth, and Alastair, Marcus suspected, because he was afraid of discovering it.

It had not helped matters that Alastair maintained a proper English reserve toward his daughters and left them entirely to the care of a series of nannies and governesses. Marcus, on the other hand, spent long hours in their company when he was home. He played with them, took them for rides on the Blackthorne estate in Kent, and generally enjoyed their existence.

Because of Penthia's accusations, the relationship between the two brothers had become painfully stilted over the years, until Marcus despaired of ever restoring their former closeness.

Lately Marcus had resorted to more and more outrageous behavior in the hope of rousing his brother from his self-imposed exile at Blackthorne Abbey. But his blackened reputation had served only to increase the reproving slant of his brother's brows.

Alastair, once as much in love with life as Marcus, had thoroughly retreated from Society, and showed no inclination to rejoin it.

"Blackthorne Abbey is your inheritance," Marcus said at last. "You may guard it however you will, Alastair. But I will not have my life dictated by the necessities of duty. Or the capriciousness of a woman."

Marcus had no intention of getting caught by parson's mousetrap. As a single gentleman, second son, and soldier, he had no obligations to anyone but himself and the men under his command. He had observed firsthand what havoc loving a woman could wreak on a man. He had seen the sober relic that duty—and a disastrous marriage—had made of his brother and vowed not to repeat Alastair's mistake.

Call him a care-for-nothing, a scoundrel, a rakehell if you would, but Marcus liked his life the way it was. If his reputation made him less of a catch on the marriage mart, then so much the better!

Marcus knew precisely why he had been invited to a late spring house party at the country manor of the Duke and Duchess of Braddock. And why his brother was so insistent that he attend. At least a half dozen young misses and their doting mamas were sure to be in attendance with one thought in mind: to provide him with a leg-shackle.

Marcus dismissed the threat that a bevy of eligible misses presented to his single state. He had enough Town bronze to know precisely how far he could take a flirtation before eyebrows rose. He occasionally took one far enough to cause a gasp or two, simply for his own amusement. But after Bonaparte's escape from Elba in March, which made further battles on the

Continent a serious possibility, Marcus was not in the mood to play such games.

He had decided to avoid the matchmaking occasion entirely by pleading family obligations. Marcus had cut short a delightful bout of drinking, assignations with demi-reps, and gambling with his best friend, Major Julian Sheringham, in London and journeyed to Blackthorne Abbey, only to encounter his brother's obstinate insistence that he must attend the party and find a wife.

"I will go, if you will go," Marcus said finally, providing a condition he was sure his brother would not meet.

"Very well."

Marcus sat up abruptly. "What did you say?"

"I have been looking forward to some shooting with Braddock," Alastair said, the first hint of humor gleaming in his eyes. "I am glad you decided to join us."

"Touché," Marcus said, raising his brandy glass in a toast, conceding defeat to his brother. As he savored the mellow liquid, he smiled. With a duke on the platter, Marcus doubted whether the matchmaking mamas would even notice a side dish such as him. He laughed and said, "When do we leave?"

"As soon as your batman can repack your bags. The twins and I have been ready to leave anytime this past week."

Marcus set the empty crystal glass on the ivory-inlaid chess table beside him, shaking his head at the way he had been so neatly maneuvered. "You planned to go all along?"

Alastair nodded. "Our hostess particularly asked if

Regina and Rebecca could be present, and it was not possible to send them alone. They have not been on their best behavior of late."

The door to the library opened with barely a sound.

His instincts honed by years of battle in the Peninsular Wars, Marcus was immediately on his feet, his eyes searching for the potential source of danger.

The twins stood in the doorway.

They were attired identically in white muslin shifts with matching pink bows holding their black curls back from their faces. Or would have been if Regina's hair was not losing its bow and the knees of her white stockings had not been smudged with dirt.

Rebecca did not have a single black curl out of place, but she was easily identifiable to Marcus by the worried look on her face. She stood frozen, her wide, long-lashed blue eyes focused warily on the formidable figure behind the desk.

Regina ignored the duke and raced toward Marcus. "Uncle Marcus! You're here!"

"Reggie, be care—!"

She leapt, and Marcus caught her in midair and pulled her to him in a quick, ferocious hug. He shifted her into the crook of his left arm and extended his right hand to Rebecca.

"Becky?"

Rebecca gave the duke, who had risen but remained behind his massive desk, one last, cautious glance before she bolted toward Marcus. He swept her up and pulled the two of them close in his embrace, inhaling the scent of honeysuckle in their hair as it brushed his face, loving the feel of their childish arms around his neck, and the burble of their excited chatter in his ears.

Marcus gave them each a smacking kiss on the cheek and said, "It's good to see you both looking so well."

"We missed you," Becky said.

"I missed you, too," Marcus replied, fighting the lump in his throat at the accusing look in her blue eyes—the eyes that so resembled his and not his brother's, which were gray. He had promised her he would not be gone long, but it had been nearly a year since he had come home to Blackthorne Abbey.

However bad a wife Penthia had been, both girls missed their mother, and they did not know how to break through the duke's reserve to make of him a comfortable father. Nor did Marcus, for that matter.

Remembering Alastair, he met his brother's gaze and saw the longing there. He yearned to say *They want to love you. Let them love you.* But he could not.

"Regina. Rebecca."

At the sound of the duke's stern voice, the girls turned to look at him.

"That is no proper way to greet a guest."

It was precisely the greeting Marcus could have wished for—and he was no mere guest. But he knew better than to contradict Alastair. He set the girls back on their feet and stood, his heart in his throat, as they curtsied formally and said in unison, "Welcome home, Uncle Marcus."

"Better," Alastair pronounced.

Rather than bowing in return, Marcus bent down on one knee and once more gathered them into his arms. "Give me another hug," he croaked through his swollen throat. But he had not needed to ask. They already had their arms around him.

When he looked up again, Alastair was gone.

Two days later, Marcus was on his way to Somersville Manor, the Duke of Braddock's summer home in Sussex. He rode with his batman, Sergeant Griggs, alongside a carriage that contained the twins, but no governess, and without the company of his elder brother.

Alastair had entered the immense bedroom in Marcus's private wing of Blackthorne Abbey early the day before and stood at the foot of Marcus's bed—which Henry II, once King of England, had supposedly slept in—waiting for him to awaken.

Marcus's head was still pounding too loudly from the port he had overindulged in the night before to hear his brother's footsteps on the carpet, but some subconscious warning soon had him sitting bolt upright on the feather mattress.

The first thing he laid eyes on was the grisly image carved into the footboard. A knight on a rearing horse had cleaved another knight nearly in half with an ax. The agony on the dying knight's face was terrible to behold.

Nausea rolled in his stomach. He squeezed his eyes shut and grabbed his throbbing head in his hands to keep it from falling off his shoulders.

Alastair cleared his throat.

Marcus carefully opened his eyes again, wincing at the pinpoints of sunlight streaming through the moth-eaten black velvet curtains. "Oh, it's you."

"I must travel to London immediately to speak

with my solicitor," Alastair said. "Some confusion has arisen about my hereditary right to Blackthorne Hall, the most profitable of my Scottish estates."

Marcus rubbed the sleep from his bleary eyes and tried to focus on Alastair. His brother was already dressed for the journey to London in somber colors that matched his temperament. "This is not a ruse to avoid the Braddock party, is it?" Marcus asked suspiciously.

"Unfortunately, no," Alastair assured him. "Look for me within the week. Will you take care of the twins for me until I join you?"

"Like they were my own." Marcus bit his unruly tongue, but it was too late. The damning words were out. Anything more he said would only make the situation worse. And yet he felt the urge to say something. "Alastair—"

"I have no doubt Regina and Rebecca will delight in your company," Alastair said curtly. He nodded stiffly—an irritated duke's version of deference—and left the room.

Marcus groaned. What had provoked him to drink so much? What had made him say exactly the wrong thing to his brother, something guaranteed to inflame a never-quite-healed wound?

It must have been the sinister spirits that haunted Blackthorne Abbey. Sometimes he could hear them moving about at night within the stone walls. Not that he would have admitted such a thing, even under torture. There were no such things as ghosts or evil spirits. But it was easy to understand why others believed the Abbey was haunted.

The east wing of the Abbey, which included the

chapel, had been ravaged in some past century, and only a few rooms were still used. The rest was decaying, the crumbling walls damp and moldy the whole year round. Curtains put up by some recent generation of Blackthornes were steadily rotting, revealing glimpses of the mullioned windows.

Once upon a time, Marcus had planned to make extensive renovations. But that was before Penthia had leveled her accusations.

Now he rarely stayed for more than a night or two at Blackthorne Abbey. When he did, he needed alcohol to dull his senses so he could sleep. He told himself it was the macabre carving on the bedstead that kept him awake. And the ghosts in the walls. But he knew it was memories of Penthia coming to this room. To this bed.

Marcus reached for the bottle of port on the side table. He needed something to take the foul taste from his mouth. And to give him the courage to face two energetic little girls who were bound to chatter like squirrels the whole way to Sussex. To be truthful, he would enjoy conversing with the twins and making them laugh—once his headache had passed. Until then, thank God, their governess would have the care of them.

He should have known it would not be that easy.

The twins' governess, Miss Balderdish, had exited the traveling carriage immediately after entering it when Reggie's garter snake slithered across the toe of her polished black shoe. She had refused to return even when Marcus held the snake before her in his hands, proving it no longer inhabited the carriage.

"It is perfectly safe, Miss Balderdish. You may get back in now."

Miss Balderdish quivered in place on the cobblestones at the front door to Blackthorne Abbey. "There is no telling what else those children may have hidden among the seats," the pasty-faced woman steadfastly maintained. "You will have to find someone else to stay shut up with the two of them in such close quarters. It shall not be me!"

Reggie had not looked the least bit repentant.

"Really, Uncle Marcus," Becky said in her best grown-up voice. "Such a to-do over a harmless little snake."

"What else have you got in there?" he said.

Two cherubic faces smiled out at him. "Nothing."

He leaned his head inside the carriage. A mewling sound issued from a leather traveling case snuggled close at Reggie's side, and something was scratching inside a wicker basket at Becky's feet. He opened his mouth and shut it again. He really did not want to know.

Marcus turned to his batman, who stood holding the reins of both men's horses, and said, "You are not afraid of snakes, are you, Sergeant Griggs?"

"Not me, Captain."

"Find a place for this, will you?" He handed the snake to Griggs. Griggs did not mind, but the two horses took serious exception to the presence of the snake.

Marcus's Thoroughbred gelding tore free and bolted, while Griggs's mount reared and trampled a lovely bed of daffodils that graced the cobblestone drive.

It took only half an hour to recover the Thoroughbred. It would take another growing season to restore the daffodils.

When they were ready to leave at last, Marcus stood at the carriage door and said, "I suppose you two can manage without a governess for the afternoon's journey, since you have me and Sergeant Griggs." He was certain there would be more female help available once they arrived where they were going. "But I expect both of you to be on your best behavior."

"We will be, Uncle Marcus," they chorused happily.

He should have known better than to believe them.

They stopped no less than four times before the first change of horses, twice for lemonade and twice for the necessary. On the fourth stop, at the White Ball Inn, a bare fifteen miles from Blackthorne Abbey, the contents of the leather bag—a highly agitated orange, black, and white cat—escaped into the barn.

Reggie stubbornly refused to get back into the carriage until the missing cat was located. Becky sided with her sister.

"We will have the innkeeper find your cat and keep her here until we can return for her," Marcus cajoled in an attempt to finish the never-ending journey.

"You cannot really intend to abandon Frances, Uncle Marcus," Becky said. "What if it were me or Reggie who was lost. You would not continue the journey until we were found, would you?"

"That would be a different matter entirely."

"You cannot love us more than we love Frances," Becky said.

Marcus shot his batman a beseeching look.

Griggs grinned and shrugged. "She has a point, Captain."

"Frances is in the family way," Reggie informed him. "What if she needs us?"

Much to Marcus's chagrin, by the time they found Frances in the far reaches of the stable, the scroungy calico cat had already delivered one solid black kitten and another that was orange with a white nose and three white paws. It was clearly impossible to remove the cat from her nest before she was finished delivering.

Marcus was not quite certain he should have allowed the two girls to watch the birthing, but they squatted down inelegantly, but reverently, in the straw at Frances's side to observe. He had no choice but to join them.

By then, a trip that should have taken an afternoon had stretched into something more. Marcus stood to leave, with the thought of securing rooms for the night at the inn, but Becky grasped his hand and pulled him back down beside her.

"Frances might need you, Uncle Marcus."

He was not sure exactly how he could have been of any earthly help to a pregnant cat, but Becky's grip on his hand precluded leaving.

"Griggs!" he called.

The sergeant appeared at his side with an ale in hand and hung a lantern on the stall where the cat had settled. The circular yellow glow kept the growing dark at bay. "I got us rooms for the night, Captain, and arranged to stable the horses. Figured we wouldn't be leavin' right away."

"You read my mind, Griggs. The ladies will be needing some supper, too."

"A private dining room will be ready and waitin' when the birthin's done," Griggs assured him before leaving them alone.

"Do you think there are any more babies inside her?" Reggie asked when Frances had finished cleaning off the second kitten.

Marcus watched the cat's stomach ripple. "Possibly. We will have to wait and see."

Nothing about the following births escaped the girls' notice. Marcus found himself guessing at the answers to questions he knew some woman should be answering for them. But they had no mother, and were currently without a proper female companion. Griggs had retired to the other end of the stable to enjoy his mug of ale in peace, and Alastair was in London. There was no one left but him.

Becky turned a curious face up to him. "Is that how we were born?"

"Human babies come out of their mothers in essentially the same way," he managed to say.

He waited for another question, like "How do they get inside there in the first place?" But he was spared that challenge.

At last, three more blind, mewling kittens had joined the first two in the straw, and Frances appeared to be reclining comfortably with her new family.

"We should let Frances rest now," he said. "Griggs has arranged for us to have dinner inside."

"We could not possibly leave Frances now," Reggie said, appalled at his suggestion. "What if a dog should come around to chase her? Frances and her kittens need us more than ever to protect them."

"Reggie is right, Uncle Marcus," Becky said. "We have a duty to protect those weaker than ourselves."

He could not argue with that.

In the end, Marcus sent Griggs to fetch them all meat pasties and lemonade, and they had a picnic in the stall. It was no trouble for him to sleep on a bed of straw, but he was surprised that the twins insisted upon it. Warm blankets from the inn provided a coverlet, and after much shifting and arranging, the twins made a nest for themselves as comfortable as the one Frances had made for her kittens.

He listened to their prayers—God blessed an unending litany of relatives, servants, and animals—and kissed them each good night. They snuggled together instinctively to keep warm. Their faces and hands were dirty, their dresses wrinkled, but they smiled up at him as though life could not be more perfect.

He moved the lantern to the far side of the stall, and it was not long—he did not say "Go to sleep now" more than twice or thrice—before he heard the deep and even breathing that signaled their slumber.

Marcus sat with his back braced against the stall, his booted feet stretched out in front of him on the straw. He worked out a crick in his shoulder and rubbed at an old wound on his thigh.

It had been rash, maybe even reckless, he realized, to set out with two young girls and no female companion. Look what had happened. No governess would have let them get away with watching a scruffy, tattered-eared cat give birth. No governess would have allowed them to eat meat pasties in the barn, or sleep on blankets in the straw.

Marcus smiled. He was glad he was there.

He closed his eyes, dozing as though it were the eve of battle, listening for the slightest sound that might mean danger to those for whom he stood guard.

He was instantly awake when the barn door creaked open, but he mistook completely where he was. This safe barn in England had become a bullet-pocked refuge in Spain, and the stealth of whoever had opened the door made him certain it was a French soldier come to kill him.

Marcus sat perfectly still, so as not to rustle the straw, but reached for a blade he carried in his boot, ready to meet the enemy.

Chapter 2

At THE ADVANCED AGE OF SEVENTEEN AND A HALF, Miss Elizabeth Sheringham was running away from home. It was the only solution she could find to an intolerable situation. Her cousin Nigel, Earl of Ravenwood, with whom she had lived since the death of her father two years before, had made advances tonight that left no doubt as to his ignoble intentions. She was certain Nigel's wife, Agnes, would be gravely disappointed if she knew of them.

Eliza had broken a pottery vase on Nigel's head in the conservatory and made her escape. Her cousin was bound to be furious when he recovered, but she would not be there to hear him ranting.

Eliza's greatest regret was having to leave behind her aunt, Lady Lavinia Sheringham, her father's spinster sister. Unfortunately, Aunt Lavinia was too old to think a long gallop on horseback was a grand adventure. She would more likely complain about the discomfort and the cold.

It was too bad. Eliza would have welcomed the company; she had a deathly fear of being alone in the dark. Aunt Lavinia was always a comfort at such times because, though she had been blind since birth, she managed to find joy and light in her perpetually dark world. Eliza had left a message for Aunt Lavinia with Cook, promising to send for her as soon as she was settled in London.

Eliza knew she would be missed at the house party being given by the Duke and Duchess of Braddock scheduled to begin on the morrow, but that could not be helped. Her friend Charlotte, Countess of Denbigh, who had arranged the invitation for her, would understand why she had run away.

In any case, her absence was probably for the best. Eliza could not seem to control her tongue with strangers. As a Child of Scandal, she had learned to expect unkindness. At first the thoughtless remarks and occasional downright meanness had left her in tears. She had grown a tougher hide, and learned to take the sting from such insults by turning the malicious comments back upon their author.

People either laughed when her barbs hit home, in which case the evening would be enjoyable. Or they turned their backs on her entirely, at which point she went to work with a will, sending scathing—and remarkably well-aimed—insults at those who, without good cause, considered themselves her betters.

Eliza was sometimes invited to a dinner or musicale merely to provide the other guests with an interesting topic of conversation. In those cases, Eliza felt obliged to give her hostess what she expected. She had sent many a matron home with the vapors and had once constrained her hostess to retire upstairs with the headache.

Eliza did not care whether Society approved of her or not. At least, that was the appearance she gave.

Beneath the tough exterior was a lonely woman who ached to be loved and accepted.

She had thought Cousin Nigel understood her feelings. But he had seen her disdain of Society and assumed a lack of honor. After all, like father, like daughter.

"Surely one more scandal cannot matter," he had said, as he grabbed her and pressed his dry lips against hers.

Eliza had experienced a nauseated panic when she caught the acrid scent of his pipe tobacco. From that moment onward, she had fallen into a black void of terror so deep it was difficult to believe even now that she was safe.

Cousin Nigel had deserved to have a flower pot dumped on his balding pate. If it were not for the sob caught in her throat at the time, she might have laughed at the ridiculous picture he had made with a mountain of petunias growing from his head.

Eliza quietly shoved open the stable door at the White Ball Inn, searching for the stallion the Countess of Denbigh had arranged to have boarded there for Eliza's use.

"I will not be riding much for the next few months," the countess had said, "and I want Mephistopheles to be well exercised."

It had not taken much effort on Eliza's part to figure out that the countess was in expectation of a happy event. Eliza was glad for Charlie. She would like to have a houseful of children herself . . . someday.

But she had known since she was old enough to understand the whispers, that no eligible gentleman was likely to offer for her. They considered her as free and easy as Cousin Nigel had. All except for Nigel's younger brother, Major Julian Sheringham. Julian had been different from the first. He had always treated her with courtesy and respect.

Her cousin had recently returned from duty on the Continent and was on leave in London. She was counting on him now to rescue her from Cousin Nigel's clutches.

She had no doubt he would. Unlike others, Julian treated her just as he would any other young lady of quality. He had shown by his behavior toward her that the scandal surrounding her father did not matter to him. That was fortunate, because Eliza had fallen hopelessly in love with Cousin Julian when she was fifteen.

He had come home to Ravenwood the first time after Cousin Nigel inherited the title from her grandfather wearing a dashing blue hussar's uniform, with red cuffs and gold lace trim. He was so kind and so handsome, she could not help but admire him.

But at fifteen, her lovely female endowments had been nothing more than wishes on her chest. Her face had been a collection of odd features—sharp cheekbones, wide-spaced, strangely golden hazel eyes, and a dash of freckles over a nose that seemed entirely too large. She had been every bit as tall as she was now, but as gangly as a newborn colt.

She had followed Julian around the entire two weeks he stayed at Ravenwood, mute as a doorknob without the acid comments that usually sustained her conversation. He had laughingly—and lovingly, she thought—called her "Brat" and "Pest" and "Trouble-maker."

He might as well have been calling her "Dear" and "Darling" and "Sweetheart." She knew that at fifteen she was too young to be seriously courted. She suspected he was being careful not to offend her tender sensibilities.

But two years had passed since then. She was seventeen—old enough to be a wife and mother. Experienced enough to converse with ease. But Julian had never returned to court her.

Eliza had no choice except to go out and find him.

Her plan was simple. She would disguise herself in some of Julian's clothes, find the hotel where he was staying in London, and convince him to marry her.

Immediately after Cousin Nigel's attack, she had dressed in one of Julian's lawn shirts, with one of his neck cloths done up in the precise Mathematical she had often tied for her father. She had placed her father's gold watch in the pocket of a lavender brocade waistcoat because she could not bear to leave it behind. Rags were stuffed into the broad shoulders of Julian's mulberry jacket to fill it out, while his buckskin breeches fit her snugly in the hips.

Wearing Julian's clothes, including a brand new pair of Hessians that had just been delivered to Ravenwood, and with her waist-length chestnut hair hidden under a gentleman's hat, she hoped to be mistaken for a boy if she was spotted on the road.

Her height would help—she stood a head above the average male—and she had bound her breasts to hide their fullness. Her voice was gravelly sounding from a childhood riding accident, and she could lower it even more if she tried. With such manly traits to aid in her disguise, how could she fail to deceive?

Eliza breathed a sigh of relief when she saw the warm glow of light in the corner of the stable at the White Ball Inn. She had dreaded entering what she had supposed would be pitch blackness inside. It did not occur to her to wonder why a lantern should be burning in a place supposedly empty of human inhabitants.

Mephistopheles's head appeared over his stall at the sound of her bootsteps, and he whickered at the sight of her. Once inside the door, she dropped her cloth traveling bag, which contained several clean shirts and underthings and a dress in which to meet Julian, and headed toward the stallion.

"Easy there, boy. We are going for a long ride," she soothed as she approached the huge beast. "I haven't any carrots or apples for you, but—"

One second Eliza was reaching out a hand toward the stall, the next her back was pulled up tight against a muscular male body. An impossibly strong arm lay pressed against her throat, and the point of a cold, sharp knife actually pierced her skin beneath her ear.

"Make a sound, and you're dead."

She bit her lip, fighting the urge to scream. The warm drop of blood crawling down her neck tickled her, making her shiver. Any second she expected to feel the knife dig farther into her flesh. Her muscles tensed in anticipation of the pain.

They stood frozen in that deadly pose for endless moments, like some awful statue.

Eventually, despite her captor's warning, fear loosened her tongue. "You're plucking the wrong goose. I have nothing worth stealing," she croaked.

"Oh, my God," he whispered.

She felt the hold on her neck easing. She was afraid to move, afraid he would stab her the instant she tried to run. But this might be her only chance to win free.

She whirled and lashed out with a balled fist, planting him a facer exactly as her father had taught her—after one too many boys had teased her—hitting as hard as she could. The villain's head barely moved to the side at the sickening *thwack* of her knuckles on flesh, but a dark, horizontal streak appeared high on his cheekbone.

She cried out in pain and cradled her bruised knuckles in her other hand. "Ow! Ow! Ow!" It felt as though she had rammed her hand into a stone wall.

The man careened into her, his shoulder hitting her stomach and slamming her to the ground. He landed on top of her and clamped her hands fast in the dirt on either side of her head.

She was too stunned to do more than lie there and stare up at him. Until she realized she had to breathe.

She gasped in a lungful of air and felt her breasts surge against his chest. Which was when she realized the binding had slipped. And her hat was gone.

His fingertips feathered lightly through the long, tangled locks that framed her face and spread out around her on the hay-littered surface. She saw the dawning realization in his eyes as he gathered a fistful of curls the rich reddish-brown of unroasted chestnuts in each hand.

"A woman," he muttered.

He was off her a second later and bent down to yank her onto her feet. She knew the danger was greater now. He would think she was weak, vulnerable because she was female. He would think he could take advantage, as Cousin Nigel had.

While he was still bent over, she lifted her knee as high and as hard as she could—another lesson from her father to be used if a boy persisted—and caught her attacker hard on the chin. That was not precisely where she had been aiming, but it worked almost as well.

His teeth clacked together, and he went bowling over backward. Unfortunately, she heard more outrage than pain in the epithets he hurled at her.

She looked for something to use for the *coup de grâce*—anything heavy to hit him on the head and knock him out before he could come after her again. A last resort, her father had said, to be used only if her life was threatened. Which surely it was.

Before she could find a weapon, a swarm of tiny, terrifying demons, eerie ghosts in white, descended upon her. One kicked her in the knee. Another socked her in the stomach. While she was bent over with pain, yet another grabbed her hair and yanked hard enough to bring tears to her eyes.

"Leave Uncle Marcus alone!"

"Get out! Go away! And don't come back!"

She would have been glad to flee, except when she stumbled toward the door, she found it blocked by an enormous hulking figure.

"Halt!" the shadowy figure commanded. "Stand where you are!"

Eliza searched frantically for another avenue of escape, but saw none. It was either charge the door or be done in by the man and his demons.

In the momentary silence caused by her indecision, she heard a child's startled voice say, "Why, it's only a young lady, Uncle Marcus, not a man at all!"

"I can see that now," he said.

"How do you suppose she makes herself look so tall?" another childish voice asked.

"I believe she simply grew that size," the man replied with obvious amusement.

Eliza stared in astonishment at the three figures who had spoken. The "demons" she had feared were merely two little girls—with identical faces—dressed in straw-laced, wrinkled white muslin.

She bit back a sharp rebuke for the comments about her height. The man deserved it, but the child was only curious. "I am one inch less than six feet tall," she said to the twins. "And I may still be growing," she added with a teasing smile, ignoring the gentleman as though he were not there.

One twin eyed her cautiously. The other smiled back.

The man who had ambushed her stood behind them, one hand on each of their shoulders. Despite his disheveled state, it was apparent from the cut and quality of his clothes that Eliza was facing a gentleman of some distinction. And now that she had the leisure to look at him, perhaps the most perfect male specimen she had ever seen.

Not a single caustic comment came to mind. "Oh,

dear," she said. And blushed. Eliza was not the sort of woman who blushed. Not at an insult, surely. It would have made her too vulnerable to the gossips. This blush had resulted purely from her intense reaction to a man's physical attractiveness. It had never happened before, and she found it somewhat disconcerting. Her reaction to him had been so very *obvious*.

"Need any help, Captain?" the voice from the doorway called.

"I believe the twins and I have everything under control, Griggs. You may go back to bed."

"Very well, Captain."

Captain. He was a soldier, like Julian. But far more handsome than Julian. Eliza killed that traitorous thought aborning. No one could be more precious to her than Julian. Besides, as she very well knew, looks did not tell the whole story about a person. Where would she be if everyone she met judged her by her looks? She had learned from Aunt Lavinia, who could not see anything at all, to take a man's measure by what he said and did.

Eliza took further comfort in the thought that even if this gentleman were dressed in a uniform, he could not possibly look as bang up to the mark in it as Julian did in his. After all, the Prince of Wales's own 10th Royal Hussars were a very select group of gentlemen.

"Why did you attack me?" she demanded when she had recovered enough composure to speak.

"I thought you were . . ." He paused, cleared his throat, and said, "Why are you disguised as a man?"

"It is a long story," she said. "Which begins in the conservatory where I—"

"Skip forward, if you please, and explain why you were sneaking in here in the middle of the night?"

"I came to get my horse," she answered indignantly, with a gesture toward Mephistopheles. "What are you doing here?"

He rubbed his sore jaw and chuckled. "Nursemaiding a mother cat and her five kittens."

"Nursemaiding a cat," she repeated as seriously as she could. The whole idea was preposterous. A bubble of laughter escaped.

His lips curled in a friendly smile that revealed twin dimples in his cheeks.

Really, she thought. *A man with dimples. They were . . . He was charming.*

She could not take her eyes off him, perhaps because she liked so much what she saw. She might have felt more like a peagoose if he had not been staring right back at her.

Something shifted deep inside her. She felt a little dizzy and put a hand to her temple, thinking maybe she had hit the ground too hard.

"Are you all right?" he asked, reaching out a hand to grasp her shoulder.

"I'm fine," she said, fighting the shiver of awareness that streaked down her spine and shrugging to free herself from his touch. "How are the kittens?"

He seemed momentarily nonplussed but answered, "They're fine, too."

"Frances has five kittens in all," one of the twins said.

"Would you like to see them?" the other asked, tugging on her jacket—or rather, Julian's jacket.

Eliza lowered her gaze to the identical girls standing side by side before her. "Certainly, if you would like to show them to me. I would rather meet you both first."

"I am Lady—" The twin who had spoken glanced at her uncle, then turned back, chin upthrust, and said, "You may call me Reggie. This is Becky, and this is Uncle Marcus. Who are you?"

"Eliza Sheringham, lately of Ravenwood." She started to curtsy, stopped herself, and executed an elegant bow.

The captain's eyes narrowed assessingly. For a moment she was afraid he might know Cousin Nigel. Or what if he had encountered Julian in one of those taverns soldiers were forever frequenting? Or maybe he knew about the scandal. Or had heard one of the tales about her objectionable behavior being bandied about the neighborhood—all of which were true, only a few of which she regretted, and for none of which she would ever apologize.

She was surprised when he merely nodded and said, "A pleasure to meet you, Miss Sheringham. It is *Miss?*"

"Yes, Captain. Miss Sheringham," she said, unaccountably blushing again. How did one control such revealing behavior? she wondered. Especially when one had no reason to be blushing. She was in love with Julian. No mere handsome face was going to sway her loyalty to her cousin.

Besides, the perfect male standing before her could not possibly find anything attractive about her figure in Julian's clothes. And her odd facial features had matured into something equally out of the common way.

Eliza soon found herself on her knees in the straw beside a motley mother cat and her five kittens, all of which, she discovered, already had names. "They are so perfect when they're born, are they not?" she said, reaching out to stroke the soft fur of the solid black kitten under Frances's and the twins' watchful eyes. "And so very helpless."

"Would you like to have Blackie?" Becky asked. "When he is grown up enough, of course," she added.

"I will probably be far away when Blackie has grown up enough to leave his mother," she said, unable to keep the wistfulness from her voice. She thought about how much Aunt Lavinia would have enjoyed having a cat to purr in her lap.

"Where are you bound?" the captain asked.

Eliza was not sure she should tell him, but since they were perfect strangers, and he could have no interest in her, she decided there could be no real harm. "I am riding to London, where I plan to meet my cousin, Major Julian Sheringham."

"Where is your baggage? And your maid?"

"My traveling bag is there by the door. I haven't any maid," she answered airily.

She did not like the look on his face when he asked, "Why not?"

She rose, and he rose along with her. "I do not believe that can be of any concern to you."

"Surely you must have some escort," he insisted, following her as she headed for the tack room to collect Mephistopheles's saddle and bridle.

"I really do not need one," she replied.

"The twins and I will be glad to accompany you," he said.

She eyed him with distrust. "Are you attempting to importune me, sir? I assure you—"

Before she could launch a verbal attack, he said, "I assure you, Miss Sheringham, I have nothing but your best interests in mind. I merely thought you might enjoy some company on your journey."

"How can we go with Miss Sheringham, Uncle Marcus?" one of the twins asked, appearing suddenly at his side. "I thought we had to be at—"

"There is no commitment we have that is more important than escorting Miss Sheringham safely to her destination," the captain interrupted, bestowing a silencing look on the child.

Eliza identified the girl as Reggie—she had noticed Reggie had a tear in the knee of her stocking.

"Can we go see the Tower?" Becky asked, quickly joining her sister.

"And watch the performing horses?"

"And go up in a balloon?"

"We may not have time—" Their uncle stopped himself and smiled down at their upturned faces. "Why not?"

He turned to Eliza and said, "Well, Miss Sheringham? It is up to you. Would you deny two little girls their first look at London?"

She could see difficulties ahead, not the least of which was how to detach herself from the trio when the time came. But she would not deny the little girls the sort of adventure she had yearned for as a child. And she did not really wish to be riding around in the dark tonight by herself.

"I would be delighted, Captain, if you and your nieces will join me on my journey."

"Then it is settled. We will travel together in the morning."

"Early," Eliza said, concerned about getting as far away from Ravenwood as quickly possible, preferably before Cousin Nigel realized she was gone.

"How early?" the captain asked.

"Dawn?"

She thought he groaned, but the sound was muffled when Mephistopheles stomped and swished his tail to rid himself of flies.

"I would rather sleep a little longer."

"I would not dream of imposing on you, Captain. Please, do sleep in. I will travel by myself."

He pressed his lips flat and said, "Very well, Miss Sheringham. We will leave at dawn."

Eliza gave him a blinding smile. "Whatever you say, Captain."

Chapter 3

 $\mathcal{I}$T WAS DIFFICULT FOR MARCUS TO GET THE TWINS settled back down in the stall with Frances and her kittens, because they were so excited by the change in traveling plans.

Marcus had kissed them both good night for the fourth time when Becky asked, "Where will Miss Sheringham sleep, Uncle Marcus?"

"I thought I would stay here with you," she replied before he could answer.

Marcus realized with a start that Miss Sheringham had already gathered a bunch of straw into a bed-sized pile in the far corner of the stall.

"There seems to be plenty of room for all of us," Miss Sheringham said, already down on one knee.

Marcus had a brief image of himself and Miss Sheringham naked and sweaty in the straw and shook his head to clear it.

"No. Absolutely not," he said, reaching out to take her arm at the elbow. He pulled her to her feet and then out of the stall completely.

"Why can't I stay here?" she asked.

A woman of the world would have known without asking. She was obviously far from that. In his most forebearing and patient voice he explained, "Because I will be here with the children. It would not be proper for you and I to sleep under the same roof without a chaperon."

"Who will know?"

"I will."

"So will I," she said. "But if we are satisfied with the sleeping arrangements, why should it matter to anyone else?"

Frankly, he agreed with her. But he knew better.

"It will not do, Miss Sheringham. Think of the consequences if we should be caught sleeping here together."

"Oh." Recognition dawned. "You mean the world will think we are two gentlemen who—"

"No, no." He fought back a laugh as he realized what she was implying. "I mean that if it becomes common knowledge that Miss Elizabeth Sheringham and the Beau spent the night together, we will be forced to the altar."

Her hazel eyes—more like a tawny gold, he thought—probed his face as though he were a rare insect under a magnifying glass. "*You* are the Beau?"

He nodded. "Is there something about what I said you do not understand, Miss Sheringham?"

"Oh, I understand perfectly. You are right, of course. It is just that I have never met a notorious rake before," she admitted candidly. "The exploits of the Beau are known even in the countryside, Captain." Her lips curled in a devilish smile. "You are not what I expected. I mean, you have been so very nice. The Beau is an infamous rakehell, a wanton gambler, a knave who preys upon women, a—"

"Perhaps we should finish this discussion elsewhere," he interrupted before the wide-eyed twins could absorb any more of her picturesque description. "And allow the children their rest."

She glanced down at the avid listeners and nodded her assent.

"Griggs, please keep watch until I return," he said.

"Sure enough, Captain," the sergeant replied.

Marcus blew out the lantern, leaving the stable in darkness, and followed Miss Sheringham outside into the moonlight. A soft breeze ruffled his hair, and he took a deep breath of fresh air, suddenly aware of how stifling the barn had been.

Miss Sheringham did not stop outside the stable, but kept walking down the rutted country lane that led away from the White Ball Inn. A swirl of wind rustled the lilac bushes that edged the meandering road, while the moonlight made long shadows of their figures as Marcus increased his pace to catch up to her.

She had tucked her hair back up inside her hat before she left the barn, and as he watched her walk, he realized her strides were long enough, and determined enough, to fool an unobservant eye into believing she was a man.

He was all too aware she was not.

She reached a stone-edged well and began drawing a bucketful of water. Without speaking, he crossed to her side and helped. By the time he set the bucket of water on the edge of the well, she had a handkerchief in her hand, and he realized what she meant to do.

"Let me," he said.

Her eyes searched his face, and he tried to look trustworthy, not an easy feat for an avowed rake.

"Very well," she said at last.

He put his hands on her shoulders and turned her toward him. He reached for the precisely tied neck cloth, but paused when she stiffened.

"May I?" he asked.

She relaxed, then nodded.

His eyes held her gaze as he slowly untied the neck cloth that held the stiffly starched collar points upright. Then he unbuttoned the first two buttons and peeled aside the fine lawn cloth to expose her slender throat. He felt her quiver as his fingertips brushed her flesh.

"Steady," he said, as much for his own benefit as for hers.

He put his fingertips under her chin to turn her head to one side, so he could see the wound he had made with his knife. In the moonlight, he could see where blood had seeped from the small cut and was soaked up by her shirt.

"The wound is not deep," he said. "But it should be cleaned."

With a shaky hand, she offered him the handkerchief. "Would you mind?"

He felt her moist breath on his hands, the soft brush of her fingertips as he accepted the cloth from her.

"Please be gentle," she whispered.

Something about her voice, the low, gravelly sound of it, made his body tighten. His pulse quickened. His breathing harshened.

Marcus struggled to leash his growing desire. He

knew his excitement rose partly from the fact these circumstances were unlike anything in his former experience with a woman. The only wounds he had tended were on soldiers during the heat of battle. And though he had disrobed more females than he cared to count, none of them had been standing in the moonlight wearing gentleman's garb.

He wondered if Miss Sheringham felt the same sensual hunger he did. He wondered if she would let him kiss her.

He realized she was staring right back at him. There was no timidity, no coyness or shyness or any of the things he might have expected from a well-bred English lady. Her lambent eyes revealed her sharpened awareness of him. But there was no invitation in those shining golden orbs to carry the situation further.

He realized he liked her better for her honesty, for letting him see exactly what she was feeling, even if she had no intention of acting upon those feelings.

He dipped the handkerchief in the pail of water, then wrung it out. The extra liquid spattered on the stones at the base of the well and ricocheted onto the Hessians she was wearing.

"I will have to do some polishing before I return these boots to Julian," she said, glancing down.

He lifted her chin again, welcoming the excuse to touch her. "Look up."

He started near the hollow of her throat and slowly worked his way upward toward the wound, cleaning away the blood, careful not to cause her any more pain than necessary.

She hissed in a breath.

"Just a little more. There. That should do it." He threw the ruined handkerchief across the edge of the wooden pail.

"Have you another handkerchief?" she asked.

"What for?"

"Have you?"

He handed her a lace-edged, elaborately mono-grammed handkerchief from his pocket and watched as she traced the stitching.

"B for Beau?" she asked, when she identified the letter.

He smiled. "B for Blackthorne," he corrected. "I borrowed it from my brother."

She dipped the kerchief in the water and wrung it out. "I hope he will not mind if you ruin it."

"He has plenty more where that one came from," Marcus assured her with a grin.

The grin became a grimace as she pressed the cool, wet cloth against his lacerated cheek where she had struck him.

"I do not think the wound is deep," she said with a smile, reiterating his words. "But it should be cleaned."

"Ouch," he said. And then, "Ow, that hurts!"

"I did not make half so much noise," she said with a teasing laugh. She dabbed once more. "There. I am done."

The second kerchief joined the first.

When she smiled up at him so innocently, so sweetly, his common sense abandoned him. He tugged off her hat and watched as a yard of soft, silky hair slid across her shoulders. He let the hat fall to the ground, then caught her chin and raised her face to his.

He gave her no chance to deny him, simply captured her mouth with his and teased her supple lips with his tongue. She did nothing to return the kiss or reject it, but held herself perfectly still.

Marcus ended the kiss, but did not step back. He searched her face, wondering whether he should dare another kiss. Her golden eyes glowed with excitement . . . and apprehension.

A breath shuddered out of her.

The silence grew between them.

Marcus took whatever a woman offered and did his best to encourage more. But Miss Sheringham was his best friend's cousin. He had realized it the moment she said her name. Over the past two years, Julian had often mentioned his "funny little cousin Eliza" with fondness.

Julian spoke of her freckles, her odd-colored hazel eyes, her too-big nose, and her thin-as-a-bed-slat body. "The minx manages to cause more trouble than a dozen other girls her age combined," he had said. But Julian had sounded more charmed than annoyed by her outlandish behavior. There was also some scandal connected to her name, but Julian had dismissed it as nothing.

The woman standing before him did not quite fit the image Marcus had formed of her. Except for the part about causing trouble.

Her freckles were enchanting, her eyes mysterious, her high, sharp cheekbones and strong chin balanced the straight nose, and he had seldom seen a woman as well-favored with shapely feminine assets. Marcus had never bedded such a Long Meg, and he wondered what it would be like to make love to a woman who was nearly as tall as he was.

In short, he was completely intrigued by her. He wanted to spend more time looking at her, holding her, kissing her. He was more than a little curious to see the female body beneath the concealing male clothes. Not just to see it, but to put himself inside it.

But she was Julian's cousin.

A kiss he could take. More than that, she would have to offer him. He waited for her to decide.

"I have never been kissed by a rake," she said at last, her eyes still dazed from the experience.

"Was it everything you expected?" he asked, his eyes glinting with humor.

"I am not in a position to judge," she admitted. "I have nothing with which to compare it."

Marcus stood stunned for a second, then threw back his head and roared with laughter. Julian was right. She was delightful. Enormously entertaining.

Then he realized what he had done. He had not meant to kiss her. Or rather, he had wanted desperately to kiss her but had not meant to mislead her. Since he had no intention of becoming a husband, he owed it to the chit not to attach her affections. An innocent like Miss Sheringham—not to mention Julian, if he ever found out—was likely to misconstrue his behavior as something more than it was.

What induced you to kiss her in the first place? an inner voice scolded.

Curiosity. Novelty. The lure of something fresh and new.

Nothing more?

There could be nothing more. He had lived life

on the edge, but he knew better than to let himself get carried away by passion. No woman was worth the trouble such emotions caused. Not even the enticing Miss Sheringham.

"Come on, brat," he said, using a term Julian had often applied to her. "It is time we got you to bed."

"Are you planning to join me there?" she asked with an arch look.

For an instant he wondered if she meant her words as an invitation. He decided she could not possibly. He shook his head as he reached down for her hat. "Oh, no, my dear. Not me. You are entirely too dangerous."

He handed the hat to her, careful not to touch her skin, and watched as she began tucking her hair back under the concealing beaver wool felt.

"You may have one of the rooms my batman secured for us at the inn before we decided to spend the night in the stable," he said. "I will rejoin Reggie and Becky."

"You must promise not to leave without me tomorrow morning," she said as they made their way back to the inn.

"You may be sure I will be your constant companion until you reach your destination," he said.

"I appreciate your kindness, Captain. More than you know."

Marcus could not remember being called kind by anyone in recent memory. He was not the least motivated to help Miss Sheringham by feelings of kindness. After all, he was a rogue and a rake. If it were not for her connection to his best friend, she would have been lucky to escape his clutches with her good name intact. But it seemed unwise to remind her of his reputation for moral corruption when they were about to set off on a journey together.

When they reached the door to the inn he bowed, one gentleman to another. "Good night, Miss Sheringham."

She executed a quite competent bow in return. As she straightened, she gave him a gamine grin and said, "I look forward to traveling with a rake. It is only too bad I will be in disguise. It will not be half so much fun if no one knows it is me riding beside you. Good night, Captain."

He stood gaping as she disappeared inside.

"What is taking Uncle Marcus so long?" Reggie whispered to her sister. "He left with Miss Sheringham hours ago. He should have been back by now."

Reggie was not the least bit sleepy. Unfortunately, even with her eyes wide open, she could not see a thing, it was so very dark. She reached out and nudged Becky's shoulder. "Are you awake?"

"Hmmm."

Barely, Reggie decided. It was awful having a sister who always fell asleep before she did. Reggie felt bereft, abandoned, alone.

She took a deep, sighing breath and let it out. The pungent odors of hay and horse and manure were not at all unpleasant. They reminded her of the time she had climbed into the loft of the barn at Blackthorne Abbey and accidentally fallen asleep.

The household had been in an uproar, she learned later, looking everywhere for her. Father had finally discovered her in the loft and woken her with a shake. He had actually picked her up in his arms and carried her down the ladder himself. The punishment he had meted out for worrying her governess had been a small price to pay for being held so very close to him for those few moments.

Reggie inhaled deeply. The smells had been the same that memorable afternoon as they were now.

"Becky?" When she got no answer, Reggie pinched her sister.

"Ummph," Becky protested.

"Do you think Uncle Marcus will try to kiss Miss Sheringham?" Reggie whispered. "I have heard that is what rakes like Uncle Marcus do. Miss Sheringham seemed to like him well enough, even after their rough and tumble fight. Do you think she will let him have his way with her?"

"Hmmm."

"I suppose not," Reggie said. She picked up a piece of straw and used it to draw circles and squares and triangles on Becky's back. The way Becky wriggled, she knew her sister was more awake than she pretended to be. "I have never seen a woman fight like a man. Did you not think she was magnificent?"

Without pausing for a reply she continued, "I want to be like her—not afraid of anything. I am sure it would help my confidence to be so tall, but it must be a nuisance to stand head and shoulders above everyone else, would you not agree?"

Becky grunted.

It was all the encouragement Reggie needed. "I was so surprised when her hat fell off, and her hair fell all the way to her waist! Would you not say it is nearly the same color as Father's favorite hound, Rex?"

When Becky did not offer a reply, Reggie nudged her with an elbow. "Are you awake?"

"Ow!" Becky rolled over to face her. "Of course I am awake. You have been talking without a breath ever since Uncle Marcus followed Miss Sheringham from the stable."

"Then why did you not answer me?"

"You seemed happy to carry on the conversation all by yourself," Becky replied.

Reggie stuck out her tongue. Unfortunately, in the dark, Becky could not see it.

"Put your tongue back in your mouth," Becky said.

"How do you know I stuck it out?"

"I can smell your awful breath," Becky replied.

Reggie breathed hard on Becky, who made a sound of disgust and rolled over, hiding her head in her arms. "Go to sleep!"

"Admit it," Reggie said, speaking directly in her sister's covered ear. "You are as fascinated by Miss Sheringham as I am."

Becky groaned in surrender. "Very well. I admit it. Now may I sleep?"

"Oww!" Reggie grabbed her nose. "Why did you hit me?"

"It was an accident," Becky said. "I was turning over to get more comfortable. I didn't know you were there."

Now that she knew her sister was also wide awake, Reggie began to ask questions in earnest. "Have you ever thought what it would be like if Father remarried, and we got another mother?"

"No."

"I have. I think it would be nice to have someone like Miss Sheringham to hold us and kiss us and tell us stories at bedtime."

"Mother never did those things."

"She must have. Once upon a time."

"Not in my memory," Becky said. "Go to sleep, Reggie."

"I can remember . . ." But the recollection was fleeting, shrouded by time. Reggie had thought it must be Mother she remembered hugging her and kissing her, because Father never had much to do with them. But what if it had been Father? Why had he stopped loving her? What had she done wrong? What could she do to make him love her again?

Reggie closed her eyes against the sting of tears. Why was Father so distant? Uncle Marcus acted more like a father than Father did.

It was her last thought before she fell asleep.

Eliza had little difficulty passing herself off to the innkeeper as a friend of Captain Wharton. And since the captain had already paid for the room, the innkeeper did not quibble about giving her a key. It was not until she closed the upstairs bedroom door behind her that she realized she had left her traveling bag, with clean clothes for the morrow, in the stable.

It would be far too dangerous to retrieve it tonight. She would go down and get it in the morning.

Quite simply, Eliza was not sure she could resist temptation a second time. It seemed she had no more willpower to refuse that handsome rogue's entreaties than a baby offered a stick of candy. She had very much liked the feel of his lips on hers. She had very much wanted to know what it would feel like to be held in his arms. Scandal be damned. She had very much wanted to be seduced by Captain Wharton.

That made no sense to her when she loved Julian so desperately. Could a woman be in love with one man and enjoy another's kisses? *Crave* another's kisses? Apparently she could. Maybe she was her father's daughter, after all.

Eliza had never been told what sin, exactly, her father had committed. It seemed impossible he could have ruined some woman's reputation. She had seen her parents together, and they were deeply in love with each other. Her father had been a good and kind man, devoted to his family. He did not drink to excess or cheat at cards or have any other vice that one associated with scandal. So what had Papa done?

It should not matter. Except she had grown more and more certain over the years that Papa's disgrace had something to do with her. Had her mother lain with another man before she married the earl's son? Was she not her father's child? Was that why the earl had disinherited his only son?

She had never asked her parents for the truth. And they had never offered it. Sometimes she suffered nightmares in which she was lost and calling for Papa. She was hungry and thirsty and her voice was hoarse from crying. But Papa never came.

It all seemed so real. She would awake drenched in perspiration, feeling desperate to escape, and realize she was safe in her own bed, in her own room. Maybe her dream had something to do with Papa's disgrace. Maybe she had been lost, and he had not tried hard enough to find her.

That did not seem a great enough sin to banish a man forever from his family and all of Society.

Over the years, partly to confirm opinions she knew had already formed about her, Eliza had defied Society to banish her. Thanks to the tabbies, she was scandalous without having done a single truly scandalous thing. She had her virtue, her personal sense of honor, and her own standards of behavior to which she had rigidly held. In one evening, Captain Wharton had convinced her to throw them all out the window.

But if kissing the Beau was wrong, why had it felt so right? Maybe that was the lure that led one to scandal. One deceived oneself into thinking that black was really white. That wrong was really right. That because someone was nice to you, he had your best interests at heart.

She had underestimated the seductive power of the Beau's charm. She would have to guard her heart more carefully from now on. After all, it was Julian she loved, Julian she would marry.

Eliza undressed down to the female chemise and men's smalls she had worn under Julian's clothing and slipped between the bedsheets. Her feet were cold, and she tucked her legs up under her chin to try and warm herself.

As she drifted off to sleep, Eliza thought how disappointed Aunt Lavinia would be when she discovered Eliza had run away instead of attending the house party at Somersville Manor. Eliza had been reluctant to spend two full weeks in polite company, since there was no way she could have blunted her sharp tongue for that long. But Aunt Lavinia had argued at length to convince her she should go.

"It will get you away from Ravenwood—and your cousin Nigel—for two weeks," Aunt Lavinia had said.

Her aunt had apparently deduced from Eliza's tone of voice when she spoke of Cousin Nigel that the two of them were not faring well together. A respite from his company would be lovely.

"With luck," Aunt Lavinia added, "you may even find a husband."

"Surely you cannot want me to leave you here at Ravenwood and go live in some stranger's home."

Aunt Lavinia made a clucking sound and rearranged her knitting in her lap. "I would hope your husband will not be a stranger to you. Or if he is," she said, deferring to the realities of English upper-class marriage, "it would not be for long. You must resign yourself to marrying and having a home of your own without me." She paused, then said, "Someday Nigel will corner you where there is no escape."

Eliza gasped, amazed that her aunt had discerned the nature of Cousin Nigel's offensive behavior. "How did you know?"

"I am merely blind, my dear. Not deaf and dumb. You must marry, to save yourself from this untenable situation."

Eliza stared at her aunt, who stared right back. "Have you considered the fact that no gentleman at the party may want to marry the impoverished daughter of a disinherited earl?"

"Considered it and rejected it," her aunt said flatly. "Look at me, girl. Your future can be as bright as you choose to make it. You must take the chip from your shoulder and give people a chance to like you. You are an amiable young lady, you know."

Eliza dropped her eyes to escape her aunt's piercing gaze. "If you say so," she muttered.

One of the things that so unsettled people meeting her "blind, elderly aunt" for the first time was the fact that Aunt Lavinia's pale gray eyes did not look sightless. When Lady Lavinia angled her head and stared at you, it appeared she was really seeing you.

Though no one had taken the time to formally educate a blind female child, Eliza found her aunt extraordinarily wise. And Aunt Lavinia was the only one of her father's family who had come to visit him after he had been disinherited. Her aunt had been Eliza's anchor in the months after her father's death, six years following her mother's, which had left her orphaned.

"There must be some other way to escape Ravenwood," Eliza said. "Can we not go back to live at Father's house? It is mine now."

"Nigel is your guardian until you are five-and-twenty, or until you marry. I doubt he will allow it. Without his approval and support, we would have no wherewithal to live. My father, the former Earl of Sheringham, assumed I would never leave Ravenwood, so he accorded me nothing in his will except the right to live here the rest of my life."

Eliza settled on the lush carpet beside her aunt's chair, and laid her cheek on her aunt's knee. The needles stopped clicking as Aunt Lavinia reached out to touch her, to stroke her face and her hair.

Eliza had learned over the years that touching

made things real for her aunt. But Eliza wondered how much her aunt could really "see" with her hands.

Aunt Lavinia could surely feel the warmth of the fire on Eliza's hair, but there was no way she could see how the flames turned Eliza's chestnut curls a burnished copper. She could feel Eliza's downturned lips, but she could not see the faraway look in her eye. She could feel the tension in Eliza's shoulders, but she could not know it came from seeing Cousin Nigel pause at the sewing room door to stare in at them. Yet, Eliza was constantly amazed at Aunt Lavinia's powers of perception.

"I am having a private *tête-à-tête* with my niece, my lord. Would you mind closing the door for us?"

Cousin Nigel scowled, but pulled the door shut.

"However did you know he was there?" Eliza asked.

"Nigel smokes a truly wretched tobacco. Something he inherited from my father, no doubt. The stench precedes him wherever he goes."

Eliza laughed. "Only you could leave an earl looking sheepish for interrupting two ladies in his care."

"Fiddlefaddlingsticks," her aunt said.

"I think you mean *fiddle-faddle*," Eliza said with a grin. "Or *fiddlesticks*." She was certain her aunt used the malapropisms on purpose. They were absurd enough to break the tension when Eliza was upset, or irritating enough to distract her when she was angry, and silly enough to make her laugh when she was sad.

When she corrected her aunt, as she always did—because that was part of the game—Aunt Lavinia would harrumph, as though anyone with any sense would have known that was what she had meant all along.

Aunt Lavinia harrumphed.

Eliza laughed and kissed her aunt on the cheek. "You are absolutely incorrigible."

"That is the kettle calling the pot black," her aunt retorted. "As I was saying, before the earl so impertinently interrupted us, I believe you would enjoy yourself at Somersville Manor. From what you have told me of your friend, the Countess of Denbigh, I am sure she will have chosen the perfect husband for you."

"What?"

Aunt Lavinia chuckled. "Dear child, I forget sometimes how innocent you are. Surely you must realize your friend will have invited a number of eligible gentlemen for you to interview as potential husbands."

"But that's awful!" Eliza said, lifting her head to stare into her aunt's sightless gray eyes. "You expect me to choose a husband from a pack of male wolves?"

"Just be sure to get the pick of the litter," her aunt said with a chuckle.

"I would rather run away than be forced into a loveless marriage," Eliza said.

"Don't speak foolishness," her aunt said in the harshest voice Eliza had ever heard her use. "What other future is there for a woman except to marry and breed up an heir for her husband?"

"It is not enough," Eliza said in a whisper. "I want more."

The problem was, she did not know what form that "more" should take. Something was missing from her life, but she did not know what it was. She had never let herself contemplate marriage, because she had been so certain no man would ever want her. But she could not stay at Ravenwood. Marry she must.

However, not just any man would do. She needed someone willing to accept a blind, elderly woman as part of the package, because she had no intention of leaving Aunt Lavinia behind. Still, stalking a husband like a deer seemed a bit unfair, if not downright unscrupulous.

"I never thought I would hear you say I should make a marriage of convenience," Eliza muttered.

"I did not say you could not like the man," Aunt Lavinia retorted. "Merely that you must choose one and button yourself to him."

"That's *buckle*, Aunt Lavinia. Buckle myself to him."

Her aunt harrumphed. "Button, buckle, it's all the same. Give love a chance, Eliza. You cannot find your Prince Charming if you do not attend the ball."

Eliza laid her head back down on her aunt's knee, the only sign of capitulation she was willing to make. When the knitting needles began clacking again, she knew Aunt Lavinia understood she was willing to do what must be done. Truthfully, if she must marry, she had already picked the groom.

Her cousin, Major Julian Sheringham.

That afternoon, Eliza wrote a letter to her friend, Charlie, the Countess of Denbigh, who was best friends with the Duchess of Braddock, asking her to please make certain that Major Julian Sheringham was invited to the party and giving his direction in London. Once Eliza had posted the letter, she felt much better about attending.

But before her letter could possibly have gotten to Charlie, Cousin Nigel had attacked her and she had fled Ravenwood. It had made more sense to go to London and speak directly with Julian, than to attend a party to which he had not yet received an invitation, and where she might have to wait an entire week for him to arrive.

Eliza turned over in the lumpy bed at the White Ball Inn and pulled the covers over her shoulder. She could hardly keep her eyes open. Yet the moment she closed them, she saw a pair of haunting blue eyes. A frustrated, gurgling sound issued from her throat. It should be Julian's dark eyes she was seeing. After all, he was the man she loved.

The Beau might be handsome, but she knew better than to be swayed by his good looks. A rake like the Beau might be tantalizing and intriguing. But scandal married to scandal? Utterly ridiculous.

Eliza needed—wanted—intended to marry a man of honesty and character, a paragon of propriety, someone steadfast and reliable who would keep both her and Aunt Lavinia safe from care and worry. The Beau flunked that test, while Julian passed with flying colors.

Nevertheless, Eliza was grateful for Captain Wharton's offer of escort. She had not been precisely sure of the way to London. Now she could make her journey with all good speed.

She pictured Julian in his hussar's uniform and herself beside him holding a wedding bouquet of wildflowers, and with a seraphic smile, fell sound asleep.

Chapter 4

"$\mathcal{D}$O YOU THINK WE SHOULD WAKE HER UP?" BECKY asked.

Reggie stepped up to the iron-railed bed where Miss Sheringham lay sprawled sideways, sound asleep. "Uncle Marcus said Miss Sheringham was quite insistent last night that we leave at dawn. That is why he sent us up here so early with her traveling bag. He was sure she would need it to dress."

Becky glanced out the window. "It is still dark outside. Maybe we could wait—"

Reggie dropped the cloth bag onto the hardwood floor beside the bed. "Uncle Marcus said we cannot have breakfast until we change our clothes and have Miss Sheringham comb our hair. And she cannot comb our hair while she is sleeping."

Miss Sheringham yawned and stretched.

"She's waking up," Becky whispered.

The lady in question merely rolled over, pulled a pillow over her head, and lay still.

"Maybe we should go get Uncle Marcus," Becky suggested. "He will know what to do."

Reggie gave her sister a pitiful look. "I can handle this." She leaned close to Miss Sheringham's ear and shouted, "Wake up, Miss Sheringham! It is time to dress!"

Miss Sheringham bolted upright as though she were attached to a spring. She stared at Reggie in confusion, then glanced at Becky as though she were seeing double. She blinked her eyes, groaned, and said, "How did you two get in here?"

"The innkeeper has another key," Reggie said. "Uncle Marcus told him to let us in." Reggie thought it was a good thing Uncle Marcus had not come with them. Miss Sheringham did not look pleased.

"Uncle Marcus said you would not mind helping us change our clothes," Becky said. She put a hand to the rat's nest of straw and hair on her head and added, "And he was sure you would be glad to fix our hair for us."

"He was, was he," Eliza muttered, crossing her arms and staring daggers at the closed door.

Reggie knew very well when she was not wanted. Who needed *her* to comb their hair, anyway. "Come on, Becky. We should leave Miss Sheringham alone to dress." She had to grab Becky's hand and practically drag her away. "Come on," she insisted. "Let's go."

"Wait," Miss Sheringham said.

When Reggie looked back, Miss Sheringham's arms were uncrossed. She stepped barefoot onto the hardwood floor and immediately tripped over the traveling bag Reggie had dropped beside the bed.

"What corkbrain put that there?" she yelped.

Reggie cringed.

Miss Sheringham's arms windmilled to keep her enormous height upright. There was so much of her, Reggie was certain she would lose the contest and fall.

Miss Sheringham surprised her with an agile hop over the bag, a shoulder slam against the wall, and a bounce right back to the bedstead, where she stubbed her toe. The foot came up, and Miss Sheringham grabbed her toe and hopped around muttering "Ow, ow, ow."

Reggie could not help it. She laughed.

Becky looked appalled. "Are you all right, Miss Sheringham?"

Miss Sheringham let her foot go and limped in a circle, testing her toe. "I believe I am."

Reggie stared at the curious mixture of under-clothing Miss Sheringham was wearing. The chemise was identifiable, but she could only guess at the other garment. "Are those men's smalls?" she asked incredulously.

Miss Sheringham glanced down and grinned. "They are. My pantalets had too many frills to wear beneath a pair of breeches. Lumps," she explained.

Reggie was fascinated, but wary of Miss Sheringham's sudden return to friendliness. She reached for the doorknob.

"Don't go," Miss Sheringham said. "Please. I would be glad to help you change your clothes and fix your hair."

"I would like that very much," Becky said. She yanked herself free of Reggie's hand and trotted back to Miss Sheringham.

Reggie's lips puckered in disgust. Becky was a sap for a smile. Her sister was so gullible! Reggie knew better. Miss Sheringham did not really want anything to do with them. She merely wanted to impress Uncle Marcus. Ladies always did.

"I hope you will call me Eliza," Miss Sheringham said. "I want us to be friends."

Eliza wanted to impress Uncle Marcus, all right. "Sure," Reggie said, her tone snide. "We'll be glad to call you Liza."

"Eliza," Miss Sheringham corrected.

"Eliza," Becky dutifully repeated with a smile.

Reggie stared, saying nothing. Good old *Eliza* was not going to whip her into line. Reggie had confronted the best governesses London had to offer, taken everything they doled out, and come out on top. *Eliza* was not going to find Lady Regina as big a flat as her sister.

Miss Sheringham turned away, apparently conceding the battle even before they drew arms. Reggie smirked in triumph.

But no one was looking.

"Where are the clothes you wish to change into?" Miss Sheringham asked Becky.

Becky pointed to a leather valise by the door.

"Would you bring it here, please, Reggie?" Miss Sheringham said.

"How do you know I am Reggie?" Reggie asked. "We are identical twins. No one can tell us apart."

"I cheated," Miss Sheringham admitted.

Reggie arched an inquiring brow.

"You have a hole in the knee of your stocking."

Reggie admired cleverness. And Miss Sheringham appeared to have her share of it. Reggie picked up the valise with both hands. It bounced against her knee as she carted it over and hefted it onto the foot of the bed. "I do not see why we have to change. We will just be putting on a shift exactly like the one we already have on."

Miss Sheringham opened the leather valise and rooted through it. "I see what you mean, Reggie," she said. "Every one of these shifts is exactly the same. What do you suggest?"

Reggie looked down at her white shift and found a spot of cherry tart, another of gravy, and several more that were just plain dirt. "I suppose it will not hurt to start the day in something clean," she conceded.

Reggie watched attentively as Miss Sheringham stripped Becky bare.

"We will all have to wait for a bath until we reach London," Miss Sheringham said. "But there is no reason why we cannot freshen our faces." She took a cloth, dampened it with water from the pitcher on the dry sink, and wiped Becky's face clean.

Reggie watched as her sister closed her eyes and tilted her face up for Miss Sheringham's ministrations. Becky acted like the water was warm and the cloth was velvet dipped in violet-scented soap. They were no such thing. Just cold water on a raggedy cloth.

Miss Sheringham had placed Becky right in front of her—not facing her, like every governess they had ever had—but with Becky's back against Miss Sheringham's front. Then Miss Sheringham bent over, her arms surrounding Becky, and held the pantalets for Becky to step into them.

Before slipping the chemise over Becky's head, Miss Sheringham said, "Arms up!" She crouched down and turned Becky to face her, tying the pink satin ribbons to close the front. She then rose and picked up a shift from the bed.

"That one's mine," Reggie said.

Miss Sheringham compared it to the other she had taken from the valise. "How can you tell?"

"The sleeve is torn."

"So I see," Miss Sheringham said. "What a clever way of marking what is yours, Reggie. It must always be a problem to identify what belongs to you, when you and your twin are always wearing exactly the same thing."

Reggie had not even realized that was what she was doing. Now that she thought about it, everything she owned was ripped or torn or spotted. Which was how she knew it belonged to her.

"Now, let us see what we can do with this hair," Miss Sheringham said to Becky. She had taken the silver-handled brush and comb set from the valise. She sat down on the bed, her legs spread wide—a posture Reggie might have used to incense her governess—and pulled Becky back between them.

"I will try to be careful," Miss Sheringham said. "But if I hurt you, just yell."

Becky glanced at Reggie from the corner of her eye, and Reggie shrugged. No governess had *ever* encouraged them to yell. Not even when they were truly hurt.

Reggie found herself crossing to the foot of the bed, where she could be closer to Miss Sheringham. She watched intently as Miss Sheringham brushed out all the tangles, making jokes as she pulled straw from Becky's hair, about how it would have made a wonderful nest for the kittens.

Reggie was sure Becky would yell at least once.

But Miss Sheringham never pulled at the tangles. She stopped and worked them out. "I used to have the same knots and snarls when I was your age," she said. "Do you know how my mother solved the problem?"

"How?" Becky asked, peering over her shoulder at Miss Sheringham.

"Braids."

"Father would not approve," Reggie said in her best stern-governess-imitation voice, which was not nearly so good as Becky's.

"Father isn't here," Becky pointed out. "I would love to have braids, Miss Sheringham."

"Uncle Marcus won't like it either," Reggie said stubbornly.

"Since your uncle asked me to fix your hair, he will have to accept the way I do it," Miss Sheringham replied with a smile. "Or do it himself the next time."

"Uncle Marcus does not know how to comb a lady's hair!" Becky protested.

Miss Sheringham grinned. "My point exactly."

By then, Miss Sheringham had plaited two braids down either side of Becky's head and gathered them into a single braid at her nape, which she then tied with the bow that had previously hung from the crown of Becky's head.

Miss Sheringham sent Becky over to the looking glass above the dry sink to inspect herself. "What do you think?"

Becky's face beamed when she turned around. "Oh, Eliza, my braids are beautiful. I love them!"

To Reggie's amazement, Miss Sheringham held

her arms wide, and Becky turned and nearly threw herself across the room, right into them.

Reggie felt betrayed. If only she was as trusting as Becky, she might be the one being hugged right now. She watched her sister enviously. Perhaps Becky was not such a cabbage-head after all.

"Your turn, Reggie," Miss Sheringham said, releasing Becky at last.

"I can dress myself," Reggie heard herself reply sullenly. Nothing had changed really. Miss Sheringham had a motive for being nice. All the tenderness, even the hug, did not mean anything. They were done for a purpose.

"Of course you can dress yourself," Miss Sheringham said. "So can Becky. But it is so much easier when one has help, do you not agree?"

Reggie nodded. She wondered how Miss Sheringham had figured out that Reggie would never go to her, and whether that was why Miss Sheringham walked over to take her hand. Reggie was surprised that she let herself be led back toward the bed.

Miss Sheringham wet the cloth again and wrung it out, then sat on the bed and pulled Reggie between her legs to wash her face.

"You have a scar I never noticed. Near your lip," Miss Sheringham observed. "Now I will be able to tell you apart even without clothes," she teased.

Reggie stared wide-eyed at Miss Sheringham. Not one governess had noticed the scar, though it had been there for as long as Reggie could remember.

She did not feel as embarrassed as she had thought she would when Miss Sheringham stripped off her clothes. She realized, now that she was the one within those encircling arms, that she felt protected by them.

Reggie stepped into the clean pantalets and felt Miss Sheringham's warm breath on her cheek as she leaned down to pull them up. Reggie caught herself watching Miss Sheringham chew on her lower lip as she studiously tied the pink bow on Reggie's chemise. She asked Miss Sheringham to help her put on her stockings and half boots before the shift went over her head and was buttoned up the back.

Then it was time for her hair.

"Let me know if I tug too hard," Miss Sheringham said.

Reggie held her breath, waiting for the quick, no-nonsense brushing she was used to.

Miss Sheringham took her time. She picked at the straw, her head bobbing around every so often to look into Reggie's eyes and make sure she was not just pretending it did not hurt.

Reggie had never felt anything so wonderful in her life. The slow, steady brush strokes made her feel weak in the knees. She wanted the brushing to go on forever.

She waited for Miss Sheringham to ask her if she wanted braids. She wanted them, all right. But if Miss Sheringham asked, she would be forced to deny herself, because she was the one who had pointed out how both Father and Uncle Marcus would disapprove.

To tell the truth, she was not at all certain Uncle Marcus would disapprove. He liked to do a lot of things that Father thought were wrong.

Reggie swallowed past the lump of misery in her

throat. Miss Sheringham would be asking any moment now.

"There. All done. Go see how you like yourself in braids." Miss Sheringham gave her a nudge toward the looking glass.

Reggie felt her heart thumping madly. She had braids? She reached up to touch. She had braids!

She walked over to the looking glass and studied the image reflected back at her. While she had been daydreaming, Miss Sheringham had produced braids exactly like Becky's, even down to the bow at her nape. She loved them.

"Thank you, Miss Sheringham." Drat! She should have called her Eliza.

"You're welcome, Reggie. Anytime."

Reggie was almost afraid to turn around, afraid Miss Sheringham's arms would not be opened wide for her. But then she saw what she was looking for in the glass. Miss Sheringham's gentle smile. And her welcoming arms waiting for a second little girl to turn and fly into them.

Reggie tried not to need it so much. Tried not to want it so much. Tried to slow herself down, so she did not look as foolishly exuberant as her sister had, leaping into Miss Sheringham's arms.

Reggie pressed herself close, hid her face against Miss Sheringham's chemise, and waited for those welcoming arms to fold around her. When they did, Reggie closed her eyes and exulted in the warm, lovely feeling.

Thank you, thank you, Eliza.

* * *

Marcus could not believe he had agreed to, even insisted upon, escorting a single, *eligible* young lady from an inn near her home to someplace she had no business going. Especially when the only chaperons in sight were a crusty old soldier and a pair of eight-year-old girls. He doubted whether they would satisfy the highest sticklers, but he did not want to involve anyone else in this escapade. The fewer people who knew about Miss Sheringham's adventure, the better.

He should be taking her back to Ravenwood. But that would mean admitting he knew who she was. For reasons he did not care to examine, he was not willing to do that.

He glanced at the upstairs window where the twins had disappeared. He had wanted very much to deliver Miss Sheringham's traveling bag himself. Griggs had intercepted him and suggested the twins do it instead. Marcus had frowned at having his plans for an early morning tryst foiled. But Griggs had pointed out, quite reasonably, that if the twins took her bag upstairs, Miss Sheringham might be willing to do something with their hair.

Marcus had smiled ruefully and handed over the bag.

While he was standing on the porch of the White Ball Inn twiddling his thumbs, the twins came tromping down the outside stairway. He was pleased to see they were neat and clean and—wearing braids?

He grinned as they skipped up to him. "You look very different this morning, ladies."

"We have braids!" Becky exulted.

"Eliza insisted," Reggie said. Her expression turned mulish, and she settled her hands on her hips.

"Eliza said if you don't like them, you can fix our hair next time yourself!"

Miss Sheringham must know he would never venture into such deep waters. "I like them. I like them," he said, laughing, his hands held up in a gesture of surrender.

"Oh, so do I," Reggie said with a dreamy look. She ran her hand softly over her hair. "Eliza was careful not to pull our hair. I thought at first she was only being nice to impress you, Uncle Marcus. But no one could like you that much," she finished ingenuously.

"I suppose not," he agreed, his mouth twisting wryly. "I assume Miss Sheringham gave you permission to address her familiarly."

The twins nodded vigorously.

"Eliza wants to be our friend," Becky said. "I like her, Uncle Marcus."

"I do, too," Reggie said.

"Then we are unanimous," Marcus said. "I like her, too."

Reggie's stomach growled. "I'm hungry, Uncle Marcus. Can we have breakfast now?"

"Where is Miss Sheringham?" he asked.

"She is still getting dressed," Becky said. "She said for us to go ahead without her. She will get something when she comes downstairs to eat along the way."

Marcus fought back a stab of annoyance. Miss Sheringham seemed to have no regard for manners. One ate at the table. *Or in the stable,* a chiding voice reminded. "Let us go eat," he said. "The sooner breakfast is done, the sooner we can leave."

Miss Sheringham turned up at the stable door a full fifteen minutes after they had finished breakfast with hot fruit tarts for everyone except Frances, for whom she produced a smelly fishhead.

"We sat down to eat an hour ago, Miss Sheringham," Marcus said in tones that conveyed his displeasure at her late arrival. "At dawn."

"They are warm from the oven," she said, tossing him an apple tart he instinctively reached out to catch. "One whiff and I guarantee you will find an empty corner of your stomach in which to put it."

"How marvelous!" Reggie said. "Another picnic!"

Marcus bit back a groan. They would be lucky if they left before time for luncheon.

Nevertheless, he found himself totally enchanted by Miss Sheringham as she strode from person to person dispensing smiles and fruit tarts. She looked even more enticing this morning, her hair hanging in chestnut wisps from beneath the hat. She sat herself down quite unself-consciously next to the children, right beside the mother cat and her kittens.

Marcus watched Miss Sheringham eat the apple tart with relish, wondering if she did everything with such gusto.

She glanced in his direction, and their eyes caught. She stopped chewing and stared at him. He tried swallowing a bite of tart, but the dough got stuck in his throat. He tried again. It was stuck fast.

He coughed, and Miss Sheringham leaped to her feet to pound on his back. "Are you all right, Captain?"

"Fine," he said, nearly choking when Griggs gave him a hard blow on his back just as he was swallowing. "Fine," he wheezed.

What was wrong with him? He had almost

choked to death because of that infernal woman! Miss Sheringham was just another bit of fluff, albeit taller and a little odder looking than the others he had bedded. Why should she discompose him so much?

He focused his attention on the twins. They had already gobbled down their tarts and—he shuddered to think what Alastair would say if he could see them—were licking their fingers clean. He opened his mouth to correct them, but realized there was not a napkin in sight. The only alternative was to wipe their hands on their dresses, which he thought could only be worse, since it would leave a permanent reminder of their barbaric eating habits.

His gaze slipped to Miss Sheringham, and he watched as she produced a damp cloth from her traveling bag to clean the children's hands. He was amazed to see Reggie and Becky voluntarily, almost enthusiastically, turn up their faces one by one so she could remove any traces of apple tart from their mouths.

It took him a moment to realize that Miss Sheringham had turned in his direction and caught him staring. She sent him an inquiring look and held up the cloth in his direction.

His ears reddened as he realized she was offering to wipe *his* face!

"You have some apple tart on your face, Uncle Marcus," Reggie said.

Before he could wipe it away with his hand, Miss Sheringham was standing in front of him, and the damp cloth was brushing the corner of his lips. Marcus was both appalled and amused by her daring. He grasped her wrist to stop her and felt her pulse beneath his fingertips. His heart began to race, keeping beat with hers.

"Captain?" She glanced at her wrist, and he released it.

And then wished he had not. He had never experienced anything so erotically exciting in his life. He kept his eyes on her face and saw the flush rise beneath her skin. She felt it, too, though he did not think she recognized it for what it was.

"Are you finished?" he asked, when the cloth had paused for the second time at the edge of his mouth. His voice was harsh with desire, irritable because he knew there was no chance of quenching it. "How much longer is this going to take?"

She gave him a beatific smile. "When a mouth has been as many places as yours has, Captain, one can never be too careful."

His eyes narrowed. Marcus suddenly realized that Miss Sheringham knew full well his reaction to her ministrations. That she might even have been prolonging the encounter to tease him. Although it seemed to have backfired slightly, since she was no less vulnerable to his charms than he was to hers.

Just when he had made up his mind to grab the rag from her hand, she stepped back and said, "There. I'm finished."

So was he. The chit had done her work well. He would be lucky if he could sit in a saddle.

Marcus caught Griggs laughing and glowered.

It was time to get them on the road, before he made a total cawker of himself. He turned to Reggie and said, "I think Frances and her kittens would be happy riding in that basket I saw on the floor of the carriage."

The twins exchanged guilty glances.

"Is there some reason why that is not possible?" he asked.

"I suppose we have to tell you," Becky conceded with a sigh. "The basket is already occupied. By Gretchen."

He hesitated to ask, but finally said, "Who is Gretchen?"

"My rabbit." Becky hung her head, but glanced up at him with penitent blue eyes. "I could not leave her behind, Uncle Marcus. She might need me."

Marcus was afraid he knew exactly what that meant, so he forbore to ask. As they rose and headed for the carriage, he said, "I think Frances and her kittens need the space in the basket more."

"I can hold Gretchen," Becky offered.

Since by then the small white rabbit was wriggling frantically in his strong hands, he doubted it. Marcus had visions of an escaping rabbit halting their journey for another night. He had no way of knowing for sure whether Gretchen was in a family way, but since rabbits were notoriously fruitful, he thought it better to be safe than sorry. Lured by the promise of a fat carrot, Gretchen was coaxed to take Frances's place in the leather valise.

"Well done, Uncle Marcus!" Becky said, clapping her hands. "I would never have thought of bribing Gretchen."

"You would be amazed what a bribe can accomplish," he said with a wry grin, thinking of all the pretty baubles he had dispensed to help an undecided lady make up her mind to indulge in an affair. He caught Miss Sheringham eyeing him with a raised brow, but refused to argue ethics with a woman who thought nothing of passing herself off as a man.

With the twins and their pets settled, he turned to Miss Sheringham. "Do you have a dress in that traveling bag of yours?"

She nodded.

"Why are you not wearing it?"

"It would not be very practical to ride astride in a dress."

Marcus's heart gave an anxious thump. "There is no need for you to ride astride when you have a carriage at your disposal."

She glanced at the elegant, well-sprung carriage that bore the Blackthorne crest. "I prefer to ride," she said, her chin lifting stubbornly.

"I am afraid I must refuse to accompany you to London if you insist on riding astride."

"Very well. I will go by myself."

She had already turned and headed back toward the stable when he caught her arm. "Why are you so insistent on doing things your way?" he demanded. "Would it not be more politic to conceal yourself in the carriage from anyone who might recognize you on the road?"

"I do not expect to meet anyone I know," she said.

"Nevertheless, I must insist—"

"You have no right to insist I do anything, Captain." Her voice was sharp-edged, and her eyes glittered with irritation. "Neither that I wear a dress, nor that I dress a child."

Marcus stiffened. "I am sorry I imposed on you to

help with the twins. Be assured I will not do so again,"
he said in a cold voice.

"You idiot!"

He was so surprised, he completely dropped his
haughty manner. "What did you call me?"

"Idiot," she repeated just as loudly. "How could
you possibly think I would mind helping those poor,
innocent children? But I would prefer to be *asked* not
ordered like some lackey. If my father had not been
disinherited, I would, in fact, outrank you. So, if you
please, I will be treated with respect."

He gave her a stiff bow. "Very well, Miss Sheringham," he said, letting his face reveal his displeasure
and disapproval. "You may ride."

She turned her back on him and marched into the
stable. Only moments later, she returned with that
black brute she called a horse, saddled and bridled.
He watched anxiously for a moment, until he saw her
not only mount by herself, but control the animal
with calm capability.

He turned to his batman and said, "Griggs, I think
it best you travel inside the carriage to keep an eye on
things."

The sergeant gave him a woeful look, but knew
better than to argue with his captain. Griggs tied his
gelding behind the carriage and, with great trepida-
tion, settled himself across from the twins with his
back to the team. The coachman from Blackthorne
Abbey took his place, and they set off for London.

Miss Sheringham seemed to fool everyone they
passed on the road with her disguise as a young man.
Unfortunately, it was not working on him.

He had a vivid memory of what her breasts felt

like against his chest and what her silky hair looked like falling about her shoulders. He had not been able to keep himself from staring at her whenever her attention was diverted by something the twins said from the carriage.

The sunlight loved her. Its golden glow highlighted the freckles on her nose and the peachlike color of her skin. One lip was temptingly swollen where she had a habit of clasping it in her teeth. He remembered the supple warmth and wetness of her mouth when he had kissed her. How she had looked up at him dazed and unsure. Sweetly vulnerable.

Marcus felt his body go rock hard and swore.

"Is something wrong, Captain?" she asked.

"Nothing that will not be cured when we reach London," he muttered.

This was all Julian's fault for filling Marcus's head with those intriguing stories about his "funny little cousin Eliza," who made him laugh.

She had made Marcus laugh, too. But there was nothing funny about the situation in which he found himself. He had kissed his best friend's innocent cousin. He had wanted to do far more and might have, if the girl had been willing. He had been lusting after her as though she were a Cyprian.

Julian would kill him.

Or maybe not, since they were, after all, best friends.

Marcus had met Julian at Oxford, and they had found in each other the sort of honesty and courage that had made them fast friends. They had both planned to join the army, for which it was necessary to buy a commission. Since Marcus's means were greater than Julian's, he had surreptitiously lost enough to his friend gambling to ensure that Julian could afford a commission with the same elite regiment he planned to join himself.

Or rather, he had thought himself surreptitious. It was not until years later, when Julian slowly but steadily lost the exact cost of his commission back to Marcus in cards, that Marcus realized he had not fooled his friend.

Marcus had met Julian's dark eyes across the table, uncertain what to say. "I only meant to help, Julian."

"I know. That is why I took the money." He smiled. "And because I could not have afforded it myself."

Marcus smiled back. "We are even now."

Julian shook his head. "I will always be in your debt."

Over the years they had fought together, Julian had repaid him time and again by saving life and limb.

Here, at last, was a chance for Marcus to even the score in some small measure. All he had to do was protect Miss Sheringham's reputation—and keep himself out of parson's mousetrap—until he could reunite the chit with Julian in London.

Marcus suddenly remembered something else Julian had said about his cousin that took on a looming importance in light of the advances he had made to Miss Sheringham last night.

"I believe she has a tendre for me. Merely a calf's love, you understand. But even so, innocent and true and utterly devoted."

Marcus felt sick to his stomach. Was it possible he had been kissing the woman Julian intended to make his bride? Surely not. Marcus was almost—but not entirely—certain Julian neither loved his cousin nor intended to marry her. But what if he was mistaken? What if Julian planned to make Miss Sheringham his wife?

He could certainly see why Julian might. She was exquisite. Not beautiful in any conventional sense. Exotic. In fact, he was certain the *ton* would find her too odd for acceptance. Too dauntless, too daring and, he was discovering, entirely too direct.

"Captain?"

"Excuse me. What did you say?"

"What is it like to be a rake?" she repeated.

His jaw dropped in stunned disbelief. Then he threw back his head and laughed.

She frowned. "What is so funny?"

"That is the first time a young lady has asked me that particular question."

"Were none curious?"

He cocked a brow. "None were forward enough to say so." He waited for a blush to appear, but none was forthcoming.

"I am in the habit of asking what I want to know," she said, looking him right in the eye.

"A quality I admire," he conceded.

Miss Sheringham's peach flesh turned a deep rose.

Strange. The insult had caused no noticeable reaction in Miss Sheringham's demeanor; the compliment had elicited an enchanting blush.

"Will you answer the question?" she demanded.

They were paddling in deep waters, but he considered himself a good swimmer—almost as good as his brother—certainly good enough to rescue them both if a storm should arise. He decided to tell her what she wanted to know.

"A rake is not much different from any other man—except that he acts upon his desires without any thought to the consequences."

She turned to him, a wary expression on her face. "For example?"

"Like gambling on horses and cards until he is rolled up. Like drinking until he is corned, pickled, and salted. Like quenching other . . . thirsts . . . as often as they arise."

"Have you seduced many women?" she asked boldly.

"Hundreds," he shot back. He looked to see if she had believed him. The silly chit had.

"I see," she said at last. "That must be what makes you such a legend among the ladies."

He shot her a skeptical glance. "Legend?"

She reined her horse close enough that their legs were almost touching. With her legs spread suggestively wide over the horse, he could not help thinking how easy it would be to reach out and stroke the damp heat between her thighs. His body throbbed with arousal.

Marcus focused on a point between his horse's ears and willed his pulse to slow.

"I had heard you were practiced at seduction," Miss Sheringham said in a nonchalant voice that denied the inappropriateness of their discussion. "But I had no idea you had so many conquests."

"I might have exaggerated the number slightly," he said.

"Why?"

His mouth curved. "To see the look of outrage on your face."

"It was an outrageous number," she retorted, reining her horse to put distance between them again. "Hundreds! I should have known better than to believe something so preposterous."

He kept his lips firmly sealed. The number was considerably less, but she did not need to know that. After all, he had his reputation as a rake to uphold.

"You would like my cousin, Julian," she said, changing the subject to something that should have been more comfortable, but was not, at least for him.

He smiled, but was careful not to look at her. "Would I?"

"Julian is a hero. He was mentioned several times in the dispatches from the front during the Peninsular Wars."

"Do you know precisely where the major is billeted in London?" he asked.

"I am sure he will not be difficult to find. How many hotels could there be?"

He bit back a gust of laughter. She had to be joking! It was a good thing he knew exactly where to look, or they might have been forced into each other's company for weeks, instead of days. He remembered suddenly that Julian was keeping a ladybird. Marcus would have to get word to his friend to send the demi-rep away. Otherwise, the major was going to break Miss Sheringham's heart.

Marcus had been so concerned about someone recognizing Miss Sheringham on the road, he had completely forgotten the fact that *he* would not go unrecognized. They had not been on the road for very long before a gentleman approaching in a yellow-wheeled curricle, whom Marcus knew from his club in London, hailed them.

"Lord Marcus!"

Marcus had no choice but to stop and greet the fellow. Diebold was a viscount, some ten years older than Marcus, but still unmarried.

Marcus was aware of the tension in Miss Sheringham, whose shoulders had squared and whose chin had come up enough to tip her nose into the air. He hoped she would not speak. Her voice was low-pitched and gravelly, but he could not believe another man would not recognize her for the female she was.

"Diebold. What brings you from London today?" Marcus said.

"Braddock is having a house party to which I have been invited. I thought to meet you there, since it seems a number of my bachelor friends are also invited. But I see you are headed in the wrong direction."

"We are going to London first," a voice piped up from the carriage.

Marcus bit back a groan.

"Oh?" Diebold acknowledged the pair of identical faces peering from the open carriage window with a tip of his hat.

Marcus began to sweat when Diebold stared at Miss Sheringham speculatively.

"I do not believe I have made your acquaintance," Diebold said to her at last.

"I am—"

"A friend of mine from the country," Marcus said before the chit could finish. "We are making a brief detour to London before I attend the Braddock party with my nieces, Lady Regina and Lady Rebecca."

"I will be glad to inform our hostess of your delay," Diebold offered.

The last thing Marcus wanted was for word to get back to Alastair that he was heading to London all by himself with the twins. He wanted a chance to explain in person the series of catastrophes that had caused their roundabout journey. "Not necessary," he told Diebold. "I have sent a note myself."

"Very well," Diebold said. "I will see you—when?"

"Soon," Marcus said evasively.

As Diebold drove away, Miss Sheringham glanced at Marcus with judgmental eyes. "You have a talent for telling clankers. I suppose one must expect that from a rake."

"You put me in an impossible situation, Miss Sheringham. What else could I have done?"

"Let me answer for myself."

"How would you have introduced yourself?"

"I would have made up a name."

He raised a supercilious brow. "You seem no stranger to Banbury tales yourself."

"I value honesty above all things," she retorted.

"Then why this charade?" he asked in a steely voice.

She was caught off guard by his attack and stared at him a moment too long, long enough for him to see the uncertainty, and fear, in her eyes. Miss Sheringham was not nearly so confident as she wanted him to think.

He wished she had not revealed the depths of her vulnerability. It brought out his protective instincts and made him ask, "What are you running away from, my dear?"

Chapter 5

"*I* MUST SPEAK TO MY WARD!" NIGEL SHERINGHAM ranted. "I know she is here. Why are you keeping her from me?"

Charlotte, Countess of Denbigh, had been unable to placate the ill-humored man. She stood by the mantel in the Duke of Braddock's drawing room, her hands clasped tightly before her, resisting the urge to shout back. "Miss Sheringham never arrived, my lord. The duchess and I expected her yesterday, but as you can see, she is not among the company here this evening."

"You're hiding her from me!"

"Why would I do such a thing?"

The Earl of Ravenwood's face turned from red to purple, and he sputtered, but no answer was forthcoming. "I am staying here until she arrives . . . or until she *appears*," he said, emphasizing the last word, as though Charlotte could produce Eliza Sheringham from thin air.

"I am sure the duke and duchess will make you welcome," she said in a frigid voice.

Charlotte left the drawing room without another word. She headed straight upstairs to Olivia's bedroom, where she found the duchess sitting in a wooden rocking chair beside a gold brocade-canopied bed nursing her son.

Olivia cried out in alarm when the door burst open.

"It is only me," Charlotte said, closing the door behind her. "I know I should knock," she said as Olivia hastily rearranged the wool blanket to completely cover her bared breast, "but I could not wait."

"What is it?" Olivia asked.

"I am afraid something terrible has happened to Eliza. Her guardian is here looking for her. She left home the night before last without a word to him and without requesting a carriage. Ravenwood checked at the White Ball Inn and discovered that Mephistopheles is missing. It sounds to me as though Eliza might be running away. That dastard must have done something to make her flee without a word to anyone."

"Now, Charlie, we do not know that."

Charlotte dropped to her knees beside the rocking chair and gripped the wooden arm, stopping its movement. "Eliza should have been here by now, Livy, unless she met with disaster somewhere on the road. What if Mephistopheles threw her? I will never forgive myself."

Olivia shook her head. "You told me you watched her on Mephistopheles, and she rides like a centaur. However, there is something odd . . ." Olivia's lips pursed, and her brow furrowed.

"What is it?"

"I was with Reeve when the Duke of Blackthorne asked to speak with him. The duke's brother, Lord Marcus, was supposed to have arrived yesterday with

Blackthorne's twin daughters, Lady Regina and Lady Rebecca. They seem to have disappeared, as well."

"Disappeared?"

"Their whereabouts are presently unknown."

"Oh, no! What if a highwayman has kidnapped them all? I must go search for Eliza. I—"

Olivia grasped Charlotte's wrist to keep her in place. "You cannot go haring off after Miss Sheringham, Charlie. There is someone else who must be considered first."

"What do you mean? I—" Charlotte met Olivia's shrewd gaze and realized her secret was out. "How did you know?"

Olivia let go of Charlotte and readjusted the blanket around William, letting her hand drift through his fine blond hair. "I cannot think of another reason why you would willingly give up riding Mephistopheles."

Charlotte put her hands to her rosy cheeks. "Does it show? Do you think Lion knows?"

"You look very happy," Olivia said with a smile. "But I doubt Lion suspects the truth. Men are oblivious to the signs until they are hit on the head with them."

Charlotte relaxed back onto her heels. "Thank goodness. I want to tell him myself—after the house party."

"I understand perfectly," Olivia said. "Once I became *enceinte*, Reeve would not allow me to do anything for myself. It was nice for a while, but it soon became quite distracting."

"What did you do?"

"I am almost ashamed to say."

"I will need help educating Lion," Charlotte said. "Please tell me."

Olivia's cheeks caught fire, and she lowered her eyes to avoid Charlotte's intent look. "I took him on a picnic and . . . and made such passionate love to him that there was no question of my stamina."

Charlotte gave a surprised laugh. "What a wonderful idea!"

"You do see you must allow someone else to go after Miss Sheringham."

Charlotte grimaced. "I suppose I must."

"Blackthorne is leaving within the hour to search for his brother and his daughters. I suppose he is the most logical person to ask for help."

"Where does he plan to start looking?"

"Viscount Diebold told Blackthorne that he met Lord Marcus on the road, but heading in the wrong direction. The twins were with Lord Marcus at the time, as well as a young man, a stranger to Diebold. Lord Marcus told Diebold he was taking a short detour to London. Even so, he has had time to reach London and travel back to Sussex."

"Why would Lord Marcus be going the other way?" Charlotte asked.

Olivia smiled. "That is not difficult to guess. A confirmed bachelor might be expected to avoid a house party laden with eligible young misses for as long as possible." The smile faded. "However, Blackthorne knew of no compelling reason why his brother should have gone to London without informing him of his direction first."

"Maybe the young man traveling with him holds the key to the mystery," Charlotte mused. "Who was he?"

"Lord Marcus introduced him to Diebold as 'a

friend from home.' Blackthorne says he has no idea who it could be."

"Did Diebold give a description of the young man?"

Olivia gasped. "Oh, dear."

"What is it? Are you all right?"

"Diebold said he hardly noticed the young man— except for his strange golden eyes—because he was too busy admiring the truly magnificent black stallion he was riding. I never made the connection until now. It must be—"

"Eliza! On Mephistopheles!" Charlotte rose and began pacing. "She must have dressed in men's clothing to ride astride. But if she is running away from her guardian, why did she not come straight here? She must have known I would protect her. Why would she go to London?"

"More importantly," Olivia said, "how did she meet up with the Beau? And why has he not brought her here? It cannot be quite the thing for them to be traveling together without a proper chaperon."

Charlotte stopped dead. "If they have been together overnight, Eliza has been compromised, even if the Beau did not . . ." Charlotte shivered at the thought of what fate her friend might have met at the hands of such a notorious rake. "He will have to propose."

"Do not get your hopes too high. If I know the Beau, he will find a way to squeak out of parson's mousetrap."

Charlotte's jaw jutted. "Not if I can help it." She headed for the door.

"Where are you going?" Olivia called after her.

"To tell Blackthorne what we have figured out. He will make his brother do the honorable thing."

Eliza had felt off balance ever since she laid eyes on the Beau that morning. Riding beside him, it was impossible not to be impressed by the man. He was dazzling, too perfect to be real. His eyes were stunningly blue, his thick blond hair fell attractively over his brow, and his smile—when he graced the world with one—revealed even, pearly white teeth. His shoulders were impossibly broad, his stomach flat, his hips narrow. His muscular legs showed to advantage in skintight buckskins. Best of all, he was several inches taller than her.

She kept reminding herself that he was a man who used his looks to seduce, that there was no honor in him. Eliza's lips curled wryly. More to the point, she must resist the temptation to fall into his arms.

That was why she had asked the Beau such pointed questions. She wanted to hear from his own lips what a dastardly character he was. She wanted to hear proof that his beauty hid a dark soul.

He had not disappointed her.

Yet he had allowed her to make the trip on horseback despite his misgivings. He was, in fact, taking her where she wanted to go. And he had lied to protect her.

What are you running away from, my dear?

Did she dare trust an infamous rake with the truth about why she had left Ravenwood? Would he take her home if he knew she had run away from her guardian? Or would he take advantage of her lack of protection to further his seduction?

She had known she would have to tell Julian about Cousin Nigel's lecherous behavior, but she was not sure she could explain the situation to anyone else. Especially not to a man with his own reputation for debauchery. The Beau would probably laugh at Cousin Nigel's antics.

She glanced at him and saw he was waiting for her answer. He looked trustworthy. But she did not dare trust him. "I have my reasons for leaving home," she said.

"What are they?" he persisted.

"I would rather not say."

"You don't trust me," he said flatly.

"Why should I?" she replied, her temper flaring. "You have confessed behavior that no honorable man would pursue. I do not intend to become another of your victims."

She thought she heard his teeth grinding. A muscle jerked in his cheek. He did not look so much attractive now, as powerfully dangerous, like he could snap her neck in his bare hands. She wondered if the thought had crossed his mind.

His hands tightened on the reins, and his horse began curvetting nervously.

She resisted the urge to apologize. Better to have him angry with her than practicing his seductive wiles. "My reasons for going to London are my own, Captain."

"Very well, Miss Sheringham. I will not pursue the subject further."

Four hours later she realized he did not intend to speak to her on any subject. The twins had asked to stop for lemonade at least once every hour, but their uncle had been adamant in his refusal to break their journey before the horses needed to be changed. At noon they stopped at the Bull and Bear, a posting inn on the fringes of London.

Eliza could see the great houses crowded in upon each other in the distance, could actually smell the mass of humanity that teemed in the thoroughfares and hear a cacophony of sounds: hooves on cobblestones, fishmongers bartering their wares, water splashing, costermongers swearing at one another, coal sliding into chutes.

"You will wait here with the twins while I locate Major Sheringham," the Beau said.

It was an order, one which he expected her to obey. She opened her mouth to remind him she did not take orders and snapped it shut again. All she had to do was let the Beau go without her. She would then be perfectly free to set off on her own. Now that she was close enough to spit at London, she was certain it would not be very difficult to find Julian on her own. Especially since she had more idea of his direction than she had admitted to the Beau.

"Very well," she said demurely. "I will wait here until you return."

The Beau's eyes narrowed on her momentarily, and she thought she might have given away the game by acting too docile. That could be easily remedied.

"Unless, of course, you intend for me to be responsible for the twins, in which case, I would rather come with you. They drink entirely too much lemonade. I would likely spend the entire time running up and down the stairs fetching more and then taking them to the necessary."

He gave her a baleful look and said, "I will see that you have a room to yourself."

She gave him a brilliant smile. "Thank you, Captain."

He made arrangements with his batman to watch over the twins, and while they all waited in a private dining room, he procured rooms for them at the inn.

When he was ready to leave, the twins followed him out onto the porch, insistent upon bidding him farewell.

And seeing more of London, Eliza speculated.

"I should be back long before supper," he said.

"Don't worry, Uncle Marcus. We will keep Eliza company," Reggie promised.

"Shh," he hissed. "Remember Miss Sheringham is disguised as a man."

"Not for much longer," Eliza assured him. "Now that we have arrived in London, I can give up my disguise."

"I will feel more comfortable if you keep it a little longer."

"I cannot allow Julian to see me like this!" she protested.

"You will have warning enough to change, I promise you," he said as he mounted his Thoroughbred. He waved one last time before he kneed his horse into the busy thoroughfare.

"Let's go inside now, ladies," Griggs said. "Time to eat."

"I will be right in, Griggs," Eliza said. "As soon as I check on Mephistopheles."

Griggs scratched his head. "I don't know, miss. Captain said I wasn't to let you out of my sight."

Eliza bit back an oath. So the captain thought she would disappear if given the chance, did he? She chuckled. Well, he was right. "Order me some bread and soup," she cheerfully told Griggs. "I will be back before it is served."

The sergeant's eyes narrowed suspiciously.

But there was nothing he could do, Eliza thought. Unless he planned to follow her around like a faithful hound.She gave him a smile that was the soul of innocence.

Reggie's stomach growled. She grabbed the sergeant's hand and tugged him toward the door to the inn. "I'm hungry, Griggs."

He looked down at her and smiled. "Very well, lass."

By the time he looked up again, Eliza was gone.

She led Mephistopheles out of the stable from a side door and asked the first person she saw for directions to Stephen's Hotel on Bond Street. It was a frequent haunt of army officers on leave, and she knew Julian was staying there while in London.

Eliza had brought along her traveling bag, which she had made sure was left in the stable when they went into the inn, so that she could change into her dress if she had the chance. But she had decided it would be easier to gain admittance to Julian's rooms as his younger brother, than as a single young lady. Julian would understand why she was dressed in his clothes once she explained why she had fled Ravenwood.

When she arrived at Stephen's Hotel, Eliza was grateful for her disguise. The only females she saw wore daring décolletages, too much rouge, and heavy black kohl on their eyes. She knew right away what they were, even though she was not even supposed to know such women existed.

Eliza only wished she had thought to bring one of Julian's old uniforms. She was nearly the only gentleman in the hotel parlor dressed as a civilian. The riot of scarlet and Clarence blue and Cossack green uniforms was splendid. The colors were reflected back a dozen times in the soldiers' patent leather boots and plumed shako hats. The last time Eliza had seen so many colorful ostrich plumes in one place, the Dowager Marchioness of Montcrief had donned them for a musicale in Kent.

Eliza explained at the desk that she was Julian Sheringham's younger brother, come to London to visit him. To her dismay, she discovered Julian was not in. She looked around and realized she would surely end up being discovered if she sat waiting among the soldiers. She could hear enough of their conversations from where she stood to know she did not have a large enough vocabulary of oaths.

"Is it possible for me to wait for my brother in his rooms?" she asked.

"I dunno, sir," the narrow-faced clerk said, appraising her down a very long nose. "Major Sheringham didn't say nothin' 'bout a brother."

"As you can see, I am here," Eliza said, taking care to keep her gravelly voice low. "I have not seen my—" She caught herself before she could say cousin. "Brother in two years. I want to surprise him."

"Guess that'd be all right. Major Sheringham can throw you out as well as I can, if you ain't who you say."

A porter let her into Julian's suite of rooms and set her traveling bag on the floor. When he held out his hand, she shook it and said, "Thank you."

He scowled, muttered, "Clutch-fisted gentry," set the key on a table inside the door, and left, closing the door behind him.

By the time Eliza realized the porter had been waiting for a coin, it was too late to call him back. She clasped her hands behind her and strode around the suite of rooms, looking for signs of Julian.

His hairbrush sat on the washstand, along with his shaving equipment. His beaver shaving brush was still damp, and she could see a puddle of water on his— she sniffed—sandalwood shaving soap. Perhaps he had only gone somewhere for breakfast and would be back soon.

The bed was unmade, the sheets tousled as though he had not slept well. She started to turn away, uncomfortable intruding on his privacy. And noticed that both pillows bore the indentation of a head.

She crossed to the foot of the brass bed and grasped the bars with white-knuckled hands, staring hard at the pillows. Maybe he had slept on both pillows. She crossed to the pillow on one side, leaned over and sniffed the coverlet. Sandalwood. Julian had laid his head there. She stroked the pillow lovingly.

Eliza paused, then leaned across the bed and sniffed the other pillow. She rose abruptly, as the cloying smell of cheap rosewater assaulted her nose.

"He has had a woman here!"

Astonishment, anger, and hurt laced her voice. She knew men had their fancy pieces, but she had not thought Julian . . . How stupid of her! She had seen the sort of females in the hotel parlor and overheard the soldiers' ribald comments. The soldiers must be inviting the ladies of the demimonde to join them in their rooms. As Julian had obviously done.

She let out a breath she had been holding too long. That did nothing to relieve the ache in her chest.

Eliza fought back a surge of jealous anger. Only a nodcock would anguish over a single gentleman's rendezvous with a paid-for paramour. She had no right to criticize Julian's behavior until he was hers. She had no doubt that when he married, he would be a faithful husband. All the same, it hurt to know Julian had not come home to her at Ravenwood. That he had stayed in London to make love to another woman.

She hastened out of his bedroom, collapsed into a padded wooden chair close to the open window of the sitting room, and took several deep, calming breaths. Her nose was assailed by the stench of the gutters, while the strident sounds from the cobblestoned street below jangled her nerves. She rose and fled toward the door but was not halfway there before she realized she had nowhere else to go.

Eliza returned to the chair by the window, pulled it far enough away to avoid the worst of the reeking foulness, and settled into it to think.

Her worst fear was that Julian would return to his rooms in the company of the demi-rep with whom he had spent the night. She did not think she could bear the comparison between herself—especially attired so indecorously in travel-stained clothes—and a beautiful, sensuous, sexually experienced woman.

So change into your walking dress.

At least if she were dressed like a lady, Julian might be more likely to see her as a prospective bride. It would still be difficult for her to compete with a "beautiful, sensuous, sexually experienced" demi-rep. She threw out "beautiful" and "sexually experienced." Julian would expect neither from her. As for "sensuous," she would simply have to rely on instinct to guide her.

Eliza had no trouble getting out of Julian's clothes. She brushed her hair, then pinned up part of it, leaving her face edged by wispy curls and a tangle of chestnut hair down her back.

Her pale blue merino day dress was horribly wrinkled from having been crumpled up in the cloth bag, but she hoped it would not be so bad once she had it on.

Getting it on proved more of a challenge than she had expected. Eliza was too used to having a maid. There was no way she could button up the dress by herself. It fell open halfway down her back, where she could not reach.

She stood pressing the square-cut neck to her throat, adjusting the short, puffy sleeves at her shoulders, when the doorknob began to turn. She felt a spurt of panic.

Oh, dear God! It must be Julian.

She could not let him see her like this! She looked for a place to hide and realized how futile that would be. At some point she would have to come out and ask Julian to help her button up her dress.

It might as well be now.

She faced the door, her heart racing, her hand

clutching the blue merino wool against her breast. And waited for Julian to enter.

Eliza gasped when she saw who was standing in the doorway.

Chapter 6

Marcus stared, dumbstruck, at the half-dressed woman in Julian's room. His body sprang to life, responding with decided interest to the female standing before him with tangled, waist-length chestnut hair cascading over her bared shoulders. Then it dawned on him who she was. And where she was.

During the hour he had been delayed helping to right an overturned cart of potatoes, and the gentleman's curricle that was also involved in the accident, Miss Sheringham had somehow found her way here. And been ravished.

He felt outraged that Julian had taken such advantage of her, even if she was besotted with him. He searched the room for his friend, ready to seek an accounting on Miss Sheringham's behalf. He would make sure Julian did the honorable thing and married her. Except, there were no dragons in sight to slay. Julian was nowhere to be seen.

Since he could not take out his temper on Julian, Miss Sheringham got the brunt of it. "Where is he?"

Miss Sheringham clutched her dress to her bosom. "Who?"

"The gentleman who lives here," he said curtly.

"I have not seen him."

"Then explain why are you in such dishabille, Miss Sheringham," he asked in a deadly voice.

"Oh." Her face pinkened as she grabbed at the puffed sleeves of the dress, pulling them farther onto her shoulders. She spoke with a quiet dignity that impressed him. "I was merely changing from Julian's borrowed clothes into a dress, Captain. You burst in here before I was able to finish."

He heard the accusation in the last half of her speech and felt himself flushing. He never flushed. But then, he had never lost the upper hand with a woman, either. Until now.

He had not stopped to knock before he entered. He had not even bothered to ask the hotel clerk whether Julian was in his rooms, because he knew his friend rarely rose before noon. Today he obviously had.

"How did you get here?" Marcus demanded, taking the offensive to rid himself of embarrassment— and the sexual attraction he was struggling to control.

"I rode here on Mephistopheles."

"Through London? By yourself?"

She nodded once in answer to each question.

He put a shaky hand to his brow. "Good lord."

His surprise at finding Miss Sheringham so deliciously unclothed, his anger at the danger she had put herself in getting here, and a growing hunger for the feast laid before him, gave his voice a sharp edge. "How did you find this place?"

"Julian sent a letter to Cousin Nigel the day he arrived in London giving his direction," she said with the throaty breathlessness of a woman in the throes of passion. But it was not passion. It was fear . . . and defiance. Her stance reminded him of a lioness, with claws that could scratch.

It dawned on him that she had deceived him on purpose. "You did not think it necessary to share that information with me?" he said through tight jaws.

She looked him right in the eye, opened her mouth to speak, closed it, and shrugged, causing her puffed sleeves to fall down her arms.

He had never seen anything quite so fascinating as the regally tall Miss Sheringham, bare-shouldered, clutching an obviously unbuttoned day dress to her ample bosom.

The situation was fraught with danger for both of them. He had to remind himself that she had not, in fact, been ravished. Yet. The sight of such a mouth-watering morsel at his mercy was tempting. He was experienced enough to know how to get Miss Sheringham into bed and to ensure that she enjoyed herself as much as he did.

He reminded himself she was an innocent, a virgin. The consequence of slaking his desire for her was a leg-shackle. He was not inclined to give up his freedom, even for such a prize.

But he imagined wrapping himself in her hair, the silky smoothness of her shoulders beneath his callused fingertips, how her lips would taste, and what it would feel like to be the first to broach her. She would be tight and hot and wet . . .

He gritted his teeth at the realization his body had gone hard as a rock. If Miss Sheringham were more worldly, she would have known to get out while she still could. He was not without conscience; he had never taken an unwilling woman to bed. But he could see no reason to refuse what a woman freely offered—with a little coaxing from him.

"Was this the way you planned to greet your cousin, Miss Sheringham?" he asked in a lazy, intimately suggestive voice.

"Of course not! I simply did not realize before I started that I could not reach a great many of the buttons on the back of this dress. I had no intention of allowing Julian to find me this way." She sounded angry and a little flustered.

Julian. Bloody hell! What madness had he been contemplating? Miss Sheringham was his best friend's cousin. Marcus had to resist temptation. He had to keep his hands off her.

She turned her bared back to him, looked at him over her shoulder—not in the least coy—and said, "Would you, please?"

He could not quite believe Miss Sheringham expected him to act as her lady's maid. He knew himself too well. If he got close enough to touch her flesh, she would be lucky to escape with her virtue.

"Pardon me," he said. "I will leave you—"

She whirled, one hand outstretched to him. "Wait! You cannot leave. I need your help."

One side of her bodice fell away entirely, revealing a thin lawn chemise decorated with satin rosebuds that barely concealed the single, luscious pink bud beneath it.

He had already started backing out the door, determined to wait downstairs for Julian's return, when he heard male voices in the hall. Any moment he would be in exactly the compromising situation he so earnestly wanted to avoid.

"Please," she said. "I would rather Julian did not find me like this."

He caught the pleading look in her eyes, fought a battle with his better judgment, and lost. He came back inside and quickly closed the door behind him.

He did not bother to hide his irritation at being forced into such a discomfiting predicament. He put his balled fists on his hips and said, "What kind of game is this?"

She gathered up her dress and clutched it against her bosom again with both hands. She kept her head high, her tawny golden eyes on his, but he watched an enticing flush begin just above her nearly exposed breasts and race its way up her throat to land as two red spots on her cheeks.

"I . . . this is not . . . I wish I could sink into the floor." She paused, blew out a breath, and continued, "But since that is not possible, I earnestly ask your help in restoring myself to the guise of respectable gentlewoman before my cousin returns."

He fought back an indulgent smile and said, "When do you expect him?"

"I have no idea when Julian left or when he will be back. I have noticed, however, that he has company."

"Company?"

Her lips pressed flat. She glanced fleetingly at the tousled sheets through the open bedroom doorway.

"Ohhhh," he said. "Company. I see." Apparently Julian's ladybird had left evidence of her existence. Too bad for Julian. And Miss Sheringham, of course.

"Would you help me, please, Captain?"

She turned her back to him again, before he could explain why he must refuse. Then he did not want to.

Her back and bare shoulders—what he could see of them above and beyond the fragile white chemise—were lovely. She had attempted buttoning the dress, but only three buttons at the base of her spine were closed. The rest of the dress lay open, with nearly a dozen buttons undone.

Marcus had always been enticed more by the promise of what lay hidden from sight than by a woman's blatant nudity. It was fun to imagine what he would find, and then to uncover the promised delights. Miss Sheringham had presented him with a charming package that was impossible to decline.

His balled hands uncurled. He took his time walking to her, the sound of his Hessians echoing on the bare wooden floor. He saw the rising tension in her shoulders as she sensed him coming closer, saw the quiver of expectation in her flesh.

When he reached for the puffed sleeves to draw them up, she jerked. "Shh," he said in a silky voice. "Don't be afraid."

"I am not afraid of you." She stared straight ahead, and her shoulders squared even more.

Marcus smiled. "Very well. Stand still while I do this."

The instant his fingertips touched her flesh, she whirled around to face him. He was forced to let go of the button he held or tear it off.

She backed away several steps and stopped, bosom heaving as though she had just run a race. "Perhaps I will wait for Julian, after all."

He gave a lazy shrug, his eyes hooded. "The choice is yours."

She looked down at herself, and an almost comical expression of dismay appeared on her face. "Oh, dear. I cannot meet Julian like this! Not with you here. He will never understand." She turned her back to him for the third time. "Hurry. Please, hurry!"

Marcus realized she had a point. Julian could return at any moment and misconstrue the situation. Nevertheless, Marcus was not inclined to rush. He intended to savor Miss Sheringham's lovely dishevelment for as long as he could.

Eliza kept reminding herself to breathe, but even when she did, it was difficult to suck air into her constricted lungs. How could she be attracted to such an irritating man? Why did the mere brush of his fingertips send frissons of sensation skittering down her spine?

The answer was simple enough. It was difficult to ignore such perfection in form and features and almost impossible to believe—except that he stood before her in the flesh—that the Beau had been so generously blessed by nature. An aquiline nose. Large, wide-spaced, bluer than blue eyes under arched brows. Blond hair that fell rakishly over his forehead in a Brutus cut.

And of course, the blatant evidence that he was physically aroused by her. She had tried not to look, but the transformation had been fascinating . . . and frightening.

Hurry, hurry! I do not want to feel like this. I am in love with Julian. I always have been, and I always will be. It is only

*because I am so inexperienced rebuffing rakes that I am over-
whelmed by these unwanted feelings. Oh, please hurry!*

The Beau took his time.

She felt the buttons being done up one at a time,
with an interminable pause between each. At this rate,
it would be time for supper before he finished. She
jumped when his knuckles brushed her flesh once
more.

"Be still," he said in a husky voice.

She wriggled her shoulders to rid herself of the
pleasant tingle of feeling that lingered.

"I cannot finish if you will not stand still," he said.
"You are going too slow!"

His hands grasped her shoulders, and his thumbs
pressed strongly against her back in a circular motion.
It felt exquisite. She bit back a moan of pleasure,
knowing she should not be letting him do this.

Eliza had seldom seen the need for most of Society's restrictions, but a chaperon would not have been
amiss just now. She fought the urge to lean back
against him. She wanted to feel his hands everywhere,
all over her. No wonder gentlemen were required to
keep their distance, if this was the result!

"Relax, Miss Sheringham. I can see your shoulders
are all bunched up." The Beau applied more soothing
pressure with his thumbs. Then his hands sieved
through her hair and moved it forward over her shoulders.

"What are . . ." The sound came out as a hoarse
whisper. She cleared her throat and finished,
". . . you doing?"

"Your hair—have I mentioned it is quite lovely?—
was in my way. I need to see what I am doing."

It sounded perfectly innocent. An inner voice warned her it was not. An instant later she felt the Beau's lips nuzzle the crest of her shoulder.

She started to lurch away, but he caught her by the shoulders with powerful hands. He held her firmly, but gently. She stood paralyzed. Why was she not struggling? She wanted to be free, didn't she?

Eliza tried to speak, to tell him to let her go, but her throat was clogged with feeling. Her breathing was erratic. Her heart pounded. "What do you want from me?"

"Only a kiss," he said, his warm breath tracing the route he intended to follow. From her throat . . . to her ear . . . to her temple . . . down her cheek . . . to the very edge of her mouth.

She shivered uncontrollably as his warm, moist breath caressed her flesh. She had never felt anything quite so exquisite. Eliza reminded herself he was a rake, schooled in seduction. She was willing to break the rules—to a point.

"You have taken two kisses already," she protested in a quavery voice.

"One more. On the lips."

"I . . . I . . ."

She would never know what answer she might have given. A noise at the door froze her in place. She stared in horror as the doorknob begin to turn.

The Beau, apparently more experienced at having his lovemaking interrupted so precipitously, finished the top three buttons in two seconds flat and took a step to her left an instant before Julian entered the room.

Eliza breathed a guilty sigh of relief that Julian

had not caught the Beau kissing her. She saw the myriad expressions flash across Julian's face at finding her in his rooms. Disbelief, delight, dismay. Then confusion, followed by suspicion.

If only she had done things differently, brought a different dress, stayed in Julian's clothes. If only the Beau were not such a scoundrel! She shot him an angry, scornful look, realizing too late how Julian might construe it.

Her gaze skipped back to Julian, who had indeed been watching the byplay. His face darkened ominously.

She did not need the Beau's male perfection. She wanted only Julian, with his dark brown eyes, his black hair that needed a trim, his broad blade of nose and high cheekbones and slashing black brows. His beloved face, his features that had so appealed to her, were contorted now by doubt and accusation.

Her nose burned, and her eyes blurred with tears. She blinked furiously. She was not the sort of miss who turned into a watering pot at the least provocation. But her meeting with Julian was not progressing at all as she had imagined.

The Beau was first to speak. He was probably used to being caught with a lady in dubious circumstances, Eliza thought cynically.

The Beau smiled as though he hadn't a care in the world and said, "Hello, Julian."

His simple greeting was not nearly enough to allay Julian's suspicion. "What in bloody hell is going on here, Marcus?"

Julian knew the Beau. And the Beau knew Julian! He had addressed Julian by his first name.

"You two know each other?" she asked, aghast.

"Julian and I are best friends," the Beau admitted with a shrug.

"*Were* best friends," Julian corrected.

"You purposely deceived me," Eliza said, her eyes locking with the captain's. "Why?"

"I was doing what I could to help out a friend," he replied.

Do you mean me? Or Julian? she wondered.

His eyes begged forgiveness. She supposed rakes never asked in words. She had actually opened her mouth to offer pardon when Julian startled her out of whatever hypnotic trance she was in. Offering pardon? To the *Beau?* What had she been thinking? He should rather ask pardon of her!

"I want to know what you are doing here alone with my cousin," Julian demanded.

The Beau was clearly incensed by Julian's antagonism.

Eliza leaped into the breach. "Captain Wharton accompanied me to London," she said matter-of-factly, "and was kind enough to wait here with me until you arrived."

Julian's scowl, and a sharp, narrow-eyed glance at the Beau, told her she had said the wrong thing, but she did not understand why it was wrong.

"Miss Sheringham means my batman, Blackthorne's twins and I escorted her to London," the Beau amended. "We were never alone together on the road, Julian. And we have been here a mere half hour waiting for you."

"Alone?" Julian queried.

The Beau nodded, tight-lipped.

The glare remained on Julian's face. "Where is your maid, Eliza?" he demanded. "What are you doing in a gentleman's apartments? What were you thinking, brat?"

He had called her brat. Was that all Julian thought of her, when she loved him so much? Eliza's stomach was in such turmoil, she feared she might cast up her accounts. She swallowed back the acid in her throat.

"I left my maid at Ravenwood. I came on horseback, Julian, since that was the fastest way to get here. I had to see you on a matter of utmost urgency."

"You could have—should have—used the post to send for me."

Eliza felt the tears scalding her eyes. There was no stopping them now, however much she blinked. She had hoped for a better welcome from her cousin. In the past, he had always grinned and given her a tight hug and a kiss on the cheek.

But their last meeting had been two years ago, when she was a child of fifteen. She was no longer a child, even if he still called her *brat*. A stone wall of propriety was stacked high between them. She had never felt so alone in her life. She stared at Julian, her heart in her eyes, willing him to reach out to her.

But he said nothing. Did nothing.

"I will excuse myself, Julian, so you may speak with your cousin alone," the Beau said.

"Wait, Marcus!" Julian said. "I cannot . . . Eliza and I should not be alone together."

"If you wish, I can wait outside the door," Marcus said.

Julian shoved a hand through his dark hair, leaving it standing on end. It was not at all unattractive, Eliza thought.

"Damn you, girl!" Julian muttered. "What a coil!"

"I must speak with you alone, Julian," Eliza said, struggling to keep her voice steady, even though her heart was breaking.

Julian shot the Beau a helpless glance, apparently trying to convey some message that Eliza could not make out. A second later, the reason for Julian's apprehension shoved open the door and took a step inside.

"What's this, lovey? More company? An orgy, is it? That'll be a coin or two more from your pocket. But the more, the merrier, I always say."

Julian sank into the chair by the door, dropped his head in his hands, and groaned.

Eliza could smell the cheap rosewater from where she stood. She felt nauseated. This doxy was the woman Julian had taken to his bed.

She put a hand to her mouth and stiffened her knees to keep them from crumpling out from under her. The Beau caught her by the shoulders and held her upright. She resisted the urge to turn to him for comfort.

Eliza was too fascinated by the creature in the doorway to look anywhere else. Julian's doxy looked surprisingly similar to those she had seen downstairs, her cheeks rouged, her eyes lined with kohl. Her lips were berry red, and her breasts were barely contained by the thin fabric of her gown. The cloth clung to her as though her slip had been dampened. Were those dark spots really her . . . ? Oh, dear.

Eliza turned without thinking and hid her face against the Beau's shoulder.

Above the steady thump of the Beau's heart, she heard Julian send the woman away. And then Julian's angry voice saying, "I think perhaps you should pay your respects to my brother, Marcus, and your addresses to Miss Sheringham."

"You are making a mistake, Julian," she heard the Beau say, his voice rumbling in her ear. His arms stayed around her, comforting her. He made no move to release her, merely explained, "Miss Sheringham turned to me because I was closest to her. You could see as well as I that she was about to faint. What would you have me do?"

She heard Julian make a warning sound in his throat.

The Beau hurried on. "There is no need for a declaration from me, I assure you. No one knows of Miss Sheringham's indiscretion in coming to your rooms unchaperoned besides me, and I have no intention—"

"What possessed you to bring her here, man?" Julian blurted. "You must have known it was no place for a young lady!"

Eliza waited for the Beau to reveal that she had come here on her own. That he'd had nothing to do with it.

A tense silence settled around them.

Eliza could not let someone else take the blame for her folly. She raised her head and stared at Julian's beloved—furiously angry—face. "Captain Wharton did not bring me here, Julian," she said. "He specifically bade me stay at a nearby inn with his nieces and wait until he could bring you to me. I came here on my own, against his wishes."

"I know Marcus too well to believe he did not

take advantage of the situation," Julian said. "What did he—"

Eliza felt the Beau's body tense beneath her hands, and only then realized she was still in his arms. She pulled herself free and turned to face her cousin. "How dare you accuse such a good friend of acting dishonorably!" she scolded. "Not to mention what such an accusation says about me."

"Are you telling me the truth, Eliza? Has he warned you not to speak? Has he touched you as only a husband has the right? Has he compromised you?"

She had never seen Julian's face look so serious. Or dangerous. A glance sideways at the Beau revealed an equally dangerous visage. He was not a man to be forced into parson's mousetrap. This lone wolf was the kind to bite off his own leg to escape. And she had no intention of marrying the wrong man because of some stupid rules she had never in her life followed.

She turned back to Julian, her own features solemn. She met his gaze steadily. "Nothing happened, Julian."

"I will excuse you while you speak with your cousin, Julian," the Beau said. "I will be outside in the hall when you have finished."

"Marcus . . ."

The Beau stopped at the open door.

"I am sorry. You must admit the circumstances—"

"No apology necessary, old chap. Your heart was in the right place."

When Marcus was gone, Julian turned to face her, his hands clasped behind his back. "Well, young lady. What do you have to say for yourself?"

"I love you, Julian. I want you to marry me."

Chapter 7

MARCUS RESISTED THE URGE TO PACE THE HALL outside Julian's door. He did not think he had ever spent a more uncomfortable fifteen minutes. What was Miss Sheringham saying to Julian? How much of what had happened between them had she revealed? Not much. Otherwise, Julian would have long since come charging through the door to queer his daylights.

Marcus reached up to loosen his neck cloth, but it was already slack from several attempts to ease the constriction there. It only felt like a noose was tightening around his neck; he was still a free man.

But for how long?

He had been surprised when Miss Sheringham lied to protect him in the first moments after Julian caught them alone together. Until it dawned on him that she had seen parson's mousetrap snapping closed on them and deftly avoided it. No wonder. She was in love with someone else.

He should have felt more guilty for putting her in such a compromising position. He could have buttoned up her dress in a tenth of the time it had taken him. Yet he could not feel sorry for the kisses he had stolen. He could still smell her hair, feel the smoothness of her skin, taste her flesh. If Julian had not interrupted . . .

She might have given him that kiss.

The muffled speaking beyond the door grew louder for a moment, but there was nothing distinct enough to give him a hint of what was transpiring between the two. Were they even now becoming engaged?

Marcus should have felt relieved at the thought. Instead, he felt sick to his stomach. He did not stop to figure out why he did not want Miss Sheringham married to his best friend. He only knew he would rather she married someone—anyone—else. Anyone, that is, but him.

He had learned his lesson from Alastair's mistake. A woman in bed for the night was a delightful frolic; making a lifetime commitment rendered a man vulnerable to an endless succession of insults, affronts, and indignities from which there was no escape.

Sometimes he wondered if Alastair's wife had been an exception. But if she was, why did so many men he knew spend so much time away from home? Why did they all have mistresses?

Marcus leaned against the papered wall, his booted feet crossed at the ankle, his arms draped across his chest in the most languid pose he could manage. He greeted several hussars from another regiment with insouciance as they strolled by on the way to their rooms.

"Is she worth the wait, Captain?" one quipped, hearing the male and female voices inside the room and drawing the conclusion that Marcus was next in line to be serviced.

"Have a friend warming her up for you, eh, Beau?" a second jibed, leering like a schoolboy ogling his first naked female.

"Never liked seconds myself," a third sallied.

Marcus should have grinned and laughed. After all, they meant no harm. But a second later the officer who had referred to Miss Sheringham as "seconds" found himself slammed against the opposite wall with Marcus's hands tight around his throat. Marcus ignored the two uniformed hussars shouting and pounding on his shoulders as though they were annoying gnats.

He saw everything through a red haze, heard nothing but the pounding pulse in his head, until a familiar voice brought him back to himself.

"Marcus! Marcus, stop! You're killing him."

Julian's face came into focus beside him, anxious and frightened. Marcus became aware that four sets of hands grasped at his own. Julian, the two friends of the soldier, and the soldier himself were all trying to tear his clenched fingers from around the poor man's neck.

The afflicted soldier's eyes bulged in terror. His face had turned blue enough to clash with his bottle green uniform.

Marcus loosened his hands. The soldier began coughing and gasping for air. Marcus backed away as the soldier reached gingerly for his wounded throat, which already bore the beginnings of bruises where Marcus's fingertips had dug deep.

Marcus stared at his trembling hands. He would have killed the man for a misplaced jest. He nearly had. He lifted glacial eyes to the other two soldiers, who flanked their friend protectively.

"He's crazy!" the choked man gasped.

"He will not trouble you again," Julian promised, putting himself between Marcus and the three men.

"I saw something like this once on the field of battle," one of the soldiers said in a quiet voice. "Fellow went completely berserk. Couldn't tell friend from foe." He took a shuddering breath. "Finally had to kill him or be killed."

The hall was silent as they absorbed his painful admission.

"Perhaps he saw one too many friends blown to bits, or got covered in too much blood, or ended up with a faceful of somebody's brains," the soldier mused.

Soldiers who had been at the front for too long sometimes reached their limit of endurance and cracked. They attacked others, or themselves. There was nothing to do but keep them quiet until they returned to normal. If they ever did.

The hussars—even the one who had been attacked—stared at Marcus with pity and compassion as they slowly backed their way down the hall.

Marcus said nothing to contradict the explanation given for his behavior.

Julian crossed to his side. "Are you all right?"

Marcus nodded, unable to speak.

"What happened? Did that cod's-head offer you an insult? Should I call him back and demand satisfaction?"

Marcus closed his eyes and put his thumb and middle finger against the pounding pulses at his temples. He still could not quite believe what had just happened. A few harmless jests aimed unknowingly at Miss Sheringham had turned him into a savage bent on strangling a man to death.

The soldiers could not have known their comments were directed toward a lady, rather than some camp follower. He had ignored—or joined in—such ribald remarks a thousand times in the past. Why had it been different this time? Thank God Julian had stopped him. Once again, he was in his friend's debt for coming to his rescue.

He opened his eyes and lowered his hand, meeting Julian's concerned gaze. "I must have gone a little mad," he said.

He felt Julian's hand on his shoulder, offering comfort and support, denying the need for more explanation.

Then it dawned on him that Julian had been ready to fight a duel for him. Julian was offering comfort. Miss Sheringham must have convinced Julian that he had not importuned her. Good girl! Then he realized Julian was alone.

"Where is Miss Sheringham?"

"I left my cousin with orders to dress herself."

Marcus felt a wave of feral ruthlessness at the thought of Julian stripping Miss Sheringham and taking her to bed while he had been standing out in the hall. His neckhairs bristled as he imagined their voices raised, not in argument as he had first believed, but in passion.

"Miss Sheringham was dressed when I left the room," he said, his eyes narrowed to slits, his lips flattened.

"She is changing into her male disguise," Julian explained, apparently unaware of Marcus's rising agitation. "I could think of no other way to remove her from here without causing a scandal."

Marcus spat an epithet under his breath and heaved out a breath of air to release his pent-up, and totally unnecessary, anger. Once again, he had misconstrued an innocent remark. Julian would never despoil his own cousin. What was putting these bizarre ideas in his head?

"You are right, of course. She will have to be in men's clothing to leave here unnoticed." His expression remained troubled, but only because he was vexed by his own behavior. What the devil was the matter with him? Maybe he *had* gone crazy. "Where are you taking Miss Sheringham from here?"

"Where she should have gone in the first place."

Marcus lifted an inquiring brow.

"To Braddock's house party in Sussex. I recently received an invitation myself. Maybe I can find her a husband there."

Marcus's heart missed a beat. "You do not plan to marry her yourself?"

"No. But she must have a husband. And soon."

Marcus paled at the implication of the need for a hasty wedding. "Who is the man?"

Julian knotted his hands behind his back. "It seems my brother Nigel has been imposing himself on his ward."

"Bloody hell!" The killing beast rose again in Marcus's breast, eager to wreak vengeance. He fought it back, leashed it tightly, and asked, "Did he hurt her?"

Julian shook his head. "She ran away two days ago after dropping a flower pot on his head."

Marcus conjured an image of the scene, fought a grin of admiration, and lost. "Miss Sheringham is nothing if not resourceful."

"I cannot help thinking she must have done something to encourage him. I cannot believe my own brother could be such a blackguard. Yet I cannot believe it of her, either. Eliza was always so uninterested in female pursuits. She was too gangly, too awkward to attract that kind of male attention when I was last home."

"Have you looked at her—really looked at her—lately?" Marcus asked. "She is not at all as you described her to me."

Julian pursed his lips thoughtfully. "She has grown taller, and her hair is longer. Though it is just as unkempt," he added.

"She is no bed slat," Marcus said flatly.

"Surely I did not call her one!"

Marcus nodded.

"I see. Yes, that has changed, too. I simply cannot see her as she is, I suppose. She always followed me around like a playful puppy, full of fun, always ready to try anything, a veritable hoyden."

"The image no longer fits," Marcus said. Then, remembering Miss Sheringham dressed in Julian's clothes, he corrected, "At least, not entirely." He looked Julian in the eye, searching for the truth, as he asked for the second time, "Do you want to marry her, Julian?"

"That is beside the point," Julian said, again dodging the question. "I have no home of my own. If I did marry her, I would have no choice except to leave her at Ravenwood when I am called back to war. You see why that would not fadge."

Marcus understood Julian's problem. Rooms at Stephen's Hotel were adequate accommodations for a soldier; they were no place for a wife. And Ravenwood could no longer be counted on as a safe haven because of Nigel. "War is not a certainty," Marcus pointed out.

"Napoleon must be subdued once and for all," Julian said. "You and I both know he will not give up without a fight. What if I am killed in battle? What kind of life would Eliza lead as a widow living at my brother's mercy?"

"You believe the solution is to get her married as quickly as possible to someone else?" Marcus asked.

"I do. Although that may not be as simple as it sounds. The scandal surrounding her is bound to make finding an eligible suitor difficult."

Marcus lifted an eyebrow. "You told me the scandal in her background was of no import."

Julian pursed his lips. "Perhaps that was an understatement."

"The scandal is ongoing?"

Julian nodded. "No one knows what caused the Earl of Sheringham to disinherit his son. Sadly, I believe the surrounding mystery has kept the scandal alive long past a time when it should have died a peaceful death. Eliza has lived under that cloud since she was a child."

"A Child of Scandal," Marcus murmured. "The sins of the fathers visited upon the sons."

"Or in this case," Julian said, "his daughter. As you

have no doubt discovered for yourself, Eliza can be perfectly amiable. Or as contrary as the most stubborn army mule. Although she has never caused a scandal, she carries the taint with her wherever she goes. Her looks are odd, and her height makes her freakish."

Marcus opened his mouth to interrupt, but Julian held up a hand to stay him.

"She does not suffer gossips gladly, and many in Kent have felt the whip of her tongue. The highest sticklers will never make her welcome. And she has no dowry to speak of. Tell me, Marcus, what does she have to attract a gentleman who wants a comfortable wife?"

"Miss Sheringham is an Original," Marcus said. "She should be valued for her uniqueness, not rebuked for it."

Julian snorted. "I will not argue the subject. You win too often."

"What makes you think she will find a man willing to make her an offer at the Duke of Braddock's house party?" Marcus asked.

"Everyone knows it is a matchmaking event. It could be no secret, with every eligible gentleman in London invited. The betting book at White's is full of wagers as to which single gentlemen will come away engaged," Julian said with a grin. "Eliza will never have a greater selection to choose from. Surely someone who attends will overlook the scandal and desire the woman. It is too bad you will not be there."

Marcus had previously told Julian he was heading to the countryside to hide. "It seems I will be there, after all," Marcus said. "My brother convinced me I must attend. I was headed to Somersville Manor when

I encountered your cousin and made the detour here to help her find you. We are both late, you realize."

"I will be on my way soon enough," Julian said. "As soon as Eliza is disguised as a young man, I am taking her directly to my great-aunt's town house in Berkeley Square. I will arrive an hour later to greet my cousin, Miss Sheringham, who has been visiting our great-aunt, Lady Sophia Minton. I am sure I can convince Aunt Sophie to chaperon Eliza on our journey to Sussex. Though, in my experience, it will take Sophie—or should I say her maid, who is at least as old as she, though neither of them will reveal how old that is—an entire day to pack."

"I had better get my own party organized and on the road before my brother misses me and begins to worry," Marcus said.

"Why would he worry?"

"I have his twin daughters with me, Lady Regina and Lady Rebecca."

"Have you hired on as a nanny, Marcus?"

"They are no longer babies, Julian. Young ladies, if you please. But a challenge to be sure."

Julian laughed. "You ought to make a good father, Marcus. You've been playing the role with your brother's children long enough to—"

Julian shot Marcus a stricken glance. "I did not mean to imply . . . I would never suggest . . ." He huffed out a breath. "Damn it, man. You know what I mean."

Julian had obviously heard the rumors that Blackthorne's twins had been sired by his younger brother. Marcus had never really thought about it, but now he realized Julian had believed them. Not without good cause, Marcus conceded.

Julian knew, better than most, that Marcus was capable of seducing another man's wife. Julian had been witness to the Beau's trysts with numerous married ladies. Julian knew the depth of Marcus's cynicism about marital fidelity: it did not exist in his social class, so far as Marcus could tell. As long as one was discreet, it was perfectly acceptable. Many a lord had second, third, or fourth children who were not his own without social stigma for husband or wife.

The Beau's perfidy in the eyes of the *ton* was in broaching a married woman before she had presented her husband with his heir. A married woman within the prohibited consanguinity for marriage. A married woman who happened to be his brother's wife.

Marcus sighed.

"I do not blame you for it, Marcus," Julian said. "She was very beautiful."

"Thank you for that," Marcus said, his lips twisted in the mockery of a smile. But he would rather Julian had not believed him capable of it.

You will make a good father.

Marcus did not intend to marry, and he did not wish to sire bastards. He had faced the fact he would never have children he could call his own. But when he was far away from home and memories of Reggie's and Becky's gamine grins and childish antics warmed his heart and made him smile, he wished things had not turned out as they had.

Marcus reached out a hand to Julian, who clasped it. "I will see you tomorrow."

"If nothing else goes awry," Julian said.

At that moment Julian's door opened, and Marcus saw Miss Sheringham, resplendent in male attire. She looked almost as jaunty as she had the first moment he had laid eyes on her, with one obvious difference.

Miss Sheringham had been crying.

"Was your visit with your cousin everything you hoped for, Miss Sheringham?" he asked.

She smiled tremulously. "Absolutely. Julian could not have made me feel more welcome." Her red-rimmed eyes and splotchy face told another story.

Marcus felt two simultaneous urges. To draw Miss Sheringham into his arms to comfort her. And to plant his friend a facer. He resisted both.

Marcus shifted his gaze from Miss Sheringham to Julian and back again. Both of them were purposefully staring at the toes of their boots.

So. More had passed between them than Julian had revealed. Perhaps Julian had kissed her. After all, Marcus had found her quite irresistible.

Or she had kissed him, expecting a proposal. Which had not come.

Marcus reminded himself that Miss Sheringham was no longer his problem or his concern. She had her cousin to take care of her now. If he did not leave immediately, he was liable to get himself back into a situation he was well out of.

"Good day, Miss Sheringham," he said. "Julian, I will look for you tomorrow or the next day."

He hurried away before he did something he knew he would regret later.

Reggie and Becky had promised Griggs they would lie down for an afternoon nap in their upstairs room at the Bull and Bear. But the moment he took himself off to the pub below, they tied several sheets together and escaped out the window. It was not difficult. They had perfected the technique at home, quite scaring the wits out of Miss Higgenbotham, the governess who had preceded Miss Balderdish.

Becky held tight to Reggie's hand as they walked the dirty, noisy streets of London. Becky grabbed her nose to keep out the stench of the running sewers that edged the cobblestones.

"What are you doing?" Reggie asked.

"It stinks!"

Reggie sniffed mightily, sucking up coal dust and bits of hay and other less salubrious debris. "It is all part of the adventure. New sights, new smells, new—" Her nose wrinkled, and she sucked a floating piece of straw into her mouth before it exited along with a clarion sneeze.

From all around them, as far away as the other side of the street, they heard a chorus of "Bless you," "God bless," "Let the devil go, child," and "Bugger, that was *loud*!"

Becky snickered. "Is that part of the adventure, too?"

"You are not supposed to know what that means."

"You told me," Becky countered.

"I can see I should have kept it to myself. If Father ever found out, he would—"

"Look, Reggie."

Reggie looked where Becky pointed. A baker's cart was being rolled down the street. It was stacked high with tarts and biscuits that smelled as sweet as the ones Cook baked at home.

"I'm hungry," Becky said.

Reggie's stomach growled at the sight of the biscuits. "Me, too. But we haven't any money to buy anything."

"Come on. I have an idea." Becky dragged her sister over to the baker's cart, where a little coltish charm and two identical toothsome smiles garnered an already-broken biscuit they could split between them.

"Maybe we should have waited for Uncle Marcus to go sightseeing," Becky said through a mouthful of butter biscuit as they continued their way down the street. She looked behind her but could no longer see the Bull and Bear. "We might get lost."

"Oh, fudge," Reggie replied. "All we have to do is ask, and someone will tell us the way back. Besides, Uncle Marcus only came to London because of Eliza. He probably would have found a way to get out of taking us to see the sights."

"But he promised—"

"He has broken promises before. Remember when he said he would buy us matching ponies?"

"Father forbade it," Becky reminded her. "Surely you must recall how long and loudly Uncle Marcus argued with him? Uncle Marcus said he had promised us, and we would be disappointed. Father would not be moved."

"I had forgotten that. What about the time Uncle Marcus promised to take us on a picnic?"

"If it did not rain. It rained," Becky pointed out.

"What about the time . . ." Reggie searched her mind, but could come up with no other examples of her uncle's perfidy. "Very well. He *usually* keeps his promises. I still say we are better off to look on our own while we can."

"Do you think he will marry her?" Becky asked.

Reggie wrinkled her nose at the abrupt change of subject—or it could have been the pile of waste in front of the butcher's store. "Think who will marry who?"

"Do you think Uncle Marcus will marry Miss Sheringham? He seemed to like her well enough."

"Uncle Marcus will never marry," Reggie said certainly. "I was listening through a crack in the door when he told Father so."

"He could change his mind."

"I would not count on it," Reggie said.

Becky sighed. "I just thought it would be nice to have Eliza in the family. Then we could have braids all the time."

"At night, when Father could not see them," Reggie reminded her.

"I wouldn't care," Becky said dreamily. "Just imagine how lovely it would be."

"I guess it would be kind of nice," Reggie said.

By the time Becky stopped daydreaming about "Aunt Eliza" and looked around her again, the street had narrowed considerably. The buildings were so close-set and narrow the sun did not reach the ground. The cobblestones lay in eerie shadows. Becky shivered, though it was not really cold. "Where are we, Reggie?"

"We are seeing the sights in London," Reggie answered, Her cheerfulness seemed forced to Becky. She glanced around anxiously, afraid to stop and ask questions, but equally afraid to keep walking. There were fewer people than before, but they wore shabbier clothes and had cunning looks on their faces. "Maybe we should go back, Reggie. We have no idea where the performing horses are, or the Tower, or anything."

"We could ask," Reggie said.

"I would be too frightened." Becky avoided making eye contact with any of the wretched dregs of humanity who passed by them. She had never encountered the like at Blackthorne Abbey. Here children and adults alike looked skinny and sharp-set and altogether frightening. "What if someone tries to kidnap us?" she whispered.

Reggie laughed. "What a ninny you are! No one will dare to bother—" She broke off as a dirty, unshaven old man bent close to leer at her, assaulting her nose with an awful, fetid smell. The stench was caused, she realized when he grinned, by a mouthful of rotted teeth.

She fought a huge sneeze and lost.

The old man drew back too late. Reggie watched as he wiped his face with a ragged sleeve.

"You'll pay the shot for that, little pigeon. See if you don't!"

Reggie quickly tightened her hold on Becky's hand. "Excuse me, sir," Reggie said with all the hauteur of a duke's daughter. "I apologize for any inconvenience."

While the old man stared at her, transfixed, she gave him the cut direct. Which meant dragging Becky across the street, nose in the air, chin high, and eyes forward.

Unfortunately, with her nose up, she could not watch out for offal on the street. She felt something squishy give way under her foot and looked down. "Oh, fudge!"

"I don't think so," Becky quipped, shooting her sister a grin as the odor of fresh manure wafted upward.

Reggie grimaced and freed her shoe. Her patent leather half boots would never be the same. She heard a sound behind her, glanced over her shoulder, and gasped. She tightened her hold on Becky's hand and increased her pace.

"What's wrong?" Becky asked, slowing down to discern what had spooked Reggie.

"Keep moving! We are being followed."

Becky glanced behind her as she was dragged along. "By the woman in the red shawl?"

"No. By that disreputable old man—" Reggie shot a look over her shoulder and realized the old man had been joined by a woman in a red shawl. She met Becky's frightened gaze and yelled "Run!"

They refused to let go of each other's hands, so they were frequently slowed by objects and people as they threaded their way through alleys and byways.

"They're catching up to us," Reggie cried. "Run faster!"

"I cannot run any faster!" Becky grabbed her side where the pain was excruciating, her legs churning to keep up with her sister. "Why haven't we reached the Bull and Bear?" she asked between aching breaths. "We must be going the wrong direction."

"We can worry about that later," Reggie said, huffing and puffing with the extra effort of pulling Becky along.

As they turned a corner back onto the main road,

a ruthlessly strong hand grabbed Reggie by the shoulder, wrenching both girls—connected by the unbreakable grasp of their hands—to a stop.

Becky shrieked in terror as she tried to yank her sister free.

Reggie balled her hand into a knotty fist and turned to confront their attacker.

Chapter 8

$\mathcal{M}$ ARCUS HEADED BACK TO THE BULL AND BEAR with the distinct feeling he had left something important behind. He should have been glad to be rid of Miss Sheringham. He would be a fool to pursue the acquaintance. It would be downright dangerous to seek any kind of private interview with her in the midst of a house party intended to match young ladies with eligible *partis*.

His interlude with Miss Sheringham must end here in London. When he arrived at Somersville Manor, he would be best served to keep an entire roomful of bachelors between them.

But curiosity ate at him. He had seen crying women before. Their noses got runny, and their eyes got red. Miss Sheringham had wiped her nose and blotted her eyes, but unless he missed his guess, she had done a great deal of weeping.

Had Julian given her a dressing-down for disguising herself and traveling to London? He imagined her giving as good as she got. But that did not explain the tears.

Had she proposed to Julian and been refused? He chuckled at the image of Miss Sheringham on bended knee. He would not have put it past her. Or had she merely been distraught because Julian, the man she supposedly loved, had refused to come up to scratch?

Marcus would never know. Because he had no intention of approaching her to ask.

"Where the bloody hell have you been? Where are my daughters?"

Lost in thought, Marcus was jerked to awareness by the familiar—though unusually harsh—voice. When he looked up, he still did not believe what he saw.

Alastair sat atop a mammoth, dappled gray creature that most resembled a medieval warhorse. Blanca was, in fact, a descendant of the fierce breed used by Blackthorne knights centuries ago to fight in heavy armor. Alastair's powerful body was tensed for action, his muscles taut.

Marcus's eyes widened when he realized the stallion was not the only medieval accoutrement his brother had brought to London with him. Tied to the saddle near his knee was an immense, jeweled sheath that held the Blackthorne Sword. The deadly Spanish steel blade, with its ruby-encrusted, gold-chased grip, had been handed down from generation to generation since Henry II had presented it to the first Duke of Blackthorne.

For as many years as Marcus could remember, the sword—whose name, Beastslayer, was etched in the blade—had hung on the wall at the entrance to Blackthorne Abbey. Why had Alastair brought Beastslayer to London? Was he planning to loan it to the British Museum for exhibit?

Marcus opened his mouth to ask but realized, even before he spoke, that Alastair had brought the sword for a much more sinister reason. His brother looked ready to eat nails and spit fire. And slit gullets.

But whose? The answer seemed unpleasantly obvious. *His.*

Marcus felt a chill run down his spine. He was a brave man. But death looked back at him from Alastair's eyes.

He shook off the feeling that he was in any danger from his own brother. They had fought over differences in the past. Both were handy with their fives. But neither had ever threatened the other's life.

Where are my daughters?

Marcus felt sick. Alastair had entrusted the twins to his care a mere two days ago. If his brother did not trust him to keep them safe for longer than a day, he should have said so before the three of them left Blackthorne Abbey, instead of running after him as if he were a thief who had stolen the family jewels.

Maybe he was a little late getting to the Braddock house party, but Alastair was not scheduled to join them until the middle of the week. He had planned to explain everything the instant Alastair arrived at Somersville Manor. Obviously, his brother had come ahead of schedule and discovered the twins missing.

Marcus muttered an oath. He had no one to blame but himself for this debacle. He was the fool who had decided Miss Sheringham could not get to London on her own. After what he had seen, she could have managed fine. And he would not now be facing an irate brother, whose wrath, so far as Marcus could see, was entirely unjustifiable.

Marcus bit back the placating words he had been

about to say and greeted his brother with a voice as cold as the one that had greeted him.

"What brings you to London, Alastair?"

"I have been looking for *you*, scoundrel! Miscreant! Villain!"

Marcus had been called worse. But never by his brother. He fought back the fury that rose in him, and the pride that demanded blood for an insult. "I trust there is some good reason you have decided to flay me with words."

"I would rather have flayed you with Beastslayer! I am trying to remember you are my brother, Marcus, but I want answers. Now. Why did you take my children and disappear without a word? Where are you keeping Regina and Rebecca?"

"Griggs—"

"I did not find them where Griggs said they would be," Alastair snarled. "If you are attempting to steal them from me—" His voice was choked with rage and pain. He gritted his teeth until he regained control.

In a hard, implacable voice he continued, "They are my daughters, Marcus. No matter who fathered them, they are *mine*. I have no intention of giving them up. If you—"

"Good God, Alastair! What do you take me for? There is a simple explanation for everything, I promise you."

"I am listening."

Marcus bit the inside of his cheek to keep from yelling obscenities. When he was calm enough not to shout he said, "I left Reggie and Becky at the Bull and Bear with my batman, Griggs, to watch over them."

"They are not there now." Alastair's voice bristled

with anger and suspicion. "What are you doing in London, Marcus? Why did you bring them here?"

"There was nothing nefarious in our detour," he snapped back.

Alastair lifted a disdainful, disbelieving brow. "Where is the lady in gentleman's disguise who has been traveling with you? Have you seduced her? Have you convinced her to run away with you and take along my children?"

"Bloody hell, Alastair! I have reached the limit of my patience with you. I have half a mind not to tell you where they are!"

Alastair grabbed for the hilt of Beastslayer.

Marcus made no move to save himself. Penthia's poison had been slow to work, but ultimately quite deadly. It would be better if Alastair killed him than to live with such enmity between them. He waited for the sound of steel on steel.

It did not come.

Alastair replaced his right hand carefully on his thigh and said, "I do not understand why you waited this long to take them, Marcus. If you wanted them, why not claim them at birth?"

Marcus clenched his teeth. His brother must already know the answer to that question in his heart. If he would only allow his heart to speak to him. But Alastair Wharton, sixth Duke of Blackthorne, no longer had a heart. His wife had turned it to stone.

Clearly, however, Alastair was not invulnerable to pain. His eyes brimmed with tears.

Marcus was not immune, either. He waited for the ache in his throat to ease before he said, "I left Reggie and Becky with Griggs while I—"

"I tell you Griggs does not have them!"

"You've been to the Bull and Bear?"

"I tracked you that far without difficulty. Griggs was willing to die rather than tell me where you had gone or the identity of the 'gentleman' with you."

Bless Griggs for his loyalty, Marcus thought. But his batman had obviously made things much worse.

"If you saw Griggs, you must have seen the twins. Griggs had charge of them. He would never have let them go anywhere by themselves."

"They snuck out through an upstairs window while they were supposed to be napping," Alastair snapped.

Marcus stared at his brother with incredulous eyes. "How did they manage that?"

Alastair slammed a gloved, fisted hand against his rock-hard thigh. "Knotted sheets. They did the same thing once at Blackthorne Abbey. I thought I had cured them of it, but apparently not. I concluded their escapade had been prearranged, that you had told them to meet you somewhere in secret."

Marcus's heart began to thud. It was inconceivable that his brother could have concocted such an unbelievable tale of corruption from such flimsy evidence. It showed how little Alastair knew him.

Did his brother really think he would encourage the twins to make a dangerous climb from a second-story window on knotted sheets? Did he not realize Marcus would have had to include Griggs in any kidnapping plan he made? Did Alastair really think Marcus would steal away children who had grown up calling Alastair "Father" even if they had been his?

It dawned on him the twins were truly lost. "Are

you telling me that Reggie and Becky are wandering the streets of London alone?"

"You do not have them?" Alastair asked, his eyes bleak.

Marcus shook his head, his expression grim. "We must find them." He looked at the lowering sun. "Before dark."

They exchanged a look of concern, not daring to reveal, even to each other, the terror for the girls' well-being that lay barely beneath the surface.

"We will find them," Marcus assured his brother.

"Griggs is looking to the south, away from Town, on the chance they went that way," Alastair said. "We can follow the main road north, searching the side roads and alleys east and west. I suggest we meet on the main road at various points to compare information."

They said nothing more, but began the search. They asked everyone they met about the twins, but offered no reward for information, afraid of putting the girls in even greater danger from someone who might think to hold them for ransom.

"I will keep them in their rooms on bread and water for a month," Alastair muttered when they met for the fourth time on the main road.

"Not if I have anything to say about it."

"You don't," Alastair retorted. "They are my daughters, not yours. I am their father. It is up to me to correct them."

"Alex—" A giant knot had formed in Marcus's throat, making it impossible to speak. He had not called his brother Alex in years. It brought back memories of a time when they had been so close they could read each other's thoughts.

He looked into Alastair's anguished eyes and saw the suffering his brother normally kept hidden behind a stony facade. He wished he could wipe away his brother's agony. He wished he had killed Penthia for her wickedness the first time she offered her bared breasts to him.

Grief settled like a rain-soaked, many-layered greatcoat on Marcus's shoulders. A stone of regret sank in his stomach. He should have spoken to Alastair long ago, whether his brother wanted to listen or not.

There were things he could say to ease Alastair's torment. But he must do it now, because he was not sure when, or if, he would ever have the chance again.

"I would never take Reggie or Becky from you, Alex. They love you. You are their father. My only role in their lives is that of doting uncle. I want no other."

Too late Marcus realized he had not actually denied paternity. He started to say the words and realized that if he did, Alastair would only think he was lying.

Alastair swallowed hard. He opened his mouth to speak, but closed it again. He seemed subdued, thoughtful, his brow etched with fretful lines that did nothing to reveal whether he believed Marcus or not.

They rode together in silence for perhaps a minute before a commotion on the next street corner drew Marcus's attention. He put out a hand to stop Alastair.

A white-haired man and a middle-aged woman

were struggling to move something they held upright between them, covered by a red shawl. The woman suddenly let out a howl and grabbed her shin, shifting sideways enough for Marcus to identify what was sticking out from beneath the shawl's fringe—four legs clad in white stockings and patent leather half boots!

Marcus exchanged a look with Alastair and saw the duke had realized, just as he had, what booty the couple were shoving along between them.

"The twins," Alastair said in a voice that was, at the same time reverent, remorseful, and wrathful.

Marcus was appalled to see the woman raise her fist and aim it at the bundle, apparently in retribution.

"Hey, you there! Stop where you are!" Marcus shouted, spurring his horse toward her.

Alastair stayed with him stride for stride on Blanca.

The woman shot Marcus a smug look of defiance, yelled an angry epithet when she shifted her gaze to Alastair, and as Marcus stared in helpless disbelief, punched out hard with her fist at the wriggling mass beneath the shawl.

His stomach clenched when one of the girls cried out in pain.

Alastair let out a roar of rage and drew Beastslayer from its sheath.

The woman blanched, stood frozen in place for an instant, then disappeared into an alley too narrow for either of them to follow on horseback.

The man was not nearly so smart as his partner. He tried to make his escape with one of the girls, grabbing her around the waist—thereby pulling the shawl completely off the other child—and throwing her over his shoulder.

The twin left behind on the ground did not, as one might have expected, stay safely where she was. Though she was bent over in obvious pain, she reached out and grabbed the trailing edge of the red shawl that was still wrapped around the captive twin, then sat down and hung on like a bulldog with a new bone.

The old man scurried back into view from the alley where he had followed after the woman, seeking to free his burden from whatever had snagged it. When he saw the child, he levered his foot to kick her away.

By then Marcus and Alastair were on the ground, not more than two strides from him.

"If you kick that child, you will lose your leg," Alastair threatened in a deadly voice.

Sweat popped out on the old man's brow. Slowly, carefully, he replanted his foot on the ground. "Now, guv'. Don't be wavin' that 'ellish sticker 'round ol' Georgie. Me and me sis was only makin' sure these wee darlin's was safe from 'arm."

While the point of Beastslayer kept the old man frozen in place, Marcus crossed to the child on the ground and bent down on one knee to check her condition. "Reggie, are you all right?"

Her eyes were wide with fright. Her gaze darted from her father, holding the sword, to the old man who had captured her and her sister.

"Are you hurt?" Alastair demanded of his daughter, as Marcus lifted Reggie into his arms. "What did he do to you?"

In a terrified voice, the old man cried out, "Tell 'im we ain't 'armed ye, ye blasted nincompoop!"

Alastair snarled and raised the sword for a killing blow, but by then Marcus had stepped between his brother and the old man, who was pale as parchment. Alastair deftly changed the angle of the sword to avoid slicing Marcus and Reggie in two.

"Are you all right, Regina?" Alastair demanded, his anger at the old man harshening his voice.

"I am fine, Father," Reggie gasped. But her face was waxy, and she held tight to her stomach, where the old woman's blow had apparently landed.

Recovering quickly, the old man piped up, "See there, guv'. Right as rain, the both of 'em. I see why a man'd wanta keep 'em," the old man said, easing the burden from his shoulder. "Like as peas in a pod, they are."

Beastslayer came up again as the old man started to let Becky drop the last foot to the ground. "Careful," Alastair warned.

The old man held his breath as he eased Becky onto her feet and let go. Without additional support, her legs gave way and she slumped toward the ground.

When Alastair let the sword clatter to the cobblestones and grabbed for her with both hands, the old man saw his chance and ran.

"He's getting away!" Reggie cried.

"I will make sure he is found," Alastair said. "And punished."

Marcus felt Reggie stiffen at the deadly fury in her father's voice, the ice in his eyes. His face was set in stone, no mercy to be found for the villains. Or for his daughters, either.

Alastair braced Becky in one arm while he dragged the shawl away from her face with the opposite hand.

Marcus caught his breath. Becky's eyes were closed, her face as pale as death. "God, please, no," he murmured.

Marcus watched as Alastair gently smoothed the sweat-dampened curls away from Becky's forehead, cheeks, and chin. He rested his fingers across her bowed lips beneath her nose, testing for a breath of life. When Alastair's shoulders relaxed slightly, Marcus knew the girl must still be alive. He blinked back the stinging tears of joy and relief and hugged Reggie tighter.

His attention was momentarily distracted when Reggie complained she could not breathe. He lifted his gaze in time to catch Alastair kissing Becky on the forehead. It was the first time Marcus had seen his brother touch one of his daughters with tenderness since the day Penthia had first made her awful accusation.

Marcus had never known whether Alastair loved Regina and Rebecca, unsure as he was that they were his. Now he knew. And felt a huge sense of relief. Even if he never returned to Blackthorne Abbey, the twins would be all right. They would be loved by Alastair as a father should love them.

A moment later, Becky's eyes blinked open. Though still groggy, she grabbed at Alastair's neck cloth and cried, "Father! You must find Reggie. She has been—"

"I am here safe, Becky," Reggie said from Marcus's arms. Marcus crossed so the two girls could see each other and watched as they reached out to clasp hands.

"You are both safe," Alastair said in harsh tones, "but not yet out of danger."

"Please, Father, do not blame Becky," Reggie pleaded. "It was my idea to see the sights unchaperoned. I am the one who should be punished."

"I was the one who thought of knotting the sheets together, Father. I should be whipped, not Reggie."

"I will make sure you both pay dearly enough for your part in this incident that you are never tempted to repeat it," Alastair said. "We will go directly home, so you will have the time and solitude to appreciate the folly of your behavior."

"But we will miss the Duke of Braddock's house party!" Reggie protested.

"Not another word," Alastair said. "You have created enough havoc for one day. I will send your excuses to the duke and duchess. You will not be allowed in company again until I know you can behave properly."

"Uncle Marcus—" Reggie and Becky said in unison.

"I am your father," Alastair interrupted sharply. "My word is final."

Giant teardrops spilled from the twins' blue eyes, turning them into dark ponds of despair. Marcus's heart went out to them. He bit his tongue to keep from interfering as he wished to do. Now that his brother was willing to accept the role, Marcus had to step back and let Alastair be their father.

Besides, this time the twins had gone too far.

They needed to realize the seriousness of what they had done, so there would be no repeat of this near-tragedy.

"Take heart, poppets," Marcus said, gently thumbing away the tears on each girl's face. "There will be other parties."

"A thousand years from now, when we are seventeen and have our come-outs," Reggie muttered rebelliously.

"Only if you have learned obedience by then," Alastair replied grimly.

The joy of knowing Reggie and Becky were safe and loved was bittersweet. Marcus exchanged a look of regret and remorse with Alastair. The blood bond that had been unraveling for years had finally been cleaved in two. Marcus had lost something even more precious to him than his time with Reggie and Becky. He had lost his brother's trust.

Penthia had won at last.

Chapter 9

"WHAT DO YOU THINK?" CHARLOTTE ASKED, EYE-ING the crowd of brilliantly gowned ladies and splendidly dressed gentlemen gathered in the ballroom at Somersville Manor.

"Of what?" Eliza replied.

"You know perfectly well what I am asking, Eliza. There must be at least eight eligible suitors in this room. I have not seen you do more than nod to any one of them. Smile. Or at least take the frown from your face."

Eliza lifted the corners of her mouth, but she knew the expression fell far short of genuine. She had nothing to smile about.

Julian had refused to marry her. Oh, he had couched his refusal in noble terms: he did not want to leave her a widow if he was killed in battle. But his answer was no.

She felt absolutely ill watching him smile indul-gently at another young lady flirting behind her fan. Miss Whitcomb could not be a year older than her, but was obviously a diamond of the first water—petite and pretty and demure.

Three things Eliza would never—could never be.

Julian had signed Eliza's dance card for the dance

after supper, thereby ensuring they would not spend the supper hour together. At a guess, she would say he was purposely avoiding her. And no wonder.

She had embarrassed herself and him with that unwanted proposal. The scene in Julian's rooms replayed painfully in her mind, as it had a hundred times since she had endured it four days ago.

"I want you to marry me," she had said, throwing her arms around Julian's neck.

She had felt his body stiffen, felt the rejection without words being spoken. He had reached up to grasp her wrists and remove her hands, then held them securely before him. After a long pause, during which he studied the toes of his Hessians, he had looked into her eyes and said with gentle humor, "It is the gentleman who usually proposes, my dear."

"I am afraid you will not ask. At least not soon enough to do me any good."

The muscles in his jaw worked, and his face turned to stone. "Who was he? Who dared—"

His hands tightened on hers until she cried out in pain. He let her go and took a step back, but she could feel the tension radiating from him, feel his dark eyes boring into hers. What had she said wrong? Why was he so angry?

"Who was the man?" he demanded, his voice menacing.

She had no idea what he was talking about. When she stared up at him, confused, he came to his own conclusion.

"Marcus! Damn him! That he should dare to bed my own cousin! How did he get you alone? When is the child due?"

"Child? Dear God, what are you saying!" Then it dawned on her what she had unwittingly said. *I am afraid you will not ask. At least not soon enough to do me any good.* Julian thought she needed a husband because she was pregnant!

He had already reached the door, muscles flexed and bent on mayhem, by the time she caught his arm.

"Wait, Julian!"

"Don't try to stop me!" he snarled, shaking off her grasp. "If Marcus was fool enough—"

"He did nothing! It was Nigel!" she cried.

Julian let go of the doorknob and turned to her. The blood drained from his face, leaving it white and drawn. "My own brother defiled you?"

"He only kissed me," she said, her voice quavering. "I dropped a pot of flowers on his head and ran away that same night. Captain Wharton merely helped me find my way to you." The captain had kissed her as well, but she did not think now was the time to confess it.

She edged between Julian and the door, then stepped close enough to notice a tiny scar cutting through his eyebrow. He had never looked more virile, more dangerous, or more attractive. She felt so lightheaded, she thought she would swoon. This was how she had always imagined it would feel to be with him. She shivered as his dark eyes focused on her.

She laid her hands against his iron-muscled chest and said, "I am not safe with your brother, Julian. And I have nowhere else to go. That is why I asked you to marry me. And . . . because I love you."

Her stomach dropped when he winced at her declaration of love.

"My poor poppet," he said, drawing her into his arms and pressing her head against his shoulder with his open hand. "I am so sorry."

Poppet! That was a name for a child—the child she had been two years ago, when he had last seen her. She was a woman now, one who loved the feel of his strong arms around her, the beat of his heart, the smell of his shaving soap. She had to make him see her as she was.

"Julian, please. I will make you a good wife. I promise I will learn to curb my tongue. I will—"

His fingertips pressed against her lips, forcing her to silence. "Shh, Eliza. Don't say any more. I cannot marry you, child."

She stared at him accusingly until his hand fell away. She swallowed past the sharp-edged lump in her throat and rasped, "Why can't you marry me?"

For long moments no answer—no excuse—was forthcoming. Finally he said, "You know Napoleon has escaped from Elba."

She nodded.

"I must go back to war, Eliza."

"It could be months before—"

"Bloody hell!" He gritted his teeth and said in a carefully controlled voice, "Forgive me. You should not be subjected to such language. It is only that this situation—"

"Is a bit unusual?" she offered.

He responded with a rueful smile. "To say the least."

"I think—"

"Let me finish, please," he said, cutting her off.

The humor was gone, and he was dead serious again. "You are too young to be a widow, Eliza."

"But you have never even been wounded badly," Eliza pointed out. "You are hale and hearty—"

"And headed back to fight again. No, Eliza. The answer is no." He tried to free himself but she threw her arms around his neck, clinging like a cat that makes a leap into space and sets its claws deep in the first solid object it finds. "Julian, please listen—"

His face hardened, and his dark eyes threatened violence. "I cannot be cajoled. Eliza, there are things you do not know . . . things I cannot tell you—" He ruthlessly pulled her hands free and took a step back from her.

"Where will I go? What will I do? I cannot return to Ravenwood," she cried. "I am not safe there."

His lips flattened. His hands fisted. "I will speak to Nigel. Under the circumstances, he cannot object if you choose to live in your father's house. Would that be agreeable to you?"

It was not at all what Eliza wanted, but it would at least keep her out of Cousin Nigel's reach. And it was all Julian was offering. "Do you think Aunt Lavinia would be allowed—"

"Of course you may have your aunt with you, and as many servants as you need. Nigel will bear the expense. I will see to it."

Julian had ordered her to put back on her male disguise so she would not cause a scandal leaving his rooms. Which meant asking him to undo the buttons on her dress.

"How did you get them buttoned in the first

place, if you cannot reach them?" Julian asked suspiciously.

Her color heightened. She knew better than to tell the truth. "It was not easy. Please, will you help me?"

He undid the buttons quickly and expeditiously, without any of the grazing touches and intimate caresses the Beau had employed. She fought back tears at this further proof that Julian did not see her as a desirable woman.

When the shoulders of the dress fell free, he hissed in a breath. And stopped.

She stood perfectly still.

His hands left the buttons and settled on her bare shoulders. He took a step closer, so she could feel the heat of him along her back, and laid his bristly cheek—dark with a day's growth of beard—against hers.

Her heart was thumping wildly. He would turn her around now and kiss her lips and acknowledge that he loved her, as she loved him.

"If things were different," he murmured. "If I were not already . . . I am so sorry, poppet."

She made a sound of protest at the childish endearment and tried to turn to him. His grip on her shoulders tightened to keep her where she was.

"Please, Eliza. I am not free to love you."

"There is someone else?"

He gave her no answer, merely repeated, "I cannot marry you."

She moaned.

He kissed her temple and let her go. "When you

are ready, join me outside." He was gone before she could plead with him further.

She had cried as hard as a person could and still not make a sound that would carry through the door. Somewhere between tying Julian's borrowed neck cloth and pulling on his Hessians, she had decided she would simply refuse to take no for an answer.

Julian would be with her for two weeks at the Braddock house party. He would see her at her best. There had to be a way to make him fall helplessly, hopelessly in love with her. If only she could figure out what it was.

She endured an awkward moment at the door to Julian's rooms, when she faced the Beau with puffy, reddened eyes, but she bluffed her way through it.

When the Beau walked away, it felt as though they had left something unfinished between them. In the hours it took for Julian's great-aunt Sophie to pack, Eliza had figured out what it was.

Her seduction.

Thank goodness Julian had arrived when he did. But she could not help but wonder what it would have been like to have the Beau kissing her when she was kissing him back.

When she and Julian finally reached Somersville Manor, there had been a very brief, very private—but very ugly—scene in the library between Julian and his brother. A swollen-nosed Cousin Nigel had left for Ravenwood as soon as his bags were packed.

Great-aunt Sophie had been enjoying herself immensely, and looked forward to meeting Aunt Lavinia, who was due to arrive within the week to join the party. She would stay to chaperon Eliza during her journey home—to the hunting box where she had grown up.

Eliza had spent the past few days being totally ignored by Julian. Charlotte was right, though. She should be wearing a smile on her face to prove to Julian that he had not broken her heart. Even if he had.

Her eyes widened as a tall, blond gentleman dressed in the uniform of Julian's regiment—the Prince of Wales's own 10th Royal Hussars—greeted Julian.

Him. What was he doing here? How dare he follow her!

Eliza gestured with her chin. "What is that soldier doing here, Charlie?"

"Who? Oh, Captain Wharton? I invited him. He does wonders for that uniform," Charlotte said, eyeing him appreciatively. "Do you not think him handsome?"

"The man is a rogue, a rake, a seducer of women," Eliza retorted. She ought to know. He had almost seduced her. If Julian had not interrupted them . . .

Charlotte pursed her lips. "I see you have heard the rumors about Captain Wharton. I suppose he is something of a rake. But one cannot expect perfection in everything."

"Fiddlesticks," Eliza muttered. "He is coming this way."

Charlotte caught Eliza's elbow before she could escape. "Stay and meet him."

"I have—" Eliza cut herself off. Julian had warned that under no circumstances must she tell anyone, especially not the Countess of Denbigh, what had transpired to cause her delay in arriving at Somersville Manor.

Now here *he* was to remind her of her entire disastrous detour. She felt like telling Charlotte that the Beau's reputation did not do him justice. She knew firsthand how beguiling he could be. Why, the man could give lessons in seduction!

The man could give lessons . . .

It was as though someone had brought a branch of candles into a darkened room. Here she stood, desperate to make Julian fall in love with her and without an inkling of how to accomplish it. And who should arrive but the most infamous rake in London. Captain Wharton was just the person to ask for advice! The Beau was practiced at seduction. He could teach her exactly how to win Julian's heart.

Her brow cleared, and her lips curved in a welcoming smile. "Captain Wharton. How lovely to see you again."

Since the moment he had entered the ballroom, Marcus had been captivated by the sight of Miss Sheringham. He was annoyed with himself for being so spellbound by the chit. She was not even pretty, with those odd-shaped, tawny gold eyes, and cheekbones that left hollows below, and a too-wide mouth.

And she was dressed all wrong.

The chit was wearing scarlet. Young ladies wore white, or pale pastels. He had seen the pointing fingers, heard the titters behind her back at the unseemly choice. He blamed the Countess of Denbigh for not taking her protégée to task. Unfortunately, the countess was as little inclined to follow the rules as he knew Miss Sheringham to be.

The square bodice was not cut low, but with Miss Sheringham's ample bosom, it did not have to be. The puffed sleeves sat at the very edge of her shoulders, leaving a great deal of deliciously bare skin. She looked like a courtesan in a roomful of virgins.

Her hair was stacked on her head in touchable, flyaway curls that dripped onto her nape, and she wore two-inch-high red satin pumps. With the extra height at top and bottom, she was taller than every unmarried man in the room, except himself. She had even surpassed Julian by an inch.

That had provoked a great deal more staring and pointing. Personally, he could not be sorry for either addition. He fought the urge to replace those curls at her nape with his lips, and he wanted desperately to feel how her body would fit against his when they were nearly the same height.

He had watched her from the second-floor balcony above the ballroom since the party had begun, long enough to know that no one except Julian had signed her dance card. He suspected the countess would inveigle her husband to dance once with the chit. But it was plain Miss Sheringham had not taken. Foolish, foolish gentlemen. They had chosen the pretty shells and left the pearl behind.

He could not resist such easy treasure.

You promised you would stay away from her. You made special plans to avoid her.

So why was he walking toward her now, like a moth drawn to flame, unable to resist the light. Like a lemming toward the cliffs above the sea?

Marcus could have been entertaining himself with a host of beauties. But none had her husky voice. Or her forthright gaze. They giggled and simpered and cast coy glances at him from above their fans. He found them insipid. And boring.

He wanted to hear her voice. See her eyes. Touch her silky skin. Put himself inside her.

"Captain Wharton," the countess said with a warm smile. "Here I was, ready to introduce you to a friend of mine, when I suddenly discover you two have met before."

Miss Sheringham had caught her lower lip in her teeth. Did she not realize how tempting she looked? Then he realized what the countess had said. "Yes," he said. "Miss Sheringham and I have met."

So, the chit had let the cat out of the bag. How much had she said?

"My cousin, Major Sheringham, introduced us earlier this evening," Miss Sheringham said without a blink to reveal the lie.

So, their encounter in London was still a secret. He had spent a great deal of time pondering what would have happened if they had not been interrupted. He would have sworn Miss Sheringham was relieved to have escaped his company that day. Now she appeared almost happy to see him. Had she had second thoughts? Did she regret the interruption of their tryst as much as he did? He bowed over the hand she held out to him. "Miss Sheringham."

"Captain Wharton," she replied.

The Countess of Denbigh looked significantly at the orchestra tuning up on a raised dais and back to Captain Sheringham. He had never seen such blatant manipulation. It would be simple to ignore the young countess. She should know the Beau never danced with eligible young ladies.

The orchestra began playing the first strains of music. A waltz. He would be able to hold Miss Sheringham in his arms. He would be able to see just how well their bodies fit together. He held out his arm. "Would you care to dance, Miss Sheringham?"

"I do not think—"

The countess nipped Miss Sheringham's rebellion in the bud. "Of course she will. Why else come to a dance?"

"To gossip," Miss Sheringham snapped, darting daggers in Miss Whitcomb's direction.

Marcus watched the Diamond staring at Miss Sheringham, obviously talking to a group of young people behind her fan. The ladies tittered nervously, and the gentlemen flushed as red as mangel-wurzels, except for Julian, who merely scowled.

The countess sent Miss Sheringham a warning look, and she bit back whatever trenchant wit she had been about to share.

"Shall we?" Marcus held out his arm, and Miss Sheringham placed her gloved hand on it.

Before they were halfway to the dance floor, she whispered, "I must speak with you privately, Captain Wharton. Can you maneuver us onto the terrace?"

As impossible as it seemed, she apparently wanted to resume their dalliance. But she had picked entirely the wrong time and place. If he left with her, the Diamond would be sure to notice. He preferred his affairs to be more discreet.

"I think not," he said.

He whirled her into the dance, vexed that he was attracted to someone so naive. Did she not realize the compromising position she would be in if they were discovered kissing on the terrace? Regrettably, he did.

"I must speak with you," she insisted.

"I am not going anywhere alone with you, Miss Sheringham."

She looked up at him, her eyes glowing with excitement. "I need your help, Captain. You cannot refuse me."

He pulled her close to escape another waltzing couple and felt her warm breasts pillow against his chest. His body responded so quickly, it was all he could do to separate them before she discovered his arousal. "What kind of help?" he growled.

"I wish to learn how to seduce a man."

He nearly collided with a palm tree. He managed to dance her beyond it and out onto the empty terrace. Exactly where he did not want to be. Especially with her.

He halted abruptly, grabbed her hand, and pulled her after him to a place where the light from the ballroom did not reach. Another couple was already there before them. He hid Miss Sheringham's face against his uniform and backed away, then led her down the steps from the terrace, gravel crunching underfoot, into the gardens beyond.

He did not stop until they were well into a high hedge that had been cut into a maze. Lanterns had been placed above the walkways within the maze, but there were plenty of shadowed places where couples could find privacy. He saw a stone bench and led her toward it. He sat her down—ungently—and stood before her, his hands behind his back, rather like a stern father before his wayward daughter.

"Now, Miss Sheringham. I believe I must have mistaken what I heard. Would you mind repeating what you said?"

"I want to learn how to seduce a man."

He rocked back on his heels. "I see." What he saw was that she was up to some mischief and intended to include him.

"I thought you would," she said happily. She bounced up and crossed to him, removing the space he had put between them. "It is because of Julian, of course. I am in love with him, but he hardly notices I am alive. I want to make him fall in love with me. You can teach me how."

He cleared his throat. "It seems you are under a misapprehension, Miss Sheringham."

Her fisted hands landed on her hips, and she tapped her red satin pump on the stone walkway. "You cannot tell me you do not know how to seduce a woman." She poked him with a pointed finger. "You are forgetting I have firsthand experience. I know how effective your methods are."

"I would never—"

Her hand flattened against his uniform, and he felt his heart speed up beneath it. "It stands to reason the same techniques could be applied by a woman with a man."

"I never said—"

She grabbed his arm with both hands. "You're Julian's friend. You want him to be happy, don't you?"

"Yes, but—"

"Then you must help me! I will make him a good wife, I promise you."

Marcus stood without speaking, unwilling to be interrupted again. When she remained silent for more than a moment, he said, "There is one fatal flaw in your plan."

She took a step back and looked at him, a V of concern between her eyes. "What is that?"

"I presume you want Julian to fall in love with you?"

"Correct."

"I am afraid I cannot help you with that, Miss Sheringham."

"But—"

He cut her off before she could touch him again. "I can teach you how to *seduce* him," he clarified. "I cannot teach you how to make him *fall in love* with you. They are not at all the same thing, you know."

"Oh." She sank onto the stone bench. "Oh, dear. I was so sure . . . I was certain . . . How could I have made such an error in calculation? You are right, of course."

The delightfully eager face she had shown him only moments before was painted in gloom. Her shoulders sagged, and she put a hand to her forehead, as though she felt faint.

"Are you all right, Miss Sheringham?"

"No," she whispered.

He wanted to rescue her from desolation. He wanted to kiss her and caress her. He wanted to do with her what he was known best for doing with women. He wanted to ravish her.

He did not know what was stopping him. She was

vulnerable. It would not take much. A soft word, a softer touch, and she would be his. He could take her right here on the ground. He knew how to make her crave what he had to offer her. She would forget all about Julian.

She loves Julian.

He swore under his breath. Honor had reared its head at a particularly inconvenient moment. Julian had rejected Miss Sheringham. That ought to be enough to leave the way clear for him.

In this case, it was not.

Miss Sheringham clearly still had her sights set on his friend. Until she gave up on Julian, he was not free to pursue her. So he might as well help her.

The words were out of his mouth before he could stop them. "I could teach you a few things that might work to garner Julian's attention. Once you have him by your side, he cannot fail to notice what a prize you are."

Her head came up. Her shoulders squared. Her eyes gleamed bright with hope. "Do you think so?"

"It is worth a try."

"Thank you, Captain. Thank you!"

She leaped up from the bench and threw herself toward him before he could curb her exuberance. His arms naturally encircled her waist. And he had his answer. She fit against him perfectly in all the right places.

"Enough of this," he said, pushing her away. "Someone might come along and get entirely the wrong idea."

She grinned. "I imagine so." She hugged herself, forcing her bosom even farther out of the low-cut gown, and beamed at him. "Where shall we start? What should I learn first?"

"I will think about it and let you know," he said. "Right now, we must return to the ballroom."

"But I want to get started right away. Tonight."

"It should suffice that we have disappeared for a few minutes together," Marcus said with a rueful twist of his mouth. "Unless I am very much mistaken, the gossips—Miss Whitcomb comes to mind—will have pointed out to your cousin that we are missing together. He should be looking for us at this very minute. I suggest—"

"Eliza? Are you in here?"

"It's Julian!" she hissed.

"Over here, Julian," Marcus answered in a loud voice.

"What are you doing?" Miss Sheringham whispered. "He will be furious with me."

"He will notice you. And that is the point, is it not, my dear?"

Her eyes went wide. "Oh. I see."

"However, I suggest we head back in his direction, and please, Miss Sheringham, stop chewing your lip. Your cousin is liable to misinterpret the reason it has become so swollen."

"Oh." She touched her damp, swollen lower lip. "You mean he will think you have been kissing me."

"Exactly."

"Perhaps a little jealousy—"

He pulled her to a stop. "A word of warning before you play at seduction, Miss Sheringham: it is a dangerous game. The consequences can be deadly.

Do not underestimate Julian. He has killed men for less reason than the one you would offer him."

"But Julian would never—"

"Julian would kill me as certainly as he would any other man for an insult to your honor. Never doubt it, Miss Sheringham. It will make this game safer for both of us."

To Marcus's utter amazement, the first person around the corner of the maze was not Julian, but the Countess of Denbigh. She was followed closely by the Duchess of Braddock.

"Good evening, Captain Wharton," the countess said with a breezy smile. It was immediately apparent she had come to rescue Miss Sheringham from his nefarious clutches. She slipped her arm through Miss Sheringham's on one side, while the duchess did the same on the other. "I have been missing my friend, Captain. Her Grace and I decided we could not wait one more minute for Miss Sheringham's return. Please excuse us."

Eliza stared helplessly over her shoulder at him as the ladies led her away.

Marcus smiled ruefully. One problem had been solved. He would not have to make excuses to Julian for what he was doing alone with Miss Sheringham. And if he was not mistaken, the two ladies involved would ensure that no slanderous repercussions resulted from Miss Sheringham's temporary disappearance from the ballroom.

"Shame on you, Eliza," Charlotte chided, a gleam of laughter in her eyes. "To steal away to the maze with the worst rake in London."

Eliza was still too stunned to speak coherently. "I never meant—"

Charlotte laughed. "Of course you did. What woman would not have welcomed a tryst with such a man? Did he kiss you? I must say it appears he did. Did you enjoy it? I hear rakes make the very best husbands."

"Charlie!" Olivia protested. "Leave the poor girl alone. You are pushing her in a direction she may not wish to go."

"He is perfect for her," Charlie said. "And she is just the woman for him."

Eliza stared dumbfounded at the countess.

"All I did was provide the opportunity for you to meet each other," Charlie said. "I hoped that fate would arrange the rest. And I see it has." She eyed Eliza's swollen mouth. "Which means, that unless you are ready to be whisked off to church without further adieu, we must make some excuse and escort you upstairs without anyone the wiser."

"But the captain did *not* kiss me," Eliza protested.

"Fortunately, you will not have to make that protest to anyone but us," the countess said with a smile. "Because you do not say it in the least persuasively."

Eliza groaned. How had everything gotten so mixed up? All she had wanted to do was learn how to make Julian love her. Instead, her hostess had her paired with entirely the wrong man! There was no time for delay. She would have to set to work immediately making Julian notice her.

That is, after she had first met privately with the Beau for her first lesson in seduction.

Chapter 10

MISTY FOG CLOAKED THE HILLS, MAKING ELIZA'S early morning tryst with the Beau seem even more furtive. Mephistopheles fought the bit, as she held the stallion to a canter. The sun barely teased the dark horizon, spilling pink and yellow into the early morning sky.

"All right, boy," she said, giving the stallion his head when her destination was in sight. "Run to your heart's content." The earth smelled fecund as the stallion's hooves tore into it. Eliza leaned forward and laughed, as the wind whipped the man's hat from her head and sent her hair tumbling in all directions.

She reined Mephistopheles to a stop at the bottom of the hill and turned him back to retrieve her—or rather, Julian's—hat. She planned to sneak back into the Braddock house as she had left it—dressed as a man. She had already tasted the sharp edge of Miss Whitcomb's tongue. She had no intention of giving Miss Whitcomb further scandal-broth to bandy about behind her fan.

Nevertheless, Eliza was determined to meet in private with the Beau. She had sent a note to him through Griggs the previous evening, suggesting the two of them ride out separately at five in the morning.

They would then meet at Braddock's Folly near the lake to begin her lessons in seduction.

Eliza was disappointed when she reached their rendezvous to discover that she was ahead of the captain. She tied the reins up, so Mephistopheles could graze, and impatiently circled the exterior of the pentagon-shaped folly.

It turned out to be nothing more than a wooden gazebo framed in waist-high white lattice. However, the lattice was entwined with marvelously scented trailing pink roses. She bent over to sniff and surprised an early morning bee at work. She gave a startled laugh and backed up to give it room. It was then she noticed a great many bees were at work gathering pollen.

Enough dew had gathered on the toes of Julian's borrowed Hessians to ruin the shine. It was a good thing she had worn her London disguise. A riding skirt would have been soaked to the knees by now.

Bluebirds had made a nest in one section of the folly's diamond-shaped lattice and chattered at her to keep her distance. She was so distracted by their antics, she did not hear the Beau's arrival.

"I have not been up this early since I was a boy at Eton."

A smile lit Eliza's face even before she whirled to greet him. She saw Captain Wharton had left his Thoroughbred gelding to graze near Mephistopheles. "I am so glad you came."

She slipped on the wet grass at the first step and would have fallen flat on the seat of Julian's breeches, if the Beau had not caught her by the waist.

He grinned down at her. "How could I resist such an eager invitation? Where would you like to start?"

"You are the expert," Eliza replied breathlessly, aware of the lack of space between their bodies and his strong grip on a part of her that rarely felt the touch of male hands. "I am merely the willing pupil."

It did not feel as though her feet were on the ground, though she knew they were. Her horse snuffled as he grazed. The bluebirds sang melodiously. Her heart beat an uneven tattoo in her chest. She stared up at him, helpless to move, unable to speak.

His eyes were hooded, his nostrils flared, his blue eyes intent on her golden ones.

She shivered unaccountably.

"Are you sure you need lessons?" he asked in a husky voice, one brow arching. "What provoked you to shiver like that?"

"I am cold!"

He laughed, breaking the tension between them, and released her. "Of course, my dear, that is the excuse one uses. The first rule of seduction: A woman's shiver is a delectable invitation to a man."

"To do what?" Eliza asked, eyes narrowed suspiciously.

"Any number of things. You see, it arouses his protective instincts. Suppose you are cold. He can remove his jacket and place it on your shoulders to warm you."

He suited word to deed and a moment later Eliza found herself ensconced in the warmth of Captain Wharton's plum riding jacket. He was left wearing white shirtsleeves and a brocaded waistcoat slightly darker than his fawn breeches. The jacket bore the distinct scents of bayberry soap and horse and . . . him.

"This gesture will leave the lady surrounded by the heat of the gentleman's body, and the gentleman wearing fewer clothes than before."

"I see," she murmured, running her fingertips along the edges of his velvet jacket. "Can every man be depended upon to respond in the same way?" she asked, trying to imagine Julian slipping his jacket, warm from his body, onto her shoulders.

"Not necessarily." He reached out to take his jacket from her. "May I?"

She shrugged out of it and handed it back to him. "Of course."

Instead of putting it back on, he threw it over the white lattice framework that framed the lower half of the folly. And set the bluebirds to chattering again.

"They have a nest close by," she said, crossing to carefully remove his coat. The chattering stopped. "See?" she said with a smile. "And there are bees at work in the flowers." She laid his jacket across one side of the wooden bannister that framed the three broad steps leading into the folly. "I will put it here, if you don't mind."

She eyed the white wrought-iron bench set within the folly, but sat herself on the topmost of the three steps instead, putting some needed distance between them. To her chagrin, he sat down right beside her.

"Now. Where were we?" he murmured in her ear.

"I was shivering," she said with a rueful twist of her lips. "And you were being protective."

"Ah, yes. Suppose you were not cold, but frightened. What better source of security than the nearest gentleman."

Her brow furrowed. "I must be missing something. What is it I am to do?"

"Seek refuge in my arms."

She blushed to the roots of her hair and tucked her hands beneath her knees. "I could not possibly."

"Come, come, Miss Sheringham," he said, rising and holding out his hand to her. "You need only take a step in my direction. I will do the rest."

She took a deep breath and let it out. "Very well." She rose and took a step toward him.

His right arm slid around her waist, the left around her back as he led her up into the folly with him. Her cheek naturally rested against his shoulder, and she could feel his warm breath on her face. The palm of his right hand slid down below her waist. In fact, he had a large handful of her trousers. His little finger might even be resting on the crevice between . . .

"Oh, dear."

She could not seem to catch her breath. The growth of roses through the supports holding up the roof of the folly filled the space with a heady perfume that made fresh air scarce. That must be the problem.

"Do you feel safe now, Miss Sheringham?"

She had never been more frightened in her life. Her body anticipated what it would feel like if his hand moved any farther downward. If it slid into her trousers and touched her naked flesh.

She shivered again.

"*Are* you cold?" he asked, looking down at her.

"Actually, you make a very fine furnace, Captain. I

believe I am quite warm enough now. And feeling absolutely safe from . . . whatever." She was prepared to wrench herself from his embrace, but such violence proved unnecessary. His hands released her without hesitation.

"Ah," he said.

Ah, what? she wondered, glancing at him from the corner of her eye. Had that second shiver given her thoughts away? Did he know she had felt physically excited by his touch? Should she make another excuse for her reaction? Or should she leave well enough alone?

She knotted her fingers in front of her and met his knowing gaze as though nothing had happened. "So, if I am standing near Julian on the terrace and happen to shiver, I can expect a similar result?"

"I cannot think why not," he said. "If you are as attracted to him as you say you are."

"I love Julian," she said defensively.

"Then, by all means, be sure to shiver when he is looking, Miss Sheringham."

"I shall," she said. "What else would you suggest?"

He rubbed at his beard.

"You haven't shaved!" she exclaimed. The shadow on his face had not been apparent earlier, but had become visible in the growing light.

"No. Do you mind?" He lifted his chin and ran a hand under it and across the day's growth of beard on his cheeks. "It seemed a shame to make Griggs go to work so early."

"I suppose I did drag you out of bed at the crack of dawn."

"Were you there? I missed seeing you," he teased. "All I remember was Griggs growling at me to get up."

She flushed. "Of course I was not—"

"I wish you had been," he said in a silky voice, stalking closer, like a large, predatory animal.

She backed up until she ran into the lattice and then took a step forward again, because she did not wish to be stung by an irritated bee. She stared at the captain warily, unable to keep images of herself in a silky nightgown, slipping beneath the covers to seek the heat of his naked body, from running through her mind.

"Very good," he said, his gaze focused on hers. "Very good, indeed. I am sure you do not need lessons, Miss Sheringham. You seem to anticipate what I would ask you to do."

"What?" she said, blinking as though she had just awakened from a trance.

He slipped her arm casually onto his and led her down out of the folly. "Lesson two in seduction: Innuendo. And knowing glances. The gentleman will provide the innuendo. You need only respond with a look that promises everything but, naturally, delivers nothing."

"Is that what I did?"

"I believe so. Were you not imagining us together, Miss Sheringham?"

She pulled herself free and planted herself in front of him, booted feet spread wide, fists on hips. "I . . . You . . . We . . . Fiddlesticks!" She could feel the heat on her face. At least she would not be shivering again anytime soon. "Will Julian be able to read my mind as easily as you seem to do?"

"I am sure if you look at Julian as you looked at me, he will receive the invitation as clearly as I did."

"What invitation?"

"To bed you, of course."

She marched across the grass toward Mephistopheles. "You go too far, Captain."

He shrugged. "I am merely offering you the benefit of my experience, Miss Sheringham. Quitting so soon?"

Eliza halted in her tracks. She had come to learn how to seduce Julian. It was be a shame to leave without finding out everything she could. She turned to face the Beau, careful not to slip on the wet grass and give him another excuse to touch her. "I want to know everything you can teach me."

He raised a questioning brow.

"Everything," she repeated.

"Very well, lesson number three: Proximity, proximity, proximity."

He took several steps toward her.

She held out her hand, palm open, to stop him from coming any closer. "I do not need a demonstration, Captain Wharton. I believe I understand the concept."

"Very well. Show me how it works," he challenged, walking forward until her palm rested flat against his chest.

She swallowed hard. "You are suggesting I stand close to Julian."

He nodded.

"Closer than arm's width."

He nodded again.

She let her hand drop and took two steps toward

him. Less than a foot of space remained between them. "This threatens propriety, Captain," she said in a quiet voice.

"To the devil with propriety, Miss Sheringham. Remember you are bent on seduction."

She raised uncertain eyes to his. "Anything closer would suggest an intimacy that does not yet exist between myself and Julian."

"Come closer, Miss Sheringham," he murmured.

She took another step and stared up at him. Now she could see the spray of darker blue around his pupils that gave such vivid color to his eyes. He remained perfectly still as she reached up to satisfy her curiosity by touching the night's growth of whiskers on his face.

She gave a surprised laugh. "It feels so rough!"

He grasped her wrist. "You are an apt pupil, Miss Sheringham. I believe that is quite close enough."

A teasing glint lit her eyes, and a mischievous smile curved her lips. "This is a great deal more fun than I had imagined, Captain."

She inched closer and gasped as the tips of her breasts grazed his chest. A frisson of excitement danced down her spine. She felt the danger, but was not ready to stop.

She watched her hands, of their own accord, slowly unbutton his waistcoat and slide beneath it to discover the hard muscle of his chest and rib cage, and the heavy beat of his heart beneath the thin lawn shirt.

She met his feral gaze and saw she was no longer facing Captain Wharton, Julian's friend, but the merciless rakehell who had seduced dozens of women without a single look back.

His hand slowly curled around her nape and drew her face toward his. His mouth captured her lips in a kiss that was as brutal as it was passionate. He bound her tight against him from chest to thighs.

She was not prepared for the kiss, for the depth of his passion, for the feel of his hard, aroused body as he spread his legs and angled her between them. She kept her teeth gritted tight against his probing tongue, but the hand at her nape held her fast, until he had what he wanted—her mouth, open to him. The sensations he aroused were both exhilarating and terrifying.

He released her at last, his eyes glittering with raw sexual need. Her heart thundered with fear, her whole body trembled, yet she stared at him defiantly, daring him to force himself on her again.

"You are no gentleman!"

"Lesson number four, Miss Sheringham," he said in a silky voice. "Never, never underestimate your adversary."

"Adversary! We are not at war, Captain Wharton."

"Oh, but we are. To capture a man's heart, you must break through his defenses, and you must do so without losing the constant battle between the sexes. If you ever give in to the power of seduction, Miss Sheringham, you have lost . . . everything."

"I am perfectly capable of protecting my virtue," she retorted.

"I doubt it. You are playing with fire, Miss Sheringham. Be careful you don't get burned."

"Are you through?" she demanded.

"I believe I am. Good luck with Julian, Miss Sheringham."

He left her standing with her mouth agape and marched over to retrieve his jacket. He stopped to put it on, no easy task when fashion demanded it fit like a second skin. He had barely settled it on his shoulders when he began yanking it off again, cursing and slapping at his back. He turned the jacket inside out and shook it hard several times.

"Is something wrong, Captain?"

"It should please you to know, Miss Sheringham, that I have just been stung by a bee."

She stared at his indignant face, then burst out laughing.

He stalked to his horse, the offending jacket over his arm, mounted, and was gone before she could curb her whoops of mirth.

Unfortunately, even after the captain was long gone, Eliza could not seem to stop laughing. Her ribs ached from the effort to catch her breath, and her legs trembled uncontrollably. Tears squeezed from her eyes. She managed to reach the steps of the folly and collapse, her arms wrapped tight around her to keep her insides from flying out.

That awful, despicable man! She wished a hundred bees had stung him. The Beau deserved his reputation. The bounder! How dare he make her want him!

Eliza wiped her hand across her lips but could not rid herself of the taste of him. She would show him! She would take the lessons he had taught her and use them to bring Julian to the point. Just see how smug he was when she stood at the altar with another man!

Mephistopheles suddenly lifted his head, ears alert, eyes searching the horizon, nostrils flaring as he tested the wind. He whinnied loudly, not a challenge, but a question. The call was answered by another horse somewhere over the hill.

Eliza felt a momentary panic. If anyone saw her dressed like this— She decided it must be Captain Wharton's horse that Mephistopheles had scented. Surely no one else was out riding this early.

A quick glance revealed the sun was fully up. The Beau's lessons must have lasted much longer than she had realized. She would have a much more difficult time sneaking back into Somersville Manor unnoticed in the daylight. However, during her two years at Ravenwood, it was her experience that only the servants got up this early. Ladies and gentlemen stayed ensconced in their rooms until much later. All was not yet lost. She need only exercise discretion, and all would be well.

That comfort lasted only until she saw a curricle drawn by a stunningly handsome pair of grays crest the hill above her.

It was Julian. And Miss Whitcomb.

She had been certain the Diamond was one of those who never raised her head from the pillow before noon. What was Julian doing with the Diamond at this hour of the morning? How had they known where to find her?

She saw Miss Whitcomb pointing, saw the frown form on Julian's face. She was tempted to make a run for it, but there was no disguising Mephistopheles.

Miss Whitcomb had criticized Eliza publicly yesterday afternoon for mounting such a "dangerous wild beast" and pointed out that she must be "as strong as a man" to control him. The Diamond had added, with a mocking laugh, "She is certainly as tall as one. In fact, Miss Sheringham towers over every man here."

Despite a pleading look in Julian's direction, he had said nothing in her defense. Belatedly, she realized he probably agreed with Miss Whitcomb. Nevertheless, she felt betrayed by his defection. He was her cousin. If only for the sake of that relation, he should have come to her rescue.

Captain Wharton had been the one to turn Miss Whitcomb's words back on her, much as Eliza might have done herself if he had not intervened.

He stood beside the Diamond and looked a very long way down his aristocratic nose at her. "You may not envy Miss Sheringham's height," he said. "But you must certainly regret the lack of her many other noteworthy assets." The captain's eyes had very obviously skipped from the Diamond's face to her bosom.

Miss Whitcomb's features turned to ice.

"Personally, I prefer my women—and of course my wine—to be a little fuller-bodied," he said.

The other young misses tittered. Their mamas glared, while the gentleman, including Miss Whitcomb's papa, chuckled and chortled behind their hands.

Miss Whitcomb turned red as a radish and discovered a tear in her hem that necessitated retiring immediately to have it mended.

Eliza did not want to think what insults Miss

Whitcomb would unleash this morning, when she realized whom she had caught wearing men's trousers.

Eliza was not sure whether to be relieved or alarmed when several more vehicles, apparently full of servants, and a landau bearing both Charlie and the duchess, followed Julian over the hill.

She led Mephistopheles over to the steps of the folly and hurriedly mounted. She tugged her hat down low and spurred the stallion around Julian's curricle, heading directly for the landau that carried Charlie, where she was sure to find solace.

Escape was not to be so easy.

"Miss Sheringham? Is that you?" Miss Whitcomb queried.

Eliza thought of riding past Julian's curricle, but Julian pulled to a stop right in front of her.

"Good morning, Julian, Miss Whitcomb," Eliza said, tipping her hat as a gentleman would.

"It *is* you," Miss Whitcomb said delightedly. "I could scarcely believe my eyes. I told Major Sheringham it must be you, because of that brutish black horse you ride."

Mephistopheles curvetted restlessly, and Miss Whitcomb gave him a nervous glance.

"What brings you here this morning?" Eliza asked.

Miss Whitcomb made a show of rearranging the large bow beneath her chin, even though her straw hat was perched perfectly on her head. "Major Sheringham and I have come with Her Grace and the countess to help plan where the tables should be set for the picnic this afternoon."

Eliza remembered hearing something about a picnic at supper last night, but she had been too busy planning how to get a note to Captain Wharton to pay attention. "Here at the folly? This afternoon?"

Miss Whitcomb carefully realigned each finger of her white gloves as she spoke. "Really, Miss Sheringham. I know you were sitting at the supper table when everything was settled. Where was your mind, I wonder?"

"Not nearly so deep in the gutter as yours," Eliza retorted.

Miss Whitcomb gasped and fanned her face. "Why, I never—" She turned to Julian, injured tears already sparkling in her eyes.

Eliza felt sick. She should have kept her tongue leashed. Why had she let the Diamond provoke her? She simply could not understand how Julian could be interested in such an unpleasant female. How had Miss Whitcomb cajoled him into attending her?

Eliza was so very glad for her lessons from the Beau. It would likely take some very special maneuvers to loosen Julian from the Diamond's groping, white-gloved grasp.

At least Miss Whitcomb had refrained from mentioning her attire. "I will leave you to your planning," Eliza said. "I must be elsewhere this morning." Anywhere Miss Whitcomb was not.

"Miss Sheringham." Miss Whitcomb's sharp voice caused Mephistopheles to jump sideways.

Eliza brought the stallion back under control and said through gritted teeth, "Yes, Miss Whitcomb?"

"Where is the masquerade, Miss Sheringham?"

"Masquerade?" Eliza said cautiously.

Miss Whitcomb smiled spitefully. "The one you are attending, dressed as a man."

"You should know, Miss Whitcomb. It is likely the same one you are attending, dressed as a woman."

Julian stared at her in open disbelief.

Eliza clamped her teeth on any apology he might demand. Surely she had the right to defend herself.

When Julian's open disbelief became obvious disapproval, Eliza put spurs to the stallion's flanks. She had left Miss Whitcomb in the dust long before she heard the Diamond's shriek of outrage. It had taken that long for the Diamond to understand the insult.

Eliza waved at Charlie and the duchess as she thundered by without reducing her speed. She watched them put their heads together and knew it was only a matter of time before she received another lecture on propriety.

Eliza did not care. She had always been different. The scandal had made it so. She did not know how to be like them. She could only be who she was. But it seemed she did not please anyone. Julian least of all.

Her eyes blurred, and her stomach churned. She could not give up now. She must use the lessons she had learned this morning at the picnic this afternoon. She would win Julian's love. She could not possibly lose him to someone as dreadful as the Diamond.

Chapter 11

MARCUS COULD HARDLY BEAR TO WATCH MISS Sheringham exercising her seductive charms on Julian. Unfortunately, she could not use shivering as a ploy. It was clearly impossible to plead either cold or fear during a warm afternoon picnic with a dozen other couples seated on blankets nearby.

But she had used proximity to good effect. Not an inch of space remained between her arm and Julian's as they stood next to each other near the lake, conversing with the ever-cheerful Countess of Denbigh.

Miss Sheringham had more natural allure than the most practiced courtesans he had bedded, yet Julian seemed impervious to her wiles. What was wrong with the man? Marcus would have forfeited his perfect face and form to have Miss Sheringham just once glance at him with the sort of adoration she offered Julian.

He did not know what it was about the girl that intrigued him. Perhaps it was their first violent meeting. Or her odd features and unusual height. Or the knowledge that she flouted the rules of Society as freely as he did. Or perhaps it was that amusing, and yes, enticing interlude teaching her the art of seduction.

He was very much afraid his efforts had been wasted. As far as he could tell, Miss Sheringham was in love with the wrong man.

As Penthia had claimed to be. *I love you, Marcus. I only married Alastair to be near you. Please, let me come to you tonight. Alastair will never know.*

He shook his head to clear it of Penthia's hypnotizing voice. She had taught him hard lessons, lessons he would never forget. No woman could be trusted. Beneath their beautiful facades, they were all manipulative, selfish creatures. Any man who tied himself to one for life was a fool and an idiot.

Captain Lord Marcus Wharton was neither.

He had confined himself to flirting with innocents, knowing the grim consequences of indulging himself further with one of them.

Until Miss Sheringham had come along.

He had made the mistake of letting himself get close enough to kiss her, to hold her in his arms, to give himself a delicious taste of what he was missing. And what he must deny himself.

He was tempted to satisfy his craving for her. His blood surged as forbidden images rose before him. Kissing her swollen lips, caressing her naked breasts and belly, putting himself inside her, the first man to do so. And the last.

Marcus closed his trembling hands into fists, denying the fierce surge of possessiveness that quivered through him. Making a commitment to one woman was not in his nature. Or his future. If he hoped to keep his sanity, he must put her from his mind. There would be other women. There always had been.

Not like her. She is unforgettable. One of a kind.

He swore and slid a finger between his throat and the neck cloth that was strangling him.

"Good afternoon, Captain Wharton."

Miss Whitcomb had snuck up on him while he was busy thinking about Miss Sheringham. The Diamond was wearing a muslin dress ruffled on top to maximize her meager assets and carried a matching yellow parasol. Before he could say a word in greeting, she had slid her arm through his and sidled up next to him.

His lips twisted wryly. The chit had proximity down to an art.

She batted her eyelashes at him above an ivory and lace fan that swayed gently over the lower half of her face. "You look warm, Captain."

She even provided the innuendo, relieving him of the chore. She reminded him of Penthia, in the days when Alastair was courting her. Marcus had been young and foolish enough then to turn rock hard at the mere suggestion that he might be "warm" in a lady's presence.

He pulled a handkerchief from his pocket to dab at the perspiration on his face and noticed the Blackthorne B stitched into it. It reminded him powerfully of the first night he had met Miss Sheringham.

Forget her. She will only cause you pain in the end.

He removed the moisture from his upper lip and forehead, smiled benignly at Miss Whitcomb, and said, "Yes, I am warm. The sun is hot this afternoon."

Nothing spiked the effect of innuendo like a literal response. Miss Whitcomb looked perplexed, but only for a moment. She twirled the parasol laid over her shoulder and said, "Perhaps you would be more comfortable in the shade."

She indicated the nearby forest with a tip of her head. The chit had moved beyond seduction to invitation. He knew better than to be maneuvered into the stand of oak and ash, where they could be found by her mama in whatever compromising position she would have him in by then.

"I have just remembered I promised to take Miss Sheringham for a cooling walk among the trees. Thank you for reminding me, Miss Whitcomb. May I escort you back to your mama?"

He caught her quick, stabbing glare in Miss Sheringham's direction before she pouted prettily and said, "Perhaps I will keep Major Sheringham company while you are entertaining his country cousin."

The girl slid a sideways look at him, to see if her effort at maneuvering him with jealousy had worked.

The latest Season's diamond held no interest for him; Miss Sheringham, however, did. He felt insulted on her behalf at the Diamond's denigrating reference to Julian's "country cousin."

"Do you ride, Miss Whitcomb?" he asked, knowing full well she did not.

"I am afraid not, Captain," she said. "Horses frighten me."

"Too bad," he said. "Miss Sheringham is a bruising rider, you know. All those fields in the country to practice on, I suppose. I think I shall see if I can get a riding party together. We will miss you, Miss Whitcomb."

He watched the Diamond struggle to keep her face from contorting with fury.

"Miss Sheringham is—"

He shot her an icy look that stopped her in mid-speech. "I will warn you only once, Miss Whitcomb. I do not wish to hear you malign Miss Sheringham again. To me, or anyone else in this party."

Her large blue eyes filled with the sort of virulent hatred he had seen often on Penthia's face. Miss Whitcomb was only eighteen. He knew firsthand how malice would harden her features as she matured. She had certainly proved herself a Diamond—right down to her coal black heart.

It was easier than he had thought it would be to separate Miss Sheringham from Julian. He fully expected several other couples to join them on their walk. He had no desire to find himself alone with her in the cool seclusion of the forest.

Before he knew it, the Countess of Denbigh had suggested that Julian take Miss Whitcomb for a boat ride on the lake and directed several other couples to join them.

That pleased Miss Whitcomb, who shot him a superior look and—without a word—made her disdain of Miss Sheringham clear to that lady.

"I think Eliza could use a little shade," Lady Denbigh said. "Her freckles are beginning to sprout."

Miss Sheringham put a gloved hand up to hide her nose, but he saw through her fingers that, sure enough, a number of brownish-red freckles were sprinkled across her nose and cheeks. He opened his mouth to say they were charming and shut it again. Clearly he could not trust himself not to go too far in flirting with the chit. Better to say nothing at all.

"I will find the earl and join you in a few minutes, if we may," the countess said.

That was a warning. Lady Denbigh was sending Miss Sheringham off alone with him, but giving fair notice he should not start anything he did not want to be observed by the couple following after.

Miss Sheringham seemed unnaturally quiet as he led her toward the cooling shade. She was wearing a straw hat, but it was pushed so far back on her head that it did little to keep the sun off her face. A whirlwind off the lake pulled the hat completely off, so it lay against her back, hanging by the soft yellow ribbon knotted at her throat.

Chestnut wisps had escaped the simple knot at her crown and graced her brow and temples. Tiny beads of perspiration had gathered above her mouth. He had the irresistible urge to kiss them off. But resisted it.

Her eyes looked troubled. She was chewing on her lower lip. The sight of her plump lower lip, damp and soft, sent the blood rushing to his loins. Sinews and tendons flexed as he battled temptation. And won.

He waited for her to speak first, but they were far into the forest—far enough that they could not be observed by those boating on the lake or settled on blankets beside it—and she still had said nothing.

"Miss Sheringham?" he said at last.

Her eyes widened, as though she was not only surprised to find him standing across from her, but astonished to find herself alone with him. Her eyes darted like a cornered rabbit, scouting avenues of escape. "I thought the earl and countess were joining us."

"In a few minutes," he reassured her.

She relaxed, but only slightly.

"You seem disturbed about something," he said. "Can I be of help?"

"I should not even be speaking to you. Not after the liberties you took this morning. But . . ."

"But . . . ?"

"It isn't working," she blurted out. "What you taught me isn't working on Julian."

"How do you know?"

"It isn't there! I don't see it when I am with him."

"What isn't there?" he asked gently. "What don't you see?"

"That look. The one in your eyes when you touched me. Before you kissed me." She cut herself off and began pacing, her strides long and agitated, limited only by the width of her flounced hem.

"I am being silly, I know," she said. "You and I were alone. Julian and I were standing among a host of people. Of course he could not share such a look with me in public."

She glanced up, and her gaze caught on his. "Oh, no," she whispered. "There it is again."

"It is only desire, Miss Sheringham. Nothing more." It could not be more than that. He would not allow it to be.

She shook her head. "No, Captain. I have seen lust in a man's eyes. You look at me with . . . something more."

He could not speak. His heart was pounding. *No. No. There is nothing more.*

She took a step closer, searching his face. "What I see in your eyes makes me feel . . . so much more . . . than I feel with Julian."

He swore under his breath. "What you feel is merely desire, Miss Sheringham."

Her brow furrowed deeply. "Desire for you? How is that possible, Captain? I do not even like you very much."

He had never wanted her as much as he did at that moment. The situation was fraught with danger, as much for him, as for her. How had a chit of seventeen brought him to the brink of sexual frenzy? It was the look in her golden eyes when she focused them on him, the same look that must be reflected in his. A look of loneliness. A look of need. Desperate need.

"Eliza . . ."

He did not realize he had used her first name until he saw the surprise on her face. He opened his mouth to correct himself and apologize for his forwardness, but the words never got out. His mouth was already on hers, and her arms had circled tight around his waist.

"Please let me in," he breathed against her closed mouth. "I want you, Eliza. I need you."

With a moan of surrender, she opened to him.

He thrust his hands into her hair, sending pins flying as the loosened knot fell free. Rich chestnut curls tumbled over her shoulders and down her back.

Some deep, dark place inside him blazoned with light as he drank his fill of her, his mouth rapacious, his hands plundering. He had never felt so out of control, so overwhelmed by passion. He could not stop himself from taking more . . . and more.

Until he tasted salty tears.

"Dear God," he whispered as he lifted his head to stare at her tear-streaked face. "What have I done?"

"Nothing I did not want as badly as you," she rasped. "I do not understand why . . . I cannot imagine what . . ." She backed away from him.

He took a step toward her, ready to offer anything if she would not leave him.

She turned to run and stumbled over an almost buried log. Arms windmilling, she tried to catch her balance.

He reached for her, but only managed to grasp a single puffed sleeve before she began to fall. He held on until the fabric tore with a loud *rrrriiiip*.

He heard the breath whoosh out of her when she landed facedown, her hands spread wide to break her fall, in a century's collection of dead and moldy leaves.

He expected her to push herself upright, but when she lay unmoving, he crouched on one knee beside her. "Miss Sheringham? Are you all right?"

She rolled over with a painful grunt, opened her eyes, and stared up into the patchwork of leaves and sun above them. "I think that must rank very high on my list of graceless exits."

He chuckled and sat down beside her. "Doubtless number one."

He put a hand beneath her back and helped her sit up, then brushed a dead leaf off her face, leaving a streak of dirt behind. It was hard not to touch her more. Hard to remove his hand.

His stomach lurched when blood began to well from a cut on her lower lip. "You're hurt!"

"I am?" She looked at her hands and elbows, but they were merely dirty.

"You've cut your lip," he said. "Have you a handkerchief?"

She reached into her bodice but came away with nothing. "I have no idea where it could have gone."

"Mine has been used," he said, nevertheless reaching into his pocket. He rearranged the fold and handed it to her.

She reached up with a fingertip to search for the cut. And found it. "Ouch." Her finger came away bloody. "Is it bad?" She dabbed at her lip with the handkerchief.

"I don't believe so." He leaned closer, to take a better look.

A triumphant female voice announced, "I told you so! I expected no less from a rake like Captain Wharton. And no more from a woman who breaks the rules of Society as conspicuously as Miss Sheringham."

"Miss Whitcomb, I believe you should return to your mama," Major Sheringham said.

"I am here, Major," a disdainful female voice said from somewhere beyond him. "Come to me, dearest," Mrs. Whitcomb implored her daughter. "These are not sights for your tender eyes."

Julian did not need to say a word for Marcus to see that he was furious. They greeted each other with stiff-necked nods.

"Julian."

"Marcus."

Marcus rose slowly, helping Eliza to her feet at the same time. She stood frozen like a statue beside him, her eyes trained on Julian's reproachful features.

"I thought you were boating on the lake," Marcus said.

"The sway of the boat made Miss Whitcomb queasy. She preferred to walk in the forest. I obliged her."

"Conniving chit," Marcus muttered under his breath. Miss Whitcomb had taken terrible revenge for his slight. Regrettably, it was Miss Sheringham who would suffer the most.

Marcus glanced at Julian, who looked ready to murder someone. It was time to start explaining.

"This is not what it looks like," Marcus began.

"It looks like you ravished my cousin," Julian said in a deadly voice.

Marcus took one look at Miss Sheringham and realized even he would be hard-pressed to believe in his innocence—or hers. Her dress was torn, her lip was bloodied, and her hair was all about her shoulders. To make matters worse, they had been sitting on the ground, his hands on her face, their faces intimately close together, when they were discovered.

"The Earl and Countess of Denbigh are not far behind me," Julian bit out. "I am afraid we cannot rely on the discretion of either Miss Whitcomb or her mama. Word of this encounter will doubtless have spread to the entire party before you and Eliza reach the edge of the forest."

"Miss Whitcomb does have a way with words," Marcus said bitterly.

"I think it best you pay your addresses to my cousin now."

Marcus opened his mouth to object, but Miss Sheringham was before him.

"Best for whom?" she demanded. "Despite the look of things, nothing happened here except a kiss. *A kiss*, Julian."

"Your dress is torn. Your lip is bloodied. It must have been quite a kiss, Eliza."

She made a disgusted sound. "I was running—" She stopped herself and said more calmly, "Captain Wharton and I were returning to the picnic, when I tripped over that log on the ground." She pointed to the half-hidden obstacle. "Captain Wharton grabbed at my arm to keep me from falling, but caught my sleeve instead, which tore. I cut my lip when I fell. The captain only knelt beside me because he saw I had hurt myself. That is how you found us."

"I suppose the pins dropped out of your hair when you fell, too."

"No. They did not," she admitted, her chin held high.

Marcus admired her quiet dignity. She could have lied. Julian would not have believed her, but he would not have contradicted her story.

"Have you an explanation?" Julian demanded.

She met his gaze levelly. "The pins fell when Captain Wharton kissed me."

A muscle in Julian's jaw jerked.

Marcus waited for his friend to confront him. He knew what was coming but still wished there were some way to avoid it.

"What do you have to say for yourself, Marcus?"

"I will make certain Miss Sheringham gets back to the house without further incident."

Julian shook his head. "I will hear a proposal before we leave this spot. My cousin has been ruined.

This scandal, atop the other, will sink her for sure. I insist you take the necessary steps to mend the situation."

Marcus lifted a supercilious brow. "Miss Sheringham and I were merely strolling through the forest, Julian, when she tripped and fell. With your support, and that of the Earl and Countess of Denbigh"—he nodded to the arriving couple—"I am certain we can pass off this incident as the innocent encounter it was."

"Innocent?" Julian shook his head as he stared at his cousin's tangled hair. "I think not."

Miss Sheringham took a step toward Julian. "You could not be more wrong, Julian. Captain Wharton has acted entirely the gentleman with me."

Marcus saw that no one present believed her, not even the irrepressible Countess of Denbigh.

"He did nothing I did not allow," she persisted.

Julian snorted derisively. "Your defense of the rogue only makes you both look more guilty, Eliza." He turned to Marcus and said, "I demand to know your intentions toward my cousin, Marcus. I expect you will be riding to Ravenwood this afternoon to pay your respects to my brother and to ask for Miss Sheringham's hand in marriage."

Miss Sheringham gasped. "I do not wish to marry Captain Wharton."

"You should have considered that before you kissed him!" Julian snarled.

Miss Sheringham turned pleading eyes to the Earl and Countess of Denbigh. "Please, Charlie, is there nothing you can do to help me?"

Marcus watched the countess wring her hands.

She exchanged a guilty glance with the earl, who said, "I am afraid your cousin is right, Miss Sheringham. This scandal will not soon be forgotten. You may avoid marriage with Captain Wharton, but you should know he may be your last chance for a suitable alliance. You are ruined, my dear. From this day forward, no gentleman of the *ton* can be expected to make you a proper proposal of marriage. I am sorry, but that is the brutal truth."

Miss Sheringham put a hand to her mouth, but an agonized cry nevertheless escaped. Her eyes welled with tears as she stared at the earl in disbelief and dread.

"I am waiting, Marcus," Julian said.

Marcus knew they all expected him to propose, even Miss Sheringham, who, in all likelihood, would refuse him. No doubt his brother would be disappointed in him if he abandoned her to her fate. But his reputation could not get much worse than it was. And he would not be forced into anything. He would rather endure the scandal.

He was sorry for Miss Sheringham's plight. But there was nothing he could do to help her without condemning them both to a lifetime of unhappiness.

Over the sudden lump in his throat he said, "I have no intentions at all toward the lady, Julian. As you would realize if you stopped a moment to think."

"Do you hear that, Eliza?" Julian said. "The infamous Beau has no intention of making an honest woman out of you. Oh, he will gladly take everything you have to give. But he offers nothing in return. I expect it must have been exciting to have such a notorious gentleman's attention, but you would have been better served—"

"Julian, please stop."

Miss Sheringham pressed her fingertips against her temples, where Marcus could see the pulse beating erratically.

"Leave her be," Marcus said rage growing inside him at Julian's attack on his cousin.

"You have no right—"

"Leave her be," he said in a deadly voice.

"I am waiting for your declaration, Marcus," Julian said.

Marcus fought the desperate urge to offer for her. *Remember Alastair's marriage.*

He felt sick inside and angry and torn. The words that came next were wrenched from some dark place inside him.

"You can wait until Doomsday, Julian. I will never offer marriage to any lady. Especially not to your cousin."

Julian pulled off one of the white gloves he wore with his hussar's uniform and slapped Marcus across the face with it.

Miss Sheringham gasped.

The earl swore under his breath and grabbed the countess to keep her from jumping into the fray.

"Pistols at dawn?" Marcus asked through tight lips.

"Presuming I can arrange for a special license to wed Miss Sheringham myself before the morrow."

Marcus felt his heart jump to his throat. "What?"

"I owe that much to my cousin," Julian said. "You were my friend. I trusted you with her. I allowed this to happen. I will make an honest woman of her, if you will not. And I will do it tonight, in case your aim is truer than mine in the morning."

While Marcus stood stunned, Julian turned to Miss Sheringham, took both her hands in his, looked into her tear-bright golden eyes and said, "Will you do me the great honor of becoming my wife, Eliza?"

Marcus watched her swallow, saw her stare into Julian's dark eyes. He knew what she was looking for. He hoped that she found it.

"Eliza," the countess said. "Please do not make a decision to marry because you think it is your only option. I will—"

"Charlotte," the earl warned. "I believe you have interfered enough in this young lady's life."

Eliza met the countess's troubled gaze and said, "I have not, and I am not now, doing anything against my wishes."

"I am waiting for your answer," Julian said.

Her voice was a bare whisper. "Yes, Julian. I will marry you."

A moment later, the countess was by her side supporting her. The earl stepped between Marcus and Julian and shook Julian's hand.

"Congratulations, Major Sheringham. You are a very fortunate man."

Marcus waited for Julian to agree, but he made no reply. Marcus felt furious with his friend for marrying Miss Sheringham if he did not want her. But he knew no way to remedy the situation unless he proposed himself. His stomach churned, his eyes misted, and his nose stung.

He simply could not bring himself to do it.

Marcus suddenly realized the earl had given him

the cut direct. The slight hurt. But it was only a taste of what he could expect in days to come.

It would be much worse for Miss Sheringham. The *ton* had a long and vindictive memory where young, rebellious misses were concerned. She had made the right decision accepting Julian's proposal. Besides, she loved the man.

Even if Julian did not love her.

Marcus had never felt so empty inside, so completely bereft.

The Duke of Braddock appeared from the trees and hailed them. "Major Sheringham. Captain Wharton. I am afraid I have bad news for you. Bonaparte is on the march. All soldiers have been recalled to their regiments. You must ride to the coast tonight. You sail for the Continent at dawn."

Marcus exchanged a look with his friend, the man who had fought beside him in so many battles. "It seems you will have to wait a while to spill my blood."

Julian met his look with disdain and loathing. "If I am lucky, some Frenchman will save me the trouble."

Marcus heard a gasp, but could not tell whether it had come from the countess or Miss Sheringham.

"My only regret," Julian said as he looked into Miss Sheringham's eyes, "is that I cannot stay and marry you now, Eliza. I offer you the protection of my name while I am gone. And I look forward to making you my wife when I return."

He turned to leave, but Miss Sheringham called him back. "Julian!"

Marcus watched her cross to Julian, put her hands on either side of his face to draw his mouth down to hers, and kiss him tenderly on the lips.

Something twisted painfully inside him. He could not seem to catch his breath. It was as though someone were squeezing his chest and would not let go.

"Goodbye, Julian. God be with you."

Julian managed a smile. "Do not fear, poppet. I will come back safe to you."

He was gone a moment later.

Miss Sheringham turned to stare at Marcus. He had never seen such a tormented look in his life.

The earl and countess stood protectively on either side of her. He wanted to explain why he could not marry her, that it was nothing to do with her, but a failing in him. He could never trust a woman, not even her. But whatever he wanted to say would have to be said in front of the sheltering couple. And he could not—would not—lay his heart open to anyone but her.

He settled for what could be said.

"Goodbye, Miss Sheringham. I cannot offer much to allay the trouble I have caused you, except to say I will protect Julian with my life. I wish you joy together."

He did not expect a reply. He had pivoted to leave when he heard her whisper.

"It was not there, Captain. I looked, but it was not there."

He hesitated, swallowed over the aching lump in his throat, and walked away.

AFTER THE KISS

The Beast of Blackthorne

Chapter 12

"UNCLE MARCUS IS CRYING," REGGIE WHISPERED.

"How do you know?" Becky whispered back.

They lay flat on their stomachs in the dark, heedless of the damage being done to their matching shifts by the damp, moldy stone floor. Uncle Marcus had been hiding out in the east wing of Blackthorne Abbey for nearly a year, refusing to receive them. Today they had decided to see him, whether he wanted to be seen, or not.

Getting in through the door had proved impossible, with Griggs blocking the way. They had been reduced to spying on Uncle Marcus through an ornate wrought iron grate set in the wall of the drawing room.

The narrow black grate, which traveled from floor to ceiling, looked merely decorative from their uncle's side of the gray stone wall, but it concealed the presence of a room on the other side that could be reached only through a secret passageway.

They had first discovered the mazelike corridors that honeycombed the stone walls of Blackthorne Abbey three years ago when they were mere babes of six. Within moments of entering the narrow passageway from a bedroom in their wing of the Abbey, they had been hopelessly lost in the coal black labyrinth. When their father found them hours later, near where they were now, weeping and scared out of their wits by cobwebs and crawling creatures, they had been more than willing to promise never to enter the passageway again.

That had been a long time ago. Dire situations required dangerous solutions. For the first time in nearly a year they they were able to see their uncle, and were shocked by what they had found.

Uncle Marcus was crying.

Becky peered through the iron grate, listening carefully for a grown-up version of the sobs or whimpers or wails that normally accompanied crying. "I don't hear anything, Reggie."

"No. But he is crying, all the same. I can see a tear on his cheek," Reggie said. "Do you think he is remembering Father and wishing he were here?"

"Perhaps," Becky conceded in a quiet voice. "Miss Stipple said this morning that it is exactly one year today since Father disappeared at sea. And eleven months and thirteen days since Uncle Marcus came home from Waterloo so horribly wounded and disappeared into this 'decayed, dilapidated, and decrepit' wing of Blackthorne Abbey."

Becky mimicked the haughty tones of their latest governess perfectly as she continued, " 'The new duke might as well have drowned with his brother, as little use as he is to you children or anyone else.' "

Becky exchanged a resolute look with Reggie. They had let Miss Stipple know such feelings were not appreciated in the most direct way they knew.

Reggie had filled her plate full of breakfast foods from the sideboard and "accidentally" spilled it in Miss Stipple's lap on the way to her seat. Becky had jumped up from her place at the table to help Miss Stipple clean up the mess. And easily managed to spread shirred eggs and porridge and a heaping spoon of jelly onto her face and into her hair.

Miss Stipple had immediately retired to her room, swearing they were "devils" and no one could control them, and as soon as she could find another position, she was "departing this madhouse!"

"We must do something to get Uncle Marcus to come out of hiding," Reggie said. "Otherwise, we are going to end up with another of those horrid governesses."

Becky put a hand to Reggie's mouth. "Shh! Uncle Marcus will hear you."

Reggie pried Becky's hand away and hissed, "Maybe I want him to hear! Maybe I want him to—"

Both girls held their breath as their uncle frowned in the direction of their hiding place. He sat slouched in one of two wingback chairs that faced the mammoth fireplace.

Becky had never seen Uncle Marcus when he did not look top-of-the-trees. Until now.

He wore no jacket, and several buttons were open at the neck, revealing a tuft of golden hair at his throat. His white shirt points were long past wilted, and his neck cloth dangled, half untied. Fawn pants fit like a second skin, but showed stains where he must have spilled his drink. His booted feet—where was the spit-polish shine?—extended before him, crossed at the ankle.

The heavy black curtains over the windows made daylight dark as night, and the flickering flames cast an eerie shadow on his face. Nevertheless, with his head angled toward them, part of the scar on his face became visible above a heavy beard and the Brutus cut he had allowed to grow wild.

No one would have recognized this man as the Beau.

Becky saw the dread on Reggie's face and knew her own expression must be equally distressed. It was impossible to look at Uncle Marcus without wincing. One imagined one's own pain at the infliction of such a terrible wound.

The distortion at the edge of his right eye from the slashing sabre cut was not nearly as bad now as it had been before the wound healed. But every time Becky saw the remaining scars, she remembered the horror of the fresh wound, instead of seeing the thin, almost white, spider web of lines that were all that remained to mark his pain.

In the first days after Uncle Marcus had returned to Blackthorne Abbey, the maids and grooms and footmen were forever gasping and averting their eyes when they caught sight of him. The maid-of-all-work screamed and fainted dead away. Uncle Marcus could have dismissed them. Instead, he had taken himself from their sight.

Little remained of the fun-loving uncle they had known. His eyes were hooded, his mouth—what Becky could see beneath the dark golden beard—was grim. The beard hid part of the thin white line that trailed from his eye, down his cheek past the edge of his mouth, all the way to his chin. He reminded her of a thunderstorm, dark and menacing, hovering ominously overhead, waiting for the right time and place to strike.

When Uncle Marcus's gaze returned at last to the crackling fire, Becky breathed a sigh of relief. She reached over to touch Reggie's arm to reassure her their hiding place had not been detected.

They watched together as, with his good right hand, their uncle traced the pheasant in flight etched on the brandy decanter that sat on the table between the two wingback chairs. His black-gloved left hand rested palm up on the arm of the chair, the fingers frozen in place like an upside-down spider missing a few legs.

Griggs, who had lost his right arm at Waterloo, had brought Uncle Marcus the refilled decanter not five minutes past, protesting, "You should not be drinkin' so much brandy, Your Grace."

In a slurred voice Uncle Marcus had replied, "Then next time bring me a bottle of port."

Griggs made an unpleasant sound and said in sarcastic tones, "By all means, Your Grace."

"Don't call me that! I don't want my brother's title or the honors that go with it. Alastair can swim like a fish. The three sailors who survived said they saw him safe into the water before his ship went down. If they made it safely to the coast of Scotland, he did, too. I have no idea what is keeping him away, but mark my words, my brother is alive. I have no right to be Duke of Blackthorne."

"Nevertheless, Your Grace, it's duke you are. And a sodden one at that, if I may be so bold as to say it."

"When did you ever let rank stop you from speaking your mind?" Uncle Marcus retorted.

"If you want the truth, here it is," Griggs said. "I thought better of you than what I've seen, Captain. You lost your brother to the sea, and Major Sheringham in a battle that claimed too many old friends."

Griggs refused to let Uncle Marcus interrupt. "It was not your fault the major died, despite what you think. There was nothin' you could've done to save him."

"I could have fought at his side."

Griggs gave a Gallic shrug. "He did not want you there."

"That was my fault, too!"

"Blame yourself, if you must," Griggs said. "But there is no changin' what happened. You could not save your friend from harm, Captain. And this time, sad to say, he could not save you, either."

Uncle Marcus closed his eyes and leaned his head back against the chair. "Miss Sheringham will never be married now, never have a husband to care for her, or children to hold in her arms," he said in a voice so soft Becky had to strain to hear it. "That is my fault, too."

"You could marry her yourself."

Uncle Marcus turned to Griggs, a look of such agony on his face that Becky nearly cried out to him. Reggie's palm trapped the sound before it escaped. She met Reggie's eyes and nodded that she was all right, and her sister released her.

Griggs laid a hand on Uncle Marcus's shoulder and said, "Miss Sheringham has been livin' with her aunt in the home she inherited from her father. There's no reason why you couldn't—"

"It is impossible." Her uncle lurched from the chair, as much to escape the comfort Griggs offered, Becky thought, as from his own restlessness.

"Miss Sheringham did not want me when I was the Beau. She would never have me like this."

Griggs's voice turned gruff. "The Beau you will never be again. But the world did not end when you lost your beauteous looks, Captain. I never believed they mattered to you, but I see I was wrong."

"If I were not—"

"You are still a whole man, with arms and legs and a face—scarred though it may be. That is more than many another came home with," Griggs charged, angling his body so Uncle Marcus could not fail to see the empty sleeve where his jacket was pinned up.

Becky could not even imagine living life without one of her hands. She needed them both to paint and to play the piano and to write her wonderful stories. Griggs had used his right hand to fight, but the war with Boney was over and both men had left the army. Griggs had learned how to manage his duties as her uncle's valet—not so different from those as his batman—with the hand he had left.

Uncle Marcus's shoulders slumped, and his head fell forward in defeat. "I admire your courage, Griggs. I wish I had some of it."

"You never lacked courage before, Captain. If only you would—"

Uncle Marcus whirled, completely exposing his scarred face and gnarled hand. "I am a monster, Griggs! The Beast of Blackthorne."

Becky was afraid to breathe in the silence that followed her uncle's anguished admission. It hurt to swallow over the frog-size lump that grew in her throat.

Griggs opened his mouth to protest, but this time Uncle Marcus cut him off.

"I know what everyone says behind my back. I know how hideous I look."

"I expect not, Your Grace, since you haven't allowed a lookin' glass in this wing of the abbey since you came here. The wound has healed. It is not nearly so bad—"

"A beast belongs in a cave, Griggs. Here I will stay."

"What about the children, Your Grace? Lady Regina and Lady Rebecca have been asking to see you."

Becky risked a glance at Reggie to see if she was paying attention and found her sister staring back at her with a look of pain and longing in her eyes that matched Becky's feelings exactly. They clasped hands and turned their gazes back to the shadowy room, waiting to hear whether Uncle Marcus would agree, finally, to see them.

After an interminable silence, he sighed and said, "They were never mine, Griggs. I am not necessary to their well-being. All Reggie and Becky really need at their age is a governess."

Becky shot Reggie a frustrated look and got an angry one in exchange as Reggie pulled her hand free. How could Uncle Marcus be so stupid as to think they did not need him? Fortunately, Griggs came to the rescue. Although Becky wished he had not chosen quite the argument he did.

"No governess can manage the little demons, Your Grace. They sent the seventh one packing today."

"Put an advertisement in the *Times*," Uncle Marcus retorted. "Find another. Surely one woman with hair and wit can be found in all of London."

"They need a father, Your Grace."

Uncle Marcus scowled, a fearsome look that would have frightened Becky if it had been directed at her. Griggs did not seem to notice it.

"Alastair is their father," Uncle Marcus said.

"The man is dead!"

"I cannot believe he is gone. I would feel more pain in here." Uncle Marcus thumped his good hand—which held a glass of brandy—against his heart, spilling some of the liquid. "My brother is still out there somewhere."

"It has been a year. The Bow Street runners you hired have searched the whole of Scotland—includin' that troublesome estate where he was bound, Blackthorne Hall—and half of England, as well. The duke has not been found. You must accept the fact your brother is gone—"

"No!" Uncle Marcus threw his glass against the stone fireplace, where the crystal shattered, sending shards flying and blue flames licking at the brandy on the grate. He began pacing the room, his gloved hand curled tight against his body.

Griggs pleaded, "For the children's sake—"

"Damn and blast, man! Do you not understand the sight of them reminds me of all I have lost? Of what I will never have? Get out!" he raged. "Leave me alone!"

Griggs left without another word.

Uncle Marcus had eventually slumped back into

his chair before the fireplace, staring once again into the fire.

Becky had felt sick inside, frightened of what the future held if he truly had abandoned them. She wanted to flee, to get as far away from this dark and lonely place as she could. She grabbed Reggie's hand to pull her away, but her sister resisted.

That was when Reggie had told her Uncle Marcus was crying. Now that she looked more closely, she could make out a single, silvery line down his cheek reflected by the firelight.

Becky shivered—from the cold stones beneath her, of course, not from fear of her uncle, despite his recent rage. Uncle Marcus would never hurt a flea. *Well, maybe a flea*, she corrected herself, literal to a fault, *but nothing larger*.

However, with his hair and beard so wild, and cast in shadows, he did look quite fearsome. And lonely. And sad.

"He does not want us," Reggie said flatly.

"We will have to change his mind."

"How?"

"I will think of something." Becky was as good at coming up with ideas as Reggie was at executing them.

"I wish Father were here," Reggie said wistfully.

"Me, too."

"Do you think Uncle Marcus is right? Do you think Father might still be alive?"

Becky saw the hope on Reggie's face and hated to extinguish it. But she did not want Reggie refusing whatever plan she presented to force Uncle Marcus out of hiding, because she believed Father might someday return and right the situation.

"Uncle Marcus is wrong," Becky said certainly. "Father is dead."

Reggie did not argue. Her eyes welled, and her chin quivered. Before the first tear could slip out, she turned and stared through the grate again, blinking fast enough to force it back.

Becky was not as strong-willed as her sister. Her watery eyes began to leak tears that felt hot as they dripped onto her cold cheeks.

Becky had hung on to hope for a long time herself, but when Father never came back, she knew he must have died. He would never go away and leave them for so long. She knew that because things had been different after she and Reggie were nearly kidnapped in London.

Father had scolded them less harshly after that, and had spoken to them more softly. He occasionally touched her or Reggie on the shoulder or brushed at their black curls. It was almost as though a different person—a much nicer one—had come home with them from London in place of the stern, distant father they had previously known.

Before Father left for Scotland to take care of some business at one of the Blackthorne estates there, he had called them into his library. Becky had been certain the other father, the cold and angry one, would be waiting there for them.

She had been wrong.

Father had not been sitting behind his desk, he had been standing near the door. The instant Becky entered the room, he grasped her under her arms, swinging her playfully high above him. She shrieked once in surprise before he pulled her tight against him, so her nose settled against his throat. He hugged her for a long time, long enough for her to become aware of the strong, steady pulse in his throat and to notice he smelled of bayberry.

At last he set her down beside Reggie.

She watched as he reached for Reggie. He seemed more hesitant, less certain of himself. Reggie stood still while Father reached to pick her up, but she stared somberly—and with Reggie, as always, defiantly—into his eyes the entire time.

He did not lift her high, simply braced her against his hard chest with his arm around her hips. Reggie hesitated an instant, still staring Father in the eye, before she relented and laid her head on his shoulder. Father held her tight and rocked her back and forth. Reggie's arms slid around Father's neck and clasped him tight.

Becky wished she had thought to hug him back. It had all happened so fast, it had never occurred to her. Father had to pull Reggie's hands away before he could set her on her feet.

Becky had clasped Reggie's hand, because she could see Reggie wanted to run, to escape before she started crying. Reggie never let anyone see her crying. Her chin had wobbled before she clenched her jaw, but once the urge to escape was past, she stood firm.

Becky waited for Father to impart the admonition he never failed to give them before he traveled away from home.

"Be good," he said.

Only this time it was a request, not an order.

There was a wry smile on his face and rueful understanding in his voice. As though he expected their high spirits to lead them astray, but hoped they would stay safe until he returned.

Becky was not certain how she knew all that from two simple words and a look. But it was absolutely clear to her that he loved her and would miss her while he was gone.

That was her last memory of Father. If only he had disappeared before that miraculous change. She would not have missed the cold and stern father nearly as much as she missed the one who smelled of bayberry and hugged her tight, and said, "Be good" in a way that really meant "I love you."

Father was dead. He was not coming back. The house had been draped in black for an entire year. The period of mourning was ended today. It was time to start living again. All Becky and Reggie had left was Uncle Marcus, who had exiled himself to this rundown wing of Blackthorne Abbey.

One moonlit night, Becky had seen Uncle Marcus from her bedroom window wearing a black, hooded cloak, racing her father's stallion, Blanca, across the rolling hills that surrounded the Abbey. She had tried staying up late enough to confront him in the stable. But she always fell asleep in the stable before he came.

The next morning she would be in bed, with no idea how she got there. Reggie said the groom probably brought her to the Abbey door, where the butler called the governess to carry her to bed. But since neither of them had been awake, Becky was left to speculate on the possibility that if she could some night *pretend* to be asleep in the stable, she might discover it was Uncle Marcus, after all.

Sleeping in the stable. Of course. She should have thought of it sooner.

"I have an idea how we can get Uncle Marcus to come out and see us," she whispered to Reggie.

"I'm listening."

"We can talk while we're finding the way out," Becky said in a hushed voice, pushing herself up to her knees and then onto her feet. Reggie followed suit. They had left a candle a little ways into the passage, and Reggie picked it up to lead the way.

"Uncle Marcus did not look dicked in the nob to me," Reggie said when they were far enough into the passage that her voice would not carry back to him.

"Who told you he was crazy?" Becky demanded.

"The groom, and he should know. Ralph has a brother in Bedlam."

Becky's brow furrowed. "Bedlam?"

"A hospital for crazy people in Lambeth."

Becky felt out of curl, imagining Uncle Marcus in such a place. It was not as easy to dismiss the groom's words as she would have liked. "How does Ralph know that Uncle Marcus is . . . not well."

"Ralph said any man who was once as handsome as Uncle Marcus would go crazy if he were so horribly scarred. The servants claim to have heard strange, beastly howls coming from this wing of the Abbey at night. *AaaaooOOOOooo,*" Reggie howled in her best imitation of a strange beast.

"Stop that!" Becky wished it were not quite so dark. She took a step closer to her sister and the candlelight.

Reggie's voice softened to a conspiratorial whisper. "Ralph says the reason no one is allowed in this wing of the Abbey is because Uncle Marcus really has become a beast, and that he'd tear a living person limb from limb."

Becky scoffed, but her heart was thumping hard. "You saw for yourself Uncle Marcus is no beast."

But she remembered the fearsome look on his face. And the frightening sound of his voice in a rage. And glass shattering against the fireplace.

Nevertheless, she defended him. "I think Uncle Marcus is only sad and lonely."

"Then why does he refuse to let us see him? We could cheer him up!"

"What if we ran screaming from him instead? What if we looked at him as though he really were a beast? Can you honestly say you would let Uncle Marcus touch you with that awful, frozen hand?"

Reggie visibly shuddered.

"We have only seen his face in the dark and from a distance," Becky continued. "Imagine what it must look like up close, in the daylight. We both know Uncle Marcus is not a . . . a beast. The tears prove it. Animals cannot cry. It is only because of the scar on his face, and . . . and his hand that they call him that."

"It looks like a bird's claw to me," Reggie admitted. "His hand, I mean. Why do you suppose he always wears that leather glove?"

"You know the answer without asking. As scary as that clawed hand looks, think how mutilated his flesh must be. On second thought," Becky conceded reluctantly, "maybe Uncle Marcus should stay where he is. Maybe that is best for him."

Reggie's chin took on a mulish tilt. "But not for us. I miss Uncle Marcus. I refuse to settle for watching and whispering behind a grate. And if I have to scare away one more fusby-faced governess to get his attention, I may resort to something drastic."

If everything Reggie had done so far did not constitute "drastic" behavior, Becky was afraid to contemplate what antics her sister might employ to drive away the next unlucky governess. Granted, everything they had done so far was intended to pry Uncle Marcus out of hiding. But so far, none of it had worked.

"I have an idea how to get him to come out," Becky said.

"I am willing to try anything," Reggie said.

That was exactly what Becky was afraid of. She continued, "When Father died, Uncle Marcus became the Duke of Blackthorne. Now he must marry and produce an heir to carry on the title."

Reggie was silent for a moment. "So?"

"Don't you see?" Becky said. "All we have to do is find him a wife. Surely the right woman can pry him out of there."

"I suppose that would work," Reggie mused. "But where are we going to find someone willing to marry the Beast of Blackthorne?"

"I came up with the idea. You figure out how to make it work," Becky said.

They had reached the spot where they had entered the passageway, and Reggie released a latch that opened a doorway beside the fireplace in their bedroom. She pushed her way past the cobwebs, and blinked rapidly as bright sunlight hit her constricted pupils.

Becky brushed frantically at a web that had caught in the curls around her face. It stuck to her fingers even after she had clawed it from her hair. "Reggie, help! I can feel a spider crawling on me. I hate spiders!"

Reggie searched for the offending insect, helping Becky brush away the sticky web. "I don't see any spider."

"It must be there. I can feel it!"

"I tell you I cannot find any spider! It is only the web you are feeling." Reggie pulled the last of the sticky spiderwebs from Becky's hair and fingers. "There. It is all gone."

Becky stood still, waiting for the trembling to stop. She saw the disgusted look on Reggie's face and said, "I cannot help it. Spiders scare me." And had ever since she was six and a spider had crawled down her arm and onto her hand in the dark passageway.

Becky crossed to the canopied bed and let her weak knees buckle as she fell back onto it.

Reggie looked thoughtful. "You have given me an idea."

"I have?"

Reggie crawled on her knees across the bed to the other side and sat cross-legged beside her. "I know how to lure Uncle Marcus's future wife to Blackthorne Abbey."

"You have someone in mind already?" Becky asked, sitting up, astounded.

"Of course. She already knows Uncle Marcus. If

you will only think for a moment, you will come up with the name yourself."

"Eliza! But how can we get her to come here?" Becky asked.

"Uncle Marcus will surely advertise in the *Times* for another governess. We will simply make sure Miss Sheringham gets a copy of the *Times* with the advertisement circled, along with a note from us begging her to come and save us from Uncle Marcus."

"From Uncle Marcus?"

Reggie nodded, a mischievous smile on her face. "She will surely have heard rumors about the monster."

Becky's eyes went white around the rims. "Monster?"

"The Beast of Blackthorne. We will simply embellish upon them and make Uncle Marcus seem as fearsome as the rumors. Tell Eliza we fear for our very lives, that the Beast of Blackthorne scares us to death."

"Like spiders frighten me," Becky said with a laugh. "I see. It will work! I know it will. I mean, to get her here. But how are you going to get her together with Uncle Marcus?"

"We will worry about that when she arrives."

Chapter 13

"*I* WILL NOT DO IT!" ELIZA BALLED UP THE *TIMES* ADvertisement seeking a "qualified governess to attend Lady Regina Wharton and Lady Rebecca Wharton at Blackthorne Abbey in Kent," and pitched it into the fire.

Aunt Lavinia sat knitting in an overstuffed chair placed close enough to the fire to catch the additional heat as the newsprint briefly flared, before turning to ash.

"I despise Captain Wharton. With good reason," Eliza said. "I have no desire to seek employment from him."

"Captain Wharton is no more, my dear. Enter the Duke of Blackthorne. His Grace, or the duke, if you please."

"I am the last person *His Grace* would want in his home, caring for *His Grace's* children," Eliza said.

Aunt Lavinia's lips puckered as though she had just sucked on a lemon.

"Don't kick up a dust at me," Eliza chided her aunt. "They *are* his daughters. I do not doubt he seduced his brother's wife. After all, he thought nothing of seducing an innocent like me!"

"That is all in the past. You must move forward, my dear."

"I cannot do it!" Eliza insisted.

"Hummingbird!" Aunt Lavinia replied.

Eliza felt the urge to laugh at Aunt Lavinia's rendition of "Humbug!" but choked it back. "I tell you, I cannot! And it is *humbug*, not *hummingbird*."

Her aunt harrumped. The knitting needles clacked furiously. "You can work for him. And you must. Or we are lost."

Panic rose in Eliza's breast. She was being urged willy-nilly toward a situation fraught with danger. She paced a well-known path before her aunt's chair, holding Charlie's letter, which had accompanied the *Times* advertisement, clutched in her fist.

Thanks to the Countess of Denbigh, Eliza had been the recipient of each of the previous six *Times* advertisements for a governess placed during the past year by the newest Duke of Blackthorne. On each occasion Charlie had prompted Eliza to apply for the position of governess.

It had been easy, at first, to throw the advertisements—and Charlie's notes—away. She would do nothing to help His Grace. Blackthorne had not kept his promise. He had not watched over Julian. The Beau had come home alive. And Julian was dead.

Eliza had mourned Julian as though he were her husband, rather than merely her fiancé. She had draped the hunting box—and herself—in black. During her year of mourning, the scandal had returned to haunt her. Country folk hid their children's faces from her when she walked down the aisle at church. The gentry excluded her from their holiday celebrations.

The Quality gave her the cut direct. Even with her aunt's company, she had never felt so alone.

Charlie had insisted Eliza come to Denbigh Castle for a visit, but Eliza had not allowed herself that comfort. She did not deserve it. Because the first thing she had felt upon hearing of Julian's death had not been grief. It had been relief.

From the moment she had accepted Julian's proposal, Eliza had known it was a mistake. It was all so clear to her—after it was too late to change what she had done.

She had thought she loved Julian. She had been so certain she did! When she had her heart's desire in hand, when Julian had proposed to her, she had realized what she felt for him was not love. It was admiration. And amity. Regard. And respect.

That should have been enough for a good marriage. It would have been enough. If the Beau had not kissed her that last time.

Something had happened inside her, something she did not understand, could never have explained, but knew had been life-altering. He needed her. And God help her, she needed him. Somewhere inside her was a void she had not even known existed. When she looked into the Beau's blue eyes, when he held her tight in his embrace, when he gave her that final, devastating kiss . . . the void had been filled.

Eliza had grieved mightily over the past year. For the loss of her one true love. And for the loss of Major Sheringham.

She had been careful to hide her true feelings for the Beau from everyone. He was a confirmed bachelor. He had proved that by refusing to marry her, even though he had ruined her reputation. She had conceded the futility of loving such a man. But she could not seem to stop. It would be humiliating to have anyone find out what an addle-cove she was.

Eliza had accepted blame for her part in the kiss that had ruined her. She had flaunted the rules, not realizing—or to be perfectly honest, not caring—how catastrophic the consequences might be. But her sin was not nearly so great as his. The Beau had known full well what would happen to her if they were caught, and had selfishly, thoughtlessly, taken the risk.

She could not forgive him for that, or for abandoning her to her fate. But she still loved him. Would always love him. Eliza fought that weakness every day. It was why she had not responded to any of the advertisements for a governess at Blackthorne Abbey.

She did not trust herself near him.

Her reputation had been blackened so badly by scandal, there was nothing left to preserve. Eliza was afraid she would give in to the Beau's blandishments—she had no doubt he would tempt her—and become his mistress. *His whore.* She knew she would hate herself—and him—if she did.

Late this afternoon, Eliza had received the seventh *Times* advertisement. Charlie's accompanying note had been laced with capitals to emphasize her sentiments.

Dearest Eliza,

I heard Marcus Wharton called the Beast of Blackthorne in my drawing room last night. I understand his face is Horribly Scarred. He lives in the Dark, and No

One is allowed to see him. Imagine the plight of those Two Little Girls!

I am not asking you to Forgive the Beau. I doubt whether you would even see him, since he is playing Least in Sight. You must consider the Children. They need Someone like you to Love Them.

At least go see him. I have no doubt he would hire you Forthwith.

> *Affectionately,*
> *Charlie*

Eliza forced back the pity she felt for the scars that had turned the Beau into a beast. He had suffered a terrible calamity. But a great many men had not returned whole from Waterloo. And a great many more had not returned at all.

She forced herself to speak calmly to her aunt, but her voice vibrated with feeling. "I am sorry for the twins. But I cannot go to Blackthorne Abbey. I am not certain what I would do if I ever laid eyes on the Beau again. I would rather not find out. Believe me, Aunt Lavinia, anyone who applies for the position would make a better governess than I would."

"What about the correspondence you received from Lady Regina and Lady Rebecca?" her aunt challenged, knitting needles clacking noisily. "Are you planning to disregard it, as well?"

Eliza bit her lower lip. "I will simply have to tell the twins I cannot help them."

Her aunt stopped knitting and focused her gray eyes on Eliza. "Then you're a worse ninnypoophammer than I thought!"

"It's *ninny*. Or *ninnyhammer*. Or *nincompoop*," Eliza said.

"You know what I mean," Aunt Lavinia replied, bristling. "How can you refuse their plea? Those two little girls seem genuinely frightened of what their uncle might do to them in one of his rages. Their safety must be considered first in any decision you make."

"Surely there is someone else—"

"Rhubarb! Those helpless babes did not write to someone else. They wrote to *you*. Their uncle has apparently deserted them. Will you desert them as well?"

"I am not the person to remedy the situation. I have responsibilities here. And it is *Rubbish!*"

Her aunt harrumphed. "I can take care of myself. And there is no coin to take care of anything else. We cannot even afford to buy meat to—"

"I would rather starve than work for him!"

Aunt Lavinia made a disapproving sound. "You say that with your belly full from supper. Wait a few weeks and tell me that when hunger gnaws at your bones."

The vegetables Eliza had grown in her summer garden last year were nearly gone, and it would be months before a new crop could ripen. They had eaten meatless stew for a month.

Eliza looked around her. She and Aunt Lavinia were using less than half the space in the two-story hunting box, since that was all they could manage to heat. She remembered what it been like—was it only three years ago?—before her father had died. A cheery fire, sparkling windowpanes, the acrid smell of his favorite pipe tobacco, which she still caught a faint whiff of now and again.

When she was very little, her father had let her help him blend his tobacco, showing her exactly how much of each type of leaves to mix together. Sitting in his lap, smelling all the different smells, measuring, oh, so carefully. It was one of her fondest memories of him.

This had been a safe refuge when Julian left to fight Napoleon in Belgium. In this quiet, solitary place, she heard no scandalous gossip about herself and the Beau. It had become her sanctuary when news of Julian's death arrived a mere three weeks later.

And it had been her prison since Cousin Nigel had come nearly a year past with the spiteful announcement that he would no longer be providing the generous stipend Julian had insisted upon for her living expenses. Nigel had halved and halved again and yet again the amount of her quarterly allowance.

Eliza and her aunt were, of course, invited to return to Ravenwood at any time they wished. She knew Nigel hoped they would be starved or frozen out. He would welcome her return to Ravenwood and his lecherous advances.

She would die first. She would willingly starve or freeze or—Eliza glanced guiltily at Aunt Lavinia, huddled beneath a blanket and shawl before the small fire. It was all very well to make sacrifices herself. But it was unfair to force cold and starvation on her aunt.

She crossed and rearranged the woolen shawl over Aunt Lavinia's shoulders and the plaid blanket over her knees, then waved away the smoke coming from the green wood that was all she had to burn. The June day was surprisingly cold, and the warped, drafty windows stole what little heat there was.

She leaned over Aunt Lavinia's shoulder and put her cheek next to her aunt's cold flesh. Her throat was clogged with remorse. This was all her fault. She should never, never have let the Beau kiss her—or have kissed him back.

"I am so sorry, Aunt Lavinia," she whispered. "So very sorry for everything."

Aunt Lavinia laid down her knitting needles and reached up to press a hand against Eliza's tear-streaked cheek. Eliza came around the chair and sat at her aunt's feet on the worn Turkish carpet. She curled her cold toes beneath her and laid her cheek on her aunt's knee.

"Dry your tears, sweeting," Aunt Lavinia said, gently brushing Eliza's hair back from her face. "There is no help for it. The cupboard is empty, and there's no coal to burn. We cannot survive here another year. You must find a living."

"Can we not go into trade?"

Aunt Lavinia shook her head. "I am afraid you are far too notorious, my dear."

"If I am so notorious, what makes you think His Grace will hire me as a governess?"

"Because he has reached the point of desperation. Because you will convince him you can best serve his needs. And because the twins will plead your cause."

"You don't understand, Aunt Lavinia. There are reasons why I cannot go to him."

"But it is not to *him* you go, but to those two innocents who wrote to you, begging for your help. I do not believe you can refuse them, even though you bear such enmity toward their uncle."

"Their *father*," Eliza muttered.

"That is not at issue," her aunt reminded her. "I believe we must think first of the children's welfare. And of course, our own survival."

"I cannot face him," Eliza murmured.

"I do not believe you will have to," her aunt replied. "Lady Denbigh's letter confirms that Blackthorne is never at home to company, not even to the children."

"No wonder Reggie and Becky are so distraught," Eliza murmured, raising her head to stare into her aunt's sightless eyes. "How can he forsake his own daughters like that?"

"I would guess he is suffering as much as his nieces are," Aunt Lavinia said, making the correction again.

"He is a grown man. They are children. He has a duty—"

"Perhaps you are the one to remind him of it."

Eliza realized she would have no peace until she agreed to go. There was no denying she must find a source of income or return to Ravenwood.

"Very well," she said. "I will travel to the Abbey and apply for the job of governess. If His Grace hires me—which I cannot quite believe—I will insist that you be included in the package."

"I can return to Ravenwood," Aunt Lavinia protested.

"And be hidden away from sight like some—" Eliza bit back her anger. Her aunt was not a freak or a monster. She merely looked at the world with sightless eyes.

"Please, Aunt Lavinia. I need you with me. I will make whatever bargain with the devil I must. It cannot be worse than what we face here."

"Very well, my dear. We will both make the journey to Blackthorne Abbey."

Eliza arrived at the impressive double doors that graced the arched entrance to Blackthorne Abbey late the following night. She was by herself, having left her aunt at a nearby inn.

She and Aunt Lavinia had traveled to Kent in the mail coach, riding backward in the two least comfortable seats. She had relinquished her blacks at Aunt Lavinia's insistence and wore a lavender bombazine traveling dress, which was still enough to discourage conversation with the two middle-aged ladies in the seats opposite them.

Because Aunt Lavinia had been plagued with motion sickness for most of the trip, Eliza had settled her aunt at the Hundred Hill Inn in the small village of Comarty before she walked to Blackthorne Abbey, two miles farther down the road. Aunt Lavinia had urged her to wait until morning, but Eliza was adamant about seeing the duke as soon as possible.

"If he closes the door in my face, or refuses to hire me after an audience, I can suffer the blow to my pride without witnesses. We can leave for home in the morning with no one the wiser."

"And find some other way to resolve our dilemma?" her aunt asked. "Balderdish!"

They both knew there was no other viable resolution. Eliza needed this position.

"I know I must convince him I am the best candidate for the job," she said. "I would not be able to sleep a wink knowing I had to face His Grace first thing in the morning. I would rather see him tonight than meet him with red-rimmed eyes tomorrow. By the way, Balderdish was one of the children's former governesses. The word you want is *Balderdash!*"

Her aunt harrumphed. "Are you certain you will not mind walking in the dark?"

Eliza managed a laugh. "Don't worry. I'll take a lantern with me. I will be fine."

But Eliza had underestimated her fear of the dark. She had not been walking for long on the country road—all by herself—before she began to regret her impulsive decision and recant her brave words.

With the moon behind a cloud, the night was black as pitch, except for the small circle of light provided by the lantern she carried. She had endured one especially scary moment when a gust of wind had threatened to extinguish the light. But the flickering candle had survived the onslaught, and so had she.

Eliza did not know why she was so afraid of the dark. She only knew she was. The fear was worse indoors than out. Indoors she felt as though she could not breathe, as though she were buried alive. At least outside, she knew there was nothing to confine her. But the terror was there all the same.

Eliza was perplexed when she arrived at the Abbey to note that not a single light burned in any window she could see. The entire household must have retired for the night. Or lived on the backside of Blackthorne Abbey.

She stepped from the cobblestone drive onto the stone porch with the distinct feeling that something massive was hulking over her. It took her a few moments to realize it was the Abbey itself. She could feel the huge, stone edifice towering above her, even though she could not see beyond the wedge of light the lantern provided.

But maybe it was not the Abbey. What if someone . . . something . . . was out there?

Her heart began to race. She listened for some sound that would tell her whether danger lurked in the darkness. She heard nothing. No crickets. No rustling of leaves. No frogs. Not even a horse or a hound.

She knocked frantically on the immense wooden door for admittance, but soon realized it was so thick, no one could hear her. She searched for and found what she thought must be a door knocker that looked like it had been placed conveniently for a giant. For once, she was grateful for her height. The massive iron ring's echoing thumps sounded reassuring, but she wondered if anyone could hear them.

No one came to the door.

She shivered and knocked again. On the third try, an ancient butler, holding a dripping candle stuck in pewter, opened one half of the double door.

Wispy white hair crowned his head, and it was apparent he had pulled on his trousers over a nightshirt as old as he was. He did not invite her inside or even ask her name. His pale blue eyes had already dismissed her before he said, "His Grace ain't receivin'."

When he started to close the door, she stuck her foot in the way and said, "I have come to apply for the position of governess."

"It's been filled," he said.

Eliza stood frozen in stunned disbelief. The *Times* had been a week old when she received it from Lady Denbigh. Of course there would have been dozens of applicants by now. And the duke had chosen one of them.

Eliza realized she was disappointed. Which made no sense, because she had never wanted the job in the first place. Her second thought was concern for the twins. Would whatever stranger the duke had hired be able to give them the love they needed? Her third thought—was interrupted by the butler.

"It's been filled by Miss Elizabeth Sheringham," he said, in what she finally recognized as a Scottish burr. "Lady Rebecca told me His Grace had hired the woman through his solicitor in London. And Lady Regina said Miss Sheringham's the only one to be admitted, no matter how many says they're here for the job. If ye ain't her, ye ain't welcome."

How could the position possibly be hers? Eliza wondered. She had not even interviewed with the duke!

Then it dawned on her what the old man had said. *Lady Rebecca told me His Grace had hired the woman . . . And Lady Regina said Miss Sheringham's the only one to be admitted.* Why those two little imps! They had been turning away applicants for a week, waiting for her arrival!

"I am Miss Sheringham!" Eliza blurted.

"Why didn't ye say so?" the butler grumbled. "Come in. Come in." He stuck his head outside and asked, "Where's yer baggage, lass?"

"I left it in Comarty, at the Hundred Hill Inn."

"I'll send a footman for it tomorrow," the butler promised. "I am Fenwick," he announced.

"I'm glad to meet you, Fenwick."

Fenwick scratched his balding head. "I ain't sure

what to do with ye, miss, seein' as how ye've arrived so late and all. I dunno where the duke wants ye to stay."

"Are the children still awake?"

The butler's lips curved indulgently. "I expect they are. Them two rarely keeps to a schedule."

"Can you tell me where to find them?"

"Up the stairs, right down the hall, last room on the left. It's Lady Regina's room, but ye'll find 'em both there. They stay together, and that's a fact. Even more since they lost their da."

"Thank you, Fenwick. I will find my way."

Eliza was grateful for the lantern she had brought, since none of the candles along the stairs or in the upstairs hall were lit. Either the new duke was a frugal man, or he liked it dark. Knowing the Beau's reputation, she suspected the latter.

Eliza was relieved to see a light showing under the last door on the left at the end of the hall. She stood for a moment, listening to muffled voices before she knocked.

"Who is there?"

"Miss Sheringham."

She heard the twins scrambling from the bed, heard their bare feet pounding on the carpet, before the door opened to reveal a room lit with so many candles that it was almost as bright as day. They wore long-sleeved white nightdresses tied with pink silk ribbons at the throat.

She identified Reggie immediately. Her childish attempt at braids had nearly fallen out of her hair, which lay tumbled about her shoulders. The silk ribbon had come untied and frayed on one side into something resembling fringe.

"I told you she would come," Reggie said, throwing her sister a satisfied smirk.

"What took you so long?" Becky asked. "We were worried that someone would *demand* to speak to Uncle Marcus, and he would find out what we were doing."

Eliza set her lantern on the dry sink and slipped off the woolen shawl she had borrowed from Aunt Lavinia, draping it over the foot of the bed before she leaned down and held out her arms to them.

The twins hesitated only an instant before they tumbled toward her. Eliza was hard-pressed to stay upright, and in fact dropped down onto one knee. Their arms clung to her neck, and they pressed their cheeks hard against hers. Her heart went out to them. She should have come sooner. She should not have let her animosity toward *him* keep her away.

"Now," she said, leaning back so she could see their faces. "Explain to me why you felt it necessary to resort to such tomfoolery."

"We don't really need a governess," Reggie said.

Eliza raised a disbelieving brow.

"Reggie is right," Becky said. "What we really need is someone to bring Uncle Marcus out of the doldrums."

"That is why we picked you," Reggie said. "Uncle Marcus told us how much he likes you."

"And we could see for ourselves how much you like him," Becky added.

Eliza flushed. "I am sorry you brought me here under such a misapprehension."

"Misap— What?" Reggie asked.

Eliza gently tugged their hands from behind her neck and stood. "Your . . . uncle and I have had a falling out since our meeting last year."

"Uncle Marcus never said anything to us about it," Reggie said.

"It happened just before Waterloo," Eliza said. "Am I correct that you have not spoken much to him since?"

The twins nodded glumly.

"Come," Eliza said. "Your feet must be getting cold. Up onto the bed."

Reggie and Becky climbed the rails at the foot of the bed like a ladder and scooted to the center of what had to be at least four feather mattresses stacked one upon the other. Eliza perched at the head of the bed with her muddy half boots hanging over the side.

"I want to hear everything you have been doing," Eliza said.

"You cannot imagine what the past year has been like!" Reggie said.

"Describe it for me," Eliza said.

"Horrible!" Becky said. "We had to get rid of *six* governesses!"

"I know," Eliza said with a grin. "I have seen the advertisements for each and every one."

Reggie frowned. "Then why did you not come sooner? You must have realized we were in desperate trouble."

"I thought you cared for us," Becky said, a worried V between her brows.

Eliza smoothed the V with her thumb. "I do," she said in a soft voice. "Very much. But I was in mourn-

ing. My fiancé, Major Sheringham, was killed at Waterloo."

"We were in mourning, too," Reggie said. "Because
Father disappeared—"

Becky pinched her arm.

"Ow!" Reggie glared at her twin, but amended,
"Because Father *drowned at sea*. That did not stop us
from doing what had to be done."

"Were all those governesses really so terrible?"
Eliza asked.

"They never listened to us," Becky said. "And they
punished us for the smallest mistake."

"Which means," Reggie said disgustedly, "for everything we did."

"Miss Tolemeister gave Reggie welts!"

"Dear God. Why?" Eliza asked, her stomach rolling.

"Because I would not cry when she applied the
rod," Reggie said, her eyes lit with defiance.

"Welts where?" Eliza asked.

Instead of putting out her hands, as Eliza had expected, Reggie turned and raised the back of her
gown.

Eliza traced three distinct, silvery lines where the
rod must have broken the skin. Her hands trembled as
she lowered the gown. "Why didn't you tell your uncle about this?" she demanded angrily.

"It would not have done any good," Reggie said.

"Uncle Marcus told Griggs that the governess was
to have as much authority as she needed," Becky said.
"We put up with each one as long as we could."

"And then what?" Eliza asked.

"We'd do something so dreadful to her, she was glad to leave!"

"I put spiders in Miss Tolemeister's shoes," Reggie said with grim satisfaction. "And a snake in her bed."

"Oh, dear," Eliza said. "Things have been much worse than I could ever have imagined."

"You will stay, won't you?" Becky said.

"I am not sure your . . . uncle will allow me to stay."

"Ask him. I am sure he will," Reggie said confidently.

"When do you propose I solicit this interview?" Eliza said.

"Right now," Becky replied. "He mostly sleeps in the daytime and stays up all night."

"Why in heaven's name would he do that?"

"He does not want anyone to see his face," Becky said. "He was wounded, you know, at Waterloo."

"I heard as much," Eliza said. But she began to wonder exactly what kind of beast the Beau had become.

"Uncle Marcus roams the east wing of the Abbey at night dressed all in black. The servants won't go near the place," Reggie said.

"I must confess, I am a little frightened to go there myself," Eliza said.

"Fenwick can direct you to the east wing," Becky said. "Once you are there, you will have to convince Griggs to let you see Uncle Marcus."

"Have you been to see your uncle?" Eliza asked.

"We spied at him through a secret opening in the wall," Reggie admitted. "But he did not know we were there."

"We saw him cry," Becky said, her voice achingly soft.

Spying? A secret opening in the wall? The Beau crying? Eliza did not know where to start asking questions, she had so many.

"You must make Uncle Marcus let you stay," Reggie said. "We don't know where else to turn."

Eliza edged herself off the bed, pulled down the covers, and said, "Slip under here and let me tuck you in."

The twins quickly complied, as agile as monkeys, and chattering just as fast. Eliza arranged the covers under their arms and tucked them in on either side, making a snug cocoon. She gave each of the twins a hug and a kiss on the forehead and received a hug and a smacking kiss on the cheek from each in return.

"Does the fire need more coal?" she asked, glancing at the bucket of coal and scoop set nearby.

"The maid has already banked it for the night," Reggie replied.

Eliza walked around the room, methodically blowing out what had to be two dozen expensive wax candles in candelabra set on the dressing table, the dry sink, a chest of drawers, an end table, a writing table, a toy chest, and a clothes press. She was careful not to extinguish her own lantern.

At last she reached the side of the large bed, where one last candle lent a glow to two identical cherubic faces.

"Have you said your prayers?" Eliza asked.

"Not tonight," Reggie said.

"Not for a while," Becky admitted.

"Close your eyes," Eliza instructed, "and fold your hands."

Reggie squeezed her eyes closed and laced her fingers tightly together. Becky's eyelashes lay like coal crescents on her cheeks, and her hands were pressed evenly together as though she were praying in church.

"Now I lay me down to sleep," Eliza began. The twins listened intently, waiting for whatever came next. "Say it after me," she coaxed.

"Now I lay me down to sleep," the twins repeated.

"I pray the Lord my soul to keep."

"I pray the Lord my soul to keep."

"If I should die before I wake."

Becky popped upright, her blue eyes wide with alarm. "I don't feel the least bit sick. Surely there is no chance I could die before I wake!"

Eliza slipped her arm around Becky and reached over to tug at one of Reggie's uneven braids. "You have not heard the last verse," she chided. "Say this one first."

Warily, the twins repeated, *"If I should die before I wake."*

"I pray the Lord my soul to take."

"I pray the Lord my soul to take."

"I see," Reggie said, turning to share her revelation with Becky. "It is like planning for the worst and hoping for the best!"

"Exactly," Eliza said. "None of us knows what the future holds for us, so we ask for God's protection."

"Can God save us from goblins?" Becky asked, wide-eyed.

"Why do you ask?" Eliza said.

"I think I see one in the hall!"

Chapter 14

$\mathcal{M}$ARCUS WAS SURPRISED TO FIND THE DOOR TO the twins' room open and a stream of light spilling out. It had been his habit during the past year to look in on them after they—and the rest of the household—were asleep. Usually by now their room was dark and still.

Though he had relinquished all contact with them in full daylight, Marcus could not give up seeing the girls entirely. Yet neither could he bear having Reggie and Becky stare at him with the horror he had seen on their faces when they first glimpsed his wounded face and clawlike hand.

He was a monster from a nightmare. And monsters confined themselves to roaming at night.

Marcus edged along the wall toward the doorway, making sure the hood of his black cloak was pulled forward enough to keep his face in shadow. He had ordered all the lamps in the Abbey, including those on the stairs and in the upstairs hall, to be extinguished each evening. In the dark, wearing a hooded black cloak, he was virtually invisible.

He listened intently outside the twins' doorway and thought he heard Miss Sheringham's husky voice. His lips curved in a bitter smile. He had heard her low, gravelly voice often over the past year. In his mind.

"It was not there, Captain. I looked, but it was not there."

He had known what she was saying. Julian was not the one she loved. Or the one who loved her back. Yet he had turned his back on her and walked away.

"It was not there. It was not there. It was not there."

Sometimes, the remembered anguish in her voice seemed so real he would swear she was in the room with him. In the first months after his return from Waterloo, the pain from his wound, anxiety over the disappearance of his brother, and grief for the death of his best friend, combined to steal his rest. During those solitary, sleepless hours, he had prowled through the darkened Abbey looking for Miss Sheringham, like a hunter seeking prey.

He had never found her.

She was far from Blackthorne Abbey, living with an elderly relation at her father's hunting box. Thank God Julian had arranged for her to have an allowance from the Earl of Ravenwood. Otherwise, Marcus shuddered to think how Miss Sheringham might have fared.

Marcus had done a great deal of thinking over the months he had spent in seclusion, mostly about what he could have done differently. Like confessing the truth to Alastair and making peace between them. Like earning Julian's respect by acting honorably toward Miss Sheringham. Like being honest with himself . . . and admitting he had fallen in love with her.

He would never forget the last, desolate look Miss

Sheringham had given him, her hazel eyes misted with tears, her lips—swollen and cut—pressed tightly together to still her quivering chin. She had not begged him to reconsider. She had merely laid her heart bare to him.

The decision had been entirely his. And he had made the wrong choice.

He regretted the fact Miss Sheringham would likely remain a spinster. He regretted the fact she would likely never have children of her own. He was not the same man he had been when last he saw her. Given a second chance . . .

But there were no second chances for him. Even if Miss Sheringham could find it in her heart to forgive him, she would never tie herself in marriage to the Beast of Blackthorne. Outside of offering marriage, there was nothing he could do to right the wrong he had committed against her.

"Now I lay me down to sleep."

It was her voice again, in his head, saying a childhood prayer. He listened for the rest of it, but instead, heard the twins repeat the same line.

Her voice again. And theirs. Hers. And theirs.

Marcus stiffened. This voice—her voice—sounded real. Impossible as it seemed, Miss Sheringham was in his home, in the same room with Reggie and Becky, saying a bedtime prayer.

He did not quite trust his mind to be telling him the truth. He would believe his eyes. If he could see her, he would concede she was really there.

He took a step closer. He only intended to take a quick glance inside the room to confirm her presence, but when his eyes beheld her profile—he had forgotten how distinctive her features were—he could not tear himself away.

Marcus realized he had been discovered when Becky pointed in his direction. He stepped out of the light and edged back down the hall several steps, until he was invisible in the darkness once again.

He waited, hoping Miss Sheringham would come to the door. He caught his breath as she took one step into the hall holding a lantern aloft that cast a glow on her face.

He could not get his fill of looking at her. Her face seemed narrower, her body thinner than he remembered. He saw one explanation for her apparent lack of appetite. She was wearing lavender, which meant she had just come out of mourning. She must have grieved deeply for Julian.

Julian's death was another wrong for which Marcus did not believe Miss Sheringham could forgive him. Her fiancé—her only hope for a return to respectability—had perished at Waterloo. Marcus had not brought his friend home safely to her, as he had promised.

"I don't see anyone," Miss Sheringham said, extending the lantern the length of her arm. "Or anything," she added.

Her gravelly voice raised the hair on his arms.

She took one step farther down the hall and looked right at him. "Is someone there?"

Marcus was well hidden in the dark but held his breath anyway.

She quickly stepped back inside the bedroom. "Whatever it was is gone now," he heard her say to the twins. "Now it is time for you to go to sleep, and for me to find Griggs and arrange to see the duke."

She was coming to see him? Now?

He did not catch the rest of what she said to the twins. He was too busy contemplating whether he should allow her an audience. He wanted to see more of her, but he did not want her to see him. Perhaps there was a way to manage it.

The light coming through the twins' doorway dimmed, and he realized she must have extinguished whatever candles were left burning in the children's room.

Moments later, she reappeared holding the lantern. It provided a yellow glow that lit her face above and a small area at her feet. She had added a fringed shawl around her shoulders. It must not have been enough to keep her warm, because the instant she closed the children's door behind her, she shivered.

The courage it took to walk down that darkened hallway was visible on her face. He stayed a few steps beyond her reach, careful not to let the circle of light from the lantern touch him. Several times she stopped and looked directly at him.

Once she even whispered, "Is someone there?"

When he did not answer, her voice sharpened. "I do not find this the least bit funny!" And then, coaxing, "Come into the light, please, and show yourself."

He remained hidden in the darkness, knowing that if he appeared like a wraith, she would likely run screaming from him.

When she started to take a wrong turn at the bottom of the stairs, he whispered, "This way."

She stood frozen. Her eyes rounded with fright,

and for a moment he thought she would run for the front door. He saw her jaw firm and watched as she headed stalwartly in his direction.

No mistake. Miss Sheringham was pluck to the bone.

Marcus had not realized how decrepit the entrance to the east wing had become until he saw it through Miss Sheringham's apprehensive eyes. The carpet on the floor was ragged with moth holes, and cobwebs hung from the ceilings. Doors creaked on unoiled hinges as she forced them open and headed farther into the Stygian gloom.

When she reached the chapel, he heard an audible sigh of relief. "I know you cannot harm me in this Holy place," she murmured, holding the lantern high enough to make out an altar with a stone crucifix carved into the wall behind it and a wooden *prie-dieu*.

She eased herself onto a bench facing the altar, and he used her respite to slip into Griggs's room and wake him.

"Miss Sheringham is here seeking an interview with the duke," he said to the groggy man. "You will find her in the chapel. Bring her to me in the drawing room."

"In the middle of the night?" Griggs asked, yawning and scratching his belly.

"Right now," Marcus said. "Go quickly. I am afraid her courage may desert her. I do not wish her to escape."

Marcus was at the door when he turned back to say, "Griggs. Send her in alone. And do not allow her to bring a light."

"How's she supposed to see where she's goin'?" Griggs retorted. "It's black as Hades in there."

"A fire is burning in the grate. That will be enough."

Marcus left Griggs and hurried back to the chapel, hoping Miss Sheringham had not fled.

She was sitting precisely where he had left her. It was clear she had no idea where to go from there. At least four doors opened in different directions.

"Now where?" she demanded aloud, as though she expected to be given further direction.

Marcus obliged her. "Wait here," he whispered. "Someone will come for you."

She whirled, startled. The lantern tipped and almost fell. She gave a cry of alarm and grabbed for it, giving him time to escape.

He made his way to the drawing room and moved one of the two wingback chairs far enough from the fireplace that he was certain no firelight could reach his face. On the other hand, if Miss Sheringham stood directly in front of him, her face would be fully illuminated.

Marcus sat in the chair and crossed his booted feet casually. He kept the hood up to prevent any chance of Miss Sheringham seeing his scarred face. He settled his clawlike hand in his lap, where it would be hidden, and grasped the arm of the chair with the other.

He heard Griggs's gruff voice as the door opened, and a *thunk* as the door closed again. His heart raced. She was here. She had come to him. But for what reason?

Marcus could think of only one reason that mattered. Was she ready to forgive him? Was she willing at least to be his friend?

"I can barely see," she said, her back against the closed door. "Is there another light?"

"There is firelight," he answered.

"If I trip over something, you will have to come and pick me up," she warned. "And I am no light burden."

He smiled. It felt strange. He could not remember smiling with humor anytime in the past year.

Marcus heard her footsteps on the stone floor and then muffled steps as she reached a no-longer-vivid Turkish carpet brought home from the Crusades. "Where are you?" she asked, peering into the gloom.

"Here."

When she turned in his direction, Marcus saw that her lower lip was clamped in her teeth. Her hands grasped the ends of the woolen shawl and wrapped it tightly around her. She took two nervous steps closer—enough to put her fully in the firelight—before he said, "That is close enough."

"Why do you keep it so dark?" she asked.

"It is my solace, Miss Sheringham."

"I suppose it must be, if your face is as badly scarred as rumor says. But I have business to discuss. I would like to do it face to face."

"I can see you quite well."

"But I cannot see you!"

He remained silent following her outburst. She must know why he liked it dark. He should not have to speak the words. He watched her bosom rise and fall as she took a deep breath and let it out.

His body stirred, surprising him. He had thought

. . . But apparently not. He felt himself smiling again.

Impatient to know why she had come, he asked, "Why are you here, Miss Sheringham?"

"I've come to apply for the position of governess to Lady Regina and Lady Rebecca."

He was glad she could not see his face. His jaw had fallen open like a hee-hawing jackass. "Governess?" he managed to say.

"I saw the advertisement in the *Times*. The seventh this year, I believe, Your Grace."

He frowned. *Your Grace.* He wanted to be the captain again. But those days were gone forever.

"Why would you want to spend your days with two such incorrigible scamps?" he demanded.

"They are not incorrigible! They are merely seeking the love and attention you do not give them," she retorted. "Someone must care for them. I am willing to take on that responsibility."

"I am fully capable of handling my responsibilities without your help," he snapped. How dare the chit suggest he was not taking proper care of Reggie and Becky!

"Did you know the six previous governesses felt free to punish the girls severely for the least infraction? That one raised welts on Reggie's back because she refused to cry when the rod was applied?"

"Who told you such a thing!" he roared, lurching from his chair.

"The twins."

Marcus was appalled. He had not imagined Reggie and Becky were being mistreated. They had said nothing to him.

How could they? You refused to see them.

Clearly he needed to choose a better governess this time, one who would not be stern or cruel with the girls when they attacked life with a bit too much enthusiasm. One who would never, ever leave welts. Someone who would give them the hugs and kisses he no longer could. Someone like Miss Sheringham.

Only, he did not think he could bear to have her so very close and not touch her, not taste her, not want her. And she would never have him. Not as he was.

Miss Sheringham stood her ground as he took a step closer to her. He saw her frustration when the hood kept his face in shadow. When her eyes finally focused on his clawlike hand, she shuddered with revulsion.

He should not have been angry at her reaction, but he was. It confirmed all his fears. She was no different from anyone else. She feared his mutilated body.

"Will you dare to touch the Beast of Blackthorne, Miss Sheringham?" He slowly extended his wounded hand toward her, palm up.

Her distressed golden eyes were focused on the spot where his face should have been. He watched her struggle to conceal her panic, as his black-gloved fingers appeared under her nose like fierce, deadly talons.

"It is only a crippled hand, Your Grace," she said breathlessly. "What is there to fear?"

To his surprise, she slowly extended her hand toward his. She had barely touched his black-gloved fingertips with hers when he abruptly withdrew.

252

His sudden move frightened her, and she put up her hands to ward off an attack. By the time she realized she was safe, and lowered her hands in mortification, he had retreated behind the wingback chair.

He was glad for the distance. His heart was pounding, and a cold, clammy sweat dotted his brow. He could not quite believe what she had almost done. What he had almost allowed her to do. His gloved fingers still tingled from her touch.

"You are brave to the point of recklessness, Miss Sheringham, I will say that for you."

"You frightened me on purpose!" she accused. "I suppose that was you whispering in the hall, as well."

He nodded.

"I don't know why I thought this could work," she said. "You are the same care-for-nobody you always were! I would not have come here at all if . . ."

She clamped her lips tight.

So. Nothing had been forgiven. Or was likely to be. Nevertheless, he wanted to hear the rest of what she had to say. "What provoked you to confront the Beast, Miss Sheringham?"

"I need the stipend I would earn as governess," she blurted. "To support myself and my aunt."

His eyes narrowed. "Are you saying you are destitute, Miss Sheringham?"

"Poor as a church mouse," she replied, chin outthrust, daring him to offer insult.

He took the dare. "You must have expensive tastes. I know for a fact Major Sheringham arranged a generous allowance through his brother—"

"Certainly he did!" she interrupted angrily. "But Cousin Nigel felt no compunction to keep a promise made to a dead man. My aunt and I can no longer live on his meager charity. I must find a living.

"I thought I could do some good as governess for the twins. I thought you and I would be able to deal with each other civilly, despite . . . everything. But I see I was wrong," she finished bitterly. "I will not trouble you further, Your Grace."

She had pivoted to leave when he said, "Perhaps we can contrive an arrangement that will meet both our needs."

She turned back to him cautiously. "What kind of arrangement?" Her face paled as she thought of one obvious possibility. "You need not offer *carte blanche*, Your Grace. I will not accept it."

"I have no desire to make you my mistress, Miss Sheringham."

He watched the flush race up her slender throat and realized she believed he no longer desired her. Foolish woman.

"Will you hire me as governess, after all?" she asked, her hands laced tightly before her.

"How badly do you want the job, Miss Sheringham?"

Her eyes narrowed. "What is your price?" she asked baldly. "What do you want?"

"Obviously the children's situation must be remedied. I need someone to care for them who will not leave at the first sign of trouble. In the event my brother does not return from the dead, I need an heir. So what I want, Miss Sheringham, is a wife."

"You must know I despise you," she whispered. "You must know I could never agree to marry you."

"Nevertheless, Miss Sheringham, my price is marriage."

He saw from the way her lips had flattened in determination that she intended to refuse him.

"There are benefits to such an arrangement you may not have contemplated," he said.

"Becoming the wife of the Beast of Blackthorne? Becoming a prisoner within these stone walls? I have considered both and desire neither!"

"Taking my name mends your reputation," he said in a steely voice. "And an heir for me means a child for you!"

He saw both reasons appealed to her.

"You must also realize that as my wife, you would never want for anything. I promise my purse would be open to you."

"Promises can be broken."

"I will have my solicitor draw up papers that guarantee you an income," he said cynically. "Will that satisfy you?"

"Will you let me see your face?"

"No." The curt response had come from somewhere deep inside him. "There is no reason for it," he said more calmly.

"If I were your wife, I would expect to discuss matters face to face with you."

"It is a marriage of convenience, my dear. I do not need you except at night. Any questions you have in the daytime can be asked through Griggs."

His words sounded brutal even to his own ears. *Carte blanche* would have been less humiliating than what he was offering.

"I must decline your kind offer," she said, her gravelly voice rasping over his skin.

"I will be waiting in the chapel after the sun goes down tomorrow with a special license and a vicar to marry us. You have until then to change your mind."

"I will not change my mind," she said, her eyes bleak and brimming with tears. "Goodbye, Your Grace. Please tell the twins I am sorry. I—"

She pressed a fist to her mouth to keep a sob from escaping, shot him one last angry, defiant—and desolate—look, and ran from the room.

Marcus slumped into the chair, extended his feet toward the fire, and let his head fall back against the cushion.

He was exhausted. He should try to sleep.

But he knew he would not. Not before tomorrow night. Not before he knew for sure whether she was gone forever from his life.

Julian, I wish you were here. I need a friend right now.

He wondered if Miss Sheringham would have felt any differently toward him if he had explained how Julian had died. Julian's revelations would only have hurt her. And what had happened afterward was too gruesome, too macabre, to be repeated in a young lady's presence. Yet over the past year, he had explained everything to the imaginary Miss Sheringham, the one who lived in his head.

When he closed his eyes to shut out the memories that haunted him, a picture of Julian's angry face appeared behind his eyelids.

"I will not fight beside a coward," Julian had said, spurring his mount to put distance between them.

"Coward?" Marcus jeered, spurring his horse to

keep up with his friend as they galloped toward the oncoming horde of enemy soldiers.

"What else do you call someone who runs from trouble," Julian accused.

They had to shout to be heard over the thunder of a hundred charging horses. "You did not have to propose to her yourself," Marcus countered.

"You left me no choice," Julian said. "I only hope my fiancée will understand why I must marry another woman. There was no time to speak with her before I left. Likely she will break the engagement herself when she hears the gossip."

"You promised marriage to Miss Sheringham when you were bound to another lady?" Marcus reined his horse around a rock in his path and angled back to Julian's side.

"It was a secret engagement," Julian snapped back. "Her father forbids the marriage."

"How could you—"

"I did what you made necessary," Julian interrupted harshly. "More lives will be ruined than you guessed, Marcus. I hope you are happy with your freedom!"

Marcus was nettled that Julian had not trusted him enough to share his secret. And appalled at the havoc he had wrought by refusing to marry Miss Sheringham.

The order came to draw sabers. When Julian had his saber in hand he turned to Marcus one last time and shouted, "I have changed my mind, Marcus. I hope you survive the battle, so I may have the pleasure of killing you myself."

Julian spurred his mount across the field, leaving Marcus in his dust.

Marcus should have followed after him. He had made a promise to Miss Sheringham to guard Julian with his life. But he was furious at Julian's last verbal stab. Why should he protect a man who intended to kill him?

By the time he realized the danger of hesitation, he was already engaged in combat and unable to breach the distance between himself and Julian on the battlefield. Nevertheless, Marcus tried to keep watch over his friend. He managed to call a warning when a lancer nearly ran Julian through. Julian flashed a thankful grin, before his face sobered with the realization that they were no longer friends.

Marcus was distracted by the sight of Julian engaging two swordsmen at once, so he never saw the slashing blow that flayed half of his face to the bone. He did not remember feeling any pain, only the annoyance of blood seeping into his left eye and clouding his vision. The Frenchman was an excellent fencer, and it took a great deal of concentration—and luck—for Marcus to run him through.

By the time Marcus had won free, one of the two French cavalrymen attacking Julian had maneuvered himself to Julian's left side and was raising his sword to strike a mortal blow. Marcus shouted a frantic warning to Julian, who ducked, keeping his head in place. But the falling sword cleaved Julian's left leg in two.

Marcus would never forget the look of shock and surprise on Julian's face when the stump began to spurt blood. Julian quickly lost his balance and tumbled from his horse, one more body among the dead and wounded that littered the battlefield.

Marcus spurred his horse, slashing through anyone who got in his way, until he reached the spot where he thought Julian had fallen. He knew his friend would bleed to death if he did not get aid quickly.

The thick smoke from the constant firing of cannons lifted for an instant, and Marcus saw the battle lines had moved, leaving him without an enemy to fight. Nothing lay before him but the dead and dying.

He dismounted and turned over bodies, searching desperately for Julian. He was sick with what he found. Blood and brains and intestines. Bodies with no legs. No arms. No limbs at all.

Tears ran down his face. He blamed them on the smoke that burned his eyes and hoarsened his voice. It shifted like fog, making it impossible to see what lay on the ground in front of him. He stumbled over bodies, knelt to see their faces, then rose and walked on.

Marcus helped the wounded when he could and tore himself from the grasping hands of dying men who begged him to kill them and end their misery.

So many lay dead, so many more cried out in agony from their wounds, and all the while, the battle raged on. The cacophony of sound drowned out Marcus's shouts. "Julian! Where are you! Julian! Answer me!"

He could not find him.

A cannonball—apparently falling far short of its target—exploded right in front of him. His horse caught most of the shrapnel, saving Marcus's life, but his left hand, which had been holding the reins, had been ripped to shreds. Marcus knew the surgeons would likely cut it off, so he was in no hurry to seek a hospital, even though the wound was bleeding badly.

Life without his hand. He could not imagine it.

When the smoke cleared, he saw there was not much left in the cannon crater to identify. Nevertheless, he continued his search for Julian . . . or his remains.

Marcus did not remember anything after that. He had woken up lying on the grass, with only the sky above him, terribly thirsty and in terrible pain. One eye was covered completely by bandages, but he searched his surroundings with the other. Griggs sat beside him on the ground, his back against the wall of some peasant's cottage.

"Where are we?"

"Field hospital. I found you and brought you here."

Griggs's upper body was swathed in a bloody bandage. His right arm was missing. "Should've stayed here with you. Lost this later," he said, gesturing toward the missing arm.

Then Marcus remembered. His hand. He lifted his left hand and felt a searing pain. All he could see through his one good eye was a tight ball of bloody bandages. "They cut it off," he grated past his thirst-swollen throat.

"No, Captain. I wouldn't let 'em." He held a canteen to Marcus's lips, and Marcus swallowed as much as he could.

"Hand won't be much use to you," Griggs explained. "But it's there. Figured if the choice was mine, I'd want to keep it. In my case, there was no arm left for the surgeons to saw off. Frenchie got it with a saber."

"I'm glad you made it, Griggs." Marcus realized the cannon had stopped. "Is the battle over?"

"Aye, Captain."

"Did we win?"

"If you can call it that," Griggs said sourly. "Never saw so many dead. Never saw so much human slaughter."

"Have you heard from Major Sheringham? Or anything about him?"

"He's missin', Captain."

Marcus heaved out a breath of air. He felt a tear trickle down his cheek. He closed his unbandaged eye and said, "I should have offered for Miss Sheringham when I had the chance, Griggs."

"Aye, Captain. That you should."

Marcus opened his eyes and found himself in the Abbey. There was no blue sky overhead, no sunlight warming him. The drawing room was dark. Nothing remained of the fire but a few ash-covered coals.

Suddenly the fire irons rattled, and the fire leaped to life. "Is that you, Griggs?"

"Aye, Your Grace."

"What time is it."

"Midnight, I'd say. Figured you might need some coal on the fire."

It made a good excuse for Griggs to check on him. Sometimes, when he drank too much, Griggs would help him to bed.

"I have some business I need you to take care of tonight."

"Something to do with Miss Sheringham?" Griggs guessed.

Marcus nodded. "I want you to ride to London and see my solicitor. Have him arrange for a special license and a vicar to perform a marriage. I need them both in the chapel of Blackthorne Abbey by sundown tomorrow."

Griggs whistled long and low. "She said yes?"

"Not yet, Griggs. I have given Miss Sheringham some additional time to consider my offer. I will have my answer at sundown tomorrow."

Chapter 15

ELIZA CREPT ON TIPTOE INTO THE ROOM SHE WAS sharing with her aunt at the Hundred Hill Inn. She did not want to wake Aunt Lavinia, because she knew there would be questions—for which she did not yet have answers.

"Have you become the next governess at Blackthorne Abbey?"

Eliza exhaled gustily. "Why are you still awake?"

"I could not sleep with you roaming about the countryside in the dark," Aunt Lavinia grumbled. She rearranged the pillows behind her, so she was sitting up comfortably. "Well, girl? What did the duke say?"

Eliza was still breathing hard, because she had run almost the whole way back. She had spent the entire two miles trying to control her rage—unsuccessfully. Now it all poured out. "I can be the next governess," she snarled. "If I marry the Beast of Blackthorne."

"By Jericho! He did it! The Beau proposed!"

"*By Jove, Jove, Jove!*" Eliza snapped back. "And *the Beau* did not propose, it was *the Beast of Blackthorne!*"

"Stop pacing and sit down," her aunt said. "You are making me dizzy."

Eliza dropped onto the narrow servant's cot that had been set up for her next to the four-poster bed her aunt was settled in. But it was too low to the floor and uncomfortable for sitting. She shoved herself back onto her feet, crossed to the foot of the four-poster, and wrapped her arms around one of the corner posts to anchor her in place.

"I would like to hear the whole of it," her aunt said. "If you please."

"He is a brute, a bully, a—a—beast!" Eliza huffed furiously.

"From the beginning," her aunt cajoled. "Come, tell Aunt Lavinia all about it."

It was too comforting an invitation to refuse. Eliza crawled across the bedcovers and laid her head on her aunt's breast, welcoming Aunt Lavinia's consoling arms around her.

"Things are in a dreadful state at the Abbey," she said. "The children have been living in deplorable circumstances. Reggie has scars on her back from a brutal beating. I cannot bear to think of the excruciating pain she must have endured!"

"It sounds as if you have come just in time," her aunt said.

"I have come much too late!" Eliza cried. "I should have swallowed my pride and taken myself in hand and—"

"Shh. Shh," her aunt said. "What is done is done. Tell me what you intend to do now."

"I must help Reggie and Becky," she said. "I cannot abandon them. But that—Beast—has made it impossible for me to do so."

"Impossible? What about his proposal of marriage?"

"He would not even let me see his face!" Eliza

raged, pulling herself free of her aunt's embrace and sitting up to search her aunt's sightless eyes. "He kept the room so dark—you know how I hate the dark! He said I had no need to see his face."

"Perhaps it would frighten you," Aunt Lavinia suggested.

"Of *course* it would frighten me!" Eliza retorted, jumping off the bed and pacing again. "His *hand* frightened me, and it is covered with a concealing black glove."

"Then perhaps he has a good reason to keep his face hidden."

"But I would be his wife! How could I lie in bed with him, let him touch me, never knowing whether . . ."

"Whether he really *is* a monster?" her aunt finished for her.

Eliza shuddered. "What if he is?"

"Think what it must be like for him."

Trust Aunt Lavinia to arouse her compassion. Eliza was sorry the Beau's perfect face and form had been destroyed. It was a tragedy for him. The world had lost something precious, as well. The Beau had been nature's perfect creation. A magnificent collection in one body of all that Society most admired in a man.

Now he was just a man, like any other, scarred and crippled and no longer perfect. The obvious contrast between having people openly admire him a year ago, and shrinking from him in horror now, made his situation all the more pitiable. But Eliza found it hard to pity him.

"I cannot forgive his neglect of the twins," Eliza

said. "It is only pride that keeps His Grace entombed in that dark place. Other soldiers have found the courage to live in the world with disfigured bodies. Why not him?"

"Perhaps because the duke suffers from more than a crippled body," Aunt Lavinia said.

"Like what?"

"A tortured soul."

Eliza balled her hands into fists. "The Beast of Blackthorne has no soul!"

Aunt Lavinia harrumphed. "Well, then. I suppose you cannot marry him. I would like to start early tomorrow for home." She began arranging her pillows for sleep.

Eliza saw how her aunt had tricked her. Though the duke was a monster, had no soul, hid his face, and lived in the dark, marriage to him was her only route to the children. If she ran away, Eliza became as responsible for their fate as their uncle was.

Seeing that Aunt Lavinia did not intend to pursue the conversation, Eliza began to ready herself for bed. But she knew she would not sleep. She had too much thinking to do.

If only the duke had not offered marriage. If only he had offered something dishonorable she could easily refuse.

Even so, there was much to dread in the life he had offered her. Never to see his eyes when he made love to her? Never to be kissed again? To lie beneath a faceless stranger who had no use for her except at night, in his bed? It was a monstrous existence.

But her other life—the life scandal had reaped— was no better. Isolated. Purposeless. Barren. At least if she married the duke, she could help Reggie and

Becky. And she might, one day, have a child of her own to love.

But she would hate the Beast for making her his whore.

And whore she would be. The Beast's offer of marriage might as well have been an offer of *carte blanche*. Its terms were not much different. She had agreed to make her body available to him on demand, and he had agreed to reward her with comfortable living conditions in return. Their children would be legitimate. She would be respectable in company again. She would be married to him before God and man.

But not within her heart. She would despise him for not caring. For treating her with contempt and contumely.

Eliza knew many *ton* marriages were no better than what she had been offered. But she wanted more—the *more* she had been searching for all her life, but which had never had a shape until now. Eliza envisioned a life of shared hopes and dreams. A willingness to travel life's rutted roads together. A mutual joy in creating and raising children. And undying, eternal love.

The duke's offer included none of that.

She wanted to say no. She wanted to walk away. But there was more to be considered than her own feelings in the matter.

Suppose she did not marry the Beast.

She and Aunt Lavinia would be forced to return to Ravenwood, unless she could find another position. Who would she find willing to overlook the scandal attached to her name? Or willing to accept an elderly, blind companion along with an odd-looking, sharp-tongued young lady?

The children would be left to the mercy of the next governess hired to care for them.

And the Beast would prowl his dungeon, alone forevermore.

You are going in circles.

Eliza laid herself on the cot and arranged her flannel gown so it covered her to the ankles. She had left the lantern burning. Aunt Lavinia would not mind, and she would not have to deal with the nightmares that came in the dark. She cocked her barefoot toes perpendicular to the bed, aligned her hands by her sides, and traced a crack across the replastered ceiling with her eyes.

She had a few more hours to ponder. A few more hours to make up her mind.

"Have you said your prayers, Eliza?" her aunt asked softly.

"I will do it now." Eliza clasped her hands before her.

> *Now I lay me down to sleep.*
> *I pray the Lord my soul to keep.*
> *If I should die before I wake . . .*

Becky's worried face appeared before her. Reggie's tumbling-down braids. And the scars on her back.

> *I pray the Lord—*

The crack in the ceiling blurred. Eliza gripped her hands so tightly the knuckles turned white. She gritted her teeth to stop her chin from quivering.

Please, please, she prayed. *Tell me what to do.*

* * *

"Rise and shine, you sleepyheads!" Eliza said, shoving the faded maroon velvet curtains back from the window to let in the morning sun. There was not a cloud in the sky—or in her mind. Sometime during the night she had realized exactly what she must do. "Slugabeds!" she chided.

Becky popped up amid the tangled sheets, eyes open wide.

Reggie sat up groggily, squinted in Eliza's direction, said to Becky "I told you so," yawned, and flopped back down.

"Uncle Marcus hired you!" Becky said, her face breaking into a relieved smile. "I was so worried he would not. Reggie was sure you would convince Uncle Marcus to let you stay and be our governess."

Eliza picked up the silver brush and comb set from the dressing table and crossed to Becky. For the first time she noticed that Reggie's nightdress was on inside out, and Becky was still wearing a bow in her disheveled black curls. It dawned on her the girls must have dressed themselves for bed.

Eliza sat down and tried untying Becky's pink bow. She knew immediately why it had been left on overnight. The ribbon had pulled tight, with strands of hair caught within the knots. It would have been impossible for either child to untie it. Eliza finally managed to get it off and began brushing Becky's hair.

Reggie immediately sat up, eyeing her sister enviously.

"Your turn will come," Eliza said with a laugh. "I am not going anywhere." She bit her lip and added, "But I am not going to be your governess, either."

"What?" Reggie said, scrambling to her knees on the bed.

Becky twisted around to gape at Eliza, and the brush caught on a snarl. "Ow! You hurt me!" she said in an aggrieved voice, rubbing the injured spot and backing up toward her sister.

"I'm sorry," Eliza said.

Reggie and Becky huddled together near the center of the bed. Eliza was sure they did not even realize they were holding hands.

"Why aren't you going to be our governess?" Reggie demanded, her blue eyes wary.

Eliza took a deep breath and plunged. "Because I have decided to be your aunt instead. I hope you won't mind."

Reggie gasped. "Our aunt?"

Becky shared a significant look with Reggie. "Aunt Eliza," she said, as though some secret message were being passed between them. "Aunt Eliza," she repeated with reverence.

Reggie looked thoughtful. "Does this mean you are going to marry Uncle Marcus?"

"He has offered for me," Eliza said, fighting the urge to jump up from her perch on the bed and pace. "I have not given him my answer. I am willing. But I wanted to make sure first that neither of you will mind."

"Mind?" Becky said, grinning from ear to ear. "Why, it's bloody marvelous!" Becky slapped a hand over her mouth. "I mean marvelous," she quickly corrected. "The bloody just came out, Eliza. I don't know why I said it. I am just so excited! And glad!"

"I will excuse you this time, young lady," Eliza

said, arching a brow. "But that word is to be erased from your vocabulary."

"Yes, Aunt Eliza," Becky said.

Eliza opened her arms, and Becky scurried over to be hugged. She turned around and plopped herself down so Eliza could finish brushing her hair.

Eliza's gaze focused on Reggie's troubled face. "Reggie?" she prodded, deftly braiding Becky's hair. "Have you some objection to the marriage?"

"Having you for our aunt . . . It would almost be like having another mother," Reggie said.

"Would that be so bad?" Eliza asked, tying off the pink bow and giving Becky a little shove off her lap to make room for Reggie.

"Maybe. Maybe not." Reggie hesitated, then scooted over and backed up close to Eliza to have her hair brushed. Once Eliza started, Reggie's eyes slid closed, as though she were having a religious experience.

Eliza wondered what the twins' mother had done that made them think twice about having another one. She tried to imagine what it might have been like to live in a household where the drunken duchess accused her brother-in-law of being the father of the duke's children. Episodes of rage and spite. Shouting and broken glass. Ominous, insidious silence.

Guessing was not good enough. She needed to know what it was Reggie feared. "What is it, exactly, you're afraid will happen if I marry your uncle?"

Reggie opened her eyes and gave Eliza a veiled look over her shoulder. "I think that once you and Uncle Marcus are married, you won't want any more to do with me and Becky. And that you'll make Uncle Marcus stay away from us, too."

Neglect. Abandonment. That was the duchess's terrible sin. And apparently the duke's, as well.

"I don't believe anything could make your uncle Marcus abandon you," Eliza said quietly. "And I already love you both too much ever to leave you."

Reggie stared doubtfully at her. She swallowed hard. "I . . . I . . ."

Eliza saw it was all too much for Reggie to believe. That she was loved. That she would never be abandoned again. That her uncle would come out of hiding at last—Eliza was determined that he would— and be the father that he had not been in the past.

"I suppose it will be all right," Reggie said gruffly. "At least we will have you for a little while."

Eliza knew that only time would prove to Reggie that she had meant what she said. At least the children were willing to accept her. That was a good start.

Eliza finished Reggie's braids and searched for a bow among the bedsheets, but did not see one. "Where is your pink bow, Reggie?"

"I lost it in bed somewhere, I guess."

"Do you have another?"

Reggie shook her head.

"We will simply have to use another color," Eliza said, jumping up. "Where do you keep your hair ribbons?"

"In the drawer of the dressing table," Becky said, hop-skipping alongside Eliza. "But we *always* wear the same color. You will have to change mine, and match it to whatever Reggie is wearing."

Eliza pulled out a bright yellow ribbon and

marched back to where Reggie sat dumbfounded. "Why?"

"Because," Becky said, crawling up onto the bed beside her sister, "we always dress alike."

"Why?" Eliza asked again. "Is there a rule that says all twins must dress alike?"

While Becky looked at her as though she had lost her mind, Eliza tied the bright yellow ribbon at Reggie's nape.

"I suppose I never thought about it before," Becky admitted. "Have you ever heard of a rule, Reggie?"

"No," Reggie said. "No rule. It is just . . . We have always done it."

The twins looked at each other in awed silence.

"I suppose you will have to wear the same shifts today," Eliza said, "but I see no reason why we cannot go shopping and let each of you choose what colors you would like best."

"Yellow," said Reggie, fingering her bow. "And green and pink and blue."

"Blue," Becky said, "And pink and yellow and green."

Eliza laughed. "I can see we will have to vary the patterns as well, or we are liable to end up with a great deal of confusion over whose shift is whose after all."

"Different patterns," Becky said with wonder.

"And different colors," Reggie added. Her brow furrowed, and she turned to Eliza. "Do you think Uncle Marcus will allow it?"

"Since 'Aunt Eliza' approves, I am sure he can have no objection," she replied tartly.

The twins looked at each other, then back at her, and laughed delightedly.

Eliza joined them.

The twins were nearly finished dressing when Becky asked, "Where is the wedding to be held and when?"

"This evening. In the chapel," Eliza replied.

Reggie looked horrified. "In the *chapel*? Why, it is crumbling down! No one is allowed in there for fear the ceiling will fall on their heads! How can you be married there?"

The absurdity of wedding a man whose face she was not allowed to see, in a chapel where the ceiling was in imminent danger of falling on their heads, made Eliza laugh.

"It will be a death-defying adventure, to be sure," she conceded with a smile. "Nevertheless, your uncle and I will be married there today at sundown."

"May I throw flower petals from a basket?" Becky asked. "I saw it done once, when a couple married at the fair in Comarty."

"I am sure we could arrange it," Eliza said. "In fact, we could decorate the whole chapel with flowers. And put candles everywhere." Flowers would soften the stark stone walls. And candles would relieve the gloom and perhaps allow her to catch a glimpse of the Beast.

"When is Uncle Marcus coming to see us?" Reggie asked. "I want to tell him—"

"I do not believe he intends to see you," Eliza interrupted. Better to let them hear the truth now, than to be disillusioned later.

Reggie left her stocking rolled halfway up her calf. Becky paused with her toe pointed at her right half boot.

"But whyever not?" Becky asked, setting her stocking foot flat on the hardwood floor. "If you are getting married, Uncle Marcus will have to leave the east wing of the Abbey and come live with us. Won't he?"

"Not necessarily." Eliza had turned her back to the children, busily doing inventory on what clothing they had and what they would need to buy. But she could see the dismay and disappointment reflected on their young faces in the looking glass before her.

Eliza rounded to face them, trying not to look as upset and frustrated as she felt. "Your uncle and I have agreed to marry. But he will continue living where he is."

"I knew it was too good to be true," Reggie said bitterly. "If marriage to you cannot pry Uncle Marcus out of there, nothing ever will!"

"How is it possible for Uncle Marcus to remain there?" Becky demanded. "Will you have to sleep there, too? With the ghosts and goblins and—"

"No," Eliza said, shivering at the thought. "I will have a room here, near you."

"Thank goodness for that," Becky said.

Reggie said nothing, simply stared at Eliza with too much knowledge in her eyes.

Did she know that Eliza would be spending at least part of every night in her uncle's bed? That Eliza dreaded the thought of it? That Eliza, who was no willing martyr, had decided she could bear anything for the sake of the children?

"I have not given up hope that your uncle will eventually decide to join us," Eliza said. "Perhaps over time—"

"It has been a year," Reggie said. "If he was ever going to come out, he would have by now."

"He was not married to me before," Eliza said determinedly. "I have no intention of allowing your uncle to languish alone in the dark. The three of us are going to make his solitude so unpleasant that he will leap at the chance to forsake it."

"The three of us?" Becky said. "You and Reggie and me?"

Eliza nodded firmly.

"What did you have in mind?" Reggie asked, the first spark of interest lighting in her eyes.

Eliza smiled ruefully. "I had not quite gotten that far," she admitted.

"We can be ghosts in the secret passage," Becky said excitedly, "and scare him out!"

"We can oversalt his beef," Reggie said. "And put water in his wine."

"We can ambush him at the stable," Becky said.

"He rides?" Eliza asked.

Becky nodded. "He gallops Blanca over the hills on moonlit nights. I've seen him. But I've never been able to catch him."

"She falls asleep in the stable," Reggie said.

"Uncle Marcus brings me inside and puts me to bed."

"You only wish he did," Reggie countered. "It is the groom and Fenwick and the governess who do it."

"Wait, wait," Eliza said. "You are both going too fast for me. Finish dressing." She rubbed her hands together as though she were preparing to make a tasty dish of something good to eat. "I can see the three of us have a great many plans to make. We might as well get started this afternoon."

"Doing what?" Reggie asked.

Eliza shot her a mischievous smile. "Making life in the east wing as uncomfortable as we can for your uncle."

Chapter 16

ELIZA HAD BEEN FULL OF BRAVADO WHEN SHE CON-
fronted the children in the morning sun. She was
not quite so courageous waiting in the cold stone
chapel for the Beast of Blackthorne to arrive. She had
pleaded with Aunt Lavinia to come to the wedding,
but her aunt had refused.

"You will have other things to do than watch out
for me," Aunt Lavinia said. "You know I cannot see
anything anyway."

"What a corker!" Eliza replied in exasperation.
"You see just fine when you want to!"

"Do you mean *clanker*, my dear?" her aunt asked.

Eliza harrumped. "I meant big fat lie!"

Her aunt grinned, and Eliza hugged her tight.
"Oh, I will miss you so much! I wish you would come."

"I will be with you at the Abbey soon enough,
child." Aunt Lavinia had sniffed and dabbed at her
eyes with a handkerchief. "I am getting my crying out
of the way early. I promise only smiles when we meet
again, my darling duchess."

Eliza looked around at the empty wooden pews in
the chapel and wanted to cry. She did not feel like
anyone's darling right now. And she was going to

need all the willpower she had to wait around long enough for the duke to make her his duchess.

Reggie and Becky stood on either side of her at the back of the chapel, resplendent in matching white dresses—with different colored sashes. Each girl wore a crown of white daisies atop her braided hair, a gift from Eliza. She had tried to show them how to make a crown themselves, but they had been too busy gathering flowers in the meadow to sit and do such quiet work.

When the twins were ready to come downstairs for the wedding, she had surprised each of them with a crown of daisies. They had laughed and exchanged a conspiratorial glance before Reggie reached under the bed and came up with another crown—this one made of wildflowers.

"We had the same idea," Becky explained. "Ours is not quite as neat as the ones you made," she said hesitantly.

Her glance slid from the neat circles of daisies Eliza had created to the wild jumble of yellow snapdragons, white daisies, blue bachelor's buttons, and bell-shaped lilies-of-the-valley that the twins had woven into a crown.

"Here," Reggie said, extending the crown of wildflowers reverently toward her. "It's our wedding gift to you."

"It's lovely," Eliza said, accepting the chaos of color from Reggie and standing before the looking glass to put it on. The crown was so large, that instead of sitting on top of her head, it came to rest—flowers crushing, stems painfully scratching and poking—

halfway down her forehead, like a band across her brow.

"It's too big," Reggie said flatly.

"Not at all," Eliza countered, trying to keep from wincing as she adjusted a few of the worst-offending stems. When she was done, she turned to face them with a radiant smile on her face. "This is exactly what a very famous queen of England, Eleanor of Aquitaine, wore at her wedding."

Reggie eyed her doubtfully.

"I swear," Eliza said, crossing her heart. "Only her band was made of ugly gold and jewels, not beautiful blossoms like mine."

She surprised a laugh out of Becky and a snort of disbelief from Reggie.

"You are so silly, Eliza," Becky said. "What lady wants flowers, when she could have gold and jewels?"

"What lady wants gold and jewels," she countered, "when she could wear a crown of delicate, scented wildflowers—never before worn and never to be worn again?"

"How lovely you make it sound," Becky said.

"It is lovely," Eliza insisted. She leaned over and gave each girl a hug and a kiss on the cheek. "Thank you, Becky. Thank you, Reggie. I will always remember your thoughtfulness."

Eliza wanted the twins to understand how important their gift was to her. That it was not the value of the gift that made it precious, but the love that had prompted the giving of it. Yet from the strange look Reggie had given her, and the confusion on Becky's face, Eliza knew they did not understand. Or if they did, could neither accept nor believe what they were hearing. Someday, in the not too distant future, both children would.

But first, Eliza had to get through the wedding. The wildflowers were beginning to wilt. Where was the groom? He had said sundown. They had not even come to the chapel until sundown. Had the Beast changed his mind?

It was too late for that. They had made a bargain. Eliza intended to see it through. Even if she had to drag the Beast kicking and screaming to the altar.

The thought made Eliza smile. And shudder.

"The decorations are so very beautiful," Becky said with a sigh, glancing around the chapel. "The flowers. And the candles."

Eliza eyed the two painted ceramic vases Griggs was arranging on the altar—unfortunately unmatched—which held enormous bouquets of dark purple irises, fern, and cascading wisteria. The twins had turned the rest of the wildflowers they had gathered that morning into two large baskets of petals, since Reggie had decided to join Becky in reenacting the wedding at the fair in Comarty. If they threw them all, she would be wading in wildflowers.

Eliza had done everything she could, with the help of Griggs and the children, to dispel the gloom in the chapel. Beeswax candles burned in every iron sconce along the crumbling wall, and from as many candelabras as she and the twins could carry from one wing of the Abbey to the other in a single afternoon.

As he joined her, Griggs muttered, "All lit up like a Spanish whorehouse. All we need are the dancin' ladies."

Eliza's lips curled, but she could not manage the

smile. She was too aware of how little time remained before she was to become a bride. "Where is he, Griggs?"

"Waitin' for company to arrive, miss. Should be along any minute now."

"Company?" Eliza asked, her stomach shifting sideways. "What company?"

Griggs shrugged. "Folks he invited to the weddin'."

Eliza tightened her grip on the ribbon-bound bouquet of wildflowers she had rescued from the twins before they dissolved it into petals. Drat the man! She could barely keep her knees from knocking, she was so scared, and the looby had invited guests to the wedding!

"Eliza! You're beautiful!"

Eliza whirled. She almost broke into tears when she saw who was standing there. "Charlie!"

The Earl and Countess of Denbigh were flanked by the Duke and Duchess of Braddock. Behind them, hat in hand, stood Cousin Nigel and his wife. Bringing up the rear, but by no means the least of the collected company, stood Aunt Lavinia.

"Oh, dear," Eliza said. "Oh, dear." She was overwhelmed with joy, with gratefulness that he—that man—the captain—had thought to invite her friends, and that he had somehow convinced Aunt Lavinia to come, as well.

And though she could not be happy that Cousin Nigel was present, she suddenly realized what the Beast must have known full well—that her guardian must give his consent for her wedding to be valid.

Eliza glanced at each of them again, her heart in her throat. "Oh, dear," she said.

"My sharp-tongued Eliza can only say 'Oh, dear'? Have you lost your wit, as well as your senses?" the countess asked, walking right up to Eliza and hugging her. "What is this I hear? Is it possible? Did the Beau really ask for your hand, and did you really say yes?"

Eliza gestured helplessly to the flowers she carried and the crown in her hair. "Can you think of any other reason I would become a walking garden?"

"That is my Eliza!" the countess said with a laugh and another hug. "See, Lion, everything has turned out fine, after all."

Eliza noticed the earl reserved agreement. Instead he said, "I have brought the special dispensation for Blackthorne to be married after dark."

Griggs held out his hand. "I will take it, your lordship."

Eliza stared as the paper changed hands. Of course. Weddings were only held between eight in the morning and noon. It had never even occurred to her that the Beast would need permission to do otherwise.

While Eliza was standing lost in thought, Charlotte, being Charlotte, introduced herself to the twins. And introduced the twins to everyone else.

Eliza was surprised to see Reggie and Becky curtsy with perfect civility to each person they met and introduce themselves politely as "Lady Regina" and "Lady Rebecca." Why those scamps! For all their "trouble" with governesses, they had absolutely *perfect* manners!

"Where is His Grace?" Eliza whispered to Griggs.

"I'm to fetch him and the Reverend Mister Hopewell once everyone is seated," Griggs whispered back.

Eliza was distracted by the Duchess of Braddock's hand on her arm.

"I am so glad for you, Miss Sheringham," the duchess said. "You are so brave . . ."

Eliza shivered. Did the duchess know something she did not? Was there more to fear from the Beast than a scarred face and a clawlike hand?

The duke put his arm around Her Grace's shoulder and said, "The duchess and I extend our best wishes to you and Blackthorne, Miss Sheringham," before leading his wife over to be introduced to the twins.

"Are you all right?" her aunt asked. "Your hands are cold."

"The chapel is cold," Eliza said, making an excuse for her bloodless hands. "As you will soon discover for yourself. Let me help you find a seat."

Eliza began to lead her aunt toward one of the front pews.

"Pardon me, miss," Griggs said. "But His Grace said only the last two rows."

"What?"

"No one's to sit closer than the last two rows."

"Steady, dear," her aunt said, clasping her hand tightly. "Come, find me a place to sit. My old legs are buckling under me."

White-faced, Eliza led her aunt to a seat on the aisle in the next-to-the-last row. "At least you will be able to smell me when I go by," she said. "I am all over flowers."

"Are you wearing the dress?"

Eliza flushed. "Yes."

Every dress Eliza had brought with her to Blackthorne Abbey had been lilac or lavender, the only colors she felt comfortable wearing so soon after her year of mourning. But lavender was the wrong color for a wedding.

Aunt Lavinia had heard her muttering and said, "Open my leather traveling valise. I believe I have something in there you can alter to fit you."

Eliza had opened the valise and gasped at what she found. "What is this?"

"Your wedding dress. It is a gift from your mother."

Eliza had been aghast. And entranced.

"Is it as beautiful as it was the day I saw your mother try it on?" her aunt asked.

"I don't know," Eliza rasped, staring down at the square, pearl-encrusted bodice, the ivory satin skirt. "It must have cost of fortune."

It had been intended as a ballgown, her aunt had said, for her mother's first ball in London. But it had never been worn. All these years it had lain in a cedar chest, to be given to Eliza on the day she married.

Eliza saw in the pearl-encrusted dress a way they could have saved themselves from destitution. "Why could we not have sold this? It would have kept us in coal—"

"This dress was the reason your father and mother left you alone with your—" Aunt Lavinia had cut herself off, agitated and upset.

Eliza had not been allowed to question her further. In fact, the dress had needed very little alteration. "Whatever made you bring it along?" Eliza had asked.

Her aunt chuckled. "I had a feeling you might need it."

When Eliza finally looked up from seating her aunt in the next-to-the-last row of the chapel, she realized Griggs had already seated everyone else in the back two rows where the duke wanted them. She watched with dismay as Griggs moved along the wall, putting out every candle from the next-to-the-last pew forward, all the way to the altar.

Griggs left two sconces burning, one in each far corner in the front of the chapel. But their meager light did not reach to the altar, which was now cloaked in shadows. The two vases had disappeared in the gloom.

"Behold," she heard one of the gentlemen say in a low voice. "The bridegroom cometh."

For a man of God, Marcus thought, the Reverend Mister Hopewell did not have much faith in his Maker to keep him safe from the evils of the world—and Marcus in particular. The man stuttered when he talked and was visibly shaking when Marcus gestured him through one of the four doors that led into the chapel.

"After you, Your Grace," the little man said.

Marcus smiled within his hood. The vicar apparently intended to put the Beast of Blackthorne between himself and any evil spirits flapping and fluttering on the other side.

Marcus forgot entirely about the little man the instant he stepped through the door and laid eyes on

Miss Sheringham. She was bathed in a glow of candlelight at the very back of the chapel, where the candles were still burning. Her jaw was firm, but her face looked as pale as parchment. She carried a bouquet of wildflowers in her hand and wore a strikingly lovely crown of them upon her head. He could smell flowers from where he stood.

He would not have noticed the gown at all, if she had not turned in that instant so that candlelight struck the profusion of pearls on the bodice. He wondered if the Countess of Denbigh had given the dress to her as a wedding gift. He was sure it cost more than he could have made in a year as a captain in the 10th] Royal Hussars.

He saw her eyes search the shadows for him. Her frightened eyes.

It was not very far from the altar to the back of the chapel. In perhaps five strides, he could be at her side. But he stayed where he was. The dark was his friend. It kept the monster hidden from those who feared it.

Please, he thought. *Do not be afraid of me.*

He noticed the dark circles under her eyes and knew she must not have slept any more than he had. He did not look much better. There had been a great deal to arrange in four-and-twenty hours.

His solicitor had come to terms with Nigel Sheringham, procuring a signed document from the earl that his ward, Miss Elizabeth Sheringham, had his permission to marry Marcus Wharton, currently in possession of his brother's title, Duke of Blackthorne.

It had been the middle of the night when he realized it would better for Miss Sheringham if the wedding were witnessed by friends. Not only to give her company, but to prove to Society that she had not been gobbled up by the Beast, but merely married to him.

And he had needed a favor from Denbigh. A special dispensation to marry after dark had never even occurred to him until the vicar had pointed out the impossibility of conducting a wedding anytime after noon.

"And it must be in a chapel, Your Grace," the little man had reminded him.

"There is a chapel in the Abbey," he had said. "It is consecrated ground."

"When was it consecrated, Your Grace?" the little man demanded. "And by whom?"

"By the Archbishop of Canterbury," Marcus snarled back, "on the day Henry II bestowed a dukedom on the first Lord of Blackthorne. Will that suffice, Mister Hopewell?"

The little man had made no more objection. But he clearly suffered a fright when he walked past the decaying walls of the Abbey and heard the windows begin to rattle and saw the tattered velvet curtains appear to move all by themselves.

Marcus did not realize the vicar had followed him into the chapel until the little man cleared his throat from a spot behind the altar.

"Are we ready to proceed?" the vicar asked. "Where is the bride?"

Marcus saw Miss Sheringham sway and then catch her balance.

"I am here," she said. She turned and gave Reggie and Becky a little shove in front of her.

When he could see the twins in the light, Marcus noticed all the changes Miss Sheringham had wrought in a single day. More braids! Different colored sashes! And charming garlands of daisies he knew she must have made for them.

He watched as Becky reached into her basket, pulled out a handful of something, and threw it high into the air. Whatever it was floated down over the assembled company. From muffled laughter and whispered comments, he realized Becky had thrown a handful of flower petals.

Miss Sheringham whispered into Reggie's ear, and he watched as Reggie threw a handful of petals from her basket. These landed in a solid clump on the stone floor in front of her. She used the toe of her patent leather half boot to spread them around.

Marcus heard more subdued laughter.

Becky looked up at Miss Sheringham. When she nodded, Becky threw another handful of petals— straight up into the air. This time the laughter was louder and more spontaneous.

Marcus watched as Miss Sheringham leaned over and whispered to both girls, presumably giving more instructions.

Becky peered down the aisle toward where he stood and shook her head. Reggie boldly took three or four steps down the aisle, just far enough to leave the glow of candlelight behind. She stood stock-still in the dark for a moment, then dropped her basket, and raced headlong back to Miss Sheringham.

Both twins clutched at her skirt, and Miss Sheringham did not seem to be able to get them to let go. She lifted her head and looked directly at him.

He knew what she wanted. It would have been a simple matter for him to calm the twins' fears. If only he had not been the source of them.

"Griggs," he said. "Please help Reggie and Becky to a seat near you."

His voice startled the children, actually making things worse. He should have spoken directly to them, not to Griggs, he realized. Now they struggled even harder not to be torn away from Miss Sheringham. Marcus took a single step down the aisle toward them, his heart aching, knowing that all they needed was someone to hug them and tell them everything would be all right.

As though she had read his mind, Miss Sheringham knelt and pulled the girls close. She whispered to them, then led them over and sat them down in the pew next to Lady Denbigh, who lifted Becky right into her lap and put her arm around Reggie.

Before Marcus quite realized it was happening, Miss Sheringham was on her way down the aisle toward him. She did not stop, but stepped over the fallen basket of flowers and walked slowly but steadily out of the light and into the darkness. When she reached a spot in front of the altar, she stopped and stared at the vicar.

"Will you clasp hands," the vicar intoned, "and pray with me."

Since she was on his left, Marcus automatically lifted his black-gloved left hand. He had already begun to exchange it for the right when Miss Sheringham laid her hand on the gnarled fingers. She looked into his face—the place where his face should be—and dared him to withdraw.

Marcus turned and stared straight ahead, feeling the heat of her trembling hand through the glove, aware suddenly, as he had not been until this moment, that tonight she would be his.

"Is there any man here who can show just cause why these two should not be joined in holy matrimony?" the vicar asked.

Marcus waited, half expecting someone to point out that the groom was not a man, but a beast. But no one spoke, and the vicar continued.

He did not hear much of the ceremony. His body was too alive with the knowledge of her. He could not think, he could only feel and see and hear.

The touch of her hand on his as he held it to take his vows. "*I, Marcus Richard Wharton, take thee, Elizabeth Eleanor Sheringham, to be my wedded wife. To have and to hold from this day forward . . .*"

The agitated rise and fall of her bosom as she said the words that bound her to him for life.

"*I, Elizabeth Eleanor Sheringham, take thee, Marcus Richard Wharton, to be my wedded husband . . . so long as we both shall live.*"

Her indrawn breath when he placed a diamond and ruby ring—a Blackthorne heirloom intended for the wife of a second son—on her finger.

"I now pronounce you man and wife," the vicar said. "What God hath joined, let not man put asunder."

It was an admonition that had particular relevance to Marcus. It was not a man but a woman who had tunneled out the walls of his brother's castle and made it collapse. But he knew now why Alastair had never

291

forsaken Penthia. He must, at one time, have loved her.

Love changed all the rules. It had caused Marcus to do what he had said he would never do. He had taken a wife, for better or for worse. But he could not believe a life without Miss Sher—Eliza—could be worse than one with her by his side. Only, she would not be by his side. Except at night. In the dark.

It would have to be enough. Half a loaf of bread was better than none at all. If he ever revealed himself to her, she would surely turn away from him forever.

"Will you kiss the bride?" the vicar asked, cheerful now that his duty was done.

Marcus realized he must have been asked before and missed the question. "No," he said abruptly. "I will not."

The vicar's smile disappeared.

Marcus was aware of a stunned silence behind him. He turned to face them. "Thank you all for coming. My wife and I will be retiring now."

He grabbed his wife by the hand and, before she or anyone else could protest, disappeared with her through a hidden stone door behind the altar.

One minute they were there, and the next they were gone.

Reggie and Becky stared after Uncle Marcus, who had dragged their new aunt right out the door without saying a word to them. They were completely alone. Who would take care of them now? The twins sat dazed as the Earl of Denbigh rose from his seat beside them, followed quickly by his countess, who eased Becky off her lap and onto the cold bench beside

Reggie. They watched the bizarre scene unfolding around them without saying a word.

"Marcus," the Earl of Denbigh shouted. "Wait!"

"Hurry, Lion," the countess urged, following him down the center aisle. "They're getting away!"

Griggs stepped into the earl's path. "His Grace said to tell you there's food and drink for everyone in the dining room. You will find comfortable rooms have been prepared for you in the west wing of the Abbey. His Grace hopes you will enjoy your stay."

"I demand to speak with Blackthorne," the Earl of Denbigh said through clenched jaws.

"I need to know that Eliza is all right," the countess said anxiously. "Please, may I see her?"

"His Grace and his bride are not at home to company," Griggs announced.

"He will speak to me," the Duke of Braddock said. "Or I will know why."

When Braddock moved toward the door where Blackthorne had disappeared with Eliza, Griggs put his one remaining hand up to stop him. The duke could easily have pushed by the sergeant, but he looked at the empty sleeve and stopped where he was.

"Will you at least take a message to him?" Braddock said.

"Of course, Your Grace."

"Tell him there are rumors in Scotland of a stranger at Blackthorne Hall, a new laird married to the mistress there, who fits the description of Alastair Wharton, sixth Duke of Blackthorne."

Reggie grabbed Becky's arm and whispered, "Father is alive!"

Chapter 17

ELIZA DID NOT KNOW WHY SHE HAD NOT STRUGGLED when the Beast grabbed her wrist and dragged her from the chapel. If she had said a word of protest, Eliza was certain she would have been rescued. But to what purpose? The Beast was her husband now. She belonged to him.

"Where are you taking me?" she asked breathlessly, as he dragged her down a long, dark hallway.

"To our room."

Our room? There was no such place. Only *his* room in this wing of the house and *hers* in the other.

He had no sooner said the words than he opened the door to an immense bedchamber, pulled her inside, and shut the thick wooden door behind her with a *thunk*. He shoved home two heavy iron bolts that effectively locked the door against intruders. And made her his captive.

Eliza's gaze shifted quickly around the room, searching for an avenue of escape without finding one. Several candles burned in the room, but none of them were anywhere near the bed, which lay in deep shadow.

That quick, futile glance was enough to convince her the Beast did not live in squalor. Brilliant tapestries hung on the wall; more subdued ones lay on the floor. Black velvet curtains shrouded the windows. And she had never seen such an impressive bed. The massive headboard and footboard were carved with scenes she could not distinguish in the dim light.

Eliza scrutinized the cloaked and hooded man who was about to prove that he was her husband—in every way. Her heart thumped wildly. Her breathing was erratic. Not from the rapid walk to get there—her legs were nearly as long as his, and she had kept up with him stride for stride. But because she was afraid of what he would do to her now.

As Eliza had learned long ago, the best defense against awkwardness in a social situation was to attack first. In this case, because she was also terrified, both her voice and her choice of words were more virulent than they might otherwise have been.

Eliza lifted her chin defiantly and said, "Here I am, Your Grace. Ready to play your whore."

His body stiffened. His right hand balled into a fist, while the clawlike left merely twitched. "My whore?" he rasped. "I rather thought I had made you my wife."

"I am no better than a whore," she accused. "You offer me nothing of yourself and want nothing of me—except the use of my body." She yanked off the crown of wildflowers and threw it at his feet. The hand-held bouquet shot directly at his head.

He moved subtly to one side, and it sailed past and landed on the floor behind him, skidding to a stop against the stone wall.

"Come, Your Grace," she said, gesturing him

toward her with both hands. "Take what you want from me, so I may leave and go back to my other life."

"Other life?"

"The real one. Where children play and servants sweep away the cobwebs and sunshine fills every room." Her gaze left him and roamed the exotic bedroom, with its medieval bed and tapestries brought back from the Crusades. "This is a fantasy you have concocted for yourself and expect me to fulfill. So be it. You have your wife . . . and your whore. I am ready to do your bidding."

"So be it, wife!" he snarled. "If you wish to whore for me, whore you shall be!"

He moved so fast Eliza did not realize what he had done until she heard pearls bouncing on the stone floor that edged the carpet.

"My dress!" she cried. The gift from her mother was ruined. But there was no time to grieve it. With the bodice gaping loose, he yanked the shoulders down, and she was in danger of losing the ivory gown entirely.

She reacted instinctively to his attack. Her hands curled into fists, and she punched out toward his face.

Her right fist never got there. He caught it with a steely hand and forced it back behind her, then used his clawed hand to force the other fist back, where he was able to grip both wrists in his right hand. He used his painful hold to force her hips forward, pressing her tightly against his body from breast to thigh.

"Whores want it over with quickly, so they can be paid. Is that what you want, Eliza?"

Eliza could feel his hardened shaft pressing against her belly, feel his hot breath against her flesh.

His eyes glittered with feral ruthlessness deep within the hood that shadowed his face. "I want it over," she managed to gasp. "Hurry up and finish!"

He released her suddenly and took a step back. "I think not. I think I would enjoy it done more slowly. After all, I am the one who must be pleased."

Her shoulders hurt as she brought her hands forward to soothe her recently manacled wrists. She could see no mercy in the Beast. His body was taut, his stance threatening.

He left her standing where she was and crossed to sit in a thronelike chair angled in the corner. He wrapped the full-length black cloak around him and pulled the hood forward, making certain his face was completely in the dark. She realized the single candle merely provided enough light to ensure she would be visible to him.

"Come here, whore."

Eliza swallowed past the painful thickness in her throat and walked toward him, her satin skirt rustling with each step. She resisted the urge to clutch at the torn bodice. He had ripped the chemise beneath it as well, exposing a great deal of décolletage. Let him look. Let him drink his fill. The Beast could slake his desire with her body. But that was all he would have of her. Nothing more.

It was hard to stand before him perfectly still, letting him look at her, waiting for him to do whatever it was he was going to do.

"Undress for me."

Eliza ogled him. "What?"

"Take off your clothes, Eliza," he said in a silky voice. "Let me see what I have bought."

It should have been impossible for her to remove the dress by herself. The heirloom laced closed in back. When he had yanked on her bodice, the aged, fragile cord in back had broken. When Eliza reached up to pull the dress down, the laces fell loose all the way down her back.

Her face flamed as she let the dress fall in an ivory puddle at her feet. She stepped over it, then reached down to pick it up, holding it against her bosom protectively.

The Beast held out a hand to her, and Eliza realized he wanted the dress. Reluctantly, she handed it over to him.

He took it from her and laid it across the wooden arm of the chair, caressing the satin fabric as though the dress still contained her warm flesh. "Take your time, my dear. I find the anticipation of bedding you immensely enjoyable."

Eliza stood before him in a chemise and pantalets that were inset with lace in pivotal places. They had been brought along with the dress for her wedding.

Now she knew why. They were meant to entice her husband.

Eliza could feel his eyes on her. Feel his desire across the short distance that separated them. To her horror she felt her own desire rising to meet his. Her belly curled, and she felt a dampness between her thighs. Her skin prickled with awareness of him.

Eliza realized she was only making things worse by hesitating. She quickly stepped out of her satin slippers and pushed them to the side with her foot, then bent over to roll down her stocking.

The Beast drew an audible breath.

Eliza looked up without standing up, saw where his gaze seemed to be focused, then glanced down. Her torn chemise had fallen completely open. Her breasts were exposed to him all the way to the nipples. Which, as she watched, hardened into tight pink buds.

Eliza resisted the urge to jerk herself upright and cover herself with her hands. Instead, she remained bent over, completely exposed, but lifted her head and stared directly at his face, into his eyes. Slowly, steadily, she rolled down her left stocking and then the right. Not until she had finished and was naked to the knee did she stand upright again.

His right hand clutched a fistful of satin. His breathing was labored, the muscles of his thighs taut.

"Shall I continue?" she asked in the same silky, insinuating voice he had used on her.

"By all means," the Beast said, his voice curt and harsh with what she was learning to recognize as leashed desire.

Before she removed any more clothes, Eliza reached up to pull the pins from the knot that had held her hair in place at her crown. It fell heavily down her back. She pulled it forward over her shoulders. It would not hide her nakedness completely, but it satisfied her need for some modesty.

"Go on," he said in a guttural voice. "Finish it."

When Eliza reached for the tie on her chemise, her courage nearly failed her. But the Beast had already seen everything, had he not? And though she played the whore for him, she was his wife.

She released the ribbon and let the chemise fall open all the way to her waist. She shrugged and the thin straps fell off her shoulders. A tug, and the chemise slid completely down her arms. She held it by her fingertips for a moment, then let it drop to the floor.

Her mouth was dry, with no spit to swallow. She untied her pantalets and let them slide down over her hips to the floor, then stood where she was, her feet tangled in the cloth. Waiting.

Marcus's mouth had gone dry. She was exquisite, her breasts high and firm, the rosy nipples budded. Her waist was narrow, her hips wide enough for easy child-bearing. He could imagine her incredibly long, slender legs wrapped around his waist as he plunged into her.

"Get into bed," he said. "I will extinguish the candles."

For an instant, her eyes revealed stark terror. Then she was gone, scrambling under the covers he had asked Griggs to turn down, yanking the sheet all the way up to her neck like a terrified virgin. Which, of course, she was.

He stared at the torn dress still clutched in his fist. He had not meant to ruin her gown, and he would find a way to mend it, but that was the least of his problems.

She had begun this, Marcus thought angrily. Calling herself *whore*. As though he had not broken every vow he had ever made to himself to make her his wife. He had been ready to treat her as tenderly as any maiden on her wedding night, to soothe her fears as best he could. Knowing how she would be repulsed by his gloved hand. Knowing that she would fear the horribly scarred face she could not see. Knowing he would have to hurt her, because she was untried.

She had denied her right to his kindness. Denied her right to his courtesy and respect. Denied her right to be treated as the inexperienced virgin she was, by calling herself whore.

Yet a part of him urged understanding, urged compassion, urged tendernesss. That small voice could barely be heard beneath the heavy beat of his pulse, the steady throb of his arousal.

Marcus rose and circled the room blowing out candles, until only one was left. His hand was cupped around it, his head bent to snuff the flame, when she made a sound from the bed.

"Did you say something?"

He saw the struggle on her face before she said, "Please. Do not extinguish all the light."

"I must," he said sadly, blowing out the last flame.

He undressed himself quickly, knowing that the longer she lay alone in bed, the more difficult it would be to broach her. He debated whether to remove the leather glove, but left it on. It was smoother than the ravaged skin beneath it.

Eliza was panting, like a cornered fox, when he slid under the covers to join her.

"Don't touch me!" she cried.

He heard the panic in her voice. "Eliza," he said, quietly, "You are my wife—"

"Your whore!" she spat.

"I have tired of this game," he said curtly. Marcus levered himself on top of her, the weight of his body enough to prevent her escape. The shock of her flesh mated to his, her breasts rising against his chest, their bodies fitted exactly at waist and belly, left him feeling dizzy and breathless.

"Get off, you oaf!" she ranted, shoving against his shoulders. "You are too heavy!"

He knew she was afraid, but her vituperative words stung. He gritted his teeth against a vitriolic response, took most of his weight on his elbows, and used his knees to force her legs apart and make room for his hips between her thighs. "There is no way to do what must be done without some pain. If you resist me, it will only make it worse."

She bit back a sob, but her body writhed beneath him, resisting him, inflaming him.

He would rather have loved her before he put himself inside her. But it had been too long since he had bedded a woman. He was afraid if he waited he would spill himself on the sheets, and she would remain unbroached. He could not bear that ignominy on top of everything else. He was determined to make her his wife tonight. There was no turning back.

He threaded his hands into her hair to keep her from escaping and began pushing himself inside her.

"Stop!" she cried, bucking to free herself. "It hurts!"

He had never before lain with a virgin. There was no way he knew to prevent the pain this first time. He bit his lip and thrust hard, breaking through the thin membrane and burying himself to the hilt inside her.

She quivered beneath him.

"The worst is over," he grated through clenched teeth. He withdrew as slowly as he could bear, trying not to injure her further, and realized with a start that the passage was not difficult, as he had expected it to be. She was not dry inside; she was slick and wet.

After the Kiss

Ready for him. Excited by him. Wanting him.

He slid back inside her and heard her groan. Her hands clutched at his shoulders. Her nails dug crescents in his skin.

"Put your legs around me, Eliza," he whispered in her ear. "Hold tight to me."

Her legs cinched tightly around his buttocks, and she thrust her hips upward, causing an exquisite friction as he thrust down into her.

He wanted to go slow. He wanted to wait. But he did not pump into her more than once or twice before he spilled his seed. He withdrew, knowing he had left her unsatisfied. Knowing how frustrated she must feel, but unwilling to admit his own fault in the matter. That he had wanted her too badly. That he had been like a green boy with his first woman, unable to control his excitement enough to ensure her pleasure before he took his own.

Marcus levered himself off his wife and shifted to his side of the bed, lying on his back staring up into the dark, his right hand behind his head, the left beside him.

He could tell from the muffled sounds from the other side of the bed that she was crying. He felt the covers pull away and realized she was leaving the bed.

"Where are you going?"

"To my own bed."

"This is your bed," he said curtly, terrified that she would refuse to return and make him use force to keep her there.

"I have a room of my own on the other side of the Abbey," she said wearily. "I would like to go there."

"In the morning," he said brusquely. "Your nights are mine. That was the bargain."

He heard her swallow.

"I cannot bear . . ."

"Get into bed, Eliza. There will be no pain the next time, I promise you."

Eliza was half-asleep when she felt something move on her shoulder. She brushed at it with her hand to get it off, but it persisted.

"Eliza. Wake up."

Her eyes opened wide, and she found herself staring into pitch blackness.

She remembered everything. How terrified she had been, alone in the dark for those few, timeless moments before he had joined her in bed. And even then, how her imagination had created a beast where none existed. He had hurt her, it was true, but she had been warned of that pain. She had only wanted to stop him because, despite everything, she could feel herself succumbing to desire. It was fear of losing her soul that had made her fight the beast—instead of loving the man.

Eliza could only be grateful she had not been able to see into his eyes—and find love missing. Grateful that he had not been able to see into hers—and find love there.

She did not understand her feelings, nor could she explain them. How could she love the Beast? How could she want him? He was willing to make a whore of her.

No, Eliza. Not him. You are the one who started the game. He is the one who ended it.

304

She quivered as she felt the Beast's hand trace her ribs back and forth until he reached her belly. His fingertips seemed so smooth, not at all callused like— Eliza suddenly knew why his touch felt so strangely erotic.

"That is your gloved hand!" she gasped.

"It is," he admitted. "A hand. In a glove."

"I would much rather feel flesh against my flesh," she said. "When I think of your hand in that glove, I cannot help imagining a black spider crawling on my belly."

"A spider."

She shivered. "A huge, long-legged spider."

"I wear the glove to conceal—"

"Neither of us can see anything!" she interrupted. "It is as dark as the bottom of a well." She found his gloved hand in the dark—resting on her belly—and began tugging at the fingers of the glove.

He tried drawing his hand away, but she caught his thumb and held on. "If am to be yours for a lifetime, then you are also mine. It is only a crippled hand, Your Grace. Let me remove the glove."

"Marcus."

"What?"

"My name is Marcus. Say it, please."

"Will you let me take off the glove?" She had the feeling he was smiling. She reached toward his face to confirm or deny it. Some instinct made him reach up at the last instant to snag her wrist and draw it away.

"Marcus," he repeated.

"The glove?" she demanded.

He made a disgusted sound in his throat. "Very well. Remove it."

"Thank you, Marcus."

She was certain he did not breathe the entire time she was tugging off the glove. When at last she had it off, she heard him exhale gustily.

"There," she said, stuffing the glove under her pillow. "That was not so bad, was it?" *And good luck finding your glove when you want it again.*

He tried to withdraw his hand, apparently no longer interested in touching her without the glove.

"No, Marcus. I believe you were touching me . . . here . . . when you left off." His hand trembled as she laid the curled fingers against her belly. She kept her hand atop his, moving it around her body where she thought it might feel good.

She could distinguish the criss-crosses on his palm where the flesh had been sewn, the indentations where flesh had been torn away entirely. But mostly, it felt like a man's hand, with wiry hair across the knuckles, five gnarled, inflexible fingers, and fingertips that, while not as callused as his other hand, still had a texture rougher than her own.

She heard Marcus gasp when her pebbled nipple grazed the center of his palm. And bit back a gasp of her own, when he circled his palm against the sensitive crest.

"Your hand seems to have a great deal of feeling in it," she said. "I thought because you held it so stiffly—"

"I feel everything," he interrupted, his voice roughened by passion. "I feel the pleasure. And the pain."

"What pain?"

"Sometimes my hand aches. No, that is not a

strong enough word. Sometimes the muscles tighten excruciatingly. My whole body rebels against the torture."

"How do you stand it?"

"You may have heard that I indulge on occasion in an excess of brandy," he said sardonically.

"Rumor says you have been disguised on more than one occasion since your brother died." She paused and added. "I thought it was grief that made you get foxed."

"I suppose it was partly that, too," he conceded. "And other things."

She wondered what "other things" might include. Ruining her reputation? Abandoning her? Coming home alive, when Julian lay dead on the battlefield?

Eliza laid his hand palm up in hers and began to massage his fingers. To her surprise, when she manipulated them, she was able to move them slightly. "Have you ever tried to make your fingers work again?"

"No."

"Why not?" she asked.

"Why bother?"

"Because you might regain the use of your hand. Because—"

He snatched his hand away. "I don't indulge in false hopes, Eliza. Hoping something will happen doesn't make it so."

"I was not hoping you would move your fingers," she responded tartly. "I intended to move them myself!"

Eliza made a quick decision. From now on, whether he liked or not, whenever they were in bed together—and from what he had said, that meant almost every night—Eliza intended to work on those fingers. She was no doctor, but Marcus had nerves to feel sensation and muscles that could clench hard enough to cause him excruciating pain. What more did he need for a working hand?

"Eliza," he murmured.

She felt the tension emanating from him. She knew what he wanted. "Yes, Marcus?"

"I want to put myself inside you."

"Again?"

Laughter rumbled in his chest. "Yes, again."

"I am yours, to do with as you wish." She knew from the protest he made in his throat, that he had wanted a different answer from her. She had not been able to give it to him. She could not surrender herself entirely to him. He could make her body sing for him—it was already humming loudly—but she had to protect the part of her that needed more than physical pleasure from him.

He did not immediately cover her body with his. This time he touched her everywhere with his hands. And to her surprise, with his mouth.

"Do people do this?" she asked.

He laughed. "I am doing it to you."

"Is it . . . proper?" she insisted.

"My dear Eliza, you surprise me. When did you ever care what was proper?"

He had a point, Eliza conceded.

When his lips closed around her breast, and he began to suckle, she grabbed fistfuls of his hair to keep him there. Her insides began squeezing and un-squeezing with incredible pleasure. "Marcus, what are you doing?"

"Does it hurt?"

She shivered as cold air hit her nipple when he released it. She pressed his head back down. "No, no. It feels wonderful. Don't stop."

He played with her breasts. He tickled her ribs. He kissed the flesh beneath her ear, brushing her throat with his whiskers.

"You need a shave!" she chided, laughing when his whiskers tickled. She knew better than to touch his face. And he was careful not to let her.

When he mounted her at last, kneeing her legs apart and placing himself between them, she braced herself for the same pain as the first time. But as he pushed his way slowly inside her, filling her impossibly full, there was no pain, only a feeling of being stretched, of knowing he was there.

"Are you all right?" he asked.

"I think so," she replied.

"No pain."

She shook her head, then said, "None."

He began to move. Only this time, his hand slipped between them, to a spot where their bodies met. He moved his thumb, and she felt an exquisitely sharp sensation. She inched her body upward, seeking it again. She arched and swayed and writhed beneath his hand, while his shaft steadily rose and fell inside her.

Eliza closed her eyes and felt the sensations building. She angled her hips and shoved upward, wanting him to push deeper, faster, harder, so she could find whatever it was that lay just beyond her reach. She circled his hips without being asked, deepening the angle between them and giving him better access to her body. "Marcus, please," she pleaded. "Please."

She felt his muscles begin to tauten, heard him make a guttural sound in his throat.

Without warning, her body began to spasm. "Marcus!" she cried.

"I'm here, Eliza."

She held tightly to him as the pleasure became so intense it was almost pain. She heard him cry out, felt his seed spill into her. And then she was drifting back down from whatever rapturous place they had gone together.

"Go to sleep, Eliza," he murmured in her ear, his breathing still harsh and uneven.

She was too breathless to answer, merely closed her eyes and let him hold her tight in his arms.

Much later, Eliza yawned. She must be sure to awaken early in the morning. She and the twins had a great deal to do.

They had a little surprise planned for the Beast of Blackthorne.

Chapter 18

ARCUS WAS NOT READY TO WAKE UP, EVEN
though he knew the day had begun. He had
been having a dream which he did not want to let go.
He was loving Eliza, looking tenderly into her eyes as
she gazed adoringly back at him.

In real life, he had let her out of his room and
rebolted the doors shortly before dawn. She had
grumbled at being woken so early, scratched her
head, demanded a lantern, and disappeared down the
hall wearing his dressing gown and a pair of his slippers.

He felt good. More hopeful than he should. She
had taken off his glove. He had made love to her
twice.

She had wanted him.

That was half the battle. Now if he could only
figure out a way to get Eliza to forgive him, they
could live happily ever after . . . at night.

He heard voices. Children's voices. Shouting.
Breaking glass. Running feet and more shouting.

Marcus leaped from the bed, uncertain what ca-
tastrophe had occurred but anxious to get there as
quickly as he could to help. And realized he was stark

naked and had no idea where he had dropped his clothes in the dark.

He found a shirt and trousers near the foot of the bed and his stockings and boots at the head. He managed to get everything on, then realized he had no idea where his cloak and glove were. On hands and knees, he discovered his cloak balled up under the bed, but the damned glove was nowhere to be found.

Crying. A child's voice, crying.

He swirled the cloak around his shoulders, disappeared inside the hood, then stuck his crippled hand into his pocket. It could stay hidden there until he could find another glove.

He shot the bolts and swung open the door—to find chaos in the hall.

Footmen were running to and fro carrying framed art and vases and even an ormolu clock! Maids were dusting cobwebs from the hall ceiling and sweeping the floors. He glanced down the hall and saw that only a hundred years' growth of ivy kept sunlight from coming in through the mullioned windows across the east wing facade—which had been completely stripped of curtains!

"What is going on here?" he bellowed.

A maid at the far end of the hall opened her mouth to scream, but caught herself and curtsied instead. "Good morning, Your Grace. Her Grace is in the drawing room."

He had not asked. But it gave him a direction to go and a good notion who was behind all this disorder.

A footman edged out of his way juggling a Sevres vase. Marcus caught it as it fell and handed it back to the fellow. The footman was careful not to look at Marcus's face as he said, "Thank you, Your Grace."

The more polite they were, the angrier he got. What had happened to shrieking in terror? What had happened to fainting dead? He was the same monster he had been yesterday. Was he not?

Marcus glared at the next man he met, who backed up against the wall, holding a painting in front of him for protection.

"Oh, it's you, Fenwick," he said, relaxing slightly in the darkened hallway. "Why is my butler engaged in moving the furnishings?"

"Wasn't given a choice, Yer Grace," Fenwick whispered, glancing down the hall toward the open drawing room door. "Her Grace said any servant who didn't come to the east wing and help this mornin'—'ceptin' Cook, who's got orders to cook yer breakfast—was discharged! And anyone who screamed, or fainted, or looked at ye the least bit funny, was discharged without a reference."

Marcus clenched his jaws. Even Her Grace's blackmail could not totally repress the servants' abhorrence for him. It had served to curb their tongues, but not the terror reflected in their eyes and bodies. He did not want them here reminding him what a monster he was.

He marched down the hall, cloak swirling, intending to ring a peal over her head.

Marcus entered his drawing room and stopped dead. Nothing was where it had been. Except she had left the dark curtains over the windows. Perhaps she had considered that necessary to curb her own terror at seeing him, he thought darkly.

"What do you think, Griggs? Keep the chairs facing the fire, or turn them facing each other?" Eliza asked.

"Sergeant Griggs!" he bellowed.

The sergeant reflexively snapped to attention, caught himself, and turned to face the duke. "Is there somethin' you wanted, Your Grace?"

"Did I not give you strict orders that I was not at home to Her Grace during the day?"

"You did."

"Then what the devil is going on here!"

"Oh," Eliza said, smiling as she crossed to him. "I can explain that."

"I was not speaking to you," he said, keeping his eyes on the sergeant. "Well, Griggs?"

"Your Grace—"

"As I explained to Griggs," Eliza said, interrupting him, "I had no desire whatsoever to have an audience with you."

Marcus turned his head away, so she could not see his face. Fortunately, she did not cross to stand in front of him, but stared at his profile instead.

"All I wished to do was rearrange a little furniture and do a little cleaning. I never intended to disturb your rest."

"I heard broken glass. And a child crying."

"Oh, the twins were moving a crystal candelabra, but Reggie jigged when Becky jogged, and it met a sad fate on the stone floor," she said with a shrug and a diffident smile. "Neither child was hurt. Becky only cried because she was afraid you would be angry with her—I understand it was a Christmas gift one year to their mother. But once I assured her you would simply be glad she was unhurt, she was content. You are not angry, are you?"

Marcus wondered when he had lost control of the conversation. "No, I am not angry." The fewer reminders of Penthia in the Abbey, the better. "But I still do not understand what you are doing here."

"If the twins and I are moving in, we—"

"What?" Marcus could not quite believe what he had heard. "What did you say?"

"I said if the twins and I are moving in—"

"No," he said shaking his head. "Absolutely not. I wish to live alone. You cannot—"

"Uncle Marcus!"

"Uncle Marcus!"

Marcus pivoted and saw Reggie and Becky running toward him full tilt. He pulled the hood completely forward, to ensure his scarred face could not be seen. "Stop!" he commanded.

They lurched to a halt six feet in front of him.

"Uncle Marcus?"

"Uncle Marcus?"

Two pairs of pleading, anxious eyes stared up at him. He knew what they wanted. To be picked up, to be hugged, to be laughed with and loved. He wished the problem were as simple as Eliza had tried to make it. He could not go back to living as he had before Waterloo. Servants could be forced not to show their revulsion, but that did not mean it did not exist, that he could not feel their fear and loathing. The same held true for the children.

What if he tried to pick up one of the twins and, as Reggie had last night, she fled from him instead? He would rather love them at a distance. Maybe he was protecting himself at their expense. But he could not do otherwise.

Marcus felt a quick tug on his breeches and looked down to find Becky standing near him.

"Uncle Marcus—"

"What are you doing in here?"

"Eliza said—"

"I have forbidden you to come to this wing of the Abbey," he interrupted. "I meant what I said."

"And I meant what I said," Eliza interjected, "when I told the children we are moving to this wing of the Abbey."

How beautiful she looked, a few curls spilling from the knot at her crown, her chin raised, her golden eyes sparkling with defiance. "You cannot move the household willy-nilly wherever you want," he said.

"Why not? There is plenty of room here."

"The place is haunted," he said flatly. He glanced at Reggie and Becky and saw his suggestion had been planted in fertile ground.

Eliza countered, "It is no such thing. I spent the night here last night and nothing happened to me."

"Oh, no?" He reached out to caress her throat and whispered in a voice no one but she could hear, "Who made this bruise, Eliza? A Beast I think. A monster in the night."

She flushed to the roots of her hair.

"Oh!" Becky cried. "You've taken off the glove!"

Marcus stared at the hand resting on Eliza's cheek. The slightly curled fingers were pale as chalk, the scars even whiter than the skin surrounding them. He quickly withdrew his hand and stuffed it in his pocket.

"Your hand does not look nearly so much like a spider without the glove," Becky said ingenuously.

"A spider?" Marcus shot Eliza a look, and she shrugged as though to say she had not coached the child.

"I thought it looked like a bird's claw, Uncle Marcus," Reggie volunteered.

Becky looked up at him quizzically. "Does it still hurt, Uncle Marcus? Is that why you do not use it?"

"The wounds are healed," he said curtly.

"But sometimes the muscles get very tight," Eliza said, looking at him. "We can help Uncle Marcus make it feel better by bringing him hot water to ease the cramping."

"Oh," Becky said, looking up at him and back down at the bulging pocket that contained his gnarled hand. "Do you need some hot water right now, Uncle Marcus? Is that why you are acting so horrid?"

Marcus felt like laughing. And crying. "My hand is fine."

"I can help too, Uncle Marcus," Reggie volunteered.

"I need nothing from either of you!" Marcus snapped. "I can take care of myself."

Marcus felt his stomach knot as tears brimmed in Becky's eyes. Reggie's eyes misted, but she blinked hard, and in moments her face was coldly emotionless.

Reggie took Becky's hand. "I told you he would not want us here." Then, watching him over her shoulder, she dragged Becky from the room.

Griggs gave him a disappointed, disgusted look and followed after them.

Marcus glanced at Eliza and found disillusionment and disapproval in her eyes.

She had no right to condemn him. This was all her fault. He did not want any help coping with the nightmarish episodes he occasionally endured with his hand. He was not convinced a little hot water was going to do much to end his suffering, and he had no desire for the children to see him in that kind of agony, or entirely castaway when he used the one method he had found that did ease the pain.

"I hope you are happy," Eliza said when the door had closed behind Griggs and the twins.

"I never asked for your help," he snarled. "And I don't want it. I told you what use I have for you. You agreed to the bargain. Take the servants and go back where you belong."

"The twins need you so badly, Marcus. Did you see how willing they were to accept your gnarled hand when you no longer hid it away as though it were something to be feared? I am sure it would be the same once they got used to the scars on your face."

He closed his eyes. He felt sick at heart. She made it sound so easy. "I am a monster, Eliza." He said the words because they helped him to remember the hopelessness of his situation.

Her face paled. "A Beast, yes," she said disdainfully. "You treated those children without kindness or courtesy. But a monster? I will not know until you show yourself to me."

She swept out of the room without another word.

* * *

Eliza was furious with Marcus for using some silly old scars as an excuse for not hugging the twins. Imagine refusing their offer of help! Imagine sending them away, when he must have seen the hope in their eyes that he would accept them back into his life.

Eliza knew, deep in her heart, it was an understatement to call the wounds to his face "silly old scars." When she had told the servants of her plan to clean and refurbish the east wing, and eventually to move there, they had unanimously objected to helping her because of those "silly old scars."

"Made me sick to my stomach when I saw 'im," one girl said.

"Gave me nightmares," another added.

" 'Twas the face of a monster!" a third whispered.

"Fiddlesticks!" she had told them all. "It is only Marcus Wharton, whom you've known all your lives, come back from Waterloo with a cut on his face from a saber."

"Ain't you afraid of him, Your Grace?" one of the maids asked.

"Would I marry a man I feared?"

It had obviously been the wrong response because, in the end, she had needed to threaten the servants to make them go.

Eliza could not blame Marcus for being leery of showing his face to the servants or the twins. But she had to figure out some way of making him show it to her. Maybe once she saw his face for herself, she would know what she was dealing with. Only then would she know whether he was right to hide himself from the world.

Whatever he was, however he looked, he had become her husband last night. Whatever the horror of his visage, she could vouch for the fact there was nothing about his body she found repellent. He was all sinew and bone. His chest was broad and powerful, covered with a soft, ticklish mat of hair. His thighs and buttocks were corded muscle, taut and firm. Surrounded by his strong arms, she had felt safe and secure in the dark.

As for the bruise on her throat . . .

Eliza could remember Marcus sucking gently on her throat beneath her ear, sending frissons of feeling skittering throughout her body. When he increased the sucking pressure and actually bit at her skin, her insides had drawn up tight. She could remember moaning and writhing. But there had been no pain. Only breathtaking, unbelievable bliss.

Despite the bruise, the Beast had done her no harm.

Eliza went in search of the twins, to remedy what harm she could from the morning, but they were nowhere to be found. She wondered if they had disappeared into the secret passageway, where she could not—would not—follow.

She had almost given up hope of finding them— until they wanted to be found—when she discovered them playing in the stable with Frances and another litter of kittens. By then, Eliza was well aware of the damage she had wrought by pushing too hard to reunite Marcus and his children.

The duke had issued orders countermanding hers. No servant was to cross the threshold of the east wing on pain of *death*, without a written order from him.

Her plan to move herself and the children into the east wing had been irrevocably canceled.

The Beast's solitude was once again assured.

Worse than having the servants look askance at her for marrying a lunatic—or being one herself—was the damage she had done to the twins' budding trust in her. She had promised them they would get their uncle back. She had failed dismally to deliver.

Eliza knew she was in trouble when she saw the twins had changed into *matching* bows.

"Hello," she said as she squatted down in the same inelegant pose Reggie and Becky had adopted next to the mother cat and her kittens. She pointed and said, "That one looks just like Blackie."

"Midnight is not ready to leave Frances," Becky said.

"You cannot have him," Reggie said.

"I see." Their previous offer of a kitten was rescinded. Along with their trust and their friendship.

"You lied," Reggie accused.

"Uncle Marcus never wanted to see us!" Becky said.

Eliza searched for words to help them understand. "Your uncle wants to see you. But he is also afraid to see you. Or rather, afraid for you to see him."

"But why?" Reggie demanded, wrapping her arms around her knees.

"Because of the ugly scar on his face," Eliza said bluntly.

"It is not as bad as it was at first," Becky said.

"It is horrible!" Reggie countered. "His eye is all bunched up on one side, and his cheek has an awful crooked line in it. But I would not mind looking at it, if only he would not send us away."

"It does make one wince," Becky agreed.

"You sound as though you know exactly what your uncle's face looks like behind that black hood," Eliza said. "How is that possible?"

"We saw him through—"

Reggie elbowed Becky hard enough to cut her off. "We just do."

"But if you've seen his face, and you believe you can bear to look at it—however horrible—why is your uncle so intent on hiding it from you?" Eliza asked, nonplussed.

"Uncle Marcus doesn't know we've seen him," Becky said. "Because we spied on him from behind the wall."

"Behind what wall?"

Reggie poked Becky again.

"Stop it!" Becky said. "We already told her about spying on Uncle Marcus from the secret passage." Becky turned to Eliza and said, "We heard Griggs tell Uncle Marcus he should look for himself and see it isn't so bad, but Uncle Marcus won't."

"Are you suggesting your uncle has no idea what he looks like?"

"There is not a single looking glass in the east wing," Reggie said.

Eliza stared at her in disbelief. "Surely you jest!"

Both girls shook their heads.

"How can he shave without—" She cut herself off. She had known from the feel of Marcus's beard and the length of his hair when they had consummated their marriage, that he must not have shaved or cut his hair in a very long time.

"Now she'll tell Uncle Marcus about us spying and get us into trouble," Reggie said sullenly.

"Eliza would never tell about the secret passageway if we asked her not to," Becky said to Reggie. She turned and, looking earnestly up at Eliza, said, "You wouldn't, would you, Eliza?"

"No, I would not. Not if you show me where it is."

"I am not sure we should," Becky said, a frown etching lines in her young brow. "Father absolutely forbid us to go in there the time we got lost. Now that he may be coming home soon, I do not think—"

"Your father—the duke—is alive?" Eliza exclaimed.

"The Duke of Braddock said at the wedding that there is a new laird at Blackthorne Hall, and that it may be Father," Becky explained.

"Does your uncle know about this?" Eliza asked.

"Griggs was supposed to tell him," Reggie said.

Eliza jumped up from the straw. "I want to see the secret passageway, but I think first I should make sure your uncle knows about this. Can I meet you in your room right after tea?"

Eliza waited to see whether they were willing to give her a second chance.

"I suppose so," Reggie said. "If you absolutely promise not to tell Uncle Marcus about the secret passageway."

"I promise," Eliza said, crossing her heart.

Eliza left the children and raced inside the Abbey, directly toward the east wing. She had just crossed the threshold when Griggs appeared and stood in her way.

"Is there somethin' I can do for you, Your Grace."

"I need to speak with my husband."

"I'll be glad to take a message to him."

Eliza started to brush past the sergeant, but he stepped in her way.

"He won't see you. Not in the daytime. I can take a message to him, but I can't let you in. Not until dark."

Eliza stared, disbelieving, into the soldier's flinty eyes. This was not the same man who had willingly abetted her invasion of the duke's domain. Obviously, the law had been laid down to him, as well. Eliza had no doubt Griggs would lay hands—his hand—on her to keep her out.

"Never mind, Griggs. What I have to say to His Grace"—and it was a good deal more than the information that his brother might be alive—"I will say to his face tonight."

Eliza spent the afternoon seething. She was careful not to reveal her anger when she met the twins in their bedroom.

"This is the panel that lets you into the secret passageway," Reggie said, pressing on part of the wall near the fireplace. The panel swung open. Eliza realized the mock facade around the fireplace in the girls' room perfectly concealed the entrance to the passageway.

When Eliza stuck her upper body inside the pitch black vault, Reggie gave her a shove and slammed the door behind her.

"It's really dark in there, isn't it," Reggie said with a laugh.

"Let her out!" Becky cried. "There are *spiders* in there!"

The feeling of being crushed from all sides paralyzed Eliza. Her legs felt strapped to the floor. Her hands felt bound to her sides. Only her eyes moved, searching for something to see, searching for a way out. Black nothingness surrounded her as though she were buried alive.

Eliza could not breathe. She was afraid to draw breath, for fear of what she would smell. She knew it would be something awful. Something that would make her sick.

The panel suddenly opened and bright sunlight streamed in around her. She drew a deep, gasping lungful of air.

"Eliza," Becky said, grabbing her hand. She tugged, but Eliza's feet were still rooted to the floor.

"Are you all right? Your hand is so cold! You look so pale!" Becky turned and glowered at Reggie. "That was not funny, Reggie. Sometime I'm going to shut you in there without a light and see how you like it!"

Eliza felt dizzy. She lifted her feet, which felt like heavy irons, and backed slowly out of the passageway. When she pushed the panel shut, a draft of air squeezed out. She held her breath as long as she could, but at last was forced to inhale. The stale, moldy-smelling odor was not familiar. It was not the one she had feared. That was another smell entirely, stronger, more distasteful, more . . . She did not quite know what.

"I only meant to tease you a little," Reggie said.

"I am afraid of the dark," Eliza confessed.

Reggie flushed, and Becky glared at her again.

"We never go in there without a lantern," Becky said.

"You will never go in there again!" Eliza said, fear making her voice sharp. She was imagining the terror of being lost inside those cold, black walls.

"We don't have to do what you say," Reggie retorted.

Eliza said nothing for a moment, merely met Reggie's gaze and held it, forcing her to acknowledge for the first time the significant change in their relationship. As Reggie's aunt, and as the new Duchess of Blackthorne, Reggie most certainly did have to obey her. Nevertheless, she explained the reason for her dictum.

"I don't want you in those passageways because it's dangerous! You could get lost and die in there."

Reggie scoffed. "We know where we're going. We haven't gotten lost in a long time."

"What if your lantern were accidentally extinguished? How would you find your way back?"

"I'd go to one of the grates in the wall," Becky said, "and shout for help."

"What grates?" Eliza asked.

"The passageway leads to grates in the walls of various rooms, where you can see and hear whoever's on the other side," Becky said.

"Show me one."

Becky and Reggie ran downstairs to their father's library with Eliza on their heels. They pointed to a simple, decorative iron grate set along the floor at the base of a wall full of bookshelves.

"See?" Reggie said. "There's one."

Eliza examined the grate standing up, but saw nothing that indicated anything was on the other side. "Are you certain? I don't see anything."

"You have to get closer," Becky said.

Eliza dropped to her hands and knees. Within an inch of the grate she felt a draft and inhaled the same stale, moldy odor she had smelled through the panel upstairs.

"Where does this passageway go?" she asked.

"They are all connected," Reggie said. "Like a honeycomb inside the Abbey. Upstairs and down, from one wing to the other."

Eliza thought of the ghosts haunting the Abbey. Not ghosts at all, she realized, but real human voices—the sound perhaps distorted by distance— carried through these passageways from one room to the next. "These passageways must have been used once upon a time to eavesdrop," she mused aloud.

Reggie and Becky settled on the floor beside Eliza. "Father said the monks who built the Abbey must not have trusted each other very much."

Eliza smiled ruefully. "I never thought of that."

Fenwick appeared at the door to the library and cleared his throat.

Eliza jumped up and hurriedly began brushing the dust off her dress and the twins' shifts, as they rose beside her. She would have to get the maids to do a better job in here. "Yes, Fenwick? What is it?"

Fenwick pretended not to notice anything amiss. "Yer aunt has arrived, Yer Grace. I've arranged for her things to be taken upstairs to the room next to yers. She's waitin' on ye in the drawing room."

"Would you like to meet my aunt?" she asked the twins.

"We saw her at the wedding," Reggie said unenthusiastically.

"Please come," Eliza urged. "I think you will get along famously with each other." She took the twins' hands and led them out the door. "Aunt Lavinia cannot see," she began.

"At all?" Reggie asked, dumbfounded.

Eliza shook her head. "The one thing you must always remember when you are with Aunt Lavinia is . . ."

The rest of the afternoon with her aunt and the twins was one of the most pleasant Eliza had ever spent. The twins loved trying to trick Aunt Lavinia in a game of hide-and-seek. She amazed them—and sometimes Eliza—with her ability to find them without ever leaving her chair.

Eliza enjoyed the day as best she could, knowing that when darkness fell, she would have to confront the Beast.

He had said she was not his whore. That it was a game she played. But he had commanded Griggs to turn her away, confirming she had no purpose except as his consort at night.

After supper, after the children had been tucked into bed, and she had assured herself that her aunt was comfortable, Eliza went to her bedroom and changed into a concealing nightgown. She was unwilling to take the chance that her husband would ask her to disrobe for him again. She crept down the stairs, with a candle to keep the dark at bay, and made her way to the east wing.

Griggs led her to the Beast's bedroom, held open the door for her to enter, and said, "His Grace will join you shortly."

The first thing Eliza looked for when she entered the bedroom was an iron grate, similar to the one in the library. She found two, not more than a foot wide, running floor to ceiling on either side of the throne-like chair. If only she had the courage to go into the passageway, she might catch the Beast unaware and see his face for herself.

Paralyzing terror rose in her breast at the thought of entering that dark abyss. She shook her head to free herself from the memory. She would never go in there again.

At least the search for a grate had helped to fill the time she waited for Marcus. She paced the room, becoming more and more nervous. She sat in the thronelike chair, paced, then sat again.

But he never came.

Eliza had made up her mind to leave when she noticed moonlight streaming through tiny holes in the black curtains. They were not as new as she had first thought. The velvet was riddled with tiny moth holes.

She shoved the worn velvet aside and looked out onto a neglected garden. She could see the barn in the distance. And on a far hillock, a ghostly white horse, ridden by a man dressed all in black.

Eliza left the Beast's bedroom on the run, headed for the barn. If she could only get there before he returned, she could hide herself and perhaps catch the Beast without his hood. She was barefoot, but she did not want to take the time to go up to her room for slippers, for fear she would miss him.

The grass was soft under her feet and wet with dew. Goose bumps rose on her arms, from the cold or the damp . . . or the dark. She shivered, pulled up her gown to keep the hem from getting soaked, and raced through the cool night air.

But as fast as she ran, it was not fast enough. The Beast was there before her. She hesitated behind a lilac bush, watching as he led the immense white horse inside.

He was wearing his cloak and hood. She could see nothing of his face.

Eliza knew she should return to the house before the Beast caught her spying on him. But perhaps it was better—if she planned to raise her voice—to do it here, rather than in the Abbey, where the sound might carry through the grates to some other part of the house.

The Beast must have left his horse for the groom to tend, because he appeared moments later carrying something in his arms. It took a moment for her to realize it was a child.

Becky must also have seen her uncle riding, gone to wait for him at the stable, and fallen sound asleep. She had been right. It was her uncle who carried her back to her room at night and put her in bed.

Marcus was not uncaring, Eliza realized. Merely unwilling to have his daughters shrink from him in horror if they saw his face.

But she must see it. Would see it. She could see it, Eliza realized, if she confronted him now. There was no way he could stop her from removing the hood while he was holding Becky in both arms. He could not very well drop the child, and if she was quick enough . . .

Eliza waited breathlessly until Marcus had reached the spot where she was hiding and stepped out directly in front of him.

"Hello, Marcus."

He froze. His features were well hidden by the hood.

Eliza knew she should do it now, before he suspected what she was about, but her courage failed her.

You must do it. Everything depends on your fortitude. Whatever is there, you can bear it. Must bear it.

But not yet, she thought. *When I have said what must be said, then I will do it.*

"I don't care much for the terms of our marriage so far," she said baldly. "I needed to speak with you today, but Griggs turned me away."

"He was obeying my orders."

"What if I had needed you for something important?" she demanded.

"Was it important?"

"Did you know your brother may be alive?"

"Griggs told me there is a chance Alastair is in Scotland, at Blackthorne Hall. So you see, there was no need after all for you to see me."

Eliza blew out a breath of air. "Is this really what you want, Marcus? Is there no other way we can arrange to live together?"

He shook his head.

Eliza made her move.

Marcus was apparently so stunned that she would dare to remove his hood, that the deed was done before he could back away. Suddenly his head was bare. And she could see his face.

Chapter 19

ELIZA FOUGHT NOT TO CRY OUT. THE SCARS WERE not as terrible as she had expected. But the damage was not as little as she had hoped.

"You have what you wanted," Marcus snarled. "Are you satisfied?"

She swallowed hard, forcing herself to look at him. With the moonlight at his back, she could not see enough of his features to get more than an impression of disfigurement.

"You need a shave, Marcus," she said as calmly as she could. "I cannot find your face for all the hair growing on it."

"There is a reason I do not shave," he said, his body rigid with tension, his voice hoarse with rage.

She fought to keep her gaze even with eyes that threatened violence. "I brought a looking glass with me to your bedroom tonight."

"I do not wish to see myself."

"Shall I describe what I see for you?" Before he could object, she said, "An unkempt head of hair. A beard that has grown wild. Two gleaming eyes. An aristocratic nose. I believe there must be a mouth beneath the beard, but I cannot see it."

She swallowed and said, "Your left eye is webbed

333

with scars at the far edge near your temple, and your eyebrow is divided by the same line that travels down your cheek to separate your beard. Coincidentally, it is not much wider than the blade of a saber.

"I would say the scar also cuts through the edge of your mouth. But it has not affected your speech that I can hear. Or any other use to which you have put your mouth," she said quietly.

She was remembering all the things he had done to her with his mouth the night past. And done very well.

"I have seen your face, Marcus," Eliza said. "And I have not fled screaming in terror."

"It is dark. You cannot see it as it really is!"

"You are no monster, Marcus. Only a very foolish and frightened man." Eliza turned to leave.

"I expect to find you waiting for me," he said, "after I have put Becky to bed."

She glanced at him over her shoulder. "And if I am not?"

"I will come and get you."

Marcus felt confused, and as frightened as Eliza had accused him of being. She had challenged everything he had believed about himself for the past year. Was it possible the wounds had healed looking less terrible than when he had last seen them? Griggs had told him as much, but the sergeant was used to seeing desecrated bodies.

Marcus was afraid to hope, afraid to believe that he might be able to move again in Society, or at least among his household servants, without them shrinking from him.

He shifted Becky in his arms, trying to relieve the pressure on his clawlike hand and headed for the Abbey. He had felt the familiar tension building in the hand late in the afternoon and known what was coming. The cramps began as muscle twitches. The muscles steadily tightened over the next several hours until the wrenching spasms began. When the agony became unbearable, he drank himself into oblivion.

He had gone riding soon after sundown in the hope that if he refused to acknowledge the pain, it would go away. Marcus had not realized how long he had been running from the inevitable, until Eliza confronted him at the stable. Under the circumstances, it had been insane to order his wife to be waiting for him in his bedroom. Rather, he should have sent her away and ordered a bottle of brandy from Griggs.

But after seeing her barefoot, her hair flowing down her back in the moonlight, her nipples poking at the thin cloth, he had wanted her badly enough to deny the pain. He would take her quickly, he decided, push her and himself to the heights of ecstasy, where the pain could not follow, then send her away before the shrieking muscles unmanned him.

On his way up the stairs to her bedroom, he shifted Becky again, accidentally waking her. He tensed, remembering that his hood no longer concealed his face.

"Father?" she asked groggily.

He realized she was still half asleep, and the hall was too dark for her to see him. "No, Becky. It is Uncle Marcus."

She snuggled against him trustingly. "I dreamed you were Father," she mumbled.

He waited for her to say more, but she had fallen back asleep. He was glad, because he had no way of getting her to bed except through the lighted doorway.

He walked as quietly as he could across the bedroom and laid her gently on the bed beside Reggie, who was sprawled out in the middle. He slipped Becky's feet under the covers and pulled the sheet and coverlet up over her.

When he leaned over to kiss Becky on the forehead, he realized that Reggie's eyes were open. And that she was staring at him with wide-eyed horror.

He quickly yanked the hood up over his face, blew out the candle, and whirled, cloak flying, to leave the room.

The sound of Reggie screaming . . . and screaming . . . and screaming . . . followed him down the stairs all the way to the east wing. He was trembling, his heart pounding, when Griggs met him there.

"See to the children, Griggs." He met the sergeant's eyes and said, "Reggie saw my face."

Marcus headed down the hallway toward his bedroom more furious with Eliza than he had been when she exposed his face in the moonlight. She had lied to him. Told him his face was bearable. Allowed him to hope.

He slammed open his bedroom door and found her bent over a black kettle set on a hob over the fire. Too many candles, he thought. Too much light. She would see his face.

And then he did not care. He saw her and wanted her and nothing else mattered.

She rose quickly and smoothed her gown over her belly and hips, revealing even more of her body than she had in the moonlight.

"Get in bed," he said. "Now."

"No. Not until you shave. I have warmed water over the fire—"

He reached her in two strides, grabbed her by the hair, and dragged her to the bed. He mantled her struggling body with his own, using his legs to force hers wide. As she bucked against him, he settled his engorged shaft in the cradle of her thighs.

"Marcus, no! Don't do this!" She pushed at his shoulders, freeing the hood, which fell back, exposing his face in the candlelight.

Her eyes went wide with shock.

His heart clutched. His stomach lurched. She had only been fooling herself. And him. The moonlight had softened the horror, had made him seem less of a beast and more of a man. The light revealed the truth in her eyes.

She could not bear to look at him.

Marcus never took his eyes off of hers as he lowered his mouth toward hers. When she tried to close her eyes, he rasped, "Look at me, Eliza. See what you have married. Love the beast, for that is what I am."

He crushed her lips with his, thrusting his tongue inside her mouth in a violent imitation of a loving act. His hand throbbed painfully, along with his shaft. He took no time to prepare her—there was no time before the pain would be upon him—simply grabbed the cloth gown and shoved it aside, freed himself, and thrust inside her.

She was not ready for him, and he knew he had hurt her without hearing her cry of pain.

"Marcus! Stop!"

She pounded at his shoulders, yanked on his beard, left bloody scratches to mar what was left of his beauty.

He paused, gasping, and stared down at her tear-streaked face. The horror was gone. Her golden eyes glared at him, daring him, defying him to continue.

Suddenly his hand spasmed, the muscles clenching tight. He was still embedded deep inside her, his body throbbing. He closed his eyes and bit his lip hard enough to draw blood, but still the groan of agony escaped.

When he opened his eyes, her gaze had shifted to his twitching hand.

"I don't—need your—pity!" he grated between cramping spasms.

"Marcus, let me help you," she pleaded.

"I don't—need your—help!" He thrust savagely, an animal in pain seeking solace. He spilled his seed inside her with a cry of rage and pain and shame.

He heard her hiss as he withdrew himself and turned from her and readjusted his clothes. She scrambled away from him, nearly falling as her knees buckled when her feet landed on the floor. She pushed herself upright and ran for the door.

He got there first and blocked her way.

"Let me out!" she cried. "I cannot bear to be near you!"

"You made a bargain, wife. The nights are mine."

She made a frustrated sound in her throat. She

could not get past him. He was too strong. And she knew it.

"You may take all you want from me as brutally as you wish, but I will give you nothing more of myself," she snarled at him. "Animal! Monster!"

He closed his eyes and turned his head away from her. God, what had he done to her? What had he done to both of them?

He opened the door and stood aside. "Leave." When she did not move, he shouted, "Get out!"

When she stood where she was, he slammed the door and bolted it, locking her inside. With the beast.

Eliza had made up her mind in an instant—of stupidity? of sympathy?—to stay with Marcus. She did not know why he had attacked her. She had not expected it. She was certain anger—and pain—must have driven him to it.

She had no idea what had provoked the anger, but before the night was over, she intended to find out. She knew exactly what had caused the pain.

Eliza crossed to the hob and checked the water in the kettle over the fire. It was more than warm shaving water now. It bubbled and boiled with a hiss. She headed for the tall chest where she knew Marcus kept his clothes and began to open drawers.

He took a threatening step toward her. "Why are you ransacking my clothing?"

"I am looking for handkerchiefs. Here they are," she said breathlessly, pulling a handful out. She shot him a bold, sidelong glance. "It seems you will have a great deal to return to your brother when he shows up again. The children. The title. And handkerchiefs."

Kerchief after kerchief she unfolded was monogrammed with a B.

"What are you doing?" he demanded.

Eliza crossed back to the kettle and dropped all of them into the pot. "Go sit in that chair in the corner," she ordered.

He shrugged and said, "It is as good a place to sit and drink as any other. Find Griggs and tell him to bring me a bottle of brandy."

She had no intention of allowing Griggs to add drunkenness to the Beast's other vices. But she was going to need the sergeant's help. "Very well, Marcus." She headed for the door.

"Eliza," he said, settling himself in the thronelike chair.

She turned to look at him. "Yes, Marcus?"

"Don't come back," he said in a soft voice.

She looked into his face, realizing belatedly that she was not seeing the scars that ruined his beauty, only the expressions of agony and despair.

"I will bring Griggs when I return," she said.

He closed his eyes and turned his head away. His right hand clenched the arm of the chair. His left hand twitched spasmodically.

Eliza was nearly running by the time she reached Griggs's bedroom and pounded on the door. When he did not answer, she shoved the door open and was startled to discover he was not there.

She swallowed hard. Could she do this alone? Would Marcus hold still for her ministrations without Griggs to lend a hand? Should she bring Marcus the brandy, after all? She knew that was the way he had escaped the pain in the past.

But Eliza had seen her mother ease the ache in her father's feet with hot water. Surely the remedy would work just as well for a hand.

She hurried back to Marcus's bedroom, figuratively rolling up her sleeves. It was not going to be easy to convince him there was another way to allay his pain besides drinking himself into a stupor.

"Where is Griggs?" he said the instant she closed and bolted the door behind her. "And where is my brandy?"

"Griggs was not in his room, and—"

Marcus pounded the arm of the chair with his right fist. "Damn and blast! I forgot I sent him up to take care of the children."

"What is wrong with the twins? Are they hurt?" she cried, hurrying to his side.

He shot her an angry look. "Reggie took one look at my face and screamed her bloody head off. I would not be surprised if she woke the entire household."

Eliza stood stunned. She now knew the reason for his wrath. "She saw your face?"

His lips twisted bitterly. "She woke up when I was putting Becky to bed. You deceived me completely, Eliza. I believed the faradiddle you told me in the moonlight. It seems the scars are not bearable. At least, not to a child."

"You cork-brained idiot! I told the truth! Waking up to find anyone—especially a long-haired, wildly bearded man—lurking in your bedroom in the middle of the night would be enough to frighten any child."

"I tell you my face—"

"If you were right, I should be quailing at the very sight of you." She walked right up and stood nose to nose with him. "Do I look the least bit frightened by your bloody face?"

Marcus frowned, but whether at the blasphemy or her apparent lack of fear, she was not sure. Eliza watched as his lowering forehead squeezed the scars at the edge of his eye into a spray of white against the darker skin. There was nothing grotesque about it; the left side of his face was simply spider-webbed with very thin, very smooth white lines. She was itching to shave him, to see what his face looked like without the beard.

That would have to wait.

She left Marcus sitting where he was and crossed to the fire, using the iron poker to lift one of the handkerchiefs from the boiling pot. She let it drip on the stone floor as she made her way back to Marcus. She reached out to see if the cloth was cool enough for her to wring it out in her hands. She pulled it off, leaned the poker against the chair, and wrung out the handkerchief, letting the excess water splatter on the floor, where it ricocheted onto his boots.

She was reminded of the first night she had met him, the first time he had kissed her . . . at the well. So long ago. A lifetime ago. She looked up and saw Marcus's eyes were focused on her. And that he was remembering, too.

She swallowed over the ache in her throat. "This should not be too hot," she said, passing the kerchief from hand to hand like a hot potato.

He eyed her skeptically.

"It has to be hot to relax the muscles."

He started to get up, and she put a flat hand

against his chest. "I will use force if I must, to keep you where you are."

He lifted a brow. "You think you can?"

She picked up the poker and brandished it. "A lump on the head would work, I believe."

His lips curled. "Very well, wife. Do your worst." The humor disappeared from his face as a spasm racked his hand.

While his eyes were closed and his teeth gritted against the pain, Eliza wrapped the hot handkerchief around his hand from palm to knuckles.

"You'll likely burn the thing to a crisp, and I can knock off the ashes and be done with it," he said when he was able to open his eyes and study her handiwork.

She was already at the kettle retrieving another kerchief. "I think I can leave this one a little hotter and put it over the other," she said.

Eliza watched the sweat pop out on Marcus's forehead as she added the steaming kerchief to his spasming hand. Saw the bead of blood where he had bitten his lip through. Watched his right hand clench the arm of the chair and dig in until his fingernails left white crescents in the dark wood. His whole body strained to survive the torment.

"I cannot do it, Eliza," he gasped between spasms. "I need something to dull the pain. This is not working."

"It will," she promised. "A little longer, Marcus." She leaned over to kiss his wounded cheek above the beard.

Their eyes met—his shocked, hers compassionate.

"Why did you do that?" he asked, watching her face carefully.

"It is a bribe," she admitted with a smile. "Someone told me once you can get almost anything with a bribe. Is it working?"

"It depends on what you want," he said, his lips quirking.

"Another thirty minutes to see if this treatment will work. If it does not . . . I will bring you a bottle of brandy myself."

Marcus looked at the ormolu clock on the tall chest. "Thirty minutes," he agreed.

Eliza knelt at his side on the hard stone floor, her knees aching as she massaged his fingers.

"That is only making it worse," he said through tight jaws, pulling his hand away.

"Let me try," she said, holding out her hand until he laid his hand in her palm.

He turned his face away, tightened his right hand on the chair, and shuddered as another spasm racked his clawlike hand.

Eliza kept the handkerchiefs as hot as she—and he—could bear. She started at his little finger and worked her way to his thumb, curling the fingers forward and straightening them out. She massaged the joints. The space between his thumb and forefinger. The palm of his hand. His wrist. And back the other direction.

It took twenty-two minutes.

"I . . . I think the pain . . . the spasms have stopped," Marcus said in wonder. He stared at his gnarled hand, which lay in her palm.

Eliza looked up at him, a relieved smile on her

face. "I am so glad, Marcus. Now that you know what to do, you can begin the treatment as soon as you suspect the muscles have begun to clench." She curled his little finger almost all the way to his palm. "Do you see how flexible this finger is? I think they all might become so, if you worked with them."

He pulled his hand from hers. "I can do this for myself now. Thank you."

Eliza rose, keeping her gaze lowered, so he would not see how much his rejection hurt. "If you no longer need me," she said, "I will go."

"Eliza," he said, his voice raw. "Don't leave."

She turned to face him, then opened her arms wide. "Here stands your whore, Marcus, whom you feel free to rape for your pleasure."

He winced.

"I cannot live that life. I deserve much, much more. I will not stay tonight, nor will I come to this room again, unless you ask me here as your wife."

"What does that mean, Eliza?"

"It means I want to be honored and respected. It means I want to share my life with you night and day. It means I want your love, Marcus, before I will give you mine."

"I admire you, Eliza."

She shook her head sadly. "It is not enough, Marcus."

"I need you."

"You need my body, Marcus. I want your soul to be the other half of mine, to fill an emptiness inside me. Until you want all of me, body and soul, you can have none at all."

"I do not think I am able to love you," he said, the words torn from him.

"Then I am sorry for both of us, Marcus. I will live my life the best I can without you—in the light. You may stay here in the darkness forever if you like. But you will be here by yourself."

Eliza unbolted the lock and left the room, closing the door with a silent *snick* behind her.

Chapter 20

"YOU MUST TELL MARCUS, ELIZA. HE DESERVES TO know."

Eliza lifted her head from the chamber pot over which it had been bent for half the morning and wiped her mouth with a damp kerchief. "What purpose would that serve, Aunt Lavinia. Marcus has had six weeks to make up his mind whether to join me and the twins or stay where he is. Obviously, he has made his choice."

"Perhaps knowing that you carry his child might change his mind," her aunt suggested, knitting needles clacking.

Eliza crawled from behind the screen where the chamber pot was kept, across her bedroom carpet, to the chair next to the fire where her aunt sat knitting. "How long did you say this lasted for Mama?"

"A few months only."

Eliza groaned. "I am not sure I will survive another month of this." She settled her back against the chair, stretched her legs out in front of her toward the fire, and played with the peach-colored ribbon that hung down the front of her dress. "I want Marcus to come out of hiding because he loves me, not because I will bear him a child. Especially since producing an heir was one of the main reasons he gave for wanting to marry me."

"Piddletush!"

Eliza turned and stared at her aunt. "What?"

"The duke could have married any woman if he merely wanted an heir."

Eliza made a face. *"Piddletush?"*

"Oh, that. Stumped you," Aunt Lavinia said with a cackling laugh. "I made it up!"

Eliza smiled. "All right. *Piddletush.* If the Duke of Blackthorne did not marry me for an heir, why *did* he marry me?"

"If you have not figured that out by now, you are more mutton-headed than he is," her aunt muttered, knitting needles clacking noisily.

"He wanted someone to care for the children?" Eliza suggested.

Her aunt scowled. "Why would a man who has remained a bachelor for thirty years *marry* to acquire a *governess?* He could have married any one of the previous six ladies if that had been his goal."

"He was desperate," Eliza said. "He had no other choice by the time he got to me."

"He could have shipped the twins off to boarding school."

"Marcus would never do such a thing! He *loves* those children."

"Aha!" her aunt said. "Now we are getting somewhere."

Eliza's forehead furrowed. "Are you saying Marcus married me because he *loved* me?" she asked incredulously.

"Loves you," Aunt Lavinia corrected.

Eliza gnawed on her lower lip. "Marcus does not believe he *can* love me. He told me so himself."

"He may not *wish* to love you. But I promise you he is smitten."

"How do you know?" Eliza demanded, hoping her aunt was right, but afraid to believe she was.

The knitting needles stopped clacking. "We are talking in circles," Aunt Lavinia said. "The point is, what are you going to do about it? Mope around like a milk-and-water miss until your child is born without a father? Or do something to pry the duke out of that murky dungeon?"

"There is nothing I am willing to do, other than what I have done," Eliza said firmly. "I will not plead or beg or demand or cajole. He is the one who must make the first move."

"Stubborn mink," her aunt grumbled.

"Very stubborn *minx*," Eliza replied with a grin.

Aunt Lavinia harrumphed.

Reggie and Becky lay on their bellies listening to Eliza's conversation with her aunt. Fortunately, the grate was under the headboard, where Eliza would never think to look. Eavesdropping had become absolutely necessary over the past six weeks. It was the only way they could find out what was going on in the house.

Ever since Reggie had woken up to find a bearded highwayman about to kidnap them out of their beds and screamed her head off—only to discover it was Uncle Marcus, of all people!—things had gone steadily downhill.

"At least now we know why Eliza has been staying

in her room every morning," Becky said. "A baby," she said dreamily. "Do you suppose she will let us hold it?"

"She will be gone before it is born if we don't do something to help get them back together," Reggie said. "Have you any suggestions?"

" 'Pry Uncle Marcus out of that murky dungeon,' " Becky suggested, in a perfect imitation of Aunt Lavinia's voice.

Reggie glanced at her admiringly. "Very good. Only, how are we going to do it?"

"I know exactly how it can be accomplished," Becky said. "But you may not like my plan."

"Why not?"

"Because we might have to go hungry and thirsty for a little while."

"How long?" Becky asked, eyes narrowing suspiciously.

"Not more than half a day, I would guess."

"I suppose that would be all right. If you are sure the sacrifice will draw Uncle Marcus out into the open."

Becky smiled. "Oh, yes," she said airily. "It will turn the entire household upside-down."

Marcus reached up to rub his hand across his smooth chin. He had been shaving himself every day for the past six weeks. He had gotten used to the feel of his face. He had even gotten used to the look of it.

He had woken up the morning after Eliza had left him feeling that he must do something to make amends. But the only thing she wanted from him was the one thing he was most afraid to give her. His love.

"You could shave off that beard of yours," Griggs

had said. "Her Grace asked me for a kettle to heat water, and made sure your shaving kit was where you could find it, and a towel and looking glass. She wanted to see your face. I must confess I miss your beauty myself."

Marcus had lifted a skeptical brow, but the instant Griggs left him alone, he began the task. He dipped his fingers in the kettle and discovered the water was still warm.

A swell of feeling made his nose sting and his eyes water. He could not believe that after the harsh way he had used his wife, she had gone down on her knees on the hard stone floor to ease his pain. No more than he could understand why he had treated her in a way that was guaranteed to turn her against him.

It had taken Marcus a great deal of thinking to realize he did not believe he deserved happiness, so he had done his best to destroy it.

The hardest part of looking at himself in the glass was admitting that the person he had really been hiding from for the past year was himself. He was the one who believed himself a monster. He was the one who was shocked by his behavior. He had seen himself through his brother's eyes, and through Eliza's, and through Julian's. Marcus was forced to admit that, while he might have had a perfect face and form, he had been a far from perfect man.

Nothing he did now would bring back Julian. Or Alastair who—if he had been the mysterious laird of Blackthorne Hall—had disappeared once again into the mist. Or Eliza's innocence.

But he could try to live a more exemplary life. He could raise Alastair's daughters as though they were his own. He could love his wife and treat her with the honor and respect she deserved.

Marcus's heart was racing when he finally soaped his face with his beaver shaving brush, picked up his straight-edged razor, and set to work.

He shaved the uninjured part of his face first. It was surprising to see himself reflected in the looking glass. Blue eyes, arched brows, aquiline nose, mobile lips, strong chin. The Beau he knew emerged as the beard fell away.

Then he focused on the other half of his face. And for the first time, faced the Beast.

The scars did the most to distort his looks around his left eye, where a web of scars shot out in a white spray. His lip was puckered slightly on one side, but as Eliza had pointed out, it hindered neither his speech nor his ability to make love to his wife. A small nick in his chin, a slight indentation, showed where the saber had stopped. The rest of the scars had faded to fine, silvery lines that showed less without the beard than with it.

His face laid bare, Marcus was forced to acknowledge who he was and what he was, and decide what he wanted to become.

That was easier said than done.

Over the past six weeks, he had often been tempted to send for Eliza, to make his apology to her, and admit how much he had always loved her. One thing had stopped him: the fear that she would not be able to forgive him. That she could never learn to love him again because of what he had done in the past. If he never begged forgiveness, he would not have to face the end of all his hopes and dreams.

Of course, if he never begged forgiveness, his hopes and dreams had no chance at all. The longer Eliza kept her promise and stayed away, the more convinced he became that she no longer loved him and the more reluctant he became to bare his soul to her.

Griggs entered the drawing room without knocking, interrupting Marcus's musing and lending significance to his announcement, "You have a visitor, Your Grace. A lady."

Marcus leapt from his chair and stood with his back to the undraped windows, his heart racketing around in his chest. He was certain it must be Eliza. His future lay in his hands. He need only say the right things. He need only convince her that he would be a husband she could be proud of, a man she could love. A man who would love her as she deserved to be loved.

The excitement he felt metamorphosed into disappointment when he saw who the "lady" was.

"You will have to excuse me, Your Grace," Lady Lavinia said as Griggs led her in on his arm. "I need a guide in unfamiliar surroundings."

"You are welcome anytime, Lady Lavinia."

"I have come on a matter of utmost urgency," she said.

"Is something wrong with Eliza or the twins?"

"I am afraid there is a slight problem," Aunt Lavinia said. "Though I am sure you will be able to correct it."

Marcus was beginning to think this was a feint by Eliza to draw him out. Some trumped-up disaster that he must avert. A way to save face for both of them. A smile curled his lips at her deviousness.

"This is not a laughing matter, Your Grace."

Marcus frowned. How had a blind woman seen the expression on his face? "I never said it was," he retorted.

"I was afraid you would think this was some trick of Eliza's to draw you out of hiding. I assure you it is not."

Marcus's heart began to pump a little faster. "You said both Eliza and the children are involved. What exactly is the nature of the problem, Lady Lavinia?"

"They all seem to have disappeared."

Becky stared at the growing pool of blood on the stones around Reggie's head. Her first panicked thought was to run for help. But she was afraid if she did, Reggie might die before she could find her way back.

Then she remembered they were locked in.

It was very dark. The lantern made a circle of light several feet wide. Outside that glow lay all the horrors Becky had ever imagined in her worst nightmares. A stretching rack and old rusty spikes and lots of other things meant to torture people.

Becky looked around her for something she could use to stanch the flow of blood, but everything was so dirty, so musty, so full of . . . of spiderwebs. She pulled off her bow—a pink one that matched her pink shift, and squatted down beside Reggie, who was dressed in yellow.

When she lifted Reggie's head to locate the oozing bump, her hands got covered with something slippery she soon realized was Reggie's blood. She let go of Reggie's head and scrubbed her hands on her shift to get it off, then looked down and gagged at the sight of herself, covered with blood.

She glanced at Reggie and realized she had to do something to stop the bleeding. She could not wait. Becky sniffed back her tears and did her best to bind the wound tightly with the wide pink ribbon.

"Reggie," she said, shaking her sister's shoulder. "Wake up."

Reggie's eyes remained closed.

Becky ran to the thick wooden door and banged on it, shouting for help.

No one answered. They were completely lost, locked in a dungeon without food or water, somewhere in the bowels of Blackthorne Abbey.

It was the skeleton in one of the torture devices that had caused all the problems. They had bent down to look more closely at the skull, when a spider crawled out of the eyehole. Becky had panicked. She had taken off with the lantern, leaving Reggie in the dark. Reggie had shouted for her to come back, but Becky had only wanted to get out, to get away.

That was when Becky had realized they were locked in. That the wooden door had somehow closed after they had passed through it and was locked tight.

"Reggie, we cannot get out!" she yelled. "Reggie, where are you!"

Reggie had appeared at her side, angry for being left in the dark. "Don't do that again," she chided.

"Now you see how Eliza felt," Becky had not been able to resist saying.

Reggie had found some wooden boxes to stack so she could reach the barred window near the top of the door. It had not been a sturdy sort of ladder, and Becky warned Reggie to be careful.

"I am being careful!" she snapped. "Hand me the lantern, so I can see."

Becky held up the lantern, but when Reggie reached for it, she lost her balance and went tumbling over backward. She had shrieked once before her head hit the stones.

She had not woken up since.

If only they had told Eliza what they were doing before they entered the secret passageway, Becky thought. If only someone knew they were down here in the dungeon, they might have a chance of being found. A slim chance, because so far she had not found any grates through which she could yell for help.

Her plan had been a good one: She and Reggie would disappear into the secret passageway. When Eliza could not find them in the house or the barn, she would go to Uncle Marcus for help. He would come out of hiding, they would reappear, he and Eliza would make up, and everybody would live happily ever after.

Things had simply gone awry. It had been hours and hours since they had walked into the honey-combed passage. They had taken a wrong turn, and it had led them down here. Even if Eliza remembered the secret passageway, she was too scared of the dark to go in it by herself. Would she break her promise and tell Uncle Marcus about it? Even if she did, it could be hours before they were found. Maybe days. Maybe weeks.

Becky remembered the skeleton.

Maybe they would not be found at all.

When the twins did not show up for morning tea, Eliza excused herself and went looking for them. She knew they had been disappointed when word came several weeks ago that the new laird of Blackthorne Hall had disappeared as mysteriously as he had arrived. If the laird had been their father, which was by no means certain, he was missing again.

Eliza had watched the twins walk to the end of the lane each day expecting Alastair's return. Eventually they had given up. Eliza had no idea what had occupied their time lately, because she had been under the hatches. No wonder they felt neglected. No wonder they had not come in for tea. Who would care? Who would notice they were gone?

Eliza searched the better part of the day without finding them. She was beginning to be seriously concerned and wondered whether she should send a message to Marcus—through Griggs—that the children were missing.

She imagined Marcus's response. Something coldly sarcastic. Something disapproving. Something bound to make her blood boil. Something sure to make her cast up her accounts—and give away the secret she was desperate to hide.

Then it dawned on her where the twins must have gone. And the promise she had made not to tell their uncle about the secret passageway. Of course, if the twins were lost—and they must be, they had been gone so long—she must tell Marcus and let him search for them. There was no way Eliza could do it herself. She would not be able to take the first step inside that black void.

Eliza was not quite sure why she went up to the girls' room instead of marching straight to the east wing of the Abbey, except it galled her that she could not even ask her husband for help directly. She had to do it through Griggs. What if Griggs denied her admittance? Would she have to wait like a supplicant while her husband decided whether what she had to say was *important* enough to merit his attention?

Eliza slid her hand along the wall near the twins' fireplace until she found the release she was seeking. The panel opened without a sound. A damp, moldy smell seeped out into the children's room. Eliza stared transfixed into the gloom. She lit a beeswax candle in a brass holder, one she was sure would burn brightly for a very long time, and stepped into the abyss.

A zephyr swirled in through the twins' open window, fluttered the curtains, and blew out Eliza's candle. Before she could stop it, the panel shut behind her with a slam.

Eliza opened her mouth to scream, but no sound came out. Her throat was too constricted for air to get past it. She was suffocating where she stood. She fell to the floor in a faint.

Only half concious, Eliza thought she heard a child crying. One of the twins. No, it was someone else. She could see the child in her mind's eye, three or four years old, with long chestnut hair, and tears streaking her face. She could feel the child's distress.

The little girl was locked in a small, dark room, and she could not get out.

Eliza concentrated very hard. If she could only see something that would tell her where the child was, she could perhaps find the little girl and help her. She searched the dark room in her vision and saw tins and tins full of . . . of different tobaccos. How did she know that?

She knew more.

Each tobacco had a distinctive smell, and one blended the crushed leaves to create a personal pipe tobacco. It was an art and a science. Her father had learned it from his father. And he was teaching it . . . to her.

Such strong odors. Russian. Turkish. Broadleaf. Burley. Fire-cured. Air-cured. Havana. Virginia. *When would someone come to take her away?* Acrid. Bitter. Musky. Spicy.

Eliza heard herself—or was it the child?—whimpering, calling for help. Calling for someone to come. To save her from the dark.

Where are Mama and Papa? Grandpapa said I cannot leave this room until they come and get me. I am so sorry, Grandpapa. Please let me out. I did not mean to spill your tobaccos and mix them all together. I was only trying to make a tobacco just for you, as Papa taught me to do. It is so dark in here, Grandpapa. Please, I want out!

Eliza could not catch her breath. She knew what was going to happen. She could see it in her mind's eye. The little girl would not get out. Not for a long, long time.

Eliza watched in her vision as the door opened

and a blinding light filled the room. The little girl squinted her eyes to see who was standing there.

"Papa," she croaked, her voice nearly gone from screaming endlessly in the dark. "I'm sorry, Papa. I'm so sorry."

Her papa pulled her into his arms and hugged her tight, as he sobbed against her throat. She tried to pull away, ashamed because she had wet herself, and she was getting him wet. Mama's eyes blurred with tears as she took her from Papa. She clung to Mama, clung very tight and would not let her go. "Where were you?" she cried. "I called and called, but you never came!"

Her eyes went wide with terror, as Grandpapa entered the room. He and Papa shouted at each other. Papa grabbed Grandpapa's throat and squeezed and squeezed until Grandpapa turned red and purple and blue.

Mama set her down, and she held tight to Mama's skirt as she pulled Papa away. Grandpapa was very angry, coughing and choking. Papa was even angrier. He said he wanted to kill Grandpapa, that he was sorry Mama had stopped him.

Mama said Eliza should forget everything that had happened in that horrible room, put it from her mind as though it had never happened. Because they were never going to mention it again. Ever.

Eliza slowly opened her eyes, but there was nothing to see in the dark passageway. She knew now why she was afraid of the dark. Why her father must have been disinherited. Why she had always felt, deep down, that somehow she was responsible. There had been no scandal. Only a little girl who had spilled her grandpapa's tobacco, and got locked in a closet and forgotten.

Eliza realized she could move in the dark. Not quickly, and not without a great deal of effort, but she could move. She felt her way across the floor to the wall, then stood up slowly and carefully, running her hands along the rough stone, looking for the latch that she knew must be there.

She could not find it.

Eliza had no choice but to move farther into the dark passageway until she found a grate—and shout at the top of her lungs for help.

Chapter 21

$\mathcal{M}$ARCUS HAD BARELY ABSORBED LADY LAVINIA'S announcement and sent her away with Griggs, when he heard a commotion in the main hallway of the Abbey. He headed for the door of the drawing room, but froze when he saw who was standing there.

Alastair Wharton, sixth Duke of Blackthorne, entered the room—wearing a kilt. He grinned at the shocked expression on Marcus's face and said, "Well, laddie, your big brother is home. How about a fond greeting?"

Marcus felt tears sting his eyes. He quickly took the few steps to close the distance between himself and his long-lost brother. He would have shaken Alastair's hand, except his brother pulled him close and gave him a bear's hug. Marcus had no idea what had caused the change in Alastair—the warm greeting, the warmer hug—but he was glad for it.

He had thought Alastair would be put off by the marks on his face, but his brother acted as though they did not exist. The scars did not look so loathsome to Marcus these days, either. He no longer winced when he caught sight of himself in a looking glass. But he had thought it was only because he was used to them. Perhaps Alastair did not see the scars, because he was not looking at the facade, but the man inside.

As Eliza had.

"Where have you been?" Marcus choked out as he slapped his brother on the back. "We were told you had drowned."

"You know better, Marcus."

"I said as much," he conceded. "But why did you not come home, Alex? Where have you been?"

Alastair scowled. "A cunning lass kept me captive through trickery. I shall have my revenge," he promised grimly. "She shall repay the debt she owes me in full. As for where I have been . . . seeing to my lands in Scotland."

"Are you the mysterious Laird of Blackthorne Hall?"

"The Laird," he said with a thick Scottish burr. "And married to its mistress."

Marcus gaped. "You are married, Alex?"

He smiled cynically. "The witch would tell you so. I say it is for the courts to settle."

"What witch?"

"My wife. But Katherine is not a fit topic for discussion. Where are my children, Marcus?"

"I hesitate to say."

Alastair frowned. "I trust they are well."

"As far as I know," Marcus said. "I seem to have lost them."

"Again?" Alastair said with a laugh and another ardent hug that left Marcus thinking one of his ribs might be broken. "You really must be more careful."

Marcus could not get over the difference in the

joyful, exuberant man who stood before him and the staid, morose man who had left a year past. "You are so different, Alex. What has changed?"

"I have realized how short life can be, Marcus," he said. "I am no longer willing to let doubts keep me from loving my children. Or let acrimony separate me from my only kin."

Marcus smiled. "Scotland is good for you, Alex. You should go there more often."

"Perhaps I will take the twins to see Blackthorne Hall next summer." He smiled drolly and added, "If we can find them."

"I believe they are somewhere in the hidden passageways within the Abbey," Marcus said. "Of which I had no knowledge until a few minutes ago. Are you aware of them, Alex? Do you know where they start and end?"

"I ventured into them a couple of times, until I got lost and nearly did not get found. Father rescued me at a point when I was resigned to dying and warned me never to go into the tunnels again. Essentially, it was the same lecture I gave the twins several years ago—which apparently went in one ear and out the other. There is an entrance in your bedroom, Marcus. We can start there."

Marcus was amazed to see a panel near the thronelike chair swing open. Each man carried a lantern, and Alastair warned Marcus to move slowly and watch his step in the dark.

"Don't get separated from me," Alastair warned. "Some of the tunnels lead to blind falls. Others to dead ends. One leads down into a dungeon."

"A real dungeon?" Marcus asked with a laugh. "With torture devices and manacles on the wall?"

"All of that and more. I nearly died there when I was eleven. Someone else's bones still reside there. The Ghost of Blackthorne Abbey."

"There are no such things as ghosts."

"Listen to the Abbey walls, Marcus. They will speak to you," Alastair advised.

Marcus shivered. They already had. "I need to talk to you, Alex."

"Can it wait?"

"No, it cannot," Marcus said as he followed Alastair into the cool, dark tunnel. The depths of the Abbey seemed an apt place to confess his sins to his brother.

"I never lay with Penthia, Alex, except the time you interrupted us. I am sorry I was not strong enough to resist her entreaties. But I never put myself inside her, Alex. I was too ashamed, when I realized what I had almost done, even to beg your pardon.

"But the truth is, the twins cannot be mine. Penthia only wanted to hurt us both. You, because you discovered us together, but would not set her aside, and me, because I would not lie with her again. Reggie and Becky are your daughters, Alex, not mine."

Alastair released a shuddering sigh. "It is good to know the truth, Marcus. But before I left, I had already made up my mind to love them no matter whose children they were. And while I was gone, I made up my mind to forgive you. I had a lesson in Scotland that taught me things are not always what they seem."

"Thank you, Alex." Marcus felt a sense of relief he

had not expected, and a great deal of hope that they would be friends again, as they had been long ago.

"I can see you were wounded at Waterloo, Marcus," Alastair said, "and lost a bit of your good looks. I trust you at least saved your charm."

Marcus smiled, amazed that he could. "Griggs kept the surgeons from cutting off my hand, but it was badly crippled until this past six weeks. I have been exercising it, and I can pick things up with it now. My charm suffered temporarily," he said with a wry twist of his mouth, "but it is enjoying a resurgence."

"Has the past year been difficult for you?"

"More than you know. I missed you, Alex." Just as Marcus finished speaking, he thought he heard a voice calling to him from within the walls. "Did you hear that?"

Alastair stopped and listened. "Someone saying your name, I think."

"It sounds like— It is! Eliza!"

"Who is Eliza?"

"Elizabeth Sheringham, now Elizabeth Wharton," Marcus said. "My wife."

Alastair turned and studied him for a moment in the glow from the lantern. "It seems I have been gone a great deal too long. The Beau has accepted a legshackle?"

"It is a long story, Alex. Suffice it to say I did *not* act honorably toward the lady, that Julian—before he was killed at Waterloo—engaged himself to her, and that after a period of mourning, she has recently become my wife."

"Miss Sheringham did not care that your looks were spoiled?"

"No, Alex. She is only concerned that I love her."

"Is it a love match then?" Alastair asked.

"It is on my side. It was for her, I think, in the beginning. But lately . . . there have been problems."

"With women, there usually are," Alastair said.

The voice called again, closer. "Marcus, where are you? Marcus, please, come and find me."

"I believe you will find the lady down that passageway and to the left," Alastair said, pointing to the place where two tunnels intersected. "I will go this way and look for the twins. When you have found your lady, retrace your steps and keep making right-hand turns. You will end up where I am heading now."

Becky sat beside Reggie, shivering in the dark. She was cold. And scared. The fuel in the lantern had long since burned out. She did not know how many hours they had been prisoners in the dungeon. Only that her stomach was rumbling with hunger, and her tongue was swollen with thirst.

"Reggie," she whispered, "are you awake?" She had been asking for hours with no response.

This time Reggie muttered, "My head hurts. Why is it so dark? Where are we, Becky?"

Becky sobbed with relief and squeezed Reggie's hand, which she had been holding in the dark. "You fell from that stack of boxes and hurt your head. Do you remember?"

A pause and then, "Are we still in the dungeon?"

"Yes. The lantern burned out a while ago."

Becky could feel Reggie trying to sit up and said, "I think you should lie still."

"My hair is sticky with something."

"It is blood," Becky said. "From a cut."

"Am I going to die?" Reggie asked tremulously.

"I . . . I hope not."

"Do you think Aunt Eliza and Uncle Marcus are looking for us?" Reggie asked.

Becky nodded, realized her sister could not see her, and said, "I am sure everyone is searching. I have been yelling and yelling, but so far no one has answered."

"Will you yell again now?" Reggie asked. "Or shall I?"

Becky thought of the headache Reggie must have, and though she was afraid to move in the dark—for fear of running into spiderwebs, and the spiders who had made them—she knew Reggie was right. She had to keep shouting for help. It was their only hope.

She had cleared a path while the lantern was still lit, and put her hands out in front of her now to be certain she did not encounter anything that might have moved of its own accord in the dark as she made her way to the door.

When she reached the wooden door, she raised her head toward the open window and yelled, "Is anyone there? We are locked in the dungeon and cannot get out. Help, someone! We are locked—"

"I can hear you, Becky."

Father's voice. Becky's nose stung, and her eyes welled with tears. Maybe she and Reggie were already dead, and they did not know it. How else could Father have responded so quickly to her cries for help? How else could he know exactly where to find them?

"We are locked in, Father," she said in a calm

voice. Becky thought she saw a glow of light at the high window, but perhaps that was wishful thinking.

"There is a key," the voice replied. "It is hidden in another place. I will be back shortly."

Becky thought she heard footsteps moving away.

"Is Father really here?" Reggie asked. "I thought I must be imagining his voice in my head."

"I could hear him, too," Becky replied. And then, expressing her fears aloud, "Don't you think it quite impossible that Father could be here? That he could have found us when no one else has?"

"Not at all. We have expected him to return to the Abbey anytime now. And he has finally arrived," Reggie said.

"On the one day we are lost, and no one can find us?" Becky asked skeptically.

"What are you suggesting?"

"That perhaps we are dead, and Father's ghost has come to take us to heaven."

Reggie moaned deep in her throat, a keening sound. "I don't want to die, Becky. I don't want Father to be dead. I love him."

Becky made her way back to Reggie as quickly as she could, took her sister's hand in hers, and pinched it.

"Ow! Why did you do that?"

"Pinch me back," Becky said excitedly. "Ow, not so hard! Don't you see? It hurts!"

"Then we are not dead!"

"And Father must really be here!"

The door swung open and Father stood there, the lantern casting eerie shadows on his face and figure. Becky sat frozen where she was, still not quite certain whether he was an apparition. He was, she realized, wearing a skirt—a kilt, she corrected, the kind Fenwick had said were worn in Scotland.

"Reggie? Becky? Are you all right?" he asked in his familiar rumbly voice.

"Reggie is hurt, Father. She fell and cut her head."

He crossed to them hurriedly, dropping on one knee beside Reggie and setting the lamp where the circle of light lit both their faces and his.

Becky looked at his face, so somber and serious. Was this the kind father she had missed so much? Or the stern one?

"Who put this bandage on?" he asked.

"I did," Becky said. "I tried to stop the bleeding."

Becky watched as he lifted Reggie right into his arms and pulled her against his breast. His eyes closed as he held her tight against him. "Reggie," he murmured, pressing his lips to her cheeks and forehead. "I am so glad you are safe."

Then he looked into her eyes and said, "Thank you, Becky. I think your nursing may have saved your sister's life."

Becky felt her throat tighten. It was neither of the old fathers who had come back, she realized, but someone new. Someone wonderful.

Father's eyes had blurred with tears. He held his hand out to her, and she laid hers in it and let him draw her close. His arm banded her waist and pulled her and Reggie snugly against him, enfolding them in a warm circle of love.

"Papa is home," he said, his breath warm against her brow.

"I love you, Papa," Becky whispered in his ear.

"I love you, too," he whispered back.

Eliza was shivering, her body pressed close to the stone wall, the only solid thing she had to hang on to. She told herself over and over that she was only afraid of the dark because she had once been locked inside a dark room when she was a child.

It helped a little. But the feeling of being abandoned, the sensation that the walls were closing in and would crush her if she did not somehow escape, persisted despite all logic against it.

Eliza saw the glow from the lantern long before she could distinguish the face of the person carrying it. Somehow she knew it was Marcus. "You found me," she said, half crying, half laughing with relief as he took the last few steps to reach her.

"I could hear you calling for me. I came as fast as I could."

Eliza launched herself toward Marcus, who quickly set the lantern on the stone floor and opened his arms wide.

"I've missed you, Eliza," he breathed against her ear.

When he lowered his mouth, hers was waiting for him. As his tongue urgently probed the seam of her lips, her mouth opened eagerly to receive him. His tongue dipped inside, tasting her, letting her taste him. Eliza quivered. This was what had been missing all her life. His body impatient for hers, hers more than ready for his, a merging of body and soul, so that two became one.

She let her tongue tease the side of his mouth,

where the scar was, and heard him make a primitive, guttural sound as he pulled her close, letting her feel his arousal.

Eliza had forgotten how wonderful the Beau's kisses could be. She put a hand to his cheek, wanting to feel his flesh against her fingertips—and abruptly ended the kiss, levering herself back to look at him. "You shaved! I can see your face!"

Marcus rubbed a hand over his jaw and grinned. "I did not think you were going to notice." She saw the tension in his body when he asked, "What is the verdict? Can you bear the Beast in all his glory?"

As if his scarred face could ever keep her from loving him! "Shaving that monstrous beard is a vast improvement," she said tartly. "At least now I can find your lips to kiss them."

She suited word to deed, and it was long moments before either of them came up for air. Eliza realized he was brushing her damp lips with his thumb. His left thumb.

"Your hand!" she cried, grabbing hold of it. "You can use your fingers!"

"Griggs has been helping me to exercise them," he said, thrusting his now-flexible left hand into her hair and sending pins flying. "I have learned a great deal about myself in the past six weeks, Eliza. Enough to know that I need you. Enough to know that I do not want to wait another moment to start our lives together."

He grabbed a handful of curls and gently angled her head back, kissing her with a passion that spoke volumes about his desire and need and hopes and dreams. "I want you with me always," he murmured, pressing kisses against her throat.

"I am listening," she said with throaty laugh. "Tell me more."

"I need you to light the dark places inside of me. I want to make children with you, to fill your days and nights with passion and laughter." He teased her lips with his teeth and tongue, doing all the things with his mouth that she had imagined he would do in the weeks they had been separated. Promising rapture. Offering heaven.

"Say you will let me love you," he whispered. "Say we can be husband and wife again."

Eliza looked deep into the Beau's blue eyes for the first time since the afternoon she had kissed him in the forest, the day she had seen in his eyes the love and desire that had been missing in Julian's.

"Oh, Marcus," she breathed reverently. "It is there. I can see it in your eyes."

He pressed his scarred cheek against her soft, smooth one and pulled her tight enough against him that she could feel the thundering pulse beating inside his chest. "I love you, Eliza."

"I love you, too, Marcus. I have for a very long time."

Their lips met in a kiss that offered more than the breath of life. It filled all the empty places inside her. Eliza heard a guttural moan of satisfaction, as Marcus took the soul she offered him, and gave her his.

"How many children do you want?" she murmured, thinking of the one growing inside her. "I mean, aside from the two you already have."

"The twins are not mine, Eliza," he said, looking

earnestly into her eyes. "I have just explained to Alastair that it is an impossibility."

"Oh. So you never . . . with your brother's wife."

He shook his head. "Never."

Then she realized what else he had said. "You *just now* explained this to your brother? The duke is here? He has returned?"

"He is so changed, Eliza! I hardly recognized him. The bitterness is gone, and he seems so much happier. He is determined to be a better father to Reggie and Becky."

"The twins!" She flushed. "I had completely forgotten about them."

"You have been a bit distracted," Marcus said with a grin.

"Have they been found, then? Are they all right?"

"Alastair went to search for them down another passageway, while I came to find you."

Eliza turned to look into the gloom. She thought of her own experience, calling and calling for help that never came. "Dear God. If the twins are still lost inside here somewhere, Marcus, they must think we have abandoned them. We must find them as quickly as we can!"

"Alastair gave me directions how to find him. He will know the quickest way to get you out of here, so I can continue the search."

"I am not leaving your side until we find the children," she said stubbornly, following closely behind him as he began to move through the narrow tunnel.

"Your aunt told me how frightened you are of the dark."

"She would."

He glanced over his shoulder at her. "You should have told me why you wished me to leave a candle burning," he accused. "It is another sin for which I must be forgiven."

"I was not afraid with your arms around me, Marcus. Truly. And now that I know what caused the fear—it is another story and can be told later—my dread is not so strong as it used to be. I will be fine if we are together."

It seemed they made a great many right turns before they finally saw the glow of a lantern in the distance.

"We must be in the very bowels of the Abbey," Marcus muttered. "It must be the dungeon! Hurry. Alastair may need our help."

But when they reached the door and looked inside, they saw Alastair with his arms around the twins, and the twins holding him tight and chattering like magpies.

"This is quite a family reunion," Marcus quipped, setting his lantern on the boxes stacked just inside the door. "May we join in?"

Eliza saw that, for the first time, the twins did not jump up and race to Marcus. She wondered if they still had not forgiven him for hiding away the past year.

But Becky piped up, "Papa is home, Uncle Marcus. Papa is home!" She seemed glad to see Marcus, but she clung to her father, rather than running to her uncle.

Reggie lifted her head so she could see Marcus past Alastair's shoulder and said, "I hit my head, Uncle

Marcus. But Papa has promised it will feel better soon."

Eliza saw the momentary flash of pain as Marcus realized he was no longer first in their lives. And then his smile, as he turned to her and squeezed her hand, accepting what had always been meant to be.

"The twins seem to have survived their ordeal," Alastair said. "Becky has a bump on her head that bled, but aside from a headache and a couple of ruined shifts, the twins got off lightly. I think we must take the door off this dungeon, Marcus," Alastair said. "It is far too dangerous for our progeny."

"I think you might be right."

Eliza saw how longingly Marcus looked at Alastair's daughters. "You will have one of your own soon," she whispered in his ear. She looked down and laid her hand on her belly. "She is already growing inside me."

Marcus looked stunned for an instant before his face broke into a broad grin, crinkling the web of scars near his eye. He grabbed her and whirled her in a circle so fast it made her dizzy.

"Put me down," she warned with a laugh, "or I shall cast up my accounts."

He set her down and pulled her against his side, his arm cinched around her waist. "I am going to be a father, Alex. Congratulate me. Eliza says it is a girl."

Alex grinned back at him. "I hear daughters are easier to raise than sons, Marcus," he said, looking with adoration at his incorrigible twins. "They are quiet, retiring, polite, and they never get into trouble."

"Did you hear that, Eliza? Daughters only, please," Marcus teased.

"I don't care what it is," Becky said. "As long as I get to hold it!"

Eliza laughed along with Marcus and Alastair. She slid her husband's scarred hand down to her belly and covered it with her own. "Very well, Marcus," she said, her gaze locked with his. "A meek and docile daughter you shall have."

"I only hope she is as wild a hellion as Reggie and Becky," he whispered in her ear. "I can hardly wait."

"Neither can I," Eliza said, imagining a daughter as fun-loving, as dauntless, and as hopelessly unmanageable as the twins. She grinned. "Neither can I."

Epilogue

"MATCHMAKING IS A DANGEROUS BUSINESS," Olivia warned.

Eliza looked up from nursing her daughter, Alexandra, and met the troubled gaze of the Duchess of Braddock, who was sitting on the sofa across the room. "I only thought, since Alastair is already married to Katherine, that we should invite her here from Scotland for a visit," Eliza said.

"If Blackthorne wants to see his bride, he is perfectly capable of making the journey to Scotland himself," Olivia said.

Charlotte wrinkled her nose. "Where is your sense of adventure, Livy?"

"I left it safe at home!"

Olivia had come with Charlotte to see the renovations Eliza had made to the east wing of the Abbey. And, Eliza suspected, so they could both make sure that Eliza and the Beau were living happily ever after. And they were, Eliza thought, as she looked around her.

Reggie and Becky were playing with Olivia's two-year-old son, William, and Charlotte's one-year-old daughter, Margaret, who were settled on a blanket in the center of the room with a selection of colorful wooden and cloth toys.

Of course children belonged in a nursery, not in the middle of a drawing room where guests were received, but Eliza enjoyed having the twins close by. And she knew Becky would not be happy unless she had a chance to hold the babies. Besides, the duchess and the countess had not missed a step when she had suggested they allow the children to join them.

In a chair directed toward the fire, Aunt Lavinia's knitting needles were clacking industriously. Eliza could tell she was listening to everything that was going on, merely by watching her expressive face. A sleek black cat lay curled on her lap, purring contentedly.

Eliza smiled to herself. It was not until Alexandra had been born that she realized her aunt had been knitting *baby clothes* all these years. Alexandra wanted for nothing. Now Aunt Lavinia was working on a wardrobe for the next Wharton child. Considering the ball of blue yarn in her lap, Aunt Lavinia was expecting a son to make his appearance next.

"I found matchmaking a perfectly delightful endeavor, Livy," Charlotte said. "And you must admit, my efforts have not turned out so badly." She glanced smugly from Olivia to Eliza.

Olivia made a very unduchesslike sound of rebuttal.

"I only intend to invite Alastair's wife for a visit to the Abbey. Surely there could be no harm in that," Eliza said, adjusting the lace-edged blanket over her daughter, who was greedily inhaling her luncheon.

"Despite the fact none of us has ever laid eyes on her, the mistress of Blackthorne Hall *is* my sister-in-law."

Charlotte thumped the heels of her black patent leather half boots against the side of the wingback chair in which she was sitting crosswise. "I say Eliza should do it!"

"Do what?" Marcus asked, entering the drawing room with Lion and Reeve on his heels. He crossed immediately to his wife and gave her a kiss on the mouth, caressing her breast beneath the blanket that hid the nursing child. He grinned at her rosy face and settled himself on the carpet at her feet.

Eliza blushed. Her friends must have seen how Marcus had touched her breast. Perhaps they thought he had caressed the baby's cheek.

When she finally got the courage to look up, Eliza realized from the other two sets of rosy cheeks across the room, that both women had been too busy enthusiastically greeting their own husbands to notice what she and Marcus were doing. She rearranged the nursing cloth but did not remove herself from the company. Over the past year, the three couples had become fast friends, and Charlotte made sure they treated each other as family.

When Reeve was settled beside Olivia on the sofa, and Lion had relaxed his arm across the top of Charlotte's wingback chair, Marcus repeated his question. "What is it you are planning, Eliza?"

"I want to invite Katherine to Blackthorne Abbey for a visit."

"Alex has no wish to see his wife," Marcus said flatly.

Eliza watched Lion and Reeve exchange a meaningful glance. What did they know that she did not? Did Marcus know it, too? Maybe she should not be interfering in her brother-in-law's life. But she could not understand how Alastair could simply ignore his Scottish wife.

"Better yet," Eliza said, half to herself. "I shall find a reason why Alastair must go to her."

Marcus reached out a finger, and Eliza watched as Alexandra grasped it. Marcus played tug-of-war with the baby, who held on tight.

"Alexandra is already obstinate," he remarked. "I shudder to think what a few years of experience will do for her temper."

"She will twist you around her little finger," Lion remarked with a grin. "Believe me, I know."

The women exchanged amused glances. Little did their husbands know, but their wives were as adept at getting what they wanted as their children were.

William began to cry, which started Margaret to wailing.

Aunt Lavinia's knitting needles stopped clacking. She set her knitting aside and said, "Would anyone like to play a game of hide-and-seek with me in my room?"

"I would!" Reggie said.

"I would!" Becky said.

The twins jumped up and pulled Aunt Lavinia to her feet, upsetting the cat, who leapt to the floor and followed them all—indignantly but regally, tail held high—from the room.

"I think it may be time for someone's nap," Charlotte said, eyeing her husband coyly. She walked over to pick up Margaret, who stopped crying immediately.

"Will you come help me lay her down?" she asked Lion.

"Excuse us, Eliza," Lion said. "Marcus, I will see you later this afternoon for billiards."

Eliza could not believe how blatantly the countess had cozened her husband into taking her upstairs—where it was obvious exactly how they planned to spend the afternoon.

To her amazement, Reeve picked up his son—who also left off wailing in seconds—took his wife's hand, nodded to Marcus, and left the drawing room without another word.

Within moments the room was empty except for Eliza, Marcus, and the baby.

"Well," she said, clearing her throat. "I guess we know what they all have on their minds."

Marcus turned and faced her on his knees, trapping her between his arms, which were braced against the chair on either side of her. "I suppose we do," Marcus agreed.

Eliza felt a primitive thrill of excitement when she saw the feral gleam in his eyes.

He bent over to kiss her breast, just above the point where their daughter suckled. Eliza felt a rush of pleasure between her thighs and bit back a gasp.

"There must be something we can do to help Katherine and Alastair mend their differences," she said breathlessly, determined to get Marcus's help, or at least his acquiescence to her plan.

"She lied to him," Marcus said between kisses.

"She kept him prisoner in a dungeon. He cannot forget or forgive her deception."

"Fiddlesticks!" Eliza bit back another gasp of pleasure. "Alex could not even remember his own name. Katherine needed a husband to keep Blackthorne Hall. She only used her wits to resolve a difficult situation. And as for keeping him prisoner—that lasted only a month."

"Until he escaped," Marcus interjected, "and made his way home. Alex is liable to strangle the chit the next time he sees her. Better to let well enough alone."

"I still think—" Eliza moaned. Her daughter had fallen asleep, abandoning the nipple, and Marcus had taken her place. Her milk let down with an exquisite sensation as he began to suckle her as a lover would.

"I need your help to get Alastair and Katherine together," she rasped as her head fell back and her eyes fell closed.

"I want no part of this, Eliza," he said.

She felt him lift the sleeping child from her lap and watched with dazed, lambent eyes as he wrapped Alexandra snugly in the nursing cloth and laid her on the blanket the other babies had been using in the center of the room.

When he returned, he met her gaze, all the love he felt for her shimmering in his blue eyes. His mouth gently touched hers, then withdrew.

"Please help me get them together," Eliza implored.

"No," he murmured.

She nuzzled him beneath his ear. "Pretty please." Her lips caressed the scar at the edge of his eye, then moved down his cheek to the drawn-up corner of his lip. She teased his mouth until he opened to her with a guttural sound of surrender.

"Very well," he said, sieving his hands into her hair and angling her head so she could look nowhere but at him. "Against my better judgment, I will help you get them together."

"Thank you, Marcus," she breathed, opening her mouth for him.

The kiss was an affirmation of their love. Tumultuous. Tender. Demanding. Delicious. Her fingertips trailed across his face, caressing the scars that had kept them apart, reminding him that it was not the Beau or the Beast she loved, but the man who was both of them. "I love you, Marcus," she whispered against his flesh.

"And I love you, Eliza." His lips found a sensitive spot beneath her ear to lavish with kisses. "Who taught you such devious—and such splendidly enjoyable—tactics to get your own way, my love?"

"A very good friend," Eliza said, remembering Charlotte's suggestions. She smiled as she found his mouth again. "Are they working?"

She laughed in delight as he picked her up out of the chair, laid her on the floor, and lovingly mantled her body with his own.

WATCH FOR
BLACKTHORNE'S BRIDE
Coming Soon!

A NOTE TO READERS

Dear Readers,

Some of you have written asking why my titles always seem to change from what was advertised in the previous book. *Daisy and the Duke* became *The Inheritance*. *Lord of the Plains* became *Maverick Heart*. And now *The Man Who Loved Her* has become *After the Kiss*. The titles I listed first are my "working titles," the ones I use when I first conceive the book until it is turned in to the publisher. At that point, the title may change because of marketing considerations or because my publisher and I come up with something we like better. Good luck finding the book you want!

My next historical romance is *Blackthorne's Bride*, a continuation of the series which began with *Captive* and continued with *After the Kiss*. Set in Scotland, *Blackthorne's Bride* tells the delightful story of Alastair Wharton, sixth Duke of Blackthorne (you met him in *After the Kiss*), who finds himself the captive of a devious Scottish lass—who bluffs him into believing they are husband and wife. Look for it in bookstores early next year!

The next book in the #1 Bestselling Hawk's Way series (number 10!) is *The Virgin Groom*. It will be a single title release from Silhouette in August (on bookshelves in mid-July). My next mainstream novel, *Heartbeat*, is a romantic suspense in which a stone-jawed Texas Ranger and sharp-tongued lady lawyer find themselves on opposites sides of the law. It will be available from Avon in September (on bookshelves in mid-August). Watch for a hardcover Christmas collection featuring me and Diana Palmer in November.

As always, I appreciate hearing from you. If you would like to be on my mailing list, please send a postcard to me at P.O. Box 8531, Pembroke Pines, FL 33084. If you send a letter with comments or questions, and would like a reply, please enclose a self-addressed, stamped envelope.

I personally read and answer my mail, although as some of you know, a reply might be delayed if I have a writing deadline.

Best always,

Joan Johnston

March 1997

Choose your one free book from the following list

The Four of Hearts Checklist

BOOKS BY MARSHA CANHAM:
___ ACROSS THE MOONLIT SEA
___ STRAIGHT FOR THE HEART
___ IN THE SHADOW OF MIDNIGHT
___ UNDER THE DESERT MOON
___ THROUGH A DARK MIST

BOOKS BY JILL GREGORY:
___ ALWAYS YOU
___ WHEN THE HEART BECKONS
___ DAISIES IN THE WIND
___ FOREVER AFTER
___ CHERISHED

BOOKS BY JOAN JOHNSTON:
___ CAPTIVE
___ MAVERICK HEART
___ THE INHERITANCE
___ OUTLAW'S BRIDE
___ KID CALHOUN
___ THE BAREFOOT BRIDGE
___ SWEETWATER SEDUCTION

BY KATHERINE KINGSLEY
___ ONCE UPON A DREAM

Dell